THE WIDE WORLD'S END

THE WIDE WORLD'S END

JAMES ENGE

A Tournament of Shadows: Book Three

an imprint of **Prometheus Books**
Amherst, NY

Published 2015 by Pyr®, an imprint of Prometheus Books

Cover illustration ©Steve Stone
Cover design by Jacqueline Nasso Cooke

Cold Wind To Valhalla
Words and Music by Ian Anderson
Copyright © 1975 The Ian Anderson Group Of Companies, Ltd.
Copyright Renewed 2004
All Rights Administered by BMG Rights Management (US) LLC
All Rights Reserved. Used by Permission.
Reprinted by Permission of Hal Leonard Corporation.

This is a work of fiction. Characters, locales, and events portrayed in this novel either are products of the author's imagination or are used fictitiously.

Inquiries should be addressed to
Pyr
59 John Glenn Drive
Amherst, New York 14228
VOICE: 716–691–0133
FAX: 716–691–0137
WWW.PYRSF.COM

19 18 17 16 15   5 4 3 2 1

Library of Congress Cataloging-in-Publication Data

Enge, James, 1960-
The wide world's end / by James Enge.
pages ; cm. — (A tournament of shadows ; Book Three)
ISBN 978-1-61614-907-9 (pbk.) — ISBN 978-1-61614-908-6 (ebook)
I. Title.

PS3605.N43W53 2015
813'.6—dc23

2014035459

Printed in the United States of America

To Michael Korte
who stood with me once at the end of another world

Acknowledgments

A thousand thanks are due to Ian Anderson, for permission to quote his lyric from "Cold Wind to Valhalla."

Ten thousand thanks to Lou Anders for his kindness, his patience, and his attentive reading that so improved my work. If you, patient reader, still don't like it, it's not his fault.

Contents

PART THREE: A COLD SUMMER   247

PART FOUR: FALL   359

APPENDICES 377

By a knight of ghosts and shadows
I summoned am to tourney
Three leagues beyond the wide world's end.
Methinks it is no journey.

—"Tom O'Bedlam's Song"

Invocation

I'll tell the tale, since you insist, but it won't be like the songs they sing. I saw much of what I'm about to tell with my own eyes, heard it with my own ears, felt it with my own heart. But I won't be saying I-I-I all the way through. I was a different person then. And any time you tell a story about yourself, it isn't about you, really. The teller is never the tale, or anyone in it.

Old Father Tyr, standing outside the world with Those-Who-Watch, shape my words like stones to build a bridge to the truth. Creator, guide my creation, which is yours also. Sustainer, give me the breath to complete it. Avenger, teach me when to end it, as you end all things in their time.

PART ONE

The Winter War

If Winter comes, can Spring be far behind?
—Shelley, "Ode to the West Wind"

CHAPTER ONE

Lone Survivor

Night begins the day, and in the darkness of night the first day of spring was being born. In the west, great Chariot was rising, bright with hope as it re-entered the world. No other moon was in the sky, but Chariot's light filled up the snow-covered plain of the Gap of Lone, and the gray-caped thain walking on it.

The thain went his way toward the base of the cliff with slow deliberate steps, as if he had all the time in the world. His gray cape of office was charred with fire and stained dark with dried blood. Fresh blood, black in the moon's blue light, was running down his legs and squelching in his shoes, staining his footprints in the new snow like mud.

Among the gray stones of the cliff face was a hollow. In the hollow hung a golden bell. The thain picked up the copper striker that lay below it. He didn't trust his trembling fingers to hold the slender stalk of metal so he gripped it with both hands, as if it were the handle of a sledgehammer. He struck the bell as hard as he could (which wasn't so very hard): three times. Then he waited there, although he could hear his pursuers loping toward him through the snow, voiceless though they were. He struck the bell three more times and fell dead in the shallow snowdrifts at the base of the cliff.

The bell rang in the little hollow. It rang in the watchroom of the Gray Tower, the Graith's guardpost over the Gap of Lone. It rang in the thains' Northtower, on the border of Thrymhaiam in the far north. It rang in Anglecross Tower in the west of the Wardlands, in Islandkeep that guarded the Southhold, in the Graith's chamber in the city of A Thousand Towers. The same bell, or an image of it, swung in all those places. The same signal sounded in all those places.

Many thains had set out to send that signal, but only the one survived to deliver the news before he died: the Wardlands had been invaded.

When his enemies found him dead, they cut up his body and rendered it down for soup, as was their custom. But they could not work the striker loose from the thain's hands, so they cut them off and left them there at the base of the cliff.

Long the hands lay there in the bitter snows, waiting for nothing.

CHAPTER TWO

Conversations in
A Thousand Towers

Two months earlier, in the dim noon of a late-winter day, two men fought a duel in the city of A Thousand Towers.

The city street, where it could be seen through the drifts of snow, was green-gray as fungus—because, apart from the paving stones and the drifts of snow between the buildings, it was, in fact, fungus. A few decades ago, a maker in New Moorhope had developed a kind of mold that could be cultured into building materials. Whole neighborhoods on the edges of A Thousand Towers were built from the stuff. Some time later, they were as rapidly abandoned. It turned out that the fungus absorbed and accumulated bad dreams, so that buildings made with it became unpleasant, even unsafe to dwell in. Destroying the fungus released the bad dreams all at once with perilous consequences. It was decided to let the neighborhoods age and decay over time, releasing their evil dreams gradually in the world. Few ever went there—only those whose business required privacy, and who didn't fear the infection of a temporary madness or two.

And that day, these two men came there, laid aside their red cloaks in spite of the cold, and prepared to fight.

"Let me see it again," said the taller man. He was Naevros syr Tol, famed as the greatest swordsman in the Wardlands or the wide world beyond.

The other man, Morlock Ambrosius, was famous for other things. He drew his sword and handed it to Naevros.

The blade was black as death, veined with bone-white crystal down its glittering length to its point. The grip was black and bound with something that felt smooth but comfortingly resistant to his hand. The sword had heft, but was lighter than a metal sword this long would be. There was a disturbing presence to the thing, not merely physical. There was a power in it, and Naevros didn't like it.

He handed it back to Morlock, the man who made it and who owned it. Morlock was also the man who had married the only woman Naevros felt he could love. There were other women, many other women, in Naevros' life, but Aloê Oaij was different, and this ugly crooked fellow with the sideways grin got to sleep with her every night.

By rights, Naevros should have loathed the man like the slime from a pus-rat. Yet, somehow, he rather liked him. Morlock could drink a table of dwarves under the table, for one thing. He didn't say much, but anything he did say was to the point. And he was the only person in the Wardlands who could fence at or near Naevros' level.

He handed the blade back to Morlock. "So that's what you won from the Dead Cor on the Hill of Storms!" he said.

"Eh," Morlock said and shrugged. Days went by sometimes without him saying much more than that but this time, thank God Sustainer, he found the strength to go on. "Not exactly. The blade Gryregaest lay shattered on the Broken Altar when I went to claim it. Later I came to understand that the Dead Cor and his weapon were one, woven together. It died when he did, at last. I took the fragments and made them, unmade them, remade them into this blade. I call it Tyrfing."

"'Tyr's grasp'?" translated Naevros. "After Oldfather Tyr, of course." Morlock had been born in A Thousand Towers, but was raised by his foster father Tyr syr Theorn in the distant north. Tyr was long dead now, but far from forgotten.

Morlock bowed his head and made to sheath the sword.

"Not on your dwarfy life," Naevros said flatly. "Our bet stands. I'll break your sword or take it in a fair fight."

"We were drunk last night, my friend," Morlock said. "There is no need for this. We could fence with wooden swords. I brought a pair with me."

"But did you bring a pair of anything else?" Naevros taunted him, waggling his hips lewdly. "Afraid I'll put your eye out? Think Old Ambrosius will be mad at you if you go back home with a broken sword?"

He was joking and he was not joking. He was fond of Morlock and he hated him. He wanted to make him laugh (as he could sometimes do) and he wanted to cut his throat (as he might someday do). He mentioned Morlock's father, old Merlin, because he knew it would sting Morlock to murderous rage. He was restless and he wanted a fight and Morlock was the only person who came close to his skill. His useless sterile skill.

That taunt did it. Morlock was furious, though he hid it well. He stepped back on the mold-gray street and came to guard. His cold, angry eyes fixed on Naevros and he waited in the pale sunlight.

Naevros drew his own sword—no wizardish wonder-blade, but a good piece of metal made for him by the weapon-masters of Thrymhaiam—and saluted Morlock with it. He lunged and thrusted; Morlock parried and riposted, and they proceeded to fight up and down the gray street, empty but for snowdrifts and nightmares.

At first glance they were ill-matched. Naevros was taller, possessing a catlike grace and a fluent, sharp eloquence with the sword. Morlock was shorter, less lithe, with something askew in his shoulders. Still, he was swift and strong. If anger never quite left his ice-gray eyes, he never let his attacks or his defense become reckless.

Apart from the recklessness of what they were doing. To fence with real swords was madness; it took even more control to refrain from injuring your opponent or being injured by him. That was why Naevros liked it. At any moment he could kill or be killed. It was like dancing along the edge of a cliff.

But the two fought for hours, as the dim sun slid from its cloudy zenith to just above the ragged gray-green peaks of the abandoned houses, and the blades never struck home on either combatant.

As a greenish dusk began to rise, they found their swords in a bind. Naevros tried to force the crooked man back. But the crooked man set his feet and pushed in turn. The taller man slipped out of the bind and leapt aside as his opponent tumbled past, blundering into a wall. The taller man eagerly leapt forward to strike at his fallen foe, but then backed away, gasping as his opponent rose in a cloud of dead spores and dark dreams to face him, his shining dark sword at guard.

Naevros then felt something like fear. He saw the crooked man wearing the blue skull-face of Death, with Death's blue blade in his hand, as the Kaeniar paint him in their Inner Temples. Most frightening of all was something Naevros felt in himself—an easiness, a welcoming of peace and rest. It would all be so much easier if—

"Enough!" he gasped, lifting his free hand in a call for rest. "Morlock, step out of that stuff! We don't want you tracking nightmares back to Tower Ambrose."

Morlock Ambrosius never said a word if none would do, so he simply nodded and stepped forward. Naevros stood back and leaned on his sword, breathing heavily, trying to settle his mind, hoping his fear hadn't shown in his face.

When his breathing slowed to near normal, he said, "We'll call it a draw, I think. If I ever want to kill you, I guess I'll have to sneak up behind you with a rock or something."

"Eh," Morlock replied. "Do you want to kill me?"

"'If,' I said. I said, 'If.'"

"That's why I asked."

"All right, then. Since you ask. I thought about it for a long time. Are you surprised?"

"No. I once thought about killing you, too."

Naevros turned and looked straight at his opponent, colleague, and friend. "Did you really, you sneaky son-of-a-thrept? May I ask why?"

"I envied your closeness to Aloê," the crooked man said, naming his wife and Naevros' one-time thain-attendant.

Naevros found he was blushing. He exhaled completely, inhaled, exhaled, and finally he laughed. "I hadn't realized you knew about it."

"Everyone knows."

"Not everyone knows it's an intimacy that rivals your marriage."

For a moment Naevros was afraid Morlock would say *It doesn't* in that flat unemphatic way of his that somehow managed to roar in the ears like thunder. And then Naevros would really have to kill him.

Morlock shrugged, and Naevros wondered briefly if that was reason enough to kill him, too. But then Morlock lifted his accursed blade and said, "This was the wrong tool for the job, anyway."

Tool? Job? Naevros stared at Morlock's impassive face and wondered if there was some phallic innuendo in play. "What do you mean?" he asked.

"If I cut your throat," said the ice-eyed man, "I might as well cut my own.

That's no way to reach her heart. She loves you too much—is loyal to those she loves."

"I see. You couldn't afford to kill me." It was interesting to see how much his rival's thinking had mirrored his own. "So you befriended me instead," Naevros said speculatively.

Morlock turned away. "No," he said, with his face averted. "That was always there."

"How do you mean?"

"You accepted me when few would accept me—trusted me when almost no one trusted me. You saw me as myself, not just my *ruthen*-father's son. That . . . matters to me. Will always matter."

Naevros had mostly done it to irritate Noreê. But, to be fair to himself, he had seen something in that surly young Morlock, something others were disposed to overlook or throw away. Over the past century, he often wished that Noreê had succeeded in her attempt to snap baby Morlock's neck. But if she had, he would have missed many an evening of drunken conversation, many an afternoon of brilliant fencing. That would have been a loss, no matter what else might have been gained.

Rather than say any of that, Naevros clapped his free hand on the higher of Morlock's shoulders and said, "Well, I'll walk you home. Maybe you'll figure out how to get rid of me on the way."

Every few days when the Graith was in Station, Aloê and a few of her friends had been meeting to watch the weather and drink tea. The Station was now ended and this was their last meeting.

It displeased Noreê that this meeting occurred in Tower Ambrose, which had bad memories for her. But she never let personal discomfort prevent her from doing what she thought of as her work. And the world's weather these days was her work—a threat to the Wardlands even greater than a thousand Ambrosii, or so she feared. In any case, she knew she would spend very little time inside her body while that body was in Ambrose.

She stood now in the sky over the Sea of Stones, a thousand miles away from her body. Normally, visionary rapture so extreme would result in physical death. But her friends had interwoven their psyches with hers, and they stayed more firmly anchored to their bodies, barely in rapture. Their strength, their collective anchor, strengthened and anchored her voyaging mind. What she did now was dangerous enough, but something short of certain death. And it was utterly necessary.

She saw mostly by not seeing. Her vision in rapture was a perception of living things, or at least potentially alive things implicit with tal. But what she was looking for was death, the absence of life or the elements of life, a black river in the sky with many tributaries from all over the world.

Its source was deep in the north—all the way to the end of the wide world, or so she suspected. It remained tantalizingly, painfully just beyond her scope of vision. If she extended herself farther, still farther. . . . What was distance to the soul? Nothing.

But it was something to the body, and she knew that if her body and soul were not to part company she must not go farther; she must turn back. After a timeless time, contemplating the ice-dark river of death inundating the world, she did retreat.

There was a comfort in turning away from the stark smiling skeleton of the dying world, to cover herself with warm flesh like a blanket, to settle for being herself and only herself again.

She opened her eyes and met the golden gaze of Aloê, who smiled a slow, worried smile in response. "You took a long time to wake up."

"I was. I was a long way away from myself," Noreê replied, her tongue feeling as thick and about as flexible as a plank of wood.

Aloê rang for tea; it was brought by a beardless dwarf Noreê thought might be a female. She had a strong distaste for dwarves, but she strove to never display or act on that emotion. She thanked the server and sipped her tea in silent companionship with her fellow Guardians.

"Do you think it's getting worse?" Aloê said, after part of an hour, at exactly the moment Noreê was ready to speak. Her intuition was powerful, subtle, enviable.

"Yes," Noreê replied. "The world's weather is growing colder. The life of the sun is being drained by something in the deep north."

"Will the Wards protect us?" Thea asked.

"For a time. For a time. But there is something there, preying on the sun."

"Someone will have to go and do something about that," Thea said.

They all nodded and talked about the details of their separate visions.

Presently Thea looked out the window and said, "Your men are home, Aloê."

"I only have the one."

"Oh. Well, Morlock is with him."

Aloê reached over to yank gently on Thea's nose, then got up from the couch they were sharing to shout out the window at the men.

Noreê drank her tea with slow deliberation. She would have enjoyed talking with Thea and Aloê some more, but now she would leave as soon as possible. She disliked how other women, even fairly intelligent women, often became twittery in the presence of men. Not all women, of course, but Aloê and Thea were apparently not among the exceptions.

Now the heavy unmatched footfalls of the two men were ascending the stairs outside the room. Her cup was dry, the teapot was empty, and she had the distinct impression she had missed several remarks by Thea and Aloê. No matter. These brief fugues often occurred in the wake of extended rapture; everyone knew about them, and that knowledge might help mask her distaste.

Now the men had entered the room, and Aloê put her lovely mouth, lips like dark rose petals, on the scarred face of that pale, crooked man. Not perfunctorily, either, but hungrily, as if it were a half-baked pastry and she was going to eat it. Disgusting.

Naevros stood aside, a patient smile on his face, and waited until Aloê turned her golden gaze on him. Then he stood imperceptibly taller, smiled imperceptibly broader. If most women were fools for men, most men were equally foolish for women, even if they didn't like them much. Noreê didn't listen to what they were saying; it couldn't possibly matter. These people had spent a century never saying what they really meant, until it wasn't even necessary to say it anymore.

Now Thea was chiming in; greetings, apologies on Noreê's behalf, yes, yes. Now they started talking about the vision. Noreê was interested to hear Aloê and Thea's account of it. Of course, most of what they said was quotation from her, right down to her assertion that "there is something there, preying on the sun."

And echoing Thea, Morlock said, "Someone will have to go see about that."

"Not you," said Noreê and Aloê in the same instant, surprising each other and everyone else.

"Why not?" Morlock asked, saluting Noreê with a mugful of tea. Her own cup was half full again. Perhaps she was really coming out of it, now. But she chose not to answer. She rarely spoke directly to young Ambrosius, never without regretting it.

Aloê said lightly, "Thea is already going. You don't want to steal her thunder."

"I suspect there'll be plenty of thunder to go around," Thea said dryly. "Let's talk it over when you're back in town again, Vocate," she said directly to Morlock.

"Couple months," Morlock said. "Maybe three."

"A halfmonth on the southeast coast, a halfmonth in and under the Northhold," Aloê said, "plus travel time."

"Soon enough," Thea said. "It'll be spring by then, with summer before us."

But what if you never see another summer? wondered Noreê. It was a cold thought from a cold future.

She sat there, drank tea almost as cold as her thoughts, and tried to pretend interest in what the others said.

CHAPTER THREE

Knife

Two months and some days later, on the twenty-fifth of Drums, in the cozy red gloom of their shelter, Aloê Oaij said to her husband, "I dreamed you were suspended between heaven and earth. Then flying knives pierced your body and all four of you fell. That's how it always ends. I've had the dream dozens of times since the new year."

"Eh."

Aloê was bitten by a century-long, never-slumbering annoyance. She sat up in her sleeping cloak and said, "That's all you have to say? Really?"

Morlock Ambrosius shrugged. "There are not four of me. I don't see how that dream can be significant."

"Noreê says it is."

Morlock was silent for a time. Finally he said, "She probably thinks there *are* four of me. Under her bed."

"You should stop napping there."

In reply, Morlock flipped a snowball at her. She fell over squawking, "Where did you get that?"

"It snowed again last night."

Aloê dodged out of the warm, fire-edged darkness of the occlusion into the fresh-blazing air of a snow-covered morning. She laboriously made a pair of snowballs (it was not a skill she had learned at her mother's knee in the Southhold) and then shouted into the occlusion, "Come out and fight! Aroint thee, dastard! If that means what I think it does!"

Aloê felt the impact of a snowball on her shoulder. Morlock had taken advantage of her concentration to sneak out of the shelter. She turned and smote him hip and thigh with flying, fragmented snow (her snowballs tended to come apart in midair), and from there it was a tangle of confusion where snow weapons gave way to hand-to-hand combat and, eventually, some uncomfortable but enthusiastic sex in a snowbank—a first, in Aloê's experience.

They repaired shivering to the welcome warmth of the occlusion and its dim red hotlight.

"After a hundred years of marriage, you still surprise me sometimes," Aloê said wryly, as they scrambled into dry clothes.

He smiled and pointed at her. She was left guessing what he meant by that—a feeling that did not surprise her, unfortunately.

Morlock packed up while Aloê unmade the occlusion. The icy bite of the unseasonably cold spring air was not as unpleasant as she had feared: maybe it was a good idea to start the day with a snowball fight and some frosty muckling. More experimentation was needed to confirm, she decided.

The snowfall wasn't deep enough to necessitate snowshoes, but it was deep enough to slow them down a bit. The day was half-gone before they reached the Shaenli farmstead, their usual last stop before ascending the Whitethorns through the Whitewell Vale.

When they got there, she found herself wishing they'd skipped it this time.

The farmhouse was burnt down to its timbers—a charcoal sketch of a farmhouse on the paperwhite landscape.

The farm animals and people were gone. But not all gone: what was left of them was bones—shattered marrowless bones covered with teethmarks.

"What happened here?" she asked Morlock.

"I think they made soup. There's the remains of a fire over there by the bone heap, and supports for a cauldron."

"That's not what I mean. Who did it? Why did they do it?"

"They came from the unguarded lands, I guess. Times have been hard there."

"*This* hard?"

Morlock shrugged and turned away. He poked with a stick in a couple of different places, brushing away the snow.

"Think they came that way," he said at last, pointing toward the Gap of Lone. "Maybe left to go up the Whitewell, into the Northhold."

Aloê had already drawn both those conclusions. "And so . . . ?"

"Something must have happened at the Gray Tower," Morlock said. "One of us should go there. The other should head north to bring warning to the peoples of Northhold."

"Well, would you like to flip for it?"

"I think I should go north, because—"

"Sh. I was joking. I'll collect what survivors I can from the Gray Tower and follow you north. Or maybe I'll take Grynidh's Underroad westward," she added reluctantly. "I should be able to raise some help from around Three Hills."

Morlock shot a gray glance at her. He knew how much she hated travelling on Grynidh's Underroad—miles of which were underground, hence the name. But he said nothing. What was there to say? If invaders were making soup out of the Guarded, she would have to put up with a little claustrophobia or stop calling herself a Guardian.

"Get along with you, then," she said.

He walked over, held her, kissed her, and walked away. He half ran in a springing long-legged stride that let him hop over the snow rather than slog through it.

She tried to imitate it as she went eastward. But, like so much he did, it was irritatingly inimitable, and she settled for slogging.

CHAPTER FOUR

Red and Gray

Along the trackless way leading to the Gray Tower, Aloê passed signs of the intruding enemy. She found another site of a cannibal soup-feast, scattered with gnawed broken bones that could only be from men and women; the blanket of new snow made it seem more innocent and more horrible than the other. She saw the intact skeleton of a unicorn: they had somehow managed to kill it and strip its flesh, but its bones had proved unbreakable. No animals remained in the destroyers' wake, not even scavengers.

She dreaded what she would find at the Gray Tower. She had spent happy months there as a thain, a long time ago now, and some useful ones more recently as a vocate. The memory of the tower said safety to her, as few places did. But now she suspected everyone there had been slaughtered and eaten. It was the only way to explain how the invaders had gotten so deep into the Wardlands without being stopped or, it seemed, even followed.

It was as bad as she had feared, and not so bad.

The Gray Tower stood on a bluff high over the Gap of Lone. It had done so, anyway. Now it was no more than a broken, blackened tooth against the bright winter sky. Aloê, climbing the path to what had been the entrance, passed heaps of discarded weapons, campfires ringed with shattered bones, shattered blue stones from the fallen tower.

There were no bodies.

But when Aloê came to the base of the broken tower she was greeted by a friendly face: Thea's. She was digging a trench around the tower's base. When she saw Aloê approaching she waved her shovel in greeting.

"How was your vacation, Guardian?" Thea called out when they were close enough for speech.

"Shut up."

"You shut up."

"Were you here for . . . ?" Aloê waved at the ruined tower and its environs.

"No, thank God Sustainer. Banyon Fourthstone was here, though. Seems to be dead now, along with everyone else."

"How'd you hear about it?"

"The boy on duty in the Maze managed to ring the warning bell before the invaders got him. Banyon sent a brief report through the message sock before he led the thains out to die."

"Uselessly?"

"Depends. They must have taken some of the invaders with them."

"And afterwards he provided the invaders with a hearty meal."

"Thank God Avenger you said that. But I've been thinking it."

Aloê tried to put herself in Banyon's place. She had never liked or respected him much; the Graith had voted him in out of respect for Lernaion, whose great-nephew he was, and Aloê thought that kind of thing was always a mistake. But what could have driven him to lead all his thains against what must have been a superior force? Maybe he couldn't stand the thought of staying safe in the Gray Tower while the Guarded suffered. Maybe that was it: *Maintain the Guard!* and all that. It covered a multitude of sins. But it didn't cover a failure of this magnitude.

"How'd you hear about it?" Thea asked, and then Aloê had to tell her about the grisly soupfest at the Raenli homestead.

"So they went up the Whitewell?" Thea asked. "And Morlock went after them alone? That's some kind of man you've got."

If I've got him, why isn't he here? Aloê thought peevishly, but she managed to avoid saying it aloud. They all had their jobs to do.

"Earno will want to know about this," Thea continued. "He and Noreê are around here someplace."

"What is it that you're doing?"

"They broke through the Wards somehow. The Maze in the Gap of Lone is gone entirely."

"God Avenger."

"And all the other gods, too. The Wards hereabout are anchored at the base of the Gray Tower, so I'm seeing what's left of them. Want to help?"

"No. But I'll be back after I've seen Earno."

Earno was the Summoner of the Outer Lands—the highest-ranking Guardian, except for his two peers, the Summoners Bleys and Lernaion. Aloê found him shoveling dirt into a pit. Noreê was shoveling alongside him, wearing the red cloak that marked her as a vocate, and quite a few gray-caped thains were also flinging dirt. Apparently the Graith of Guardians had become a company of ditch diggers.

"A dark, cold day, Guardians," she greeted them all.

Earno nodded, but did not stop throwing dirt. Aloê was about to ask what they were doing when she realized this must be a mass grave for the remains of the people who had died here. She sighed. There was no shovel that wasn't being used so she began throwing double handfuls of dirt from the heap into the pit.

Before they were done, Thea had come to join them, dragging her cloak behind her and carrying her shovel. Aloê took the shovel and finished the burial while Noreê and Thea stood conferring over the contents of her cloak.

When the pit was full, Earno threw down his shovel and turned away. Apparently any ceremony, if there even was one, preceded the burial. Aloê stayed to say a few quiet words to the departed spirits of the dead Guardians. She wasn't sure that it did any good, even for her, but she had caught the habit of talking to ghosts from Morlock's dwarvish kin.

When she lifted her head she saw the thains were making fires and setting up shelters. Earno was assisting them. Noreê and Thea were still standing together talking. Aloê joined them.

Thea's cloak contained a set of bluestone wedges shot through with crystal: the anchors for the Wards on this side of the Maze.

"What's wrong with them?" asked Aloê.

"Nothing, in a way," Noreê replied. "They are structurally sound. But they bear no more talic imprint than any other piece of stone—less than some. I'll look at the other anchors, but I expect to find the same."

Aloê nodded. It had to be something like this, of course. The Wards were not a physical barrier, in the ordinary sense. They were a vast talic web that made it difficult, not impossible, for a conscious entity to decide to enter the Wardlands—or to execute a decision already made. A skilled seer or a sufficiently determined individual could make it through the Wards. But in the

Gap of Lone a shifting, multifarious set of Wards were (or had been) in place that would allow anyone to enter—but only by taking a long and constantly shifting path over the plain. If the horde of cannibals had walked in with no warning, either they were all seers of a very high order or the Maze must have been completely suppressed somehow. The question was . . .

"How?" Aloê asked Noreê.

The white-haired seer shook her head. "I don't know. I'll stay here and see what I can do about it. If the Wards can be broken beyond repair . . . the Guard is not maintained."

"Maintain the Guard!" whispered Thea through pale lips.

Noreê said, "I think you two should go north after the cannibals. Take as many of the thains as you can pry loose from Earno. We must save as many as we can of the Guarded."

Aloê met Thea's bright, brown eyes, and they both nodded.

"A good plan," said Aloê. "We'll meet you back here when the battle is done."

"I hope you will," said the cold, white woman. "Go as soon as you can, if you would be guided by me. I fear our world is ending, but we must fight as long as we can. . . ."

On the first night of the month of Rain (ill-named in that bitterly cold year), deep in the southern marches of the Whitethorn Mountains, Sharvetr Ûlkhyn was shaken out of his nest by an insistent knabe.

Sharvetr had been the Longtooth of Graytown for five years now, and he had almost grown to like the job. But he did not like it—he would *never* like it when he was awakened in the middle of the night to deal with some terrible crisis. A cow that had failed to return to its pen, or the terrible discovery of a horde of cookies secreted by some ill-informed youngling.

So he snarled, "What is it?" at the knabe who came to wake him, and be damned to kithness.

The knabe, a female named Vyvlidh, said curtly, "Morlock's here. He says there's trouble."

"Thanks, kithling. Where's my kilt?"

"You're wearing it."

Sharvetr rolled out of his nest and strode away to the guest hall. Morlock was sitting there, drinking wine from the guesting cup. He set it by and stood as the Longtooth entered.

"Longtooth Sharvetr. I come with bad news, I'm afraid."

"Morlock, my oldest friend: you are welcome here with whatever news you choose to bring, or none. Sit. Drink your wine. We'll talk it out."

Morlock was an old friend to everyone in Graytown. He was one of the few who had argued against killing the mandrakes, born by the hundreds in the Year of Fire, hatching out of the teeth of slain dragons.

The mandrakes had been planted carefully in an empty valley of the North and tended like plants. When their minds awoke they were taken and taught the New Way of Theornn, gently but urgently, as if their lives depended on it.

Which they did. The Graith of Guardians was ruthless when it came to threats, or even potential threats. If the mandrakes could not resist the dragon-change, they were too dangerous to live in the Wardlands.

But the New Way blossomed in the hearts of the Gray Folk: the words of patience, hospitality, generosity, loyalty. Most resisted the dragon-change, and they took on themselves the honor and burden of destroying or exiling the occasional throwback.

Now Morlock sat on the couch and Sharvetr sat beside him and listened to his troubles.

"Khnauronts, are they?" Sharvetr said at last. It was the word used in Dwarvish of a being that eats the flesh of those that think and speak—often, but not exclusively, used of dragons. "They took the wrong turn in the Whitethorns, then. I doubt they would relish a bite of one of the Gray Folk, eh, *ruthen*-Morlock?" The Gray Folk, like Morlock and his Ambrosial kin, had blood that burned in open air.

"It's true," Morlock agreed. "But there are the folk of Ranga and its colonies—of Haukrull Vale—the Silent Folk in Kwelmgrind Vale—"

"Say no more," Sharvetr stopped him. "We are of one blood, *harven coruthen*, with all the people of the North. They could have killed us in the tooth, yet they let us live and taught us the New Way, so that we could be people and not mindless greedy animals. We will do what we can do to help. I take it kindly that you have come to us first. Unless you have already . . . ?"

"No, I go next to Thrymhaiam, and then to the Silent Folk. I hope I'm not too late."

"Then send a message through us to Thrymhaiam. You go to the Silent Folk. Your friend Naevros syr Tol is here—"

"He is?"

"He is, although he does not say why."

"Can we go to him, Longtooth? There's no time to lose."

"We can, but unless I am mistaken, here he comes to us."

Naevros burst into the greeting room and fell shouting on Morlock and embraced him. In the century or so that Morlock had known Naevros he had never seen him do something like that; he was embarrassed and honored and confused. He gently pounded Naevros on the shoulderblades with his fists.

"Now we're talking!" Naevros said, letting go of Morlock at last. "You know of the invasion, of course?"

Morlock told him what they had seen at Raenli farmstead.

"I was visiting with Illion's people at Three Hills when the news came to us, via message sock," Naevros explained. "The Graith sent me to rally the peoples of Northhold. Because half a millennium ago I was born in a fishers' cottage on the Broken Coast. Ridiculous. But you were on the road and no one could reach you. My apologies, Longtooth," he said, turning to the elected leader of the Gray Folk. "I should have told you my news when I arrived, but I was not sure what to ask—what I should ask—I—"

"You are not our blood, *harven ruthenclef*, as Morlocktheorn is," Sharvetr said with steel-cold civility.

"Yes. Exactly."

"*Ruthen* Sharvetr," said Morlock quietly.

"I understand, *ruthen*. He does not know our ways and no offense is meant."

Naevros raised his eyebrows at the word *offense* and would have spoken, but Sharvetr raised a long seven-jointed gray finger.

"Though you are not *ruthen*, I choose you as *harven*. We are of one blood, you and I. Ask what you would of me, kinsman, for blood has no price."

Naevros' eyes crossed momentarily at the thought of being blood-kin to a mandrake. But his practiced suavity soon came to his aid, and he said, "The Gray Folk chose their Longtooth wisely. I beg pardon for any offense, and swear kith with you and your folk on any terms you choose."

"There is no oath. Say or say not."

"I say it, then, and say too that you honor me too much."

"You are my *ruthen*'s friend. That is already much. We'll speak no more of honor, but of this danger in the land."

Morlock understood, as Naevros apparently did not, how angry Sharvetr was; many found the long-snouted, gray-scaled faces of the mandrakes hard to read.

"Have you told him, Longtooth, about the banefires?" asked Naevros.

"I have not."

"The night is deep and clear. Shall we go look?"

They went, with Naevros and Sharvetr refusing explanations until Morlock had seen what they thought he should see.

Morlock was deeply concerned. The banefires had been set on the grave-hills in the Northhold a thousand years before. They were magical prisons for the Corain, the undead sorcerer-kings of the Coranians. While the banefires burned, the dead Corain could no longer wander the land by night and afflict it, stealing bodies and lives. That was ominously like the Khnauronts.

Naevros led the way through the tunnel-like corridors of Sharvetr's house to a doorway that faced north and west.

The sky above was dense with stars. The major moons, Chariot and Horseman, stood high and bright above the ragged horizon to the west.

The land below was not utterly dark. Beyond the shuttered lights of Gray Town, Morlock could see Ranga's mining town, a sullen brownish glow to the north and east. He knew where Thrymhaiam was, farther north, but there were no lights to be seen: dwarves didn't like to break the darkness with light unless they must.

Due north were the gravehills, where the not-quite-dead Corain had been buried, and later imprisoned. Banefires were still burning there, as they had burned every night for a thousand years or more. One terrible night a century ago, the banefire on the Hill of Storms, oldest of the gravehills, had gone out when the Dead Cor within it died.

But now there were more banefires missing—a long, meandering gap into the heart of the gravehills. At the end of the gap was a cluster of campfires. "The camp of the Khnauronts, or so I guess," Sharvetr said, pointing.

"Are the—the Khnauronts freeing the Dead Corain?" Naevros said in his ear. "Are they eating them? What are they doing?"

Morlock shook his head. He didn't know. But, "We need to know. *Ruthen Sharvetr*—"

The Longtooth was only a red-eyed shadow against the lit doorway behind him, but Morlock saw him hold up his hand. "You Guardians will go into the gravehills. I will send a messenger to the Little Cousins under Thrymhaiam, and another to the Silent Folk beyond Kirach Starn. I think you had better write them a letter yourself, Morlocktheorn. Many of them dislike the looks of us."

"*Ruthen*—"

"*Ruthen*, enough. Blood of yours is blood of mine, whether they know it or not. I only speak the truth."

"And we should send a line south to warn the Graith of what we know," Naevros added.

"*Harven*," said Sharvetr, "it will be done. If you write that, and Morlock writes the others, then we can dispatch the messengers and go back to our several nests."

Sharvetr Ûlkhyn was not greedy for gold, or power, or rage, or any of the things that led to the dragon-change. But he loved to sleep nearly as much as he loved those of his blood, be they *harven* or *ruthen*.

CHAPTER FIVE

Evening in the Gravehills

The gray plume of smoke coiled in the darkening sky over the invaders' camp, deep in the gravehills.

Evening soup, thought Naevros glumly. *Just like mama used to make.*

His mother's cooking was infamously bad—one of twelve or thirteen reasons he rarely saw his parents in recent centuries.

He and Morlock had been worming their way into the gravehills for most of a day, trying to keep out of the invaders' way. So far it had worked, and this was their reward: a cold spring twilight was falling; they were days away from anything Naevros considered a civilized place to sleep; and a thousand paces away or less, a ghoulish tribe of cannibals was preparing their evening feast.

And, in fact, just when things seemed their worst, they actually got worse (as Naevros often found to be the case). As darkness rose into the sky, the major moons opened their eyes above, and blue light bloomed on the gravehills' ragged heights. These were the banefires, those magical prisons for the Dead Corain, buried in the graves that gave these hills their baleful name.

The banefires' blue light revealed nothing but itself. It cast no shadows and shed no heat. In fact, the gathering night grew suddenly colder as the banefire light leapt up on hilltops all around them, including the hill they were standing on.

Beyond the blue ridge of fire upslope from them there was . . . something. Something within the flames ringing the hilltop. Something that moved and looked vaguely like a man.

As Naevros watched in fascination, he heard a voice whisper his name. His name. . . . It was his name—yet no one had ever called him by it. Only this voice knew it; only this voice could touch that part of him. He climbed, against his own will, a step or two upslope. He heard the name that was secretly his again, louder this time.

"Naevros," Morlock whispered, and drew him back.

"Eh?" Now he had lost the name, like a dreamer loses a dream on awakening.

"Don't look into the flames. The Dead Corain can draw you to themselves through the banefire. They hunger for your tal and your living flesh."

"Do they?" Naevros shook his head and said, "Well, they can stand in line with everyone else. I'll get around to them eventually."

Morlock's shadowy face wore a shadowy smile. He led the way around the hill's shoulder, and Naevros followed him, taking care not to look at the dead shape whispering beyond the blue flames.

Eventually, Morlock went down on his stomach and squiggled forward like a worm across the hard windswept slope of the hillside. Naevros nearly rebelled at that. But anything Morlock was willing to do, he could do as well. He got down on his belly and squiggled. But—damn it!— he thought he did it with a certain style.

When they rounded the edge of the gravehill they could see the Khnauront camp in the valley below. But there were also many Khnauronts moving about on the slope of the gravehill opposite. What they were doing was not exactly clear in the evil light. But they were walking parallel with the ring of fire, not toward it—that much was clear.

As Morlock and Naevros watched, the banefire on the gravehill opposite guttered and went dark.

Morlock retreated instantly behind the shoulder of the hill and then drew to a halt. His face was unreadable in the shadows.

"What happened?" Naevros whispered finally.

Morlock whispered back, "I think somehow they killed the Cor who was trapped behind the banefire of that hill. The flame only goes out when its prisoner is dead."

"How do you know—?" Naevros started to ask, and then he remembered a story about Morlock. He changed his question: "Are they that desperate for soup stuff that they're digging up half-alive mummies and boiling them down?"

"Doubtful," said Morlock's shadow. "They want something else. The

Dead Corain were entombed with great treasures. Maybe . . ." His voice trailed doubtfully off. "Anyway: for the time being, this is keeping them from attacking the Rangan settlements, or Gray Town, or Thrymhaiam. Maybe we can pin them down here. Somehow."

As Naevros was about to remark, *And at least we weren't seen*, he noticed two skeletally thin ragclad figures creep around the shoulder of the hill he and Morlock were lying on. Morlock was looking past him with unaccustomed alarm, which meant there were probably other Khnauronts bracketing them on that side.

The two vocates leapt to their feet.

"Has to be quick," Naevros gasped.

Morlock said nothing but drew Tyrfing with his right hand and a long dwarf-forged stabbing spear with the other. He dashed north, while Naevros unsheathed his sword and turned south.

It had to be quick before they sounded an alarm and called the rest of the Khnauronts down on them. If they hadn't already.

The Khnauronts: it was the first time Naevros had seen them so close. They looked like men who had been a year dead, their flesh sunk down into their bones. They wore no armor and very little clothing of any sort. They carried a pair of weapons: a long serrated blade with a forked tip and something that looked like a short staff. Except, he saw as he grew closer, they were hollow, like tubes.

As he dashed up to the nearest one, he shattered the tube first. He didn't understand it, and therefore it was the most dangerous thing.

Whatever the Khnauront used for muscles, it was pretty effective. The one whose tube he had broken stabbed at him instantly with the forked blade. Naevros caught the fork with his own sword and twisted it out of his enemy's hand. Without bothering to shake his blade free, he thrust straight through the Khnauront's throat.

One down. So he briefly thought.

But the Khnauront's body didn't go slack. When he made to withdraw his blade, he found that the Khnauront's throat, flesh, and bone (so he guessed from the grind he felt through his blade) had already healed around his sword. Meanwhile the other Khnauront was attacking him.

With his left hand he snatched at the forked blade of the first Khnauront, trapped between the Khnauront's leathery flesh and the guard of Naevros' own sword.

With his hand on the grip of the unfamiliar weapon he brought it up in a swift parry to strike aside the stabbing weapon of the second Khnauront. He glanced at the second Khnauront's staff, fearing whatever use it might have. But he saw it was not being directed at him. The second Khnauront was pointing the tube at the throat of the first Khnauront.

Was it a healing device rather than a weapon? Naevros wasn't sure.

The weaponless Khnauront was flailing with his arms, striking out at Naevros and the second Khnauront with equal hostility. Did he have good reason? Or was he deranged?

Naevros swung his sword so that the Khnauront still impaled on it was between Naevros and the other enemy. Then he kicked the impaled Khnauront on the chest with his right foot, and kept up the pressure with his foot until his sword was free from the closed mouth of the wound.

The weaponless Khnauront danced with frantic hate, spinning around and around with his arms and one leg extended, striking with equal fervor at Naevros and his fellow Khnauront.

The second Khnauront kept his tube or staff or whatever it was directed at the first Khnauront.

The dry white lips of the Khnauront's wound opened in his neck again and emitted a whistling hiss. He dropped to his bulbous skeletal knees. His head fell askew, nearly severed anew by the wound Naevros had made, which had so spectacularly healed and was now spectacularly unhealing.

That was what the tube was for. It fed off life, the tal of the wounded or dying, and the Khnauronts were as prone to devour each other as anyone else.

He threw the forked blade like a spear, straight into the slack, gaping mouth of the second Khnauront. The Khnauront flailed a bit and then ran straight at him, keeping the tube directed at his dying comrade.

Naevros deflected the forked blade with his own and grabbed at the tube.

The second Khnauront began a freakish dance much like the first had, only it had a weapon to stab with. But Naevros parried the forked blade with his own and kept his grip on the tube and spun against the Khnauront at every turn. Between the two of them, they soon snapped the Khnauront's wrist and Naevros snatched the tube free in triumph.

He turned the tube on the second Khnauront.

Naevros didn't expect anything to happen. Obviously, whatever the tube was, it didn't take great intelligence to operate. These beasts (he could no longer think of them as even approximately human) clearly had none to spare. But he expected that they were in rapport with the instruments, somehow, that one couldn't just pick up one and use it.

But, as it turned out, he was wrong about that.

The shock of new life rushing into him was almost more than he could stand. All of a sudden he was many people, many voices. He saw their lives and deaths. He could do all that they could do; he knew all that they knew.

And then he was the master and they were all and forever part of him. He knew the Khnauront kneeling before him had been a farmboy until extreme poverty forced the farmer to fire all his workers. The ex-farmboy had returned in the middle of the night, using his knowledge of the house, and stolen one of the children. He ate it with great satisfaction over the next few days. Then, as there was no other place for him in the world, he had joined the Khnauronts.

Then all the other voices, all their knowledge and their suffering and joys were gone. He could not get in contact with them any more than he could get in contact with his liver: they were that ineluctably a part of him. But their strength was now his.

He turned away from the fallen Khnauronts, both dead now, and went to Morlock's side of the hill.

There is no time in a match with the sword; that was one of the things Naevros loved about fighting. Each moment is an eternity leading to another.

But the night was darker, significantly darker, than it had been. He guessed his duel against the Khnauronts had taken some time. He was interested to see that Morlock had not killed even one of his opponents yet.

Naevros usually preferred sex with women, as often as he could get it, but he considered himself a connoisseur of male beauty. As such, he usually had little regard for Morlock, a man without commanding height or any other particular charm in his appearance or manner.

But what Morlock could make that misshapen body do was indeed remarkable. The strength he could command! The grace with which he could apply it! And there was something about his eyes. . . . Naevros had to admit that Aloê's choice was not completely ridiculous.

Naevros watched with impartial interest as the crooked vocate slashed a dark, dripping wound in the sagging, leathery stomach of one of the Khnauronts. It healed visibly . . . but much slower than his enemy's had. The second Khnauront fed off the first, extending his claw-faced tube toward the healing wound. But the second Khnauront had already been wounded in the eye, Naevros saw, and the first Khnauront was feeding off that. . . .

Why had Morlock not finished them off? Naevros wondered. Naevros felt a natural pride in his own abilities, but he knew those of his sparring partner equally well; surely Morlock could have finished off at least one of them by now.

As he watched Morlock watching them, he guessed that . . . that Morlock was *curious*. Yes, that was it. He was wounding them, watching them, waiting to see what would happen.

Naevros realized that here, at last, he had a chance to be free of his rival once and for all. He could, for instance, trip Morlock and walk away while the Khnauronts finished him off. No one could blame him: there were always casualties in war. And he would bring a secret that would help defeat the Khnauronts completely. Aloê would grieve, of course, and Naevros would have to wait. But he knew he could wait as long as he had to. This was his chance indeed.

He didn't take it. He raised the claw-faced tube in his hand and drained the wounded Khnauronts. The torment and the ecstasy swept over him as before, but it was less distracting. There was a sense of satiation, almost of bloat.

Did the Khnauronts cultivate their starved, stringy frames to be more receptive to the stolen tal from their victims? Was the constant quest for this ecstasy what had gnawed away at their intelligence—their souls? For the first time, Naevros understood the Khnauronts: what they were, and why they did what they did. It wasn't the hunger for food. It was the hunger for *that*: the burst of life that came from someone's death. And now he knew that hunger himself.

The Khnauronts fell sprawling, losing grip on their weapons. Morlock advanced cautiously and severed the hands holding their tubes. He impaled the hands each through the wrist with his sword, like chunks of meat on a skewer. Then he carried the skewered hands, still gripping the claw-faced tubes, over to Naevros.

"Let's go," he whispered. His throat was dry; his face was wet; his stance was weary. Naevros felt for him the smug pity that the well-fed rich feel for the hungry poor.

"What are those?" Naevros said, gesturing at the hands. "Souvenirs?"

"The wise should see these things and learn from them," Morlock said. "Noreê, Illion, the seers of New Moorhope."

"But you don't want to touch them."

"No. You," Morlock said, nodding at the tube in Naevros' hand, "are a braver man than I am."

Naevros remembered the cold, gray gaze as Morlock watched the Khnauronts feed on each other while he fought both for his life.

"You'll do," he told his friend and enemy.

They fled westward then, bearing their trophies and the news that would restore the Guard, at least for a little while.

CHAPTER SIX

The Hill of Storms

War was not a business at which the Graith of Guardians excelled. The Guard was supposed to keep enemies outside the borders, and the Wardlands did not indulge in wars of conquest.

An army needs a command structure, and the Graith was designed to provide nothing of the sort. All the vocates were free agents who could disregard direct orders even from the summoners, and the summoners were coequal in authority and reputation, at least in theory. Thains were bound to follow orders of senior Guardians, but even they were known to disobey. In fact, the most disobedient thains were viewed as having the most potential as vocates.

The force of Guardians that went north along the Whitewell, in response to the summons of Sharvetr Ûlkhyn, was an army replete with commanders and woefully short on common soldiers. The Summoner Earno was there, with an attendant cloud of thains and vocates. Aloê Oaij and Thea Stabtwice were there, and they had been joined in the jaws of the mountain pass by dry, dark Summoner Lernaion and fifty attendant thains.

In the end, it was Aloê and Thea who ended up leading the group by the simple expedient of getting up early and walking in the direction they thought most advisable. They listened politely to everyone who gave them advice in the course of the day, but they only conferred with each other.

That changed one morning on the slopes below Gray Town. The mountain village was completely abandoned—not in a panic, it seemed, and not because of attack from the Khnauronts (as Sharvetr had named them—as good a name as any). The Guardians spent the night indoors there, and the next morning they cautiously descended into Northhold.

They were negotiating a tricky path down a steep slope, dense with shik-needle trees, when one of the conifers spoke to then: *"Rokhleni!"*

Aloê and Thea both halted, and the trail of Guardians behind them did likewise.

A short stocky shape detached itself from the tree and walked up to them. It was a female dwarf, her dark, plaited hair streaked with gray. She was clad in mottled grayish green; there was a longbow and a quiver slung over her broad shoulders and a long knife in her belt.

"Harven Rynyrth!" called Aloê. "Well met, *Rokhlan!"* added Thea.

"Harven Rokhlanclef Aloê," said Rynyrth kyr Theorn. They were *harven* to each other because Rynyrth was the daughter of Oldfather Tyr, and Morlock was his harven son. "And *Rokhlan* Thea. We are well met indeed, but not by accident. Eldest Vetrtheorn knew that Guardians would be travelling north to fight the Khnauronts, and he told us to meet you. I'm glad the Graith sent you two."

"We sent ourselves," Thea said.

"Yes, I see that," Rynyrth replied with a half-smile, glancing up the slope at the trail full of Guardians. *"Weidhkyrren!"* she called out. "Greet your allies!"

The needle-thick trees gave birth to a company of short, stocky, militant dryads. Aloê's guess was that their company had doubled in size.

The *Weidhkyrren* from Over Thrymhaiam are the huntresses and farmers of the underground realm. Aloê had come to know a few of them over the years, especially their leader Rynyrth, who she would without question want at her side if it came to a life-or-death fight. Vetr the Eldest of Theorn Clan was a steady, honest fellow. His sister Rynyrth was dangerous.

"What are your people armed with?" Rynyrth asked. "The latest from my brother Morlock says that distance weapons are best against these beasts."

Thea displayed her spear. Aloê shamefacedly presented the knife she had scavenged from the burned-out Raenli homestead, and a club that had, until recently, been a tree branch.

Rynyrth examined them gravely. "I know you are dangerous with any weapons," she said. "But my *weidhkyrren* bring songbows with gravebolts, enough to arm most of you."

Aloê dropped her club and sheathed her knife with great relief, accepting the new weapons offered by the dwarves. Thea was more reluctant: she was used to her spear, which was strong enough for stabbing but balanced for throwing. But there was no denying the greater force of the songbow, so she slung her spear over her shoulder for emergencies and adapted to the needs of the moment.

The gravebolts were much like ordinary arrows, but the shaft of each one contained an impulse well.

"The gore," Rynyrth explained to Thea, tapping the pointed arrowhead, "bears a talic oculus. See that silver ring around the point? You take the bow; you aim the bolt at what you would strike. If the target has a talic presence, the arrow will perceive it. The pattern in the arrowhead freezes at the moment of release from the bow. The bolt will travel straight from the release to the target. Don't count on a rise and fall, as you would with a normal arrow."

Rynyrth drew a gravebolt from her own quiver. She showed a mark on the shaft to the Guardians: it looked a bit like a pine tree with the branches missing on one side. "Note the rune. Your gravebolts will fly at the note of your songbow, no other." She spun the arrow a few times to fill its impulse well and then fitted the bolt to her bow. She took aim at a nearby tree; she released the arrow and the bow sang it on its way. It struck the tree with splintering force and the tree shed a year's worth of new needles. Rynyrth retrieved the gravebolt and showed it to Thea and Aloê: it was undamaged. She replaced it in her quiver.

Thea was impressed. "What is its range?" she asked.

"It will vary from *weidhkyrr* to *weidhkyrr*. We find a gravebolt usually travels three or four times as far as an ordinary bowshot."

"And it always hits its target."

"There is no always. The target must have a talic imprint, and that imprint must be more or less stable. But usually a shot means a strike."

"It's not very sporting."

Rynyrth's dark eyes crossed with amusement. "Listen, *Rokhlan*, I don't know how it is with you. We do not shoot for sport. For sport we sing and dance; we climb trees; we juggle; we do many things. When we shoot, we kill."

Aloê almost spoke to interrupt the tension she saw developing between the two females, but Thea laughed and put her hand on Rynyrth's shoulder and the moment passed. Thea was much like one of the *Weidhkyrren*, Aloê reflected. She never fought without purpose, and then she fought without quarter.

From that moment their dual leadership became a triad. In principle, Guardians could not command the Guarded, and in addition Rynyrth was a sensible female who had seen combat before, albeit not since the Year of Fire when dragons invaded the Northhold.

They paused for part of that day so that the Guardians could acquaint themselves with their new weapons and so that the two groups could acquaint themselves with each other. Rynyrth had news, too, that the senior Guardians needed to discuss. Lernaion and Earno, their resplendent white cloaks somewhat the worse for travel, joined the informal council but listened more than they spoke. There was an art to being a summoner; Noreê called it "leading without command." Aloê didn't fully understand it, but she was glad that the males didn't try to steal the thread of conversation.

Rynyrth used the butt of her songbow to sketch out a rough map of the gravehills on a patch of soft ground. "Eldest Vetr is sending his bowmen—" She used the Wardic word with a wry inflection "—here, in the northwest. The Gray Folk, all but the children and their caregivers, hold the hills in the south."

"Where is everyone else?" asked dry, dark-skinned Lernaion. "We found their town empty."

"They are under Thrymhaiam, enjoying the courtesy of their *ruthen* kin, the Seven Clans." Again, Rynyrth smiled as she spoke: there was some tension there, Aloê knew, between the dwarves and the mandrakes. Or was it between the male and female dwarves?

"Word from your fellow vocates, Naevros, and my *harven*-kin Morlock is that they will rally the Silent Folk beyond Kirach Starn and attack from the west. They say they will drive the Khnauronts before them."

"Bold words," observed Thea dryly.

"Maybe. That *harven*-kin of mine is reckless enough to earn a hero's grave." She drummed her fingers thrice on the wood of her songbow. "Not in this war, we hope, Oldfather Tyr."

Aloê did not disagree with any of this, but there were more urgent matters to discuss. "Then we stand in the east and await the retreat of the Khnauronts?"

"You stab at the matter's heart," Rynyrth said agreeably.

"Then I recommend we take up station on and around the Hill of Storms," Aloê said. "It is the tallest of the gravehills—best for watching, best for defense, and it commands the passes to the south, if the Khnauronts try to flee that way."

"You speak my thought, *harven*."

"Agreed," said Thea.

The summoners said nothing, but turned away to call their junior Guardians back to the march. The red-cloaked vocates among them had as much right as anyone else to participate in the decision just made, but none of them seemed to have been interested. Aloê was often struck at how often the independence of the vocates was merely theoretical. As soon as most Guardians got the right to stand among the Graith at Station and wear the red cloaks of vocates, they sought out one of the summoners to follow, as if they were still thains. It was odd to her . . . but in this case it made for a quicker result.

They pressed their march and halted at last in twilight on the dark shoulders of the Hill of Storms, or Tunglskin, as the dwarves called it. Thains, vocates, and *weidhkyrren* sat side by side, drank water or bitter ale from bottles, and munched cold provisions. There was not much talk.

Aloê, Thea, Rynyrth, and the summoners stood atop the hill, in front of the Broken Altar. Once the first and greatest of the Corain had been imprisoned here, but he had been slain at last and in truth during the Year of Fire by a bewildered young man whom Aloê had later married. She took some comfort from that thought but didn't speak of it. She spent part of the time going through her quiver and making sure the gravebolts all bore the same mark as her songbow: a tangle of curves with a sharp protrusion or two—something like a rose. There was little chance her *harven*-kin would have made a mistake and included the wrong gravebolt in her quiver . . . but it is the kind of life-losing chance that sometimes happens in combat. Anyway, there was little else to do.

As night arose, the three moons opened their eyes: Horseman glowering and red in the west, Chariot perhaps halfway up the vault of the sky, with Trumpeter rising, searingly bright in the west.

"*Khai, gradara*," whispered Rynyrth to the rising moon.

As if in response, the banefires were kindled on the gravehills—but not on all of them. There was a cloud of darkness in the heart of the burning blue graves.

"Rokhlan Earno," Rynyrth said, "why do they kill the dead Corain? We know it is so because the Guardians said it in their message, and because we in Over Thrymhaiam watched the banefires go out, one by one. But we don't understand. Why kill the dead?"

"Dead is a relative term," Lernaion began, but Earno, talking over him, said, "Incidental, I think. The banefires are tal-sinks—they are meant to drain away the tal of the dead Corain. Unfortunately, they learned to master them and use them to drink the tal of living beings nearby. It is the tal implicit in the banefire web that the Khnauronts crave. We think they live on tal as much or more than they live on flesh."

Aloê could feel Lernaion's unspoken anger, Earno's obvious indifference. There was a cleft between the summoners, that much was clear.

She turned her insight outward, to the darkness in the gravehills. She saw no smoke in the sky, tasted no distant fire on the cold wind. If the Khnauronts had made camp, it was far away indeed.

Rynyrth, too, had been looking into the dark gravehills, and now she lay down on the face of the hill and embraced it like a child embracing her mother. Presently she leapt up.

"*Lukharnadh hai, ruthenen!*" she cried. "Be ready, too, Guardians of the south! I hear dwarvish boots on these hills. I hear the tramp of many slender feet. The battle is joined and comes toward us!"

Guardians and dwarves alike leapt to their feet. Rynyrth ran up and down their lines, arranging them in ranks of three.

Aloê reflected that the command of three had shrunk to one. A glance at Thea's face, rueful in shadows, showed that her comrade was thinking the same thing. But the anarchy of the Wardlands worked because people were willing to let the work be done by the one who could do it best. In this place, in this hour, it was Rynyrth.

Rynyrth returned to them, saying as she approached, "Each fighter has only so many gravebolts, and the Khnauronts drink life, as Rokhlan Earno has told us. A warrior without bolts, or who has been wounded, must make place in the front for another. The unwounded shall be a wall for the wounded."

"Earno told you," said Lernaion, "yet I think you knew it already."

"It was in *Harven* Morlock's last message to us."

"Hmph. He takes a lot on himself."

Aloê didn't like where this conversation was going. It wasn't for Guardians to be keeping needful knowledge from the Guarded, but Lernaion seemed to think that Earno and Morlock should have done so. She wondered if Rynyrth would be offended, but the dwarf said only, "He was ours before he was yours. He will be ours again when you are done with him. You will pardon him, I hope." As she spoke, she unslung her songbow, drew a gravebolt from her quiver, twirled it and set it to the bow. The Guardians, more slowly, with less practiced hands, did likewise.

They all waited as the stars spun slowly beyond the moons overhead, and the rumbling in the hills grew louder.

There were lights, now, casting distorted shadows on the steep gray hillsides—real lights, not the deceptive glare of banefire. Aloê could hear the clash of metal on metal but no voices yet.

Stick-thin figures stumbled into sight, lit indirectly by the approaching lights. Most clutched a wand with a clawed end in one hand and a stabbing weapon in the other; some had only the stabbing weapons. The wandbearers pointed their wands at the wandless, who thrashed about and fell and crawled and were suddenly still.

"You see it, *harven*?" Rynyrth hissed in her ear. "These beasts eat their wounded, like pus-rats. Those clawed sticks: those are the lifetakers."

More Khnauronts flooded into view. There were very many of them—hundreds or thousands—many times the little company stationed on the Hill of Storms.

But they were not alone. Beyond them, driving them, came a cohort of bearded dwarves. They marched in close ranks; each dwarf bore a glass shield in one hand and a spiked silver mallet. Floating above them like banners, supported by nothing Aloê could see, were coldlights illumining the battle.

The dwarven soldiers used the spikes on their mallets to stab, but swung the weights to break weapons or lifetakers when they could. Their progress was slow but relentless.

The slopes opposite them suddenly bristled with gray shadows and fire-red eyes: the Gray Folk, driving another mob of Khnauronts before them.

"The moment will be soon," Rynyrth said. "When they know we are here, blocking their retreat, they will charge the hill or attempt to flee up the valley to our south. We must be ready."

"We should tell the others," Thea said.

"My people know, and they will tell their allies, as I tell you."

Now, at last, they heard the distant sound of shouting. Opposite the Hill of storms, to the west, Aloê saw a cloud of torches, dark human shapes among them. She thought some of them were carrying pitchforks.

It was the so-called Silent Folk. They came from cities and towns and had no strong allegiances or families to protect them, so they banded together in the League of Silent Men and the Guild of Silent Women. A few decades ago they had settled a valley in the North.

They were farmers with no great sense of discipline or purpose or the dangers of war. They could only be armed with improvised weapons. But they had come to defend their land in this moment of danger. Of all those in this fight, they were the most at risk.

At their head, as she had expected and feared, Aloê saw a crooked, red-cloaked figure; he carried a sword in each hand and no shield. Another red-cloaked form, taller and more regular, stood beside him with shield and sword.

Before she could say, even to herself, *Don't do that, you idiots!* the two red-cloaked figures leapt into the thick of the retreating Khnauronts and began cutting a swathe through their midst. When the dwarves saw this, they finally began to chant, "*Ath, Rokhleni! Ath*, Ambrosius*! Ath*, Naevros*! Ath! Ath!*" Their line bent into a wedge, and the sharp end drove deep into the Khnauronts.

"Ambrose! Ambrose! The bond of blood!" called out the Gray Folk in fell voices as they dropped down on the Khnauronts like an avalanche from the hills.

The Khnauronts were in full retreat. The descent of the Gray Folk had closed off the retreat to the south. They turned toward the slopes of the Hill of Storms.

"Now!" called Rynyrth, lifting her own bow to the ready. "Sort friend from foe and strike for your blood, *harven* or *ruthen!*"

The songbows sang; the gravebolts flew, bright with moonlight against the dark ground; ragged ranks of skeletal Khnauronts went down in the cold light of the dwarvish banners. Aloê saw with disgust that the Khnauronts did indeed use their wands on each other, "eating their own wounded," as Rynyrth had put it. Every time she saw a Khnauront do that, she aimed a gravebolt at him. Let the eaters be eaten.

Morlock and Naevros' wild whirling course had carried them through the mob of Khnauronts, and they turned again to strike into the heart of the fragmenting mob.

Now the ragged wave of Khnauronts was climbing the slope of Tunglskin. The gravebolts thinned their ranks, but the survivors fed on the tal of the fallen. The enemies were close enough that Aloê could actually see their black wounds closing like mouths. Their faces were full of ecstasy rather than fear or hate.

When there were only a few paces between the foremost of the enemy and the line woven of dwarves and Guardians, Aloê gripped her bow with her right hand just below its runic rose, wielding it like a club; she drew her knife with her left. Then she leaped out of the line and tore into the Khnauronts, smashing their wands with the weight of her bow, stabbing and parrying with the long knife.

Rynyrth followed her, shouting, "*Ath, Rokhlan! Khai, Oaij! Ath! Ath!*"

Glancing about to be ware of friend and foe, Aloê saw that Rynyrth was also wielding her bow like a club. For a stabbing weapon, she carried a forked spear of the kind the Khnauronts used.

Lernaion's bitter, dark eyes were lit with rapture. He stood wavering, like a man about to fall asleep on his feet. But any Khnauront that approached him fell lifeless to the ground.

Earno had seized a fallen Khnauront by the heels and was swinging him in a circle, striking down his enemies with his enemy.

There were moments of wild chaos as all the lines of battle met and mixed on the dark slopes of Tunglskin.

Then the surviving Khnauronts were throwing down their weapons and speaking or weeping with dry, birdlike clicks. They didn't seem to be surrendering so much as despairing. These had no lifetaker wands. The Khnauronts with wands fought to the death, or until their wands were broken.

Now the battle had ended, but the chaos continued to swirl in Aloê's mind and heart. She was wounded, she saw: twice in the left side, once in the left arm. She had lost her knife somewhere. She felt frail and crunchy, like a dry cicada husk.

Moonslit moments, separated by moonless dark. She saw Rynyrth and a band of *weidhkyrren* forcing the defeated Khnauronts to kneel. She saw Deor, his dark eyes fierce, his face unwontedly grim. He didn't seem to see her, and somehow she could not speak to him.

She heard someone speaking, almost whispering, nearby her. "They will make that crooked man king someday. At least in the North."

She turned toward the voice. It was Lernaion's, and he wasn't speaking to her. He was speaking in Earno's ear, a dozen paces away, but somehow she could hear it, as if this were a dream. And she heard Summoner Earno's curt response as clearly: "Shut your lying mouth."

She looked around for Thea. There were Guardians gathering by the two summoners, but she was not among them. She saw the Gray Folk and the Dwarves mingling on the lower slope, talking in their harsh language—like rocks breaking, she often thought. She saw Morlock and Naevros at the bottom of the slope, leaning on each other in their weariness. She would have gone to them if she had the strength, but which one should she go to? Thea would know. She would at least have an opinion.

Aloê looked over her shoulder. At last she saw her friend, where she had fallen in the line, a pale shriveled form on the dark summit of the star-crowned hill.

There must have been other things, but she never remembered them later, and I will not tell them now.

PART TWO

Rites of Spring

I hate the dreadful hollow behind the little wood,
Its lips in the field above are dabbled with blood-red heath,
The red-ribb'd ledges drip with a silent horror of blood,
And Echo there, whatever is ask'd her, answers "Death."
—Tennyson, "Maud"

CHAPTER ONE

What Really Happened

The price of victory is work. The defeated need only flee or die, but those who win the battle must tend the battlefield like a bloody garden, and even take care of their late enemies, living or dead.

The price of fighting a war at all is forgetfulness. In the thick of fighting, few if any have the leisure to ask how it started or why.

In her time, Noreê had fought with sword and knife and naked fist to maintain the Guard. She would do so again. But, as she and her thains-attendant rewove the maze in the Gap of Lone, she had leisure to think of many things.

One was how to make a stronger defense of the Maze. This was mostly a matter of geometry, redrawing the shifting lines of talic force in the Maze so that they tended to reinforce each other rather than work against each other. She developed the necessary pattern in part of an afternoon and taught it to her assistants that evening.

The rest of the time she thought about this strange enemy. Had the Khnauronts, those mindless cannibals, the Strength and the Sight to shatter the Wardlands' immemorial protections? It seemed unlikely.

Were the Khnauronts merely shock troops, sent to pave the way for a more formidable strike force? That was Noreê's secret fear, and to forestall it she drove herself and her attendant-thains night and day to refashion the Wards over and above the Gap of Lone.

But as days passed, and the Maze was remade, and no new enemy came, Noreê was compelled to entertain another hypothesis.

The attack of the Khnauronts was a distraction. Something else, someone else, had entered the Wardlands while the Maze was broken down.

She left her thains-attendant to complete the new Maze by themselves. They were delighted by the trust she showed in them, and even more, she realized, by the prospect of her absence. Unlike Jordel, she was not the type of vocate who drew the affection and loyalty of younger Guardians—and, in fact, she rather despised the type.

She walked at random east and south as her mood took her. As she walked, she let her mind drift away from her body in light rapture. She looked for nothing. She watched everything.

The snows of winter were slowly receding, but the greens of spring had not yet appeared. It was oddly like a warm stretch of days in late autumn. Perhaps in this year would come the last of all autumns. She could feel the weight of the death in the world, the hunger of many who would never eat again. It spoke in the silence of her dreams, whether she waked or slept.

She walked much, ate little, and dreamed all the time. Her course, if plotted on a map, would have looked aimless, but it had an aim in view.

Her thinking was this: Whatever or whoever had entered the Wardlands secretly had come too long ago for conventional methods of trailing. But they had come here for some purpose. The nearer they got to their purpose, the more of a shadow it would cast in the future. That talic shadow would fall, with increasing clarity, on the present. All her unlooking was to look for that. All her indifference was to highlight that difference.

Not many seers could feel the cold drift of talic change rebounding from a future event that might never in fact happen. But she was one, and she was here; the task was hers to do. She never shrank from such tasks, however repugnant they were.

So she walked and dreamed and slept and dreamed and sat and dreamed and waited.

The answer came straight to her one morning as she sat in meditation beneath a leafless maple tree. She looked up to see a man standing awkwardly in front of her. He wore a flat black cap to cover his baldness, and from the way he hid his right hand behind him she suspected he had murdered a close relative, possibly his father. He spoke hesitantly, "I'm sorry to interrupt your thought, Vocate."

"You haven't." She felt the chill breeze of the future in this sweaty, fidgety man.

"But you are the Vocate Noreê?"

"I am."

"There is—I don't want you to think I'm a mere informer. I don't expect to be paid, or anything."

"Be sure that I will not pay you. I rarely touch money. I have none with me now."

"Oh." The man stood still, the fidget struck out of him at the thought of someone with no money.

"You were going to say?" she reminded him.

"Oh. Yeah. There's. In the town there's a stranger, and I don't think he's one of the Guarded. He hardly speaks Wardic."

The future-chill in her mind transferred itself to this stranger. "What is his name? Can you describe him?"

"He says his name is Kelat, but I think he's hiding something. He doesn't even seem to know where he's from."

"Can you describe him?"

"He is taller than I am—skin paler than mine, or most people's—hair yellowish. He is staying at Big Rock House."

"At the southern edge of town," she predicted. That was what her insight told her, and the man said, "Yes."

"Thank you," she said and stood, ignoring his belated offer of a hand up. She walked away.

"And you have no money at all?" the man said plaintively.

"Is that why you killed—for money?" Noreê said to shut him up. And it worked: she never heard him speak again.

Insight, as Noreê knew better than most, arises from the interplay between the mind and the world of talic impressions below the level of consciousness. It was dangerous to be guided by it because it arose from the unconscious without the benefit of reason. So do actions of prejudice, of madness, of folly. To walk in the way of insight was to risk slavery to these kinds of blindness. It was one of the risks she often took for the Guarded, and she knew that they often had to suffer from her mistakes—her prejudice, madness, folly.

But not today. The wind from the future grew colder and clearer with every step she took. She spent a few minutes in un-meditation to bind her awareness more closely to the chaos of matter and energy that most people thought of (wrongly) as reality.

As she walked into Big Rock House she saw a blond man, of average height or a little taller, paying his score.

"Your name is Kelat?" she asked.

He turned to look at her. His brown eyes were vacant, like a dreamer's. His leather jacket was stitched together from the skin of garbucks from the plains north of the Dolich Kund. It was probably older than he was. The laces in his boots were woven from shent, probably harvested from the coast of the Sea of Stones. He was almost certainly a Vraidish barbarian, one of the horde that was gradually conquering the fragments of the old Empire of Ontil.

"I think so," he said. "Sometimes I think I had another name. Or will have."

The bald man behind the counter met Noreê's eye and wiggled his ears. Around here that was like saying, *Crazy . . . but what can you do?*

What Noreê could and did do was hit Kelat on the left temple; then, while he was stunned, she took hold of his neck and stopped blood flow until he passed out.

When Kelat was sprawled on the beery floor of Big Rock House she said to the old man, "This Kelat is an invader. His intent here is unknown. I need to take him to A Thousand Towers so that the Graith can question him on the Witness Stone."

"You'll want to talk to the Arbiter of the Peace, then," the old man said. "She can lend you a cart and horses, maybe a couple of boys to keep Kelat in line."

"Will you go fetch her?"

"I don't want to leave my cashbox."

"Which house is hers, then? I'll go myself."

"Aren't you the one they call Noreê?"

"They do call me that."

"I guess my money's safe with you. And I guess you're welcome to as much of it as you want. You and your sister cured my grandson of a madness once. That was before you were in the Graith—when you were still among the Skein of Healing at New Moorhope."

"Ah." Those had been simpler days. She missed them sometimes. But she did not choose to end up like her sister, who had opened up so many doors in her mind that eventually there wasn't much of a mind left. "I'm sorry; I don't remember your name."

"I think you never knew it, Vocate. It is Parell."

"Parell."

The old man flipped part of the counter back, bowed low before her, and strode off to fetch the Arbiter.

The Arbiter was a young woman, less than two centuries old, with improbably orange hair and black eyebrows. Noreê knew much about people and what they thought, but she did not understand why people dyed their hair. Both the attendants that the Arbiter brought with her had dyed hair as well, so maybe it had something to do with the local chapter of the Arbitrate.

They came riding in a donkey-drawn cart, and as soon as introductions were made all around, the attendants bound Kelat's sleeping form and loaded it into the cart.

"Do you want a force to accompany you?" the Arbiter asked, as Noreê climbed into the driver's seat.

"Only if you want someone to drive the cart back to you," Noreê said.

"That's not needful. Just return it to one of the Arbiters in A Thousand Towers. Or keep it, if it's any use to you."

Noreê nodded and was about to depart when she remembered something. "Arbiter, that man who told me of Kelat. . . ."

"Bakell. I know him."

"I think he's a murderer."

"I think so, too. He probably killed his father, but we can't prove it. He may have buried the corpse in his house, where we can't get at it. What can you do?"

"You could buy the house. Or someone else might do it on your behalf, to allay suspicion. He seems like someone who would do almost anything for money."

"Possibly, but then he'd just move the body and any other evidence out of the house before the sale was complete . . ."

Noreê waited for the Arbiter to complete the thought.

". . . and then we could catch him at it!"

"It seems likely," Noreê agreed.

"Thanks, Guardian. Ever think of joining the Arbiters?"

"Often. Goodbye."

She had a bad feeling about the Arbiter—something would go wrong with her, or to her, in the near future. Noreê didn't choose to know about it. She spoke to the donkey and it started up the town's single street. Another word led the donkey to turn up a track leading to the Road.

Money she did not need and could not use. It was others who paid— sometimes with their lives—when she met them. She was sorry for it, sometimes. But she did not do these things for herself; it was for the Guarded. So she told herself, not always quite believing it, as the donkey pulled the cart onto the Road and headed south, toward A Thousand Towers.

Before she reached the city, a passing thain told her the terrible and wonderful news from up north. The Khnauronts were defeated, Thea was dead, and they spoke of Morlock Ambrosius like a king. Like a king.

Thinking of a day in Tower Ambrose more than four generations ago now, the day Morlock Ambrosius had been born, she told herself, "I did what I could." She knew that was true. And she added, "I will do what I must." And that was true as well.

CHAPTER TWO

Blood's Price

Grief is love. That's the deadly thing about it. You cannot live with grief chewing away at your insides like a cancer. The pain is too great. No one can stand it. But to kill the grief, you would have to kill your love for the one you lost. That is a survival too much like death: to be alive, without love, without caring. Even if you could do it, you would not.

It was fortunate, in a way, that Aloê had been wounded, and that some carnivorous Khnauront had fed from afar on her life. (That was what they told her had happened.) She hardly had the strength to live or grieve. She felt them, grief and the longing to live, felt them struggling within her, shadows fighting in the sandy emptiness of her heart, and it was all she could really feel. But she didn't even feel that much. Her life was ebbing and she was grateful, in a dry, gray way.

Morlock was often there. She sometimes saw Naevros, too, and Deor, and Rynyrth. Once she asked one of them, she could not remember which, where Thea was, and while they hesitated, she remembered and turned her face to the wall.

And once she heard Morlock saying, "My life is hers. Take it all, if there is need."

And Deor was there, too, with his broad face made for laughing, but he wasn't laughing now as he said, "And mine. Blood has no price!"

"I won't be a part of this!" said a third person angrily. Aloê didn't know her. She was wearing the saffron robes of an initiate to the Skein of Healing, though. They were usually smiling, as if they knew some secret that you didn't, but this woman was not smiling. The secret in her mind had turned unpleasant.

"Get out, then," Rynyrth said impatiently. "We don't need you here."

"I cannot permit—"

"Lady, you stand on the western slopes of Thrymhaiam and I am the daughter of Oldfather Tyr syr Theorn. You do not permit me or deny me here. Go!"

The lady in yellow left and Rynyrth turned to Morlock. "Do you think it will work?" she asked him in Dwarvish.

As dry and empty as Aloê felt, she nearly laughed at that. If Morlock had made it, it would work. Whatever it was.

Morlock said, "Unclear. The pattern has been renewed, and seems to be effective. But the trigger for the spell is the desire for life. If she has lost that. . . ."

"We must try."

"Yes."

"Who . . . ?"

"Who do you think?" Morlock asked impatiently. "Who will die if she doesn't live? I know you two love her also. But it's not the same."

"Then!"

Aloê felt two pairs of hard, blunt, dwarvish hands lift her out of bed. As she stood, waveringly, on her own feet—not sure she wanted to stand, not willing to say she was unwilling—someone put something into her hand.

She looked at it uncomprehendingly. If Morlock had made this, it was not up to his usual standards. A spiderweb of silvery seams covered its surface, as if it had been shattered and repaired. It was a wand, about the length of her forearm, but not as heavy as it should have been. The end pointed away from her had a sort of clawed mouth. . . .

It was one of the lifetaking wands.

She looked up to see Morlock standing in front of her. He had a knife if his hand. When her eyes met his, he slashed his bare forearm with the knife and fiery blood sprang forth.

The two shadows struggling within her struggled no longer. Finally, they agreed on something. She learned then that grief is not only love; it is also hate—hate for whatever lives when the loved one is dead. The longing to live and the longing to punish everything alive had found something to agree on.

The lifetaking wand sang in her hand and she knew the evil ecstasy of stealing someone else's life.

She cried out, in delight and horror, and Morlock fell to the ground in a shower of burning blood.

As she came wholly alive she realized what she was doing and she threw the wand from her as hard as she could.

She ran to Morlock where he had fallen and knelt beside him. He was breathing at least, but his eyes were clenched shut and his breathing was broken by croaking sounds, as if he were choking on phlegm.

She ripped a piece of cloth off his shirt and carefully bound up the gaping wound in his arm. It wasn't the first time she'd had to tend to his injuries, so she managed to do it without burning herself. She put her hand on his face and waited for him to stop choking.

His breathing grew more even. His eyes opened and looked into hers.

"That was stupid," she said.

He coughed once, twice, and sat up. "Worked," he said.

"You could have died."

He looked at her with those luminous gray eyes and said nothing.

"Sorry to interrupt this tender moment," Deor said gruffly, holding out his cape, "but this is fireproof. And you're dripping fire all over the place. And we are surrounded by pine trees."

Morlock smiled with half his face and took the cape, wrapping it around his wounded arm.

"So," she said, remembering words that had come to her through the gray fog of despair and grief, "you brought me to Thrymhaiam?"

"Yes," said Morlock. "Our *harven*-kin insisted. In fact—"

He stood. She looked up at him astonished as he reached down and picked her up. He carried her in his unwounded arm out the door of the little hut and into the thin golden light of the ailing sun.

They stood on a steep slope on the western side of Thrymhaiam. The valley below was full of folk—mandrakes, dwarves, men and women, all waiting there, waiting for something.

Morlock lifted Aloê up and held her triumphantly over his head in the thin sunshine. "Put me down, you champion idiot!" she shouted.

The crowds below roared. It was like a storm at sea; it went on and on; there was no stopping it.

Aloê was amazed. Why did it mean so much to them? Was she, as a person, so important to them? Had she come to stand, in their minds, for all their dead and wounded, and their triumph in her healing was a way to overcome their grief? Was it because she was Morlock's mate?

She didn't like that thought. But she remembered a voice saying in the night, *They will make that crooked man king someday. At least in the North.* And she remembered another voice saying, *Shut your lying mouth.*

She wanted to agree with the second voice. But she began to fear that the first voice might be right.

The crowds were still cheering when Morlock turned and carried her back into the lodge. He laid her gently down in the hateful bed where she had spent so many empty hours, but it was not so bad now. Thea was still dead and Aloê still grieved for her, but the spring sunlight was pale on the windowsill, reminding her that the world itself was dying. She had work to do, while her own life lasted, however long that was.

She was alive enough to feel hungry and tired, though. A *weidhkyrr* named Khêtlynn brought her a bowl of broth and a mug of beer from the cooking lodge of the *weidhkyrren*, and she gratefully accepted them. After Khêtlynn left she napped until the woman in yellow returned to sew up Morlock's wound. The healer wore odd metal-mesh gloves to do the work. The thin sunlight and flecks of bloody fire glittered on the metal as the healer worked patiently, and Aloê nodded off again.

When she awoke, she found that Morlock was in bed beside her. Horseman was rising, its blank eye staring through the western window of the lodge. In the unforgiving light Morlock looked uglier than ever, and so tired—his eyes like bruises as he snored there. She remembered with wonder what he had done for her, and what he had said about her as she was dying. Now part of her life was his. She felt the honor; she felt also the burden. She kissed him gently on his weary eyes and slipped out of bed.

It was chilly for a spring night, but she wore her red vocate's cloak, wrapping it close around her. The grass on the slope was winter-dry and sparse, hissing against her shoes. Horseman was not in the sky, but great Chariot stood somber in the east, and little Trumpeter was high in the western sky, still full of light and hope. The major and minor moon gave her plenty of light to pick her way down the slope. She wasn't sure where she was headed but she had to get out and see something.

There was a camp in the valley below, almost like a town full of lights and people. She drifted toward it.

There was a fire surrounded by fire-eyed Gray Folk at the edge of the camp. They rose and spoke to her politely in their crunchy language, called her *harven*, and asked her to sit with them. She begged off, saying she wanted to shake her legs a bit. The idiom made their eyes stretch wide and she had the sense they were about to laugh. But they didn't laugh, and when one of them said, "Our word of respect to your husband, *Ruthen* Morlock," they all bowed their serpentine heads and touched their scaly chests. A voice whispered in her ear, *They will make that crooked man a king someday*. She turned away from them and it, striding deeper into the camp.

She saw Naevros syr Tol coming toward her up the narrow path between shelters, and she wondered what they would say to each other. Had he been among the crowd, cheering with the rest, when Morlock had held her up triumphantly in the sun? Had he been wounded in the battle? Who else that they knew and loved had been killed in the stupid war now ended?

He brushed past her without speaking. That astonished her. She almost turned and spoke to him, but then strode proudly on instead. Perhaps the bond between them was finally broken. Perhaps it was time for that: it was a time of endings.

Suddenly weary, she leaned against a wooden booth. She felt tears on her face, but only an emptiness inside her, frighteningly like the grayness of despair and near-death she had recently escaped.

"What brings you wandering into the night, *Rokhlan*?" asked a familiar voice.

She opened her eyes to see Deor looking up at her.

"*Ath, Rokhlan!*" she replied politely. "I needed to walk and breathe some fresh air. I was tired of that house of sickness."

"I understand that," Deor said, "but have you overdone it, perhaps."

"No." She stood tall and smiled down at him. "No! But . . . something bitter just happened to me."

He said nothing, but smiled and waited. He was a wordy fellow, but a good listener—a rare combination.

She found herself saying, "I walked past Naevros just now. I think he saw me—he must have seen me. But he didn't say anything to me." She halted then, afraid that what she had said might sound disloyal somehow.

He put his hand on her arm and said, "It has been a hard time for everyone. I assure you, Naevros was as worried about you as any of us. But relief from one pain can make us newly conscious of another."

"I suppose." She gripped his arm with her free hand and he released her. "And what have you been keeping busy with?" she asked. That he was busy was a given: she had known Deor almost as long as she had Morlock, and she had rarely seen the dwarf at rest.

"We've got to herd the surviving Khnauronts down to A Thousand Towers where the Graith can have a look at them and decide whether to expel them or kill them."

"No doubt."

"Well, Lernaion and Earno are sitting with their legs crossed, weaving a little version of the Wards for each of the prisoners. Then they are going to stitch them together into a kind of ghostly honeycomb. Then they'll be more herdable, you see."

Aloê thought about this plan for a moment, then said, "It must be an enormous undertaking. Surely there are hundreds of survivors from the battle."

"No longer."

"Oh."

"I guess you mean, 'Why not?'"

"I guess I do."

"The Khnauronts without their lifetakers are a fragile bunch; there isn't much that keeps them alive. All the wounded died. We had binders from the Skein of Healing working night and day to no avail."

"Odd."

"It's odder than that, *harven*. Many of the unwounded folded their hands and died. They looked—that is—"

"Yes?"

"They looked like you looked, until today. Empty. They'd given up. I'm sorry—"

"No, I understand. But some survive."

"Yes! We made them soup, you see. Some ate it when it was set before them, some didn't. The ones who ate lived."

"Perhaps you should have offered the others pie. Not everyone likes soup."

"Eh! I wasn't born to run a refectory for ghouls. They can eat soup or starve, as far as I'm concerned. But that's not the funny thing, *Harven* Aloê."

"There's a funny thing?"

"Well, more of an oddly disgusting thing."

"That is a little different."

"Shut up, can't you? I'm trying to talk here!"

She bowed low, waving her arms in a parody of a courteous flourish.

"I like how you put that," Deor said. "Anyway, you know how Southers cut up someone to find out how they died?"

Aloê smiled. She had been born on an island off the southern coast of Laent—about as far south as you could go and still be in the Wardlands. "I've never actually done it myself, but—"

"God Avenger!" whispered Deor, genuinely dismayed. He put a hand over his mouth, as if to prevent more offensive words from pouring out.

"*Harven* Deor!" she said patiently. She grabbed his free hand and held it in both of hers.

He slowly lowered his hand from his mouth. "It's just that I forget sometimes—no, never mind!"

"Never mind it, Deor, truly."

"What I really meant was, it's those strange women from New Moorhope who do it, the yellow-robed healers."

Some of those women were men, but Aloê wasn't surprised that the difference wasn't clear to a dwarf. It wasn't always clear to her, even back when she was studying the arts at New Moorhope. She nodded.

"They opened up some of these dead Khnauronts, you see. Actually, I think they opened them all up. And the ones who died from not eating, well, they couldn't have gotten any good from food anyway. Their innards or vittles, the parts that are used for nourishment—I don't know what the Wardic word is—"

"Use the Dwarvish one."

"Their *shykkump*."

Aloê thought she recognized the word—it represented the tract from the gullet to the anus, if she wasn't mistaken. She nodded.

"All that," the dwarf continued, "was useless, and much of it was gone, absorbed back into the walls of the body."

"All right. That is oddly disgusting."

"Yes. They were dead from the moment they lost their lifetakers. Lernaion thinks that the ones who could still eat were just recent recruits—their *shyk-kumpen* would have dried up over time, too. But Earno thinks that it might have been a rank-marker, with the inferior Khnauronts slurping down soup, and the superior ones feeding off their *tal*."

"They seem to be much at odds lately." (She remembered: *They will make that crooked man king someday.* And: *Shut your lying mouth.*)

"The summoners? Indeed. I could almost wish that Bleys were here to step in between them. But the downside would be. . . ."

"That Bleys would be here, yes." The oldest summoner was loved by few, if any, of his fellow Guardians.

Deor took her to see the captive Khnauronts, in an open field on the far side of the camp. They lay or sat each one alone, and Aloê thought she could see the faint imprint of something unseen in the pale, dry grass around them. Some were sitting upright with folded hands. Others held bowls of soup in their hands, lowering their faces to the liquid and slurping it up like animals. Yet others lay staring at the sky or sleeping.

The field was ringed with spear-armed, gray-caped thains. At a near corner, she saw the Summoner Earno, his legs crossed, his eyes glowing with rapture. Far off, across the field, she could barely descry another white-mantled figure: Lernaion, she supposed.

The wet succulent sounds of slurping were the only ones in the moonlit field.

"Do any of them talk?" she asked Deor.

"They can't!" Deor pointed to his throat. "No, um, *vyrrmidhen*."

"No larynxes." How did they communicate with each other? Did they not communicate at all? It was strange indeed. "They will have to be examined on the Witness Stone."

"So the summoners say."

Aloê's stomach moved audibly within her.

Deor glanced at her with a raised eyebrow. "Queasy?"

"Hungry," she admitted. The sounds of the soup-sucking ghouls were indeed disgusting, but the smell of the broth drifting through the cold air was like a breath of meaty heaven.

"God Avenger strike me dead."

"Avert!" she said automatically. "But do you suppose . . . ?"

"Of course! The Guardians, the Gray Folk, the Silent Folk all have refectories set up. Or we could go under Thrymhaiam."

"No . . . I should return up the hill to—" Morlock "—the sleephouse."

"Come in here. We'll get you something better than soup."

She found herself sitting on a long bench, eating some sort of roasted bird and the most delicious bread since bread was invented. The rest of the hall was dark, and Deor sat beside her, talking cheerily of this and that, eating roasted mushrooms and drinking wine. He persuaded her to drink some of the wine, and the drink might have been a mistake on her part. She was already weary, and the wine sent her right to the edge of sleep. She had little flashes of awareness as Deor half led, half carried her up the long slope to the sleephouse. Then he was tucking her into bed beside the still-snoring Morlock.

"I'm off in the morning with Earno," he whispered. "If I don't see you then, I'll see you in A Thousand Towers. Be well, and good fortune to you, *harven*."

"*Harven*," she muttered, and then he was gone. She wished she had sent a word of goodbye to Earno. She regretted it when she awoke alone, long after noon, and knew they must be gone. She regretted it still more when she realized later that she would never speak to Earno again.

CHAPTER THREE

Death of a Summoner

Ten days before he was murdered, Summoner Earno woke with a dry throat and a guilty conscience. The sun was rising over the high Hrithaens to the west. He had told Deor to wake him when the stars spun around to midnight so that he could watch over their charges through part of the darkness. But here it was, deep into day, and he was just waking up.

He shook off his bedroll and leaped to his feet to see Deor standing beside him.

"Don't trouble yourself, *Rokhlan*!" the dwarf said soothingly. "I and the sentinel mannikins watched through the night. The Khnauronts have been fed, and I was just about to make a little breakfast for myself."

"You should have woken me, my friend. You need rest, too."

"Yes, but I can sleep while I walk."

"You—" Earno peered at the dwarvish thain. "In fact? That's not just an expression?"

"In fact. Not day after day, but occasionally I should be able give you a full night's rest. You looked like you needed it last night."

"Thanks. I did."

Deor's notion of breakfast always involved hard-boiled eggs and sausage tarts, when they could be procured. Eggs were difficult meat to transport on a walking tour such as theirs, but Deor had packed away a surprising number of sausage tarts in a box lined with a kind of preservative gel. Earno found the tarts inedible when they were fresh, much less when one had to brush off fragments of salty gel. But there was tea and flatbread and broth to be had; they met Earno's modest needs for the present. He thought longingly of a cookhouse near his home in A Thousand Towers: he promised himself a month straight of suppers there when he got home (a promise he would not be able to keep).

Earno did not know he was about to be murdered. He avoided casting mantias or other kinds of foretelling because he was aware of the danger of causal loops, with a prediction effecting itself through his own reaction to the prediction.

But he had not risen to the level of Summoner of the Outer Lands without attaining some depth of insight. And what insight he had was making him restless, very restless, indeed, as if time were running out—for himself, for the people he cared about, for the whole world. And his reason confirmed what his insight was whispering.

He thought of something he could do, something he should have done before leaving the Northhold: warn Morlock of a particular danger. He could write a letter and give it to Deor. That way, even if something happened. . . . He didn't finish the thought. That, too, might become a self-fulfilling prophecy.

As he herded the pitifully few surviving Khnauronts southward, he composed the letter in his mind. The Khnauronts were completely passive, willing to go anywhere they were directed, and the wardlet woven around them kept them from wandering off the Road. They had a halfmonth left to travel, he guessed, but the Road was clear and straight. He sounded judicious phrases through his mind until he was satisfied with them. When it was time to call a halt for the night, the letter was done: all that remained was to put the words down on paper, and he did that by coldlight during the first watch. By the time he woke Deor for the second watch, the letter was written in dry ink, sealed, and safely tucked away. His conscience was never completely clear, but it was a little clearer as he went to sleep that night.

The fifth day before he was murdered, Earno received a note through the message sock he always carried with him.

The psychic weight of a message sock was not something most were willing to burden themselves with. A sock that had been anchored to a location or a vessel was one thing, but a seer transferring a sock from one place to another had to devote part of his strength to continually sustain the talic *stranj* between locations that allowed the socks to function, so that a note inscribed on the palimpsest attached to one sock was instantly mirrored on the palimpsest of its twin. Earno felt, as summoner, he could not afford to be out of contact with the Graith, so he always carried one, paired to a sock in the Arch of Tidings, back in A Thousand Towers. Lernaion, in contrast, rather enjoyed being inaccessible when it suited him, and Bleys travelled so rarely that the issue hardly ever came up.

The sock message that day was from Noreê. She told about the stranger Kelat whom she had captured, and concluded, *I am coming north to meet you. Keep to the Road.*

Earno read with interest the note on the palimpsest, and laughed when he came to the end. He showed the letter to Deor and said, "Noreê is a fine vocate, but a touch high-handed. Anyway, what would anyone do but keep to the Road? Is there another way south to the city?"

"She is the enemy to my blood," Deor said flatly, as if that was the limit of his interest in discussing Noreê. This choked off a possible line of conversation between them, and they spent most of that day in silence as Earno meditated on the burden of long hates, such as Noreê had for the Ambrosii, or the dwarves had for Noreê. Was it a weakness in him that he could not hate so long and steadily? Once he had done so. He could hardly regret it: the exile of Merlin and Earno's ascent to the rank of summoner were the result. But nowadays he liked most people he knew. He appreciated their oddness. He felt himself to be quite ordinary, perhaps too ordinary.

On the morning after he had been murdered, Earno Dragonkiller, Summoner of the Inner Lands, awoke with a searing headache and a bad taste in his mouth. He coughed up a clot of red-black phlegm and spent a shocked moment staring at it as it lay glistening like jelly in his hand.

"What's that?" his friend Deor syr Theorn wondered. "Breakfast?"

"Blecch," muttered Earno and wiped his hand on the dry, brown grass.

They saw to it that their charges had something to eat and drink, and then breakfasted themselves. Earno's bacon and porridge had a difficult time making its way down his throat. There was a soreness there, a swelling, and nothing tasted right. He scraped his bowl out on the ground, packed it away, and started the task of herding their charges through another day.

The wardlet around the prisoners was choosy about who or what it let past. That was convenient in preventing runaways. It was inconvenient when the Road passed through a wood. Sometimes they had to broaden the way, with Earno or Deor lopping limbs off trees while the other watched the prisoners in case they made a collective run for freedom (though they seemed disinclined to do so).

Earno found this work interesting: he rarely got to work with his hands anymore. But it was not very interesting; nothing was, somehow. He thought about the porridge and bacon he had failed to finish that morning. Worth killing for? Worth dying for? (Earno did not doubt that the Graith would decide to kill the captured invaders.)

The whole day was like that damn porridge: more than he wanted; a little difficult to get down.

The second day after he had been murdered went a little easier. Eating was a chore, but no longer a pain. And before they had walked long in the morning, they were joined by Noreê, who true to her word, had ridden up from A Thousand Towers to see if they needed any help.

It was interesting, but not very interesting, to hear Deor and Noreê spar with frosty courtesies. It was interesting to taste the relief he felt when the responsibility for the prisoners was shared by another Guardian. Their future deaths had been weighing heavily on Earno's mind (not that he thought that they deserved to live, just that the delay was a little wearing, a little wearing). The horse she rode was interesting: a gray palfrey all the way from Three Hills.

But not very interesting. Something had gone out of the world, some flavor or color that gave intensity to life, and Earno wasn't sure what it was.

On the fourth day after he had been murdered, Earno almost felt himself again. Whatever had afflicted him was nearly past, he felt—and that was true, although he didn't know what it was. He was borrowing Noreê's gray palfrey to see if he could put it through its paces. He looked up and saw Morlock and Aloê riding toward him, on the other side of a narrow stream, tributary to the River Ruleijn.

Morlock rode even more awkwardly that Earno did, and that almost made the old summoner smile. When he saw Morlock he was always reminded simultaneously of the proudest and most shameful times in his life, and somehow that made him almost smile as well. He didn't feel much of anything these days; he had borne the burden of a great secret so long he could hardly feel it, or anything, anymore. But it was a comfort to remember that he had once felt so intensely; it gave him hope he would do so again. The thought of sharing his secret, sharing the burden, was also a relief.

They were smiling at him, raising their left hands in greeting. He raised his own in response, and now he did smile. He urged the gray palfrey forward and it stepped down into the middle of the stream and stopped, the water foaming below the horse's knees.

Something was wrong. Morlock and Aloê were looking at him, eyes wide with shock. There was a warmth, a wetness running down his neck and chest, staining his white tunic red, mingling with the coarse gray hair of the horse's mane. He heard himself gulp air, although his mouth was closed. He reached up to feel the rough, blood-spewing, lipless mouth that gaped in his throat.

Then he fell from the horse's back into the clear, cool water.

At last, in the last moment, it returned, that strange bittersweetness, the tang of life, of really feeling and being. The bright, crystalline color of the mountain stream, the taste of his own blood in his mouth. He was alive again, wholly alive. Then, on the fourth day after he was murdered, Earno died.

CHAPTER FOUR

The Last Station

Fleeing from a nightmare, Morlock awoke entangled in the limbs of his glorious, darkly golden wife. He had, for one moment, the cruel comfort of believing that all of it was a nightmare: the dying sun, the cruel war with the Khnauronts, the deaths of so many of his friends, the dreadful murder of Earno.

But, as he lay still to avoid waking Aloê, he looked out the window at the cool silver-blue sky of spring and sorted the darkness of his dream from the darkness in the waking world. They were not dissimilar. He hoped that didn't mean they were true dreams.

Aloê was dreaming, too, and from the expression on her sleeping face the dreams were as unpleasant as his. He was moved to wake her when she whispered, "Don't go! You'll never come back! You'll never come back!"

He wondered if she were in rapture, adrift in the chill winds from the future. "I have gone before," he said quietly, "and I always came back."

"This is different," she sighed. She seemed to stop breathing entirely and he was moved to alarm. But before he could act, she opened her golden eyes and looked straight into his.

"Bad dream?" he asked.

"'Good morning, beloved,'" is the usual greeting," she remarked, "but I suppose when a couple is entering their second century of marriage—"

"Good morning, beloved. Did you have a bad dream?"

"Yes, sweetheart. And you, too?"

"Yes."

"Yours first."

"Can't remember much. My leg hurt. I was sick and—I was sick or something—"

"Don't get coy on me now, Vocate."

"I was vomiting. It was dark and . . . and you weren't there. You were never going to be there."

She was silent for a long time. "In mine," she said, "I saw you going away in the dark. The further you went, the older you got. You were all twisted and horrible. Yes! Yes! Even more than you are now! I couldn't stop you. I don't know why."

"In the dream, were you all right?"

"What do you mean? Alive, healthy, or what?"

"All that."

She closed her eyes for a moment, opened them. "Yes, I think so. I was sorry to lose you, but I was alive."

He sighed in relief.

She looked at him quizzically. "Is my death the worst thing you can imagine?"

"The very worst."

She smiled gently and said, "Beloved." But he wasn't surprised when she didn't say, *I feel the same way*, because he knew she didn't. She did say, finally, "We've lost so much. We mustn't lose each other."

He held her close. They lay together in silence for a while until they heard Deor shouting somewhere in the stairway, "I don't suppose anyone will want to GET SOME BREAKFAST BEFORE THEY GO TO STATION?"

The hardy Westhold steeds that they had ridden south were still enjoying the meager comforts of Tower Ambrose's stables, but they decided to walk to Station rather than ride there. Deor accompanied them, as their thain-attendant, but he would not be allowed to speak at Station: that was a right for full members of the Graith, which Deor never intended to be.

Aloê and Morlock had broached the subject to him only last night. There were vacancies among the vocates, after the defeat of the Khnauronts, and no one among the thains was as well-respected as Deor. But he laughed at their offer of promotion. "Look, *harvenen*," he said. "I am here, at the behest of the Elder of Theorn clan, to serve your interests and keep out of his beard (may it never grow thin). How could I do either of those things as a vocate? No, shut your faces. When the time comes that I can no longer be a Guardian, I will go home and raise children under Thrymhaiam, as God Creator intended."

The day was not warm, although summer was approaching. No one felt like discussing the weather, though, so they walked mostly in silence down the winding elm-lined streets until they ran into Vocate Jordel and his brother Baran, accompanied by a gray-caped cloud of thains. No silence could long withstand Jordel's relentless assault and they were soon talking about everything under the sun, except the state of the sun.

Where the River Road joined Shortmarket Street, they came across a company of thains armed with long spears. At their head strode bitter white Vocate Noreê. In the midst walked a dirty ragged figure, manacles on his arms and legs.

Morlock felt, and felt strongly, that anger was a weakness. But he felt its red fire infecting his eyes. He stepped in front of the troupe and said to Noreê, "Who is this?"

Stiffly she replied, "The invader I captured at Big Rock. He is a stranger in the land and here for no good purpose."

"How do you know?"

"I know things you will never understand!"

"Everybody does. Everybody knows something that someone else does not, and never will." He turned away from her and said to the thain nearest him, "Stand aside."

He was prepared to draw Tyrfing and fight if need be, but there was no need. Noreê was shouting behind him, and the hapless thain glanced in terror back and forth between Noreê and Morlock. Morlock simply waited, and in the end the thain stood aside.

"Stranger," he said to the chained man, "what's your name?"

"Kelat," said the stranger vaguely. "I think. I think that's part of it, anyway."

"You must go before the Graith and account for yourself."

"So the vocate tells me. I will, if I can."

"My name is Morlock."

"I've heard that name, I think."

"Eh. Show me those." Morlock pointed at the manacles.

Kelat lifted his arms and Morlock looked keenly at the fastenings. It would be easy enough to pick the locks, but. . . . He took the locks on each of the manacles between thumb and forefinger and twisted them until they broke.

"You may be king in the North," Noreê shouted behind him, "but you are not king here!"

Morlock ignored her blasphemy. He crouched down and broke the locks on Kelat's legs as well. As he rose to his feet, Kelat shook off his chains and said, "Thanks."

"It's nothing," Morlock replied. "Jordel," he said, over his lower shoulder, "where is the nearest bathhouse? Zelion's isn't it?"

"How would I know? Why ask me?"

"You have lived in this city for three hundred years, and your house doesn't have a rain room."

"I keep meaning to have one put in. . . . I see your point. Yes, Zelion's, and he's open in the mornings."

"Then." Morlock closed his eyes. "Deortheorn. You will take Kelat here to Zelion's bathhouse. See that he's cleaned up—" there was a smear of dried blood on his temple "—and his wounds tended to. Get him some clean clothes to wear and get him breakfast. Then bring him to the Chamber of the Graith."

"*Akhram hav, rokhlan*," Deor replied. It was an act of significant discourtesy, according to dwarvish standards, to speak in a language not shared by all present. But Deor always claimed that courtesy was overrated, and this was one occasion when Morlock agreed with him.

"I forbid this," Noreê said. Morlock turned to meet her ice-blue eyes.

"It doesn't matter that you do," Morlock said. "But if you choose to send one or more of your spearmen to keep watch on the prisoner, I won't object."

"No," said Noreê thoughtfully. "Let it be on your head when the Graith calls for him and he is not found."

Morlock grunted and gestured at Deor.

"Come along, you dangerous monster," Deor said cheerily. "Let's get you fixed up. I'm Deor syr Theorn, by the way."

"I'm Kelat. At least . . . I think I am. . . ."

The dwarf led the mystified stranger away up Shortmarket Street. Morlock looked again at Noreê and strode through the spear-thains as if they were not

there. He and the others walked on to the Chamber of the Graith while Noreê
and her thains lagged a little behind.

"That was well done," Jordel said in an unwontedly low tone of voice (for
him). "I knew she was keeping this fellow prisoner, but I never thought to ask
how they were treating him, I'm ashamed to say."

"We all share that shame," Morlock said.

"Was kind of hoping for a fight," Baran admitted grudgingly. Morlock
punched his massive arm and said, "Another time."

"I wish you hadn't knelt before him," Aloê said, after a brief silence, and
Jordel laughed as if this were a joke. But Morlock was pretty sure it was not.
She cared much for appearances; they'd had many bitter conversations about
such things.

They came at last to the city's red, ruined wall, half as old as time. The
Chamber of the Graith was there because in ancient days it had been a voluntary order to defend the city against its enemies. Now the city had better
defenses than mere walls, but they remained as ruined monuments of those
dark days.

The Chamber itself had its back up against the edge of a bluff over the
River Ruleijn, the river that does not run into the sea.

A flight of twenty-two stone steps rose from the street to the Chamber
entrance; on either side the stairs were flanked by bluestone plinths bearing
granite statues of gryphons. Today, sitting beside or upon the gryphons, there
were many figures cloaked in red or gray. It was the time of Station, when the
Graith stood in council, and the war in the north was over. For many of the
Guardians here, these were occasions for celebration. Morlock thought of the
bloody mouth that had opened in Earno's throat, and did not feel like celebrating.

Some friends of Aloê's greeted her: Callion the Proud and Styrth Anvri,
each with a single thain-attendant. Morlock exchanged polite words for a
while, then clasped Aloê's forearm and walked away. He was not in the mood
for small talk. He rarely was.

He mounted the steps and entered the antechamber. Thain Maijarra was
there, blocking the way to the domed inner chamber. It had been her place of
honor since before Morlock was born.

"Vocate Morlock," she said, and lifted her spear to let him pass. He
nodded and entered.

The two remaining summoners, Lernaion and Bleys, were standing over by a window, conferring. Lernaion, dark-skinned, gray-haired, and lean, towered over the bent, hairless, turtle-like Bleys. They both looked over at Morlock and, apart from their snowy white mantles, the thing most alike about them was the displeasure stamped on both their faces.

"If you will pardon us, King of the North," Bleys said in his warmest, most ironic tone, "my colleague and I would confer in private."

Again Morlock felt the heat of anger mastering his strength. He was about to stride forward and do—something, he didn't know what—when a hand firmly gripped his shoulder.

"Summoner Bleys," said Naevros syr Tol, "this is the council chamber of the Graith of Guardians—that is to say, the vocates. The Summoner of the City may be here to convene us, but you are merely here by sufferance. Be a civil guest, or leave."

Bleys smiled quietly and turned away, as if from a conversation of no consequence. No doubt he thought himself the victor, and Morlock, as he cooled, had to admit that the old man had drawn blood. But first blood was not last blood; he was an experienced enough duelist to know it.

"Thanks," he muttered to his friend.

"It's nothing," said Naevros, and let him go.

The domed chamber began to fill with Guardians, red-cloaked vocates, and their attendant thains. Morlock and Naevros climbed the stairs of the dais and stood at the oval table, where only vocates and the Summoner of the City had a right to stand. They were joined presently by Aloê and her friends, and Illion the Wise soon followed.

"I met Noreê coming in," he said to Morlock. "I'm afraid she is no longer your friend."

Morlock smiled slightly, but did not feel amused. These bitter gray ancients and their undying hate for him. What had he ever done to earn it, except be the son of his *ruthen* father? But he was not like Merlin. He would never be. He had shown them and he *would* show them.

Summoner Lernaion mounted the steps and strode to the near end of the oval table. In a stand there rested the silver Staff of Exile. Opposite him stood the Witness Stone, and around the long empty oval stood the red-cloaked vocates.

The summoner lifted the Staff of Exile and pounded on the dais with the blunt end, calling the Station to order. The Guardians all fell silent and a few laggard vocates took up places at the long table.

As the room grew quiet, Morlock felt his spirit grow quiet. This was his place. He belonged here; he had earned it, in spite of Merlin and in spite of all the people who had hated him because of Merlin.

Lernaion said, "I summon you to stand and speak, for the safety of the land and the good of the Guarded. Maintain the Guard!"

"Maintain the Guard!" replied all the Guardians under the dome.

"The war in the north is over," said Lernaion, "but the struggle to maintain the Guard goes on. We are met for at least three purposes today. We must decide the fate of the Khnauronts who survive: shall we kill them out of hand or expel them from our land, or is there some third choice? Then: one of our own order is dead, certainly murdered. We must chart a course of vengeance for this crime. And lastly we must investigate this stranger who came walking into the land under cover of the Khnauront's invasion. Speak, vocates: what shall we settle first? Or is there some other more pressing matter for the Graith to consider?"

"The stranger Kelat is not here," Morlock said. "He was in a bad way—hungry, wounded, filthy, bewildered. I sent him with my thain-attendant to be tended to. Thain Deor will bring him here presently."

"Or not," said Noreê drily. "In which case. . . ."

"Let's deal with cases as they arise," Naevros said. "I saw the man, and his condition shocked me. Are we homeless barbarians roving the unguarded lands? Even they know laws of hospitality and decency."

"He's not a guest," observed Rild of Eastwall. "He's a stranger, perhaps an enemy. Should we set him on cushions and feed him candied fruit?"

Illion the Wise said, "If we intend to put him on the Witness Stone, he should not be weak or weary. The rapport is a strain, even for the strong. What he deserves is irrelevant. We don't judge; we defend."

Noreê would have said more, Morlock thought, but she glanced at the faces of her peers and then stood back with her arms crossed: the debate was over. She never fought to fight; she only fought to win. Morlock respected that about her.

"Then we turn to the case of the captured Khnauronts," Lernaion said. "Death? Exile? Some third way? Speak, vocates."

"Exile?" said Aloê. "They are not among the Guarded. They don't belong here. We are really sending them home, if we send them anywhere."

"Where is their home?" asked Jordel. "Shall we question them on the Witness Stone, or are they too weak for the trial?"

"My colleague and I questioned them yesterday, with the assistance of Illion and Noreê. Some did die."

Jordel, not the most patient man in the world, was already rapping on the table before Lernaion was done speaking. "Excuse me! Excuse me! If you are asking us to settle the question, you must settle our questions first. Who are these people? Where do they come from? Who sent them here?"

Illion said, "They mostly come from the lands east of the Sea of Stones. Many of them have forgotten what names they originally had. None of them know anything about the Wards, or much of anything else. They live to eat; that's all they care about."

Noreê said, "Jordel, I share your frustration. I, too, expected answers. But it may be that the true commanders of the Khnauronts were the ones whose bodies had absorbed their guts and were living on stolen tal alone—"

A storm of questions arose at this; most of the vocates were unfamiliar with the ins and outs of Khnauront anatomy. Noreê and Lernaion handled these questions capably between them, and then Noreê continued, "And so I think that the Khnauronts who survive should not be thought of as full members of their tribe, or whatever we are to call it. They were more like. . . ."

"Emergency rations," suggested Aloê.

"Exactly, yes. They were a source of tal for the commanders when there was no other."

"Their minds have been sculpted, I think, to this end," Illion said. "Their emptiness and single-mindedness is unnatural."

"Could they be cured?" asked Jordel.

"By all means, let us send them to the Skein of Healing!" cried Rild. "We can set our thains to knitting woolen underwear for their comfort! Let no expense or trouble be spared for these outlanders who broke through the Wards and invaded our lands to kill and kill and kill!"

Many of the Graith rolled their eyes or shook their heads at this hysterical ranting, but Morlock was sorry to see many vocates, and thains, too, nodding in approval.

"By all means, if you like," said Jordel when Rild paused for a breath. "But my thought was that if they could be cured, they might be able to tell us more than they have."

"Doubtful," said Illion reluctantly. "I wish it were otherwise. But I think what's gone is gone. They might be made somewhat more . . . awake than they presently are. They will never be the people they once were."

"Then, unless it conflicts with Vocate Rild's elaborate plans for their rehabilitation and comfort, I suggest we herd them onto a boat, sail it to the unguarded lands, and dump them on any convenient coast."

"Might be a kindness to kill them," Baran said.

"A cruel kindness, I guess? You're too subtle for me brother. But I must say I can't say that it matters much. They seem unable to harm us or anyone anymore. They seem equally unable to do themselves or anyone else any good."

Kothala of Sandport said, "If the enemy who sent them here in the first place finds them and gives them new lifetaking wands, then they could do much harm indeed."

This was a new thought to many, and a disturbing one.

"This is not a decision that has to be taken today," Illion said. "Time may bring them healing, or memory, or death. We should follow at least part of Rild's kindly suggestion and send to New Moorhope for seers who may glean more from the empty fields of their minds than I was able to do."

Lernaion was dismayed by this, but he looked around the table and realized the weight of opinion was with Illion.

"If we put that matter aside," Lernaion said, "what of our colleague's death? When we take the oath of Guardians and become subject to the rigors of the First Decree, the Graith assumes the role of our protector and vengeancer. It is too late to protect our lost friend, Earno—"

Morlock, to his astonishment, heard Aloê mutter to herself, "Shut your lying mouth." He wasn't sure if anyone else heard her; evidently Lernaion did not.

"—who lies dead and murdered alongside the Road. What shall we do for him?"

"I could not disagree with the summoner more!" shouted Rild.

Lernaion's dry, dark face bent with annoyance and surprise. "Some of your peers here saw him die. I myself saw his body, which lies now in occlusive stasis on the very spot where he fell. Are you saying that Earno is not dead?"

"No, of course not! But you seem to be suggesting that his death ends the threat. But it may be only the beginning! If Earno can be murdered by magic, which one of us is safe? Which one will be next?"

"Our conversation will go smoother if you address yourself to what I have said, not what I seem to have suggested. Because what I mean, I say."

"But—"

"We didn't join the Graith to be safe, but to pledge our lives for the safety of others," Illion observed.

"Yes, but—"

"Rild," Jordel interrupted, "I urge you to shut your mouth. Shall I put the question? Vocates, I want Rild to be quiet, for his good and ours. We have matters of moment to discuss."

Rild stood back, startled and offended. His glance slid around the room and he spoke no more.

"Because, listen to me, Guardians," Jordel continued, "I think we're starting in the wrong place. The question is not *what* we should do, but *who* should do it. Everyone here knows what must be done. We must find out who murdered Earno and why. To that end, we must elect one of our Graith to be investigator and vengeancer on our behalf."

"I accept your correction," said Lernaion patiently. "Who, then? We must choose carefully. It would be a strange irony if the investigator were also the criminal."

Jordel waved his hand. "Oh, I saw that play. And what was the point of all that stuff about his mother? I thought it overrated, honestly."

"With equal honesty, I assure you I have no idea what you're talking about. Fortunately, it doesn't matter at all."

"That's what I was saying!"

"It isn't, but put that aside. Who, vocates, will be your investigator, your vengeancer?"

Many, now, were looking at Morlock. He turned away from them to meet Deor's dark, amused eye. Deor always enjoyed watching the Graith at Station, which he compared to a puppet show that was popular in his youth, where every puppet in the cast took a turn beating the others with a stick. Deor nodded when he saw Morlock looking at him. Morlock didn't need to wonder what he would have said if they could have talked. Blood has no price! Earno was an odd man, but a *rokhlan* and a hero, and (after an awkward start) had been well-loved by Theorn Clan—better than he knew, perhaps.

But Morlock did not choose to undertake the task of vengeance. He said, "I name Vocate Aloê Oaij."

Startlement flashed like lightning across the chamber. Aloê turned to look at him, her golden eyes agape, her dark, rosy lips poised for a grin.

"No one could be better for the task," Noreê said coldly. "I say the same name."

"God Avenger!" cried Jordel. "If Morlock and Noreê agree on something, does anything more need to be said? Anyway. Who's shrewder? Who's braver? Who's more dedicated to the Guard? She was a friend of Earno—she has friends all through the Wardlands. She's a seer and a fighter. Let me tell you this story—maybe you've heard it before—"

"Does anyone disagree?" Lernaion said hastily. "Aloê, are you willing to take up the task?"

Aloê bowed her head in thought. Then she said, "I accept it. God Avenger have pity on the killer, for I'll have none."

Naevros pounded the table and there were shouts of assent that echoed all around the chamber. Vocates left their places at the long table and went over to congratulate her. Morlock stepped off the dais to let them pass. Looking up he saw his red-cloaked, dark-skinned, golden-haired wife crowned with the stars painted on the dome's ceiling. She seemed more than human to him in that moment, as in many others, and he laid the memory of her away in a secret temple of his mind. When the vocates drifted away back to their places he stepped up again and would have said something to her. But she stabbed him with a bitter, golden glance, and he realized that she was angry with him, though he didn't understand why.

He shrugged and said, "Tell me later."

"Yes."

Lernaion rapped the Staff of Exile on the table and said, "Guardians, to order."

"Lunch!" called out someone hopefully. The voice was disguised, but Morlock thought he recognized it as Deor's.

The cry was echoed a couple times around the long table, and a wintry smile bent Lernaion's brown lips. "The Guard now," he said. "Lunch later.

Guardians, I see that the stranger Kelat is with us. Let us do now as we have done before, and join our minds, strength to strength, and seek the truth in the mind of this stranger. I ask that you permit my colleague Bleys to join us at Station, so that he may prepare Kelat to bear witness."

"Guardians!" cried a voice near the Witness Stone. "Vocates and Summoner Lernaion! I say no to this. I urge you all to say no as well."

Looking over, Morlock saw that the speaker was Gyrla Keelmaker. Her face was red and sweating, and she leaned on the table as she shouted out her words. "Many of you know me," she continued, "but some of you may not. I don't come to Station to tell witty stories or make myself admired. The sooner it's done, the sooner we can go about our real work. But my brother was Thain Stockrey, and he is dead today because of this Bleys and the games he played with the Witness Stone. The Graith chose not to exile him for those crimes, though God Avenger knows he deserved it. You probed his mind with the Witness Stone and found its uncleanness to be of use to the Guard. 'We don't judge; we defend.' I've heard it a million times. Well, I *do* judge, and I tell you I will not stand in rapport with that monster and the Witness Stone. Neither should you. Look at him! Look at him! How can you trust him?"

Bleys stood in a patch of chilly light from the windows. His head was bowed, his pink, hairless face frozen in a smile. The names of Kinian and Stockrey would haunt him to his grave, Morlock thought, without any sympathy at all.

Lernaion's dark face grew darker with anger, but he spoke patiently. "Who better than Bleys?"

"Anyone! No one!" cried Gyrla. "But if you speak merely of skills, there are not a few who can see as deeply as Bleys into the unseen world, and who do not have the blood of fellow Guardians on their hands."

"You would persuade me better if your tone were calmer," Lernaion said in a level voice.

"When she finds no one will listen, a Guardian's voice may grow shrill," Noreê said thoughtfully. "I agree with Gyrla in this. Our rapport will be deeper, our union closer, if Bleys is not part of it. I don't trust him either, and I doubt I am alone here."

There was a general growl of agreement and Lernaion glanced thoughtfully around the table. "Very well," he said. "It is for you, Guardians, to decide who stands at Station with you. Illion and Noreê: after Bleys, you are called the greatest seers in the Graith. Will you prepare the witness for the Stone?"

"Wait a moment," said Jordel.

"Have you an entertaining story to tell us, Jordel?" Lernaion said, his long calm fraying to the breaking point.

"Thousands," said Jordel agreeably, "and I'll tell them to you some time over wine and shellfish. But for now, just one point. I don't trust Bleys either. He keeps his white cloak thanks to you and Earno. But now Earno is dead, and for all we know, you may be next. When we are in rapport with each other and the Stone, Bleys may work some harm against us. I hope you don't mind my being so frank, Summoner Bleys?"

"If I were allowed to speak in this assembly," said Bleys warmly, "I would assure Vocate Jordel of my willingness to harm him. As it is, I prefer to stand silent."

"I guess that's irony?" Jordel said. "Anyway: who'll guard the Guardians while we question the witness? It must be someone Bleys couldn't get around somehow."

"Let him do it!" said Noreê, pointing at Morlock. "They hate each other almost as much. . . ." Her voice trailed off.

". . . as much as you hate us both, my dear?" Bleys suggested in his most grandfatherly voice.

"My peer," Lernaion said heavily, "be silent." He turned to Morlock. "I don't know if Noreê spoke in malice or in jest. But I think she's right. What do you say?"

Morlock weighed his options and at length said, "Yes." He stepped off the dais and went to stand by Bleys.

Deor came over and stood on the other side of the old summoner.

"Well, well," said Bleys in a genial whisper that was audible through the whole room. "A scion of Theornn on each side of me. I almost feel one of the clan."

Neither Morlock nor Deor rose to the bait, but Naevros made a throat-clearing sound of disgust and walked past the other vocates, nearly shouldering Lernaion out of his way. He walked down the steps of the dais and went to stand next to Morlock.

"I stood with Morlock in the North and I stand with him now!" Naevros shouted up at Lernaion, who was staring coldly down at them.

"We see that," Lernaion said evenly, and turned away.

Morlock felt his face grow hot. The tangle of emotions between him and Aloê and Naevros was more than he could easily understand. But Naevros' good opinion had always meant a great deal to him, even before he had known who Aloê was. He pounded Naevros on the arm and said nothing; there was nothing he could have said.

Bleys looked as if he wanted to say something; his mouth was working as if he had just discovered it contained a live scorpion. But in the end he, too, was silent.

They watched as Illion and Noreê led the stranger Kelat to the Witness Stone.

Morlock had been present at a handful of such events, including one that had preceded his birth, when his mother Nimue Viviana had stood on the Witness Stone. They always filled him with a certain dread. But he did not like standing aside while Aloê went into rapture without him. If there was danger, he felt they should share it. But he had made his choice and would stand by it.

Aloê noted the passing of Illion and Kelat only vaguely. Her thoughts were focused inward, preparing her mind for rapport. The union involved would be superficial, but she did not want her anger against Morlock spilling out into the minds of her peers; it wasn't their business. She wrapped her private thoughts in a cloak of solitude and hid them deep within her.

Her insight told her that her peers were ready for rapport. She took the first, shallowest step into vision.

She was one-yet-separate with laughing Jordel, bitter Noreê, angry Gyrla, frightened Rild . . . all of them, all of them were there with her. She did not sense the stranger, though—could catch no echo of Kelat in all the voices in her head.

The rapport was odd. Fiery. The talic world was blood-bright, smoke-dark. Something was wrong. Something was wrong and it was her. She heard her voice speak the words of the dragon and knew her will was lost.

Morlock watched the faces of his peers change from wakeful purpose to sleepy emptiness. Then they changed again. Jaws clenched, fists closed and opened in unison all around the table.

"Something's gone wrong," he said to Bleys.

"Yes," said the summoner, without any of his carefully artificial grandfatherly warmth.

"It's like dragonspell," whispered Deor. "Look at their eyes! You can see the redness through their lids."

Dragonspell was notoriously infectious. "Deortheorn, get every thain out of the chamber instantly," Morlock said. "You had better go as well, Naevros."

"I have a talisman against binding spells," Naevros observed. "But I'll help Deor with his herding while you seers discuss . . . whatever this is."

Bleys and Morlock waited while Deor cleared the room and the great doors of the chamber were closed and barred from the outside.

"Well, Vocate," Bleys said. "What shall we do?"

"I don't know," Morlock admitted. "Tea from *maijarra* leaf will unfix a dragonspell, but first we must break the rapport somehow."

"Difficult," Bleys said, "without entering into it. Dangerous if we do: we may end up captives ourselves."

"Kelat must be the source," said Morlock. "But I looked him in the eyes this morning, and I would swear he was not spellbound."

"Odd, though," Bleys said. "Did you talk with him? I did once. Something not there. Or maybe there was something there that didn't belong. . . ."

The Dragon spoke.

Each of the Guardians standing at the long table, and Kelat as well, opened their mouths and spoke in an ill-tuned chorus, "Greetings, Guardians! I thank you and your colleagues for stepping into the trap I so carefully prepared. I am Rulgân the Kinslayer, also called Silverfoot. My plan is to steal something from you if I can, deal with you if I must."

"An honest thief," remarked Bleys, with a return of his habitual irony.

"Of course!" the many-throated monster replied. "How I had hoped that you, Master Bleys, or you, young Ambrosius, would be among my captives. But I am foiled at every turn, I see." Dozens of throats barked in unison: the dragon was laughing.

"You might not have found us so easy to master, o son of fire and envy," Bleys replied.

"You would have thrown open the door and welcomed me in!" disputed the dragon through the mouths of the vocates. "That was the genius of my plan."

"What do you want?" Morlock asked.

"Morlock Ambrosius, you are a practical man! I did not understand that at one time. And so I dismissed you. And then I hated you, for reasons we both know. And later I scorned you. But now I know that you were right all along: choose what you want, and give all else to get it! For me, for a long time, that one thing was knowledge. I paid much for it, as you know—mutilated and staked to the floor in that temple of the Gray Folk. But it was nothing to see all that I saw, through so many different eyes—hear what I heard through so many different ears. And to act! To murder! To love! To steal! To save! To die in triumph, and yet slink away in terror to survive! I have lived so many different lives, drunk deeply of so many wells of sin and truth. The price was nothing. It was nothing."

As the dragon spoke through the mouths of their colleagues and friends, Morlock and Bleys by unspoken consent began to sidle toward the Witness Stone and Kelat.

When the dragon paused, Morlock said quietly, "I congratulate you."

"I know that you do. You said something like that when you saw me in my temple, and I thought you were amusing yourself at my expense. Later, when I knew so many truths, I realized the truth of this. The greed for knowledge is greater than the greed for gold, or any mere thing."

"Greed is greed," Morlock said indifferently.

"So the dwarves taught you; so I taught the mandrakes, as their god. I know how to tell truths, Morlock, and also lies cunningly fashioned like truth."

"I see that you have assimilated a broad range of literary classics."

"You two-eyed fool, the world has been my library! I have read deeply in it. I see what you are doing now, by the way, and I let it continue only because it will do no good. But let me show you something. Yes, let me show you something."

Every other Guardian standing at the table reached up with both hands and began to choke himself or herself.

Aloê was one of them. Morlock saw her slim hands grip her long, graceful throat and squeeze. He repressed several conflicting impulses and said, "Rulgân! Do not anger us past the point of reason. You offered a deal."

The brown hands relaxed their grip, fell down at Aloê's side. The same was true of the other vocates.

"I wanted you to know," the dragon said, through Aloê's mouth alone, "that I know what your pearl is. Yes, and I know exactly what lengths you will go to defend it—defend her. No, candidly, I do not want to anger you beyond reason."

All the dragon-possessed Guardians spoke in their unlovely chorus, "But I have the power to take it from you, your pearl of great price. You will deal with me because you must. Or you will tolerate my theft because you must."

"What are we talking about?" Morlock said. "What is it you want?"

"I thought it was knowledge," the dragon said slowly through the many mouths. "If it were, I would have had it by now, and moved on to certain experiments I have often thought to try. . . ."

"Knowledge of what?" Morlock asked. Bleys' eyes were glowing. The old seer had entered visionary rapture. Morlock hoped his conversation would distract the dragon from whatever Bleys was attempting.

"I wish to travel on the Sea of Worlds," the dragon said in a crowd of voices.

"To gain more knowledge?"

"To continue my life! Has it escaped your notice, young Ambrosius, that this world is dying, this vast case for your so-small, so-precious pearl? I wish to flee, but I cannot. You could, but you do not."

"I haven't given up hope."

"You don't know what I know! But you could. Do you follow me? I offer my knowledge for my escape, the lives of these people you care about for my own life."

"That is your deal? Why don't you just take the knowledge you crave?"

"I hoped I could," the dragon's stolen voices said ruefully. "But I see from one, and then another, that what is really needed is skill: the skill of piloting through the shifting currents of the Sea of Worlds. Perhaps even a talent. Knowledge may be stolen, but skill must be acquired and talent is inborn. No, I will need someone to pilot me to a better world, a world with more life in it, if I am to live forever."

"You plan to live forever?"

"How else can I know everything that can be known?"

Morlock shrugged his crooked shoulders. "You can't!"

"You certainly won't. This world is doomed and I know who is killing its sun. That is the knowledge I propose to trade to you, Guardians. In return I want safe passage to a fresher world. I will self-bind not to harm my pilot, whomever you choose for the task."

The pale glow in Bleys' eyes faded. He met Morlock's eye, glanced down to Morlock's sword, then inclined his head slightly toward Kelat.

For a wordless communication, Bleys' meaning was fairly clear. He wanted Morlock to kill Kelat. That would break the chains binding the Guardians at Station.

This was a reasonable plan—in fact, a fairly obvious one. Morlock was not inclined to kill someone on Bleys' mere say-so, however. He ascended into vision himself—the slightest step into the visionary world, with barely a thin permeable veil between his awareness and the world of matter.

He saw the Guardians at Station, a coronet of souls writhing in fierce, brilliant agony. Intertwined with their spirits was another coronet of fiery thorns. That passed through each of the Guardians at Station and returned back to its source: the stranger Kelat.

He heard a dim thought, like a voice speaking in a distant room: Bleys was right—killing Kelat would break the ring and free the Guardians. But. . . .

Morlock's body did not move, but his awareness focused on Kelat and the Witness Stone. The coronet of fire passed out of Kelat and through the Guardians and through Kelat again, like a great wheel. But there was a smaller spiked wheel of flames that passed between a fiery locus in Kelat's brain, through his arms, into the Witness Stone, and out of the Stone into Kelat's other arm.

Morlock's mechanically inclined imagination saw them as meshing gears of fire. Break either one, the device would be powerless. . . .

He drew Tyrfing. With the blade to focus his power, he could move a little, even in deeper rapture than this. He approached the Witness Stone.

Rulgân shouted out threats and promises through the many mouths he had in thrall, but Morlock did not heed them, could not really hear them: he felt their vibrations in the coronet of fire.

He dropped out of visionary rapture. He swung his sword and struck his target: the Witness Stone.

"No, you fool!" screamed Bleys when, too late, he realized Morlock's intent.

The Stone shattered. The Guardians cried out in many voices—not their own, but not all one any longer.

"I am broken in pieces!" shrieked Noreê.

"Your pearl will dissolve in the wine of death, fool!" snarled Illion.

Kelat simply screamed and screamed without words.

Morlock jumped up on the dais next to the Stone and the screaming stranger.

Kelat's crazed eyes fixed on Morlock and his sword. "Kill me!" he begged. "It's in me! Inside of me! It hurts so much! Oh, Death and Justice, kill me now!"

Morlock, no particular friend to Death or Justice said, "No." He struck Kelat strategically on the side of the head and the stranger fell from the dais to the floor. Morlock jumped down to make sure he hadn't broken his neck in the fall and was relieved to find he was still breathing.

Next to the dais, Bleys was weeping over the fragments of the Witness Stone like a child whose favorite toy has been broken. "Why did you do it?" the summoner sobbed. "Do you know what you've done? Do you know what's been lost? To save the life of an invader, an outsider, mere bait in a trap, you have destroyed long ages of accumulated wisdom!"

Morlock looked down at the groveling old man with a mixture of pity and contempt. "The trap will lead us to the trapper, Bleys. And if this is the last age of the world, your accumulated wisdom will disperse in darkness anyway. Look to the stranger! Don't let him die or awake again."

Morlock ran around the long oval of the dais until he reached Aloê. She was slumped across the Long Table, her limbs spasming wildly. Naevros was already standing over her, but he stood back as Morlock approached. Morlock vaulted onto the dais and picked his wife up in his arms.

Her eyes were open but wild. Her limbs were still thrashing, like a baby who hasn't learned how to use her arms and legs. On her throat were dark handprints, and on one he saw a deeper cross-mark: the imprint of the ring on her finger, the ring he had made for her.

He wondered if he should go into vision and try to search for her spirit. Who could advise him? Illion, Noreê, and Lernaion were as bad as this or worse. Bleys was babbling like a dotard. Earno was dead. . . .

Aloê's golden eyes focused on him.

"Crazy bastard!" she whispered hoarsely, and bit him on the upper arm.

Then he knew that all would be well.

CHAPTER FIVE

Evening in A Thousand Towers

Stations of the Graith did not normally end with most of its members being examined by binders from the Skein of Healing, but this had been an odd one. It was necessary to know that there was no lingering dragonspell in those who kept the Guard. Many had bruised throats to look after as well, but no one had been fatally injured.

"And I, for one, am disappointed," remarked Jordel, lounging with calculated nonchalance on a window ledge in Tower Ambrose, where the recently set sun still lit the sky behind him with chilly red. "All these great warriors," Jordel complained, "and not one had a grip strong enough to break his own throat."

Baran, his brother, sitting on a couch nearby, grunted. "Neither did you."

"I know!" Jordel said, pointing at his heavily bruised skin. "I'm deeply ashamed!"

"We're all ashamed of you, J," Aloê responded from a nearby chair. "Though not all for the same reasons."

"I'll do better next time," Jordel promised.

After the Station broke up in chaos, Lernaion had led the vocates who openly belonged to his faction away to some sort of private meeting. The members of Bleys' faction, in contrast, were still consoling their leader, sobbing over the broken Witness Stone. Noreê and Illion had put a wilderment on the dragon-haunted stranger, Kelat, and conducted him to one of the nearby Wells of Healing for purposes they did not say. The remaining vocates not aligned with any summoner's faction had scattered to their own places of refuge.

One of these was Tower Ambrose, where the group of friends and peers Jordel called "the Awkward Bastards" frequently resorted after a Station. There were some of the usual faces missing: Thea, who would never be seen again, and

Illion. But Jordel and Baran were there, and Naevros and Keluaê Hendaij and a few others. The tower's staff had all gone home for the night, so Morlock and Deor were down in the kitchen whomping up something like a meal.

Aloê sat, wrapped in her red cloak, in the chair that had always been Thea's when she visited, and listened more than she talked. She had a sense that something was ending—the world, of course, was growing colder, and everything was very bad. But the thing she feared, and part of her longed for, was standing nearer than the end of the wide world outside these walls. She could not say what it was, and did not wish to. But she could think about nothing else.

Three pairs of footfalls grew closer: the long, steady stride of her husband; his *harven*-kin Deor's quicker, shorter steps; and a third, the wooden strokes of the Walking Shelf.

The three entered in that order, to general cheering. The Awkward Bastards were hungry—hungry enough that there had been serious talk of walking down to the Speckles, the infamous rusty-ladle cookshop just a few hundred steps down the River Road. The scents and sights carried in by the Walking Shelf were enough to banish such thoughts forever.

"Please hold your applause to the end!" Deor said. "This may not be up to Tower Ambrose's usual level of catering. You don't know the meaning of danger until you've worked in a kitchen with Morlock."

Morlock shrugged and said, "Walking Shelf, go: offer trays to people."

The brass eye atop Walking Shelf revolved in a circle and then the shelf stumped over to Jordel. It grabbed a tray off the shelves in its interior and offered it to him."

"All the trays are the same," Deor said apologetically. "Fell free to swap around whatever you don't want."

"It's like school," said Keluaê to Naevros, who smiled suavely. There had been no school in the three-boat port town where Naevros grew up, Aloê knew, but she doubted that Keluaê could tell. Naevros could handle any conversation—except the ones that mattered most. He was a mirror image of Morlock, who never seemed to be able to speak unless the conversation was a matter of life or death. Often she wished she could make one whole man out of their scattered traits, and not only in this context.

Morlock served out wine, red or white, whereas Deor busied himself with the tea urn. When Walking Shelf had given everyone a tray, Morlock said, "Walking shelf, go: stand in a corner." It looked around with its brass eye, stumped over to the nearest corner, and stood still.

Morlock had a tray of his own by that time and a mug of tea. He came and sat on the floor next to Aloê. He knew why she was sitting there, of course. She reached out the hand she wasn't eating with and tangled it in his crazy hair. She saw Naevros looking, saw him look away. She didn't bother to stop on his account. She had made her choice, the right choice, a century ago.

There was contented semisilence for a while, as the Guardians slew their hunger with weapons of food and drowned their thirst in oceans of drink.

"Morlock," said Sundra Ekelling after a time, "you *are* the master of all makers."

"Injustice!" sputtered Deor. "In the kitchen, *I* am the master. Eight parts of what you are eating is my work, and one of the others is either underdone or overdone."

"You lay wonderful eggs, Deor," Jordel remarked.

"You may laugh, Vocate, but laying an egg is relatively easy compared to cooking it properly—neither seared paste nor raw, slippery glook."

"Whoever made these wonderful little filled flushcakes has my eternal gratitude," Sundra said.

"Oh. Well. I suppose they're not so bad. Those *are* Morlock's, to tell the truth. Master of all makers of pancakes, you should call him. But apart from that: what a menace! Morlocktheorn, won't you have some wine?"

So Deor had noticed that, too. It was a little thing, but connected to the deep fear within her.

Morlock shook his head: he would drink no wine.

Deor persisted: "If you don't like the ones we brought up I could run and get you something else from the cellar. We have some golden Plyrrun, from that sunny island off the coast of Southhold. Salty and sweet and refreshing all at once. Or Barkun, from Westhold. That's a fine, bold red wine."

"No, Deortheorn," Morlock said. "The day's work isn't done. I never drink while I'm working."

"There!" shouted Deor. "I made you say it! Go on, then, Morlock: what's your evening's work, and how many precious talismans of the Graith's magical armory will it destroy?"

"Deor," Naevros said mildly, "give the man a rest. We all had a long, bitter day."

Deor's flat, gray face looked wounded. "It's him that doesn't want to rest. I meant no criticism of my senior in the Order—" he rolled his eyes at this "—and in Theorn Clan." He did not roll his eyes. "I enjoy breaking things, personally, and it is many hours before I must sleep. Come on, Morlock!"

Morlock shook his head. "Thinking now," he said. "Talk later."

"This may take a while, then," Jordel said. "These people who are particular about thinking always take so long to choose their words! Now, me, I never bother to think before I talk, which reminds me of the time—"

He was instantly pelted with rolls, bits of stray bread, and catcalls.

"I'm going to ignore that," he said, "partly because I know you don't mean it, and partly because your suffering is to me merely the butter on this delicious bread. This was back when—you'll remember this, Naevros—"

Jordel's stories at their best—and this was a pretty good one—required audience participation: cries of disgust or disbelief, exclamations of confirmation or denial, alternate versions of events in more temperately colored prose, occasional doses of applause. It served Jordel's end of making everyone forget their troubles—except Morlock, who sat eating and drinking his damned tea and thinking, thinking, thinking.

They were sitting in the roseate aftermath of Jordel's ridiculous anecdote when Illion appeared in the doorway, his apple-nosed jester's face looking unwontedly serious.

"I tried to ring the bell," he said, in apology, "but this big eye just opened in the door, and then the door opened to let me in. I thought it was really weird, and I want one."

They shouted for him to come in, and they got him a cup of wine. They were going to make up a tray for him out of their leavings, but Walking Shelf woke up when he came in, reached inside itself and brought forth from a hidden warming box a tray for Illion. It stumped over and handed it to him.

"Thank you," Illion said to it bemusedly.

"Walking Shelf, go: go back to the corner," said Deor in a singsong voice, then he glanced at Morlock. "So you were right. How did you know Illion was coming?"

"I didn't know," said Morlock, "but I did ask him to."

"I'm glad you did," said Illion, perching on a chair and setting down his food and drink on a nearby table. "The hospitality of Tower Ambrose is strangely excellent and excellently strange."

"Like the compliments of Illion the Wise," Jordel said wryly.

"Let him eat! Try the rolled flatcakes, Illion. They're good."

Illion ate and drank, and the conversation became general. Morlock didn't partake in it unless someone addressed him in particular, and then he answered as briefly as possible. He got up to pour himself some more tea, then came back to sit by Aloê and drink it. He was waiting.

Eventually Illion pushed away his food, accepted a refill of wine, and turned to Morlock. The waiting was over. "Listen," he said, "why did you break the Stone rather than kill Kelat? Either would have broken the hostile rapport."

"Something in him," Morlock said.

"There was, and it was still in contact with Rulgân. You have no doubts about who the speaker was?"

"None."

"Well. I didn't say so earlier, but: good work, Guardian. My throat thanks you, from the bottom of my heart."

Morlock opened his free hand and waited.

Illion sighed and drew something from his pocket. It was like a gem, the kind often used as a focus of power. It looked like a white diamond veined with red ruby. "Here it is," he said. He tossed it to Morlock.

Morlock held it up to the light, and thought, and said nothing. Aloê watched him.

"You cut it out of his *brain?*" Deor asked. "Is he dead? Oh, of course he is."

"No," Illion said, "he didn't die. Not permanently, anyway. We sealed his brain, his skull, and his skin and Noreê took him off to the lockhouse in the west side where the surviving Khnauronts are being kept."

"Will he die?" Morlock asked.

Illion shrugged and drank. "We all will, Morlock."

"Some sooner than others, if that icy witch has her way," Deor remarked. "Telling truths, Guardians," he said when some protested.

"Is he sane?" Morlock asked Illion.

"Yes. He remembers things about his life, for instance, that he didn't before. He'll remember more, in time. And we inscribed a protection against dragonspell in kharnum letters on his naked skull, so he won't fall prey to that trap again."

"Good of you."

"It was Noreê's idea." He turned to Deor. "I know why you say what you say. But there is more to her than you know."

Deor raised his mug in salute. "I honor you for defending your friend, Illion."

"It's not just that. It's about justice."

"Aha, but what about that thing you people are always saying? 'I don't judge; I defend.'"

"Perhaps I'm in the wrong line of work," said Illion. "I like justice, when I can get it." He turned back to Morlock. "What do you think of the thing, Morlock the Maker?"

"I think this gem did not grow in the veins of the ground," Morlock said thoughtfully. "There are makers in the unguarded lands who can do work like this, but they are mostly dwarves."

"Unlikely that they would take a commission from a dragon. Or do you think this was stolen?"

"No, I think it was crafted to be a vessel of power for Rulgân in particular. It vibrates with draconic force."

"And therefore . . ." Illion said, and waited.

Morlock didn't speak.

Jordel said, "You can't suppose that someone in the Wardlands made it for him?"

"I have supposed it," Illion said, "and it's not impossible, you know. The Wardlands are wide and there are many people in them, thinking their own thoughts and going their own ways. Maybe someone's path brought them to this. But no, I think there's something else even likelier."

"Old Ambrosius, of course," said Sundra. "What do you say, Morlock?"

"Yes. I think so." Morlock tossed the dragonstone back to Illion.

Illion was startled, but quick of hand. He caught the stone and said, "That's odd. I thought you would want this."

"Keep it," Morlock suggested, "in case Rulgân launches another attack against the Wardlands. But I think Kelat will be of more use to me. That is, if he can travel."

"Oh ho!" Deor said. "The evening's work has taken shape, I guess. We're going to break into the lockhouse, kidnap Kelat, and carry him back to the unguarded lands for a dragon hunt. Am I wrong, *harven?*"

"No," said Morlock.

"Yes," said Aloê, "about one thing. That is the night's work, not the evening's. If my husband is going on a deadly mission into the unguarded lands, you will need to spend a pair of hours preparing for the journey. And he needs to spend that time with me."

"*Ath, rokhlan!*" Deor said, bowing low. "*Ev xemennen akkram hav!*"

Aloê stood and offered Morlock her hand. He rose and took it. She led him from the room, heedless of Naevros' carefully averted eyes.

CHAPTER SIX

A Parting; a Meeting

Among other things, Aloê said, "I love you" and "You are in danger" and "They think you could be king."

He did not answer the first in words at all, nor did she need him to. To the second he said, "There is no safe place anywhere. It may be we only choose where and when to meet the end." To the third he said, "What?"

"Lernaion said it, after the Battle of Tunglskin. Earno called him a liar. I was half dead at the time, but I remember hearing it."

Morlock sat silent, thinking. "This explains some things Lernaion has said to me of late."

"Such as?"

"False courtesies, as if I were his senior in the Graith. As if he need ask my permission for things. As if I were king, I guess."

"Who do you think the Graith listens to more—especially after today?"

"Let them listen. When I talk, I have things that need saying. But I am not king, nor am I even Summoner of the City. I don't wish to be, Aloê."

She turned away from him on the bed and drew a coverlet over her naked shoulders. "Why not?"

"Why not?" he repeated, astonished.

"You heard me!" She turned and glared at him. "It's not like you to waste words, beloved. I say, 'Why not?' and I want your answer."

"No one person should have supreme power in the land. Attempting it is grounds for exile. It is why my *ruthen* father was exiled, Aloê."

"So what?"

"It doesn't matter to you? It matters to me."

"Say, then, you will not be king. You will be High Vocate of the Wardlands, leader of our Graith, and no more."

"King in all but name? Why would I want that?"

"Don't you want people to see that you are. . . ."

"That I'm what?"

"Better than everyone else!"

"I'm not. And I will not follow in my father's footsteps."

"You followed them into the Graith."

"To be a better Guardian than he was. A better man."

"And you are. Don't you think I know that? Don't you think everyone does?"

He was silent for a long time and she said, "I've shocked you."

"No," he said slowly. "We have lived together for a century, Aloê. We have met, heart to heart and mind to mind in rapture many times. I knew you were ambitious. I didn't know it took this precise form, though."

"You should think about your choices, beloved."

"I have made my choice, Aloê."

"No, beloved. You may have one before you that you don't understand yet."

"Tell me."

Her golden eyes searched his face. "You're not angry at me? If we're going to fight, let's fight. I don't need an ironic fencing match just now."

"I'm not angry. You see many things I would never see. Tell me."

"What if your choice is between ruling the Wardlands or being exiled from them, with no third option? What then?"

"I can't see how that would happen."

"If people think you *could* breach the First Decree, they may exile you before you have the chance."

"Not without giving me a chance to defend myself."

"Are you joking?"

"No. That's what I think."

She was silent for a while. Then she said, "I won't go with you."

He shrugged uneasily. "Of course not. You must stay here to avenge Earno."

"Thank you for that, too, but that's not what I mean. If they exile you, I'll stay here. My life is here."

He bowed his head and thought long before he spoke. Finally he said, "That is what I would want for you. To be here, to do your work, to have your life."

"That's what you would want for *me*. What would you want for *yourself*?"

"You," he said, smiling.

"Then we both can't have what we want."

He shook his head. "It won't come to that."

"If it does. . . ."

"If it does, you have told me. Have you nothing else to tell me before I leave for the end of the world?"

She did, but not in words. Their mouths were busy otherwise for an hour or so.

Morlock took a run through the rain room, put on clean clothes, and descended to the atrium of Tower Ambrose. Deor was waiting there with two packs. Morlock looked at them dubiously. One seemed too large. The other was larger.

"You always leave it to me to pack," Deor began.

"And some call Illion 'the Wise.'"

"Yes and—Was that irony at my expense, *harven*?"

"Everyone is accusing me of irony."

"That doesn't seem to be an answer. Oh, never mind. I want you to look over your pack. I don't want any snide looks if I forgot to pack your favorite razor or something."

Morlock grumbled at the gigantic backpack, evidently meant for him. "I hate a heavy backpack," he said.

"Who doesn't? I've given you the barest necessities."

Morlock unlaced the pack and began to search through it. Then he just dumped the contents on the floor of the atrium and began selecting items for repacking. He took flatbread, dried meat, and a waterbottle and put aside all other foodstuffs. A firemaker, a few tools, three books, and a bedroll completed his kit. He laced up the considerably lighter backpack and called for Walking Shelf to gather up the rest and take it away.

Deor sighed. "I suppose you'll want to go through mine as well?"

Morlock shook his head. What Deor carried was his business. But Morlock did not propose to spend the rest of his life wandering in the unguarded lands: the barest necessities would do.

"Shall we wait for Aloê?" Deor said uncertainly, as Morlock bound his sword and a stabbing spear in their scabbards to the frame of the backpack.

Morlock thought of Aloê as he had last seen her: her dark face angry under a bright glaze of tears. He shook his head.

Deor shrugged and shouldered his own backpack. They went out through the front door, which closed and locked behind them.

As they stepped into the street they both looked back and saw Aloê standing on the balcony above the door, a shadow framed by the dim light behind her.

"Hurry back," she said.

"All right," said Morlock, and turned away. He felt then he was walking away from everything that mattered to him.

Around the side were the modest stables of Tower Ambrose, and when Morlock stopped by them Deor said, "Oh, no. Not on one of those things."

"We must cross the city as fast as we can. What do you propose?"

"What do I propose? I propose that you, the master of all makers, fashion some sort of device that enables a man or a dwarf or even both to travel a decent distance in some way that preserves their dignity and comfort and that in no way involves contact with vicious, sweaty, herbivorous beasts!"

As Deor raved, Morlock was already opening the stable doors. Reluctantly, Deor assisted in saddling a couple of herbivorous beasts, a horse named Nimber for Morlock and a pony named Trundle for Deor. They cantered west along the River Road southwest for a while, then took the Vintners' Way due west. The road was unlit except by Chariot and Trumpeter, both red and gloomy over the western horizon: it was the last day of the month of Marrying. But the way was clear and they travelled steadily until Tower Ambrose was lost among the thicket of towers reaching into the starlit sky.

Vintners' Way ran west into mountain country, and they followed it through the ruinous western wall of the city into the neighborhoods beyond as far as the nightmare-painted streets of Fungustown.

"I never like coming here at night," Deor whispered. "Or in twilight. Or in the daytime."

Morlock grunted.

The only building lit up in Fungustown was the lockhouse. It had been a block of apartments when it was built. Noreê and her attendant-thains had not changed the walls at all, but simply put the prisoners in the windowless basement.

Morlock reined in Nimber two streets away from the lockhouse, or tried to. The horse didn't seem to want to stop, so in the end he simply undid the bindings on his pack and jumped off with it. Deor, with an undeniable degree of smugness, brought Trundle to a halt. He was about to give Morlock a demonstration of how to secure his steed with reins to a lampless lamp post, but before he got a chance to speak Trundle shook loose and followed Nimber up the dark street.

"Where did you get those ridiculous beasts?" he asked Morlock.

"Borrowed them from Illion," said the other quietly.

The horses, Westhold bred and trained, had enough sense to get home. Deor shrugged and decided not to worry about them. He was a little worried about how they would tackle the next stage of the journey, but at least it wouldn't be on horseback.

They soft-footed up the street but turned before they reached the crossroad that would bring them to the front of the lockhouse. They snuck up the street behind it and approached the house from the rear.

It was too much to hope for that the back of the house would be completely unguarded. But, in fact, there were only two thains there, and they were less than attentive. Their spears were standing against the wall of a nearby house, and they sat on the curb playing dice in the pale glow of a coldlight.

"Three crosses," said the shorter of the two, a woman seemingly. "That's twenty-one to you." She handed the dice and cup to her watchmate.

He took them and shook them and said, "I don't like this duty."

"I don't enjoy looking at your face, either."

"It's nothing to do with that. You said no grudges, Krida."

"So I did. Are you going to roll, or just make knuckly music all night long?"

"Rolling." The dice clattered onto the streetstones and grew still. "Night and day. Top that, wench."

"I topped your mother," said Thain Krida, accepting the dice cup and dice.

"Who hasn't? Shake 'em up, Guardian."

Krida rattled the dice in the cup and threw. "Spider-face. Chaos in shiny nuggets! Go again?"

"Sure. Why not? For another meat pie?"

"I'm tired of buying you meat pies. How about a bowl of red cream?"

"Sure. You go first: loser's privilege. I'll tell you what it is with this duty, Krida."

Krida, shaking the dice cup, guessed, "No, let me guess. Nightmares from the evil walls? Stink from the prisoners? Guilt from profiting by your watchmate's bad luck?"

"No. It's this: I joined the Graith to keep the Wardlands safe. But now we have a prison. What's next? Tax collecting? Treason trials? We get to genuflect before some self-styled king and laugh at his stupid jokes?"

"Throwing," said Krida flatly. After the dice skittered to a halt she said, "A snake and a bird. Not so bad."

"But you're not saying anything, so I guess you think I'm a bung-biter."

"I do think you're a bung-biter, but that's not why."

"Answer me straight or keep the dice and play against yourself."

She handed him the dice and the cup, and she said, "I don't know, Garol. I don't like guarding a prison, either, but no one said it was permanent. Noreê says that a king is what she's trying to prevent—those Ambrosiuses."

"Doesn't she seem a little crazy to you on the subject?"

"You didn't know Old Ambrosius? I guess not. Listen, if Noreê, who walked against the Dark Seven, is scared of that guy, there's reason for it. He had reason to hate Earno, and now Earno is dead, dropped dead, murdered in the middle of the Wardlands in the sight of three Guardians, and no one knows who did it! That tells you who did it. Old Ambrosius, or maybe the young one."

"Ah."

"They say he was there. I don't like all this stuff. Dwarves and mandrakes and God Sustainer knows what else walking around the place like they belonged here. I remember when this was a free country for *people*—just people, not every weird shtutt that wandered over the mountains. It started to get bad when the Northhold came under the Guard. And who was responsible for *that*?"

"The Graith."

"Who *really*? It was that Old Ambrosius."

"You weren't even born back then. What do you know about it?"

"I hear things. You would, too, Garol, if you bothered to listen."

"All I know is, I didn't sign on to be a prison guard."

Krida groaned. "Shut up and roll."

Standing in the shadows, Morlock mimed tossing something. Deor would have preferred a clearer clue, but he nodded and gestured at his eyes. Morlock nodded and closed his eyes.

Deor crouched and groped on the ground for a suitable rock. It took him a while to find one, but when he did he tapped Morlock on the elbow to let him know it was almost time to act, and then he threw the rock as hard as he could at the watch-thains' coldlight.

The glass shattered and the light went out. Deor saw the two goggling at each other in the glow of the dispersing lightwater.

Morlock brushed by him, running up the alley in his soft shoes, his eyes still tightly closed. A man's eyes would not adjust as quickly to darkness as Deor's did, but the dwarf thought his *harven*-kin was overdoing the caution a bit. He followed him into the fray.

There was a scramble under the wall of the lockhouse as the guard-thains tried to find their spears in the dark. They hadn't yet thought to call for help, then Morlock and Deor were on them.

Morlock seemed to be throttling Garol, which to Deor's mind was a little extreme. The attack also wasn't really an option for Deor, as Krida was an arm-length or so taller than him.

He set his feet and punched her as hard as he could in the stomach. But his aim was a little off and his stone-hard fist fell on her pubic bone. She bent over, gasping for air, and he hit her hard under the chin when it came into reach. She rolled unconscious on the street next to the dice and cup. Morlock lowered Garol there beside her—still breathing, Deor was glad to see, but quite unaware of the world.

Morlock took a wedged digging tool from a pocket in his sleeve and Deor did the same. They went to work on the base of the wall.

The first inch or so was painted stucco; after that they started getting into the dried fungus. Deor wondered whether they should cut breathing masks for themselves from their cloaks, but Morlock didn't even seem to consider it, so he didn't bother to make the suggestion. The nightmares were not physical;

they were just trapped in the dried flesh of the fungus, like an old man's soul in a dying body.

The feeling of dread that he had dreaded came over Deor with startling suddenness. For a dwarf, digging is usually a happy occasion, but this was not like digging through honest dirt and rock. The outer layers of fungus were oddly crispy, like mummified human flesh. The core of the wall was harder, less layered, like ancient dried-out bone. Deor knew that he was lying there next to Morlock digging through a wall. But at the same time he felt that he was digging into a gigantic skull. Soon they would break through and confront the gigantic carnivorous maggots that had devoured the giant's brain and were ravenous for new flesh.

"You're not my father and never were!" Morlock snarled, holding his digger like a knife. "My father is dead! His ashes rest in the Holy Halls under Thrymhaiam!"

That startled Deor out of his skull nightmare. Morlock was having a nightmare about Merlin, of course. He knew his *harven*-kin often did.

"I wish Oldfather Tyr was with us now," he whispered to Morlock. "There was nothing that he feared."

Morlock shook his head—not like he was disagreeing; like a man waking. Then he whispered, "We must be close to the interior. The nightmares will be thickest there."

"Joy of joys."

They dug.

The horror that Krida felt for mandrakes and dwarves was not hard for Deor to understand. He himself felt it for Other Folk at times, especially when they were dead. A dwarf's soul, he knew or believed, mounted into the sky and fled the world through the gateway in the west on the morning after its body's death. But there was nothing in any teaching about the souls of men and women doing the same thing. They lingered, like mist, in the dark places of the earth; they haunted graveyards and possessed dead bodies.

Deor knew where he and Morlock were and what they were doing, but at the same time he became convinced that they were digging into the mausoleum of a human graveyard. He had seen them, great buildings just like this but full of corpses rotting in boxes. And Other Folk went there and left flowers and had picnics and engaged in their bizarre and ugly mating practices on grass fed by the filth of rotting flesh. It was deeply disgusting. He hated those places and he couldn't imagine why he had come to this one. Soon they would break through to the interior and it would be filled with bodies. But they would not be dead bodies. Not anymore. . . .

His digger broke through into empty darkness. Not far away were staring eyes, gleaming silver in the moonlight.

"Stand away," Morlock directed, and Deor didn't need to be told twice. When Deor was clear, Morlock swung around so that his feet were facing the pitted wall. He braced himself and kicked until the hole was big enough to crawl through.

"Rope," he said.

Deor was a little surprised that Morlock was about to hang himself, but on reflection he decided that it was really the only escape. He handed Morlock the bight of rope hanging from his belt.

Morlock drove his digger between two paving blocks and anchored the rope to it. Then he loosed the bight and, with the free end in hand, slithered feet first into the hole.

Morlock saw eyes—dozens of them staring at him in the bar of moonslight falling after him into the cellar. He heard the hiss of many mouths breathing, smelt the stink of many bodies and their waste.

"Kelat!"

"That's me!" said a voice just behind him. "You killed me and buried me once, but you won't do it again!"

Something sharp slashed the side of his neck. He leaped away but not before his blood fell burning to the ground.

The moon-wounded darkness of the pit gave way to a blood-colored twilight as Morlock's blood burned on the fungal floor. Kelat stood astonished in the dim, fiery light, watching burning blood drip off the sharp stake in his hand.

If there was ever any chance of talking to Kelat through the haze of nightmares, it was obviously lost. Morlock kicked the stake out of Kelat's hand and continued the kick to land with his full weight on the pit of Kelat's stomach.

Kelat oofed out the air in his lungs but was not so bemused that he didn't get a grip on Morlock's foot. He twisted it viciously. Morlock was compelled to spin with the twist, or limp through the rest of his life. He landed on his back in a pile of filth. Kelat charged him, shouting in a language Morlock didn't know; he thought it might be Vraidish. He kicked Kelat in the knees and the stranger went down, striking his head against the cellar wall. He did not get up again.

Morlock climbed to his feet and went over to check on Kelat. He was still breathing, thank God Sustainer. Morlock hefted up the twitching stranger, clearly in the grip of a nightmare, and stuffed him like a sack of beans up through the gap in the cellar wall. Deor began to help from the other side, and soon the way was clear for him to leave.

He turned and looked at the Khnauronts. They were huddled up against the far wall, watching him in the dim light of the fire burning on the floor. He was tempted to let the fire burn—let them all die. They deserved it. But it wasn't up to him to decide what they deserved. He stamped out the bloodfire and climbed up the rope through the gap into the free air of the alley.

Deor was there, examining Kelat's skull with his fingers as the stranger breathed stertorously and muttered gibberish or Vraidish.

"He'll live," the dwarf said, banishing at least one of Morlock's fears. "We weren't exactly quiet."

"Let's get away quickly."

"Sew you up first," Deor said, taking an incombustible needle and thread from a couple of pockets.

"You'll burn your fingers," Morlock said.

"So what?" Deor said, and had him sit down in the street as he deftly sewed up Morlock's wound (jagged, but not serious), then smeared it with a healing paste, then anointed his fingers with the same.

"Thanks, *harven*."

"You'd do the same."

They went to pick up Kelat and started carrying him down the alleyway.

Thains with long hooded spears began stepping out of the shadows.

"Chaos in a wheelbarrow!" Deor cursed.

They dropped Kelat in the street.

Into the moonslit street strode a tall woman with white hair, wearing a red cloak.

"Surrender, Guardians!" called out Noreê in undisguised triumph. "You will not take the prisoner away. But you will explain yourselves at Station tomorrow."

"You have no authority to stay us, Vocate," Morlock called back.

"I do have the *power* to do it, Vocate," Noreê replied. "Stand away from the prisoner and you won't be hurt."

"Approach the prisoner and you *will* be hurt," Morlock replied. "What I say, I say to you all. I am on the Graith's business and I will kill anyone who stands in my way. Maintain the Guard!"

"Maintain the Guard!" replied several of the thains reflexively, but Noreê shouted over them, "Brave words, Guardian! But you can't fight your way through my thains; there are too many of them."

"The odds were worse at the Hill of Storms," Deor remarked. He unslung his axe and flourished it.

Morlock drew both sword and spear. He and Deor stood back to back.

"Thains, unhood your spears and advance," Noreê directed. "Do not kill the dwarf if it can be helped."

Most of the thains shook the hoods off their bright spears and advanced slowly up the street. Glancing about, Morlock saw that there were thains cautiously advancing from the shadows on all sides of them. And there were others who stood indecisive behind them.

"*Khuknen vei vedorna,*" Deor remarked in a low voice ("Their hearts aren't in this") and Morlock agreed, "*Zhai!*"

Morlock had become fairly skilled at using a thain's spear, and he thought that if he could take one away from the first unfortunate who approached him, their odds would go up. His stabbing spear was well-balanced for throwing, and that might take them off guard. If they could open up a hole in the wall of thains, it would be well to pick up Kelat and retreat into a narrow area between the houses, where their opponents' numbers would matter even less. . . .

Then there were other shadowy forms running into the street, hooded men coming through the gaps between the buildings, filling the empty moonlit streetstones between Morlock and Deor and the other Guardians. None of their faces could be seen, but each one wore a ring made of blackiron on his right hand.

It was the Guild of Silent Men. Morlock lowered both his swords and waited on events.

"Guardians, stand down!" said one of the Silent Men. "I am Teyn, Master of the Guild of Silent Men. I speak also for my colleague Seetch, now in the North."

"But you don't speak for the Graith of Guardians," Noreê said, as her thains hesitated. "This is an internal matter of the Graith, and I warn you to stay out of it."

"If it involves Ambrosius, it involves us. His blood is ours and ours is his."

Noreê stepped forward to look at Teyn's face, still half hidden in his hood. She glanced over to Morlock as she said, "You must be mistaken. No member of the Graith may be associated with another order, or he is subject to penalty under the First Decree."

"He may not be associated with us, but we associate ourselves with him! I warn you, Guardian. You wield your power under our sufferance, the sufferance of the Guarded. The enemy of the Guarded is the enemy of the Wardlands. Do not make yourself our enemy. We will fight our enemies here as we fought them in the North."

"I accept the limits on my power," Noreê said slowly, as if she especially enjoyed saying the words, "and woe to those who do otherwise. Morlock! Do you insist on seizing the Graith's prisoner with the help of these . . . gentlemen?"

"I say what I have said: get out of my way. I am on the Graith's business."

Noreê smiled like a shark and said, "Guardians, stand down. We will not go to war with the Guarded."

The thains lowered their spears and hooded them—many with visible relief. They filed away into the night.

"Good luck on the Graith's business!" Noreê called to Morlock before she, too, turned away. "The Graith will have some business with you when you return."

"What's that about?" Deor asked, bewildered at Noreê's sudden about face.

Morlock thought he understood it. Noreê believed she could prove Impairment of the Guard against him. Certainly other vocate who had joined leagues with the Guarded against the Graith had been sent into exile. He thought of what Aloê had said and wondered if she was right.

He grunted and shrugged.

"Oh. Now I understand," Deor said wryly. They reslung their weapons and went to talk to Teyn.

"Morlock Ambrosius," said Teyn, reaching out both hands. Morlock grasped them with both of his and said, "Teyn." He wished that the Silent Men had not intervened, but it would be churlish not to recognize the generosity of their actions. The Guild had nothing to gain, and perhaps much to lose, by angering the Graith. But they had risked that for his sake.

"Can we be of any more help?" Teyn asked anxiously. "We know the Silent Folk in the North fought hard at your side; we are willing to do the same."

There was an old rivalry, Morlock remembered, between Teyn and his colleague Seetch (long since married and moved to the colony of Silent Men and Women in the North). Perhaps there was some of that in tonight's events.

"There are a couple wounded thains behind the lockhouse, and a hole in the wall," Morlock said. "You might see to them."

"And, in truth, some of your people could help us carry the prisoner," Deor added. "Morlock has some transport arranged, but it is a ways away, I believe. We expected Kelat to be walking. Candidly, I am surprised the man is still unconscious."

"He did have brain surgery earlier today," Morlock pointed out. "That was before I bashed his head against a wall."

"Eh, *harven*. If I'm ever imprisoned in a lockhouse, please don't break in and rescue me. But, Teyn. . . ."

"Certainly!" Teyn called a few Silent Men over and gave orders: so many to accompany Morlock and Deor, so many to repair the lockhouse and tend to Krida and Garol, so many to return to the Hall, and so on.

Eventually they were walking westward again, past the front of the lockhouse (where some resentful looking thains had resumed their guard post). Teyn went with them, talking of this and that with Deor.

". . . and no matter what Morlock has planned for the next stage in the journey," Deor said, "at least it won't be horses. When I'm on one of those things, I feel as if I'm a mile from the ground! And one never knows when they will turn aside to eat some grass or chase a rabbit."

"I don't think they do that, Thain Deor," Teyn said mildly.

"It hasn't been proven, I admit, but consider the evidence! Rabbits eat grass; horses love grass. Why wouldn't they eat rabbits?"

"Or the reverse."

"The grass eating the rabbits? I've seen grass like that in Tychar. Mindless, vicious, carnivorous, poisonous. Never trust a vegetable, Teyn; they will only make you sad. What in the secret name of God Creator is *that*?"

They were deep in the Low Hills now; dwellings were rare and the paving on the road was coarser and narrower. But there was a dark shape—no, several dark shapes darkening the air between them and the moon.

"Here we are," Morlock called up into the night.

"We see you!" replied the night. "Stop moving. And ware claws."

"'Ware claws,'" repeated Deor, and there was no real danger of him moving.

Three winged pieces of night landed on the road before them. Their pelts or feathers were black, at least in the blank, cold light of the major moons. Their hindquarters were like horses with long feathery tails, except that they had claws instead of hooves. Their wings were as wide as dragons, and their forequarters were like birds of prey—dark hawks with silver eyes.

And they were saddled, and the saddles held riders. Deor relaxed when he recognized the riders.

"Good night and greetings to you, Guardians!" he called. "What brings you flying this way?"

Naevros dismounted from the nearest hippogriff and said, "The same that brings you, Guardian!"

"I was afraid of that," Deor remarked quietly, and looked reproachfully at Morlock.

Naevros greeted each one of the Silent Men by name, which surprised Morlock, and then he embraced Morlock, which surprised him even more.

"There was trouble at the lockhouse, I see?" he guessed, nodding toward the snoring prisoner.

Morlock nodded.

"Maybe I should have been there," Naevros said ruefully.

"No," Morlock said, thinking of Noreê and the danger of exile. "Besides," he said, noticing the stink of sex rising from Naevros' clothes, "you had other work."

Naevros snickered in a way that made Morlock think less of him, pounded Morlock on his higher shoulder, and let him go. Had he embraced him to show friendship or advertise his conquest? Naevros thought of his sexual experiences that way, Morlock knew: as conquests.

Now the other vocates had dismounted: Sundra and Keluaê. They approached to greet Morlock and Deor, and to be introduced to the Silent Men. Some account was given of the raid on the lockhouse and its aftermath, with Deor and Teyn doing much of the talking.

The scents of Sundra and Keluaê mingled oddly with Naevros' in the cold night air. Had he had sex with one or both of them? It was none of Morlock's business. After Morlock had sex he usually sponged himself off before meeting people, but perhaps that was excessively prudish. Had he been raised by human beings, he felt he might understand these things better.

"And now, I suppose . . ." Sundra began, looking at Morlock with eyes like pools of shadow in the moonlight.

"Yes; we must go," Morlock agreed. "Thanks for bringing your friends, Sundra."

"They brought us! As you saw. They know full well that the times are full of danger; they feel the sickness in the sun, the coldness in the sky, better than we can understand. And they will take you far along your way. But. . . ."

"Say on, Vocate. We won't be offended."

"Hippogriffs are not horses. You will not direct them. If you attempt it—well, do not."

"We won't," Deor assured her, faintly but sincerely.

"The saddles are for your convenience, and they are a great concession. I must ask you to take them off and discard them when the hippogriffs have taken you as far as they choose."

"We'll take them off and destroy them," said Morlock, loud enough for the hippogriffs to hear. He hoped they understood Wardic.

"Good! They call themselves 'the Free People' and they much despise anything that can be tamed."

Morlock nodded.

"Goodbye then!" said Naevros. "Good luck! Send word when you can!" He embraced him again.

Sundra and Keluaê also stepped forward to embrace . . . Deor, of whom they were extremely fond. They shook hands with Morlock, and Teyn held up his hands when Morlock turned to say goodbye to him and his Guildmen.

"There are no words of parting between us, Ambrosius," Teyn said. "We are always together. Good luck on your quest. Your luck will be the world's luck, I think."

Morlock nodded and turned away. With Deor's help, he lifted Kelat across a hippogriff's saddle and bound him there. Deor and he each mounted a hippogriff.

They stayed there without moving, waiting for something, some sign.

"My friend," said Morlock, "bear me where you will, as far as you will."

The hippogriff leapt into the air and the others followed, their wings booming like storm winds on the chill evening air. They turned toward the red moons lowering in the east and flew away.

So Vocate Morlock Ambrosius left the Wardlands on the wings of a hippogriff and the winds of the world, never to return.

CHAPTER SEVEN

A Needle of Sunlight

The hippogriffs landed them among the foothills of the eastern Whitethorns in the hour before dawn. They had stayed to watch with their star-silver eyes while Morlock kindled a fire and burned the saddles. Once the saddles were largely embers they unfolded their wings and took to the sky again, black shadows against the cold gray sky of morning. Neither Morlock nor Deor ever heard them make a sound with their mouths. Nor did Kelat, but he didn't seem to be hearing anything: he was still unconscious.

"That," said Deor, "was the worst thing you have ever done to me. But at least I know now that nothing can ever be worse. No method of travel could possibly be more hellish than flying those speechless beasts over half the chaos-begotten world."

Morlock thought it was reckless to make suppositions of this sort, given that their journey had hardly begun. What he said aloud, however, was, "Eh."

"That's easy for you to say. Too easy, if we come right down to it, *harven*."

"Eh."

"Have it your way. What are you going to do with our friend here?"

"I am going to stab him through the eye with a needle of sunlight."

"Well, I suppose you feel that's—Is that some kind of metaphor?"

"No."

"Why are you going to do such a ridiculous thing?"

"When I was staying at New Moorhope after—it was some years ago—"

"Yes, *harven*, I remember it. Go on."

"The healers there woke a woman from a coma this way."

"Urrrr. All right. What if it doesn't work? He's not much good to us as he is. In fact, he'll die if he doesn't wake up eventually. Unless you can think of a way to get water and nourishment into his veins while he sleeps."

Morlock grunted.

"I wish you would expand on that, Morlock."

"Eh. It's a solvable problem. But it doesn't solve *our* problem. We might let him die, and try to extract knowledge from the dead brain, or we might extract his brain from his body before it dies and try to bespeak it in some way."

"Well, well. Let's make this sun-needle thing work, then."

"Yes."

Morlock set up an immaterial shell of impulse foci around the fire, making it into an impromptu furnace. Deor found a deposit of sandstone and quarried some to bring back. Using some tongs he happened to have in his backpack (unlike Morlock, he did not believe in travelling light), he placed the fragments in the invisible furnace to begin the glass-making process.

By then, Morlock was deep in rapture, lying like a dead man next to Tyrfing, the crystalline blade glowing black-on-white and white-on-black.

"If you don't mind," Deor said to Morlock, "I'm going to have a nap. We may be up all night again."

Morlock said nothing, but Deor didn't expect it. He went and wrapped himself in his bedroll and dreamed for five solid hours about flying in the dark over the Wardlands. It was like a nightmare, only he was never afraid.

He awoke in midmorning. Kelat was still unconscious, and his breathing seemed shallower than it ought to be.

"Brains," said Deor disgustedly, and went over to the invisible forge.

The sandstone was now a globe of dark molten glass with a skewer of golden light in its heart. Morlock was still in deep rapture, keeping the glass hot and guiding the harvest of sunlight.

Deor made an early lunch of grilled sausage, softtack bread, and stromroot sauce. He brooded while he ate: there must be something he could do while Morlock did the real work.

Deor was not the master of all makers; this he knew. He was a plausible seller of goods, a skilled juggler, a good fighter, a decent cook and storyteller, and all these things were valued by his people. But he was not much of a maker, and this was the thing they (and he) valued most.

But he guessed that Morlock's needle of sunlight would be a precarious instrument to wield in colder lights: moonlight and starlight. If this attempt were going to work—and he very much wanted it to work ("Brains!")—then Morlock would need a Zone of Perfect Occlusion. Deor set about establishing one near to the invisible furnace.

The Perfect Occlusion is an immaterial barrier that does not allow light to pass. To Deor's mind, it ought to have been reflective, but a well-formed occlusion looks like a space where there simply is no light. The geometry of the Occlusion puts the light elsewhere.

Deor was no champion at multidimensional geometry, but he had developed a trial-and-error method that worked, given enough time. With no one to talk to, no books to read, and nothing else to do, he had plenty of time. By the time the sun had passed its midpoint and the chilly spring day was at its closest approach to warmth, he stood in triumph next to a stable Occlusion—a half-globe of darkness six paces in diameter. Six of Deor's paces, admittedly—about three or four of Morlock's rather oversized strides. That should be big enough.

He was revisiting his decision to bring food instead of books when he remembered that Morlock had tucked a few volumes into his pack. Deor snuck over to look at them.

One was in a language that Deor didn't read or recognize. One was a book of mathematical philosophy. One was a book of stories about monsters; it wasn't clear whether the stories were true or not. Rather discontentedly, he settled down on a comfortable rock with the book of monsters and read for a time.

As the red, cold sun sank nearer the eastern horizon, Morlock rose to his feet. Deor looked up and saw that Morlock was still in the rapture of vision. He plunged his glowing sword into the dark orb of molten glass.

The sword faded. The light behind Morlock's closed lids also faded, and he opened his eyes.

Deor tossed the monster book into Morlock's open pack and said, "Over here, *harven*."

"See it," Morlock croaked. "Thank you. Bring Kelat, eh?"

"Shouldn't you rest? If—"

"Time is short. Hurry."

Deor grabbed the nigh-lifeless form of Kelat and dragged him by the collar into the Zone of Perfect Occlusion.

Morlock had already entered. The globe of glass was cooling unevenly; in the light cast by the narrow spiralling blaze of sunlight in the globe's core, Deor could see cracks opening in the surface of the globe.

Morlock speeded up the process by putting the globe down on the dark ground and twisting his blade like a knife.

The globe of dark glass shattered and the thread of light lay bare. Morlock picked it up in his right hand. It cast strange shadows on his face; Deor didn't like it. (But he remembered the alternatives. Brains!)

"Pull one of his eyes open," Morlock croaked.

Deor wondered which one he should choose. He crouched down beside Kelat and held open both the stranger's eyes. They were stark and staring in the strange light, their pupils gaping wide in the dark.

Morlock thrust the needle of light into Kelat's left eye, spearing the dark pupil in its exact center.

Kelat's eye like a thirsty mouth drank down the light. Darkness fell like a thunderbolt in the Perfect Occlusion.

Kelat began to scream and thrash.

"Out with him!" Morlock hissed.

Morlock must have had the stranger's feet; Deor grabbed one of his arms and they dragged Kelat into the dim light of a cool spring evening.

Now Kelat was sobbing with his face in the dirt. He lifted himself onto all fours and then sat back heavily, staring around him with weeping eyes.

"What's your name?" Deor said, curious whether the stranger remembered it.

"I'm Kelat," said the stranger. "You . . . you were in the dream. So was the other. I saw the other one in hell. Is he a devil?"

"No."

"He looks like a devil."

"What does a devil look like?"

"Him."

Morlock hawked and spat. He went over to his waterbottle and drank. Then he came back and offered the bottle to Kelat.

The stranger took the bottle suspiciously and sniffed at it. Then he looked relieved and took a sip. At last he drank deep and handed the bottle back to Morlock. "Thanks, friend."

"Why a friend, now, and not a devil?" Deor asked. "Or is he both?"

"The devil doesn't drink water," Kelat said, as if everyone should know this. "But I still don't understand why you were in hell, or how I got out."

"It wasn't hell," Deor explained, "just a jail. Although there were resemblances, from the little I saw of the place. I'm Deor syr Theorn, by the way. This is my friend and *harven*-kin Morlock Ambrosius."

"Yes," Kelat said slowly. "Yes—I was afraid of that."

"Why 'afraid'?" Deor asked.

"I will not say at this time. I owe you both much, but some things I must keep to myself."

"Can you say why you came into the Wardlands, and how?"

"Was that where I was?"

"I'll take that as a no."

"No. No. I think the dragon sent me. He put—he had someone put something in me. In my—in my face—or in my brain. I don't feel it there anymore. Two of your order took it out of me."

"You know our order then?"

"Of course. You are members of the Graith of Guardians."

"You speak Wardic extremely well."

"We call it 'the secret speech' in the unguarded lands. I had a Coranian tutor who helped me with it."

"How many languages do you speak?" Morlock asked.

"The secret speech, and Vraidish, and what they call Ontilian. But I cannot read the old script."

"And that is why you were sent on this mission?" Morlock asked. "Because of your skill with languages?"

"I sent myself!" Kelat insisted. "At least . . . I set out on my own. But it was not to the Hidden Land . . . the Wardlands, as you call it. There was a dragon in the empty places west of the Sea of Stones; the Gray Folk there worship him as a god. He is said to know many things. I thought he might know how to heal the sun."

"Rulgân Silverfoot," said Deor.

"His right foreclaw is metal, it is true," Kelat said. "But there is a gem there that keeps it alive. I found him. I . . . I was trapped by him. It was he who sent me to you. I don't know why. Most of that time is a dream to me. I remember talking, or him talking through me, but I don't remember the words."

"Could you find him again?" Deor asked.

Kelat bowed his head and thought. "I will not be taken prisoner again," he said. "I will not let that thing in my mind again. But I do want to face him again, yes. And kill him if I can, before the sun goes dark. But why do you want to find him?"

"We want what you wanted," Deor assured him, "to heal the sun. Rulgân may know who is killing it. If we can find that out, we can stop it. But that will be our errand, not killing dragons—as enjoyable an occupation as that may be."

Kelat looked at Morlock. "He talks," Kelat said. "Does he talk for you?"

"About this we are of one mind," Morlock said.

"Well, I will take you to find Rulgân Silverfoot. I owe you much. I was standing in the gate of Death's city when you called me back."

"Eh."

"That means," Deor said, "'Maybe you can return the favor sometime.' Morlock doesn't say much. I say we eat and sleep and start out sometime after midnight."

Morlock nodded and turned toward his backpack, no doubt to break out the flatbread and dried meat.

"Morlock syr Theorn," Deor said sternly, "I beg you to leave that stuff alone until we have to choose between it and death by starvation. I have food enough for all three of us tonight, and we can seek more tomorrow. Now—I'm thinking sandwiches of toasted cheese, sausages, and a few pieces of fruit. I have a bottle of Old Vunthorn we can share as well. Really, Kelat, you must take my word on this. Morlock may have dragged you out of jail and out of the jaws of death, but I'm the one who just saved you from hell."

CHAPTER EIGHT

Vengeancer

About the time that Deor was serving out toasted cheese sandwiches, Aloê Oaij was peering into the eyes of a corpse.

After Morlock and Deor left Tower Ambrose for the lockhouse and points unknown, she returned to her bed and lay there for a while on Morlock's side, thinking about one thing or another, but not really trying to get to sleep.

A gravedigger and a healer—that was what she needed. And time. Time that was passing as she lay there.

Eventually she got back up, took a run through the rain room, and dressed for the road: clean but well-worn clothes of black and brown, and a weather-faded red cloak she rarely used anymore. She left, telling the lock not to expect her back for a day or two.

The stable opened politely at her approach, and she went in to saddle her red palfrey, Raudhfax. She seemed glad to get some exercise, and no more inclined to sleep than Aloê was.

Aloê rode her first to the Chamber of the Graith. There were only two thains on guard at the front; she recognized neither, but they evidently knew her, standing aside to let her enter without a word being spoken.

Inside the dome she saw Bleys and a few others—Guardians cloaked red and gray, and a couple of black-robed savants—huddling around the wreckage of the Witness Stone. Well, if anyone could heal the Stone, it would be Bleys.

But Aloê wasn't here to deal with the stone. She proceeded to the Arch of Tidings, one of several little rooms running around the base of the dome that formed the great central chamber. It held a number of message socks in identity with various fixed points in the Wardlands.

The thain on duty there gave her pen, ink, and a palimpsest to write on. She also seemed inclined to chat. Aloê dismissed her with a single lifted eyebrow and sat down to dash off a message to the Lokh of Necrophors at New Moorhope. Then she slipped it in the sock for New Moorhope and hoped someone was on night watch in the message room there.

The Lokh of Necrophors was a voluntary order of gravediggers and morticians. Aloê knew she would need help in studying the body of the murdered Summoner Earno, and she hoped the Lokharch could send her a necrophor experienced in handling murder victims.

She was prepared to wait hours for an answer, and perhaps leave in the morning without one, but to her surprise, as soon as she withdrew her palimpsest from the message sock she saw that the reverse had been inscribed with a response.

Vocate Aloê: Greetings from New Moorhope. I am Gramart of Tren, a necrophor of the third degree. I happen to be on watch here; we junior necrophors often take the late shifts. I venture to write you to say: a necrophor was dispatched to the site of Earno's most-to-be-mourned murder at the request of his family. She is Oluma Cyning, an experienced sifter of strange deaths. She knows to expect a vocate at Big Rock House, although she does not yet know it will be you. Good fortune to you, and bad luck forever to the murderer: Earno was a good man.

Aloê scribbled *Many thanks! A.O.* beneath this and returned it to the sock.

She stopped for a moment or two to chat with the thain outside the message room. She felt a little guilty about brushing her off earlier. She felt less guilty when it turned out that the girl was excited to discuss the "fit of madness" that had caused Morlock to destroy the Witness Stone. Aloê walked away while the burbling thain was in mid-word.

There was a Well of Healing not so far from here; she recovered Raudhfax from the watch-thains outside and rode her along the old wall-road until she came to Wall-Well.

The Skein of Healers always dug a well outside their hostels of healing. Aloê had no idea why, although she had studied with them off and on over the years. But she was grateful for herself and for Raudhfax tonight: she was suddenly dry as a summer street—thirsty enough to drink straight from the well bucket. And Raudhfax drank as deeply after Aloê filled the trough beside the well.

The door to the healing hostel was open and unguarded; they always were. She walked in to find two yellow-robed healers playing a game with word tiles.

"Yes, Vocate?" said one of the healers, with a supercilious air.

"Your throat bothering you?" asked the other, who either had a quick eye for bruises or had attended the aftermath of the day's Station.

"No, thanks," she said to the second healer, ignoring the first. "I'm headed north to investigate the death of Summoner Earno and I was hoping one of your order could come and assist me with the gorier details."

Master Snide said snidely, "Binder Denynê was dispatched some days ago and is awaiting a vocate at Big Rock House."

"Don't mind him," said the other healer. "He hates nightwork and he's losing at Wordweave and these things make him grumpy."

"Thanks for your courtesy," she said to him, "and good luck in your game. All night long."

She spun about and strode out the open door.

It was a long way to Big Rock, but the Road was clear, the moons were bright, Raudhfax was game, there was no way that she was going to sleep tonight.

"Let's go!" she said, leaping into her palfrey's saddle. Raudhfax snorted and clattered away up the street. She needed only a word or two in Westhold horser dialect to turn west and then north to find the great Road.

They were not far north of the city when she felt rather than saw three shadows pass between her and the moons. She was conscious of the ill omen, but she would not let it keep her from her work. She would not let anything do that.

They arrived in the hour before dawn at the inn at Big Rock. There was only the one, built into the side of the gigantic boulder that gave the little town its name. The ostler and the cook were already up, so she kissed Raudhfax's nose and told her she was a champion and then went in to consume as much egg-pie and smoked fish as the pantry could conveniently yield.

"Your healer and gravedigger friends are both already here," the cook explained when she no longer felt Aloê was going to die from hunger or thirst. "The householder put you all in the big room in the front of the house—there are three beds in there."

"Do you suppose I can sneak in there and grab a few hours' sleep without waking them?" Aloê asked wistfully.

"The door is very quiet, Vocate—I'm sure you won't disturb them."

The door was quiet on its hinges and opened with hardly a sound; Aloê did not in fact disturb them. But they weren't sleeping. They were wriggling around on one of the beds with their heads lodged between each other's legs. Aloê closed the door as quietly as she had opened it and went back down to the kitchen.

"Another room, possibly?" she asked.

With a thousand apologies and a face burning with shame, the cook took her up the back stairs and admitted her to paradise. Paradise was a drafty, closetlike room in a corner of the attic; at its center was a bed that was softer than clouds in a summer sky. Aloê muttered incoherent but utterly sincere thanks, fell into the bed fully clothed, and slept most of the day.

When she awoke and crawled out of her closet paradise, she found it was midafternoon. Wandering around the upper floors of the inn, Aloê found nothing like a privy or a rain room. There was an empty room with a tub and a pump, but Aloê guessed it must be some sort of laundry: the coarse brushes and bitter, stinking soap on the bare, water-stained board beside the tub could not have been meant for use on people.

She descended the back stairs to the kitchen, where she found a woman in a blue gown eagerly discussing food with the cook while a thin-faced, apricot-colored woman in yellow watched enviously, perched on a nearby stool.

"Vocate Aloê!" cried the cook—with a certain relief, Aloê thought. "Here are Necrophor Oluma Cyning and Binder Denynê from the Skein of Healing." *And now they're you're problem*, her pointed glance seemed to add.

"Necrophor—Binder—good day," Aloê said.

Blue-gowned Oluma jumped across the kitchen and slapped both sides of Aloê's right hand in greeting. "Good morrow, Vocate! Or close to evening now. I trust you had a good ride up last night? I saw your horse this morning; she's a beauty. Do you want to look at my seconding papers? I've got them up in our room. We've got a great room at the front of the house; I don't know why they didn't show it to you this morning. When—"

"Be glad to look at your seconding presently," Aloê said hastily, "but I've been asleep all day—"

"And you're hungry!"

"Well, yes, but—"

"Thirsty, too, I bet! Lundê, what have you got for a midafternoon breakfast?"

"I have an even more urgent need, though," Aloê said, while the cook (Lundê, it seemed) considered the question put to her. "And I couldn't find a privy upstairs," she added, when no one seemed to get it.

The cook slapped her forehead. "Fate on a pitchfork! The little cubbyhole you're in probably doesn't have a honeygourd in it?"

"I did not see one," Aloê said truthfully, not adding that she would not know one if she did see it.

"It's smell it you'd've done, if there were one in there," Oluma said cheerfully. In response to Aloê's baffled look she added, "They call it a honeygourd because it's anything but sweet, you see?"

"I think so," Aloê said thoughtfully. A honeygourd must be some kind of chamber pot. Well, she had roughed it on the road often enough. But a *house* without indoor plumbing? She hadn't seen a thing like that in decades. "So, where . . . ?"

"There's an earth closet out back," said Lundê, nodding at a doorway. But she kept an amused eye on Aloê for her reaction.

Aloê realized that she could not afford to play the white-gloved, effete citydweller. "Thanks, Lundê! Ignore any earthquakes or thunder you hear from that direction."

Lundê gagged theatrically, and Denynê's face scrunched up in distaste, looking somewhat like a dried apricot, and Oluma laughed and slapped Aloê on the back, sending dangerous shockwaves through her bladder.

"Back in a time," Aloê said, before the worst happened, and fled out the door, and up a well-worn path through the weedy side garden toward a rickety outbuilding whose purpose was tolerably obvious.

Once she was inside with the door shut, she confronted a saddle-like seat that she was apparently supposed to plant herself on. She hung her cloak of office on a nearby peg, skinned off her riding pants and underwear and hung them alongside it, then squatted over the seat. The wood there, unlike the rest of the building, was polished and oiled from contact with many behinds. She could not bring herself to touch it, but managed to hover over it. She waited for the moment of release.

"Vocate Aloê Oaij," said a thin voice weaseling its way through the thin door.

"This is not a good time," she said with absolute sincerity.

"Vocate Aloê Oaij, I am Binder Denynê of the Skein of Healers. I did not have a chance to introduce myself to you earlier."

"I'm not giving you the chance now. Go away."

"I don't know what you saw this morning, or what you thought you saw—"

"GO AWAY!" roared Aloê.

Little miffed-sounding footsteps receded into the distance, and Aloê heard off in the dim afternoon Oluma's painfully jovial voice cry, "I *told* you to leave her alone!"

Later, a much-relieved Aloê sponged herself off in the tub room (which was indeed intended for human occupants, it seemed) and changed her clothes, returning to the kitchen to find dinner being served and a new occupant at the kitchen table, a tall woman with orange hair and black eyebrows.

The newcomer stood as soon as Aloê entered. "Guardian," she said stiffly. "I'm the Arbiter of the Peace in Big Rock and roundabouts. I brought a couple of horses for your seconds so that you can ride out to the murder scene."

"Thanks, Arbiter!" said Aloê, and would have said more, but the Arbiter walked out of the room.

Aloê shrugged and sat beside her seconds.

"She's a pretty good sort," said Oluma in a worried tone, "but I think the last vocate through here sort of high-handed her. You'll like her better when we get a few drinks into her tonight."

Oluma was more worried about it than Aloê was, and Denynê was worried about something else. They had their secondings with them, though: witnessed documents that they accepted the authority of Aloê for the purposes of the investigation into Earno's death. Without them, her orders to these Guarded would put her in danger of exile under the First Decree. With them, she could order them around like thains—but she would not, of course. That was no way to get skilled work out of someone.

Aloê tucked the secondings into her sleeve and then ate a quick dinner of seared landfish and earthapple crisps alongside her seconds.

"What's to do for the rest of the evening?" asked Oluma. "Do we show you around Big Rock and introduce you, or—"

"Let's ride out and look at the body," Aloê said.

"A night exhumation!" Oluma said. "I love them! Although, strictly speaking, the body hasn't been *in*humated yet. Still, it should be equally creepy, don't you think?"

"Let's hope so."

Oluma ran off to get her bag of tricks, and Denynê took the opportunity to say urgently to Aloê, "Vocate Aloê, I don't know what you saw or what you thought you saw this morning, but. . . ." Her voice trailed off.

Aloê met her orangey-brown eye. "Yes?"

"Well, I. I just. I just want to assure you. That I would never. I would never ever. That is, never again."

"Never what?"

"Oluma seduced me, is what it is. We were waiting, and I was bored, and she is agreeable—don't you think she is?"

"I do. I'm glad for you."

Denynê drew back, appalled, as if the small distance between their two chairs had become a deep chasm spouting fire. "What do you mean? I assure you that I am a person devoted to my craft of healing and to the Skein of Healers."

"What does screwing Oluma have to do with that?"

"We were not *screwing*!"

"Boinking? Cleaning the carpet? Kissing the fish? Diving for pearls?"

Lundê squawked out a laugh and hurriedly stepped out the side door.

"Why do you have to be so offensive?" Denynê said plaintively. "I won't do it again!"

"It's nothing to me whether you do or you don't," Aloê assured her.

"But you . . . you wouldn't. . . ."

"Engage in sex with my partner in a task for my order? But I do so. Constantly. I'm married to a Guardian, Denynê."

"But before you were married. You wouldn't have. You wouldn't have. . . ."

"I did though," said Aloê, smiling as she remembered a few wonderful moments from long ago, and some horrible ones, too—all equally pleasing somehow from this distance. "But I think I know what you mean at last," she said, remembering her concern about whether Morlock and she would be able to work together after they started messing around. "I would say: don't worry about a problem until it is a problem."

"And if it is?"

"We'll talk then."

These matters, once so puzzling to the young Aloê, did not trouble her much anymore. The mystery to her in this situation was what Oluma saw in the dried-up apricot named Denynê. But that was not a mystery she had to solve, unlike the death of Earno.

She and Denynê stood and walked toward the front of the house. Oluma was standing with her bag just outside the door of the kitchen, shifting nervously from foot to foot; clearly she had overheard at least part of the conversation.

They went to get their horses from the stable. She was glad to see that her seconds were both capable horse handlers. Aloê hadn't exactly grown up with horses herself, but knowing how to ride and tend to the beasts was a useful skill that she had been compelled to learn . . . and that certain males who lived with her had never learned very well. She smiled as she saddled up Raudhfax, wondering how they were doing.

As they rode out into the brisk spring evening, they passed by a big house in the shadow of the Big Rock. The Arbiter was standing in its arched doorway, but she turned aside as Aloê and her seconds passed.

"I can't imagine what's gotten into the Arbiter!" fretted Oluma. "It's almost as if she dislikes you."

Aloê slipped this matter into her mental pocket containing all the mysteries she didn't have time to solve, and rode away to the field where her dead friend lay waiting for her.

The pale golden sun was gone from the gray field beside the quiet little brook; it was nearly gone from the sky. Earno's body lay on its back in a private pool of sunlight, staring at the cool blue-edged clouds with empty eyes. The anchors of the stasis spell, seventeen of them, ringed the body with their pointed faces turned inward, like pale chipmunks standing at attention.

"Is this how you found him, Vocate?" Oluma asked.

"No—that's not how it was at all." Aloê thought back to that terrible day. "He was alive when we came in sight of him. We were riding up from the south, Morlock and I. The others were beyond the stream, shepherding the Khnauronts toward it. Earno was on horseback—and Deor, he is never on horseback if he can help it. Noreê was walking next to him, talking about something. I'd never seen them so close together by choice. Deor hates her.

"Earno saw us and smiled. He rode his horse across the stream. When he was in the middle of it, that great wound opened up in his throat and he fell down dead in the stream. He was dead when we pulled him out of the water."

"How quickly did you set up the stasis field?" asked Denynê.

"Almost as soon as we realized he was dead. Though there was some dispute about it."

"Oh?"

"Yes: Deor wanted his body incinerated and the ashes decently buried. Dwarves are like that about people they care for. But Noreê and Morlock ignored us and started setting up the stasis spell. That was funny, too, because—" She didn't finish.

"They hate each other," Oluma finished. "That's what people say, anyway."

"Yes, but they agreed on this without even talking. Perhaps that's the only way they could agree on anything."

Aloê circled the body slowly, looking for details.

"I've never seen a body in stasis before," admitted Oluma. "It's amazing! You can still see the water droplets in his hair and on his skin! His clothes are heavy with it. His eyes are as clear as if he were still alive."

It *was* remarkable, and that fact helped Aloê keep her patience. "What else do you see?" she asked.

"I would have expected more blood," Denynê remarked. "But perhaps the stream washed it away."

"Yes!" Oluma agreed. "The lips of the wound are—they are almost dry and . . . and *crumbly*."

Aloê nodded in agreement. She had seen the same thing, but it was so odd she wanted to know that the others saw it, too.

"I'm going to counter-inscribe the spell," she told her seconds. "Stand a few paces away, please."

They stepped back into the ring of shadow surrounding the shining corpse. Aloê took a diamond-tipped stylus from her pocket and crouched down by one of the spell-anchors. She carefully inscribed an eversion rune on its outer face. She felt the emotional bite of the spell taking hold, but it was a thin whisper against the silent roar of the stasis spell. In the end, she had to inscribe variations on each of the anchors before the light faded and Earno's face fell sideways, giving the wound in his throat an unpleasant likeness to a wry mouth.

She used a coldlight, a mirror, and a magnifying lens to examine the final image in the summoner's dead eyes. It was, as she had feared, nothing useful—the sky, apparently, seen through a layer of water.

Aloê breathed through her mouth during most of this process because of the stench rising from the open wound.

"I think this stasis spell must have failed," Oluma remarked, kneeling beside her and following her technique with interest.

"Hm?" Aloê murmured.

"That stink!" Oluma said cheerfully. She was *not* breathing through her mouth. "That's from a body that's been dead a few days."

"I can't see either Morlock Ambrosius or Noreê Darkslayer making such a mistake," remarked Denynê dryly from well outside the stink zone.

"Not separately," Oluma agreed. "But perhaps together? Maybe they were working at cross-purposes. Maybe that's where the error crept in."

"Possibly," said Aloê, driven into speech, "but not probably. You must consider that Earno was murdered before his death—perhaps some days before."

"Uh? Oh! I forgot about that part."

Aloê would never forget about that part. She said next something that she knew she must but had dreaded since the moment she undertook this task: "Let's look at that wound."

"Yes!" cried Oluma, as if her best-beloved had asked her to dance at the festival of Harps.

"Gleh," Aloê replied indistinctly.

She held the dead man's head steady while Oluma probed the wound with a thin, faintly glowing scrutator and a polished speculum on a long stem. The edges of the wound were gray as a piece of moldy bread, and they were almost serrated in appearance.

"Never seen anything like it," Oluma admitted. "Denynê, honey, could you have a look here?"

"Don't call me that!" hissed the healer.

"Denynê?" Oluma asked, bewildered. "I thought—"

"Never mind!" Denynê hissed, and bent over the corpse. "Eeuuuccch."

"You're being disrespectful to the dead, dear."

"He'll never know it!" snapped the healer. "Hm. Hm. I've never seen anything like this either. Severed blood vessels the proximate cause of death, of course. The throat wound looks almost as if it were sutured, and the sutures were somehow removed, and the process of decay hastened. Oluma—"

"Sweetheart?"

"*Shut. Up. With. That.*"

"I'm only—"

"Only do this: put that scrutator next to the severed jugular."

"Which one is the—?"

"Any of the big blood vessels that have been cut through. Please. If you don't mind."

Oluma shrugged and did as Denynê asked. "You see?" Denynê said to Aloê, genuinely excited. "The ends are frayed and somewhat grayish. What happened to the integument happened to them as well."

"Excellent." Aloê had drawn the same conclusion about the throat wound, but she hadn't noticed the blood vessels. "There was never any suture, I think," she added. "The force binding the wounds together was immaterial, a sealing spell not so very different from the stasis spell I just counter-inscribed."

"What broke the seal?" asked Oluma. "Was it made to dispel after a certain stretch of time, or—"

"The stream!" said Denynê.

"Yes: that," Aloê said. "Running water has a talic presence, almost like a living being. It can shatter certain types of spells. Earno was murdered some time before he died, several days' travel up the Road, perhaps. Then the murderer put this seal upon their work and walked away, in the certain knowledge that Earno would come to grief before he reached A Thousand Towers."

"Would such a spell require anchors, like the stasis spell?" asked Denynê.

"Yes." Aloê traced her finger from one side of the wound up to the corpse's jaw. "Do you see anything here?"

Denynê and Oluma both looked closely. Oluma tapped the blunt end of the scrutator several times and the light it shed increased markedly.

"The skin is very loose," Oluma said. "Earno was a man of a certain age."

"Loose . . . and fragile also," Denynê said. "I see a line of disruption on the surface. It looked almost like an old scar for a second. But there is no scar—no gathering of tissue below the surface."

"A stress mark from the spell, I think," Aloê said. "There are others. We may find physical anchors at the end of the stresslines."

"We will need to make incisions," said Oluma with a certain satisfaction.

"Yes, but we will also need to follow the trail of the summoner back up the Road to find the scene of the actual murder. Are either of you gifted trackers?"

The healer and the gravedigger both looked a little blank in the scrutator's pale light.

"Then," Aloê said, "one of us should go back to ask for assistance from the Arbiter of the Peace."

Oluma's face was growing less bemused and more contented every moment. She would soon have the vocate to herself and have a chance to make up for previous missteps. So Aloê guessed, and she almost hated to say what she had to say next: "Oluma, you had better go."

"Me?" cried the necrophor, startled. "Why me?"

"I expect you know the Arbiter better than Denynê does, and you certainly know her better than I do."

"Er. Yes. There is that. I am a people person," the gravedigger observed.

"Hurry back," Aloê said.

Soon Oluma had mounted her steed and was clattering away in the night and Aloê and Denynê were undressing Earno's dead body to cut him open.

"Oluma really would be better for this task, I think," Denynê ventured to say, as she selected instruments from a rollup carrier.

"Possibly," said Aloê. "But I don't trust her."

Denynê did not pretend to not understand what Aloê was talking about. "I think," she said at last, "there is no malice in her. It is her sense of humor. I'm afraid. . . . Well, they tell me I don't have one."

"Nothing's duller than someone who makes everything into a joke," Aloê said. "Unless they're actually good at it. I don't think Oluma is."

"Well, it was probably best to send her after the Arbiter. She knows Ulvana far better than I do, and they seem to get along well."

Ulvana. Ulvana. The name struck a chord in Aloê's memory. "Is this the Honorable Ulvana Claystreet, from A Thousand Towers?" she asked.

Denynê thought long before answering. "I don't know her surname," she said at last, "and, of course, Arbiters have to forswear all other ranks and associations, much like your own order. But I think she did move here from A Thousand Towers. Did you know her there?"

Aloê was listening in her mind to another voice, screaming, *Love! You unspeakable trull! Don't you see how he hates you?* The voice was her voice, and she was trying hard to remember the face of the woman she had screamed at more than a century ago. It might be the same face as the Arbiter here in Big Rock. It might be.

"Not really," said Aloê at last. "But I think we did meet at least once, long ago."

Denynê nodded without much interest and stuck a thin bright blade into Earno's dead white face.

CHAPTER NINE

The Lacklands

D eor's food ran out within a day and they were thrown back largely on the resources of Morlock's travel rations. They travelled eastward through the foothills of the Whitethorns, a meandering path that kept them well away from inhabited lands. But they saw little that approached game, except a few scrawny goats that were more trouble than they were worth to catch. So Deor declared after several hours of trying to catch one, anyway.

Mushrooms, however, were relatively plentiful, and Deor delighted in each different patch of fungus that he found. Kelat ate none of it, and even Morlock was (to Deor's mind) surprisingly choosy. But in general the world seemed ill-stocked with foodstuffs.

"There is some hunger everywhere, and all the time, these days," Kelat said. "The sea yields better food than land lately, but that means that too many people fish the waters."

"Things aren't so bad in the Wardlands," Deor said.

Kelat shrugged. "I hardly remember it. That . . . that stone was in my head. In the wide world, it *is* so bad, and worse every year."

Kelat thought that the best chance of finding Rulgân Silverfoot was in Grarby, a town full of monsters on the northeast coast of the Sea of Stones, where Rulgân was worshipped as a god.

"I remember it," Morlock said. "Is Danadhar still there?"

"The God-speaker?" Kelat was surprised and impressed.

"He wasn't the God-speaker when I knew him," Morlock said. "But that was long ago."

"He has been God-speaker as long as anyone remembers," Kelat said dubiously.

Morlock shrugged and said no more.

Eventually they had to leave the foothills and travel south.

"We must be careful as we cross the River Tilion," Kelat said. "The Vraidish tribes are settled there, and their Great King is opposed to any dealing with dragons." He rubbed the side of his head ruefully. "I understand that better now, I think."

Morlock said nothing to that either.

No one lived in the Whitethorns or their shadow, but when they turned south they found themselves crossing land that had been cleared and levelled for farming, woods that had been thinned by axemen harvesting the wood for building and fuel, roads that had been worn in the land by the passage of people and their goods from town to town. They saw all the evidence of human habitation except for the humans.

They came at last in the evening to a town built up at a crossing of three little roads. There was a market in the center of town; there were fetish poles for the Old Gods of Ontil; there were houses that Deor guessed were hundreds of years old—a great age for a dwelling not made by a dwarf.

All the windows were dark; no smoke came from any chimney; no word or footstep other than their own could be heard in the whole place. The town was dead; even the animals were gone.

"What happened here?" Deor asked.

"The world is dying," Kelat replied. "The people went south, I guess."

Morlock said nothing, but found a decent-sized house with a fireplace. No one felt like using one of the empty beds, so they lay in their bedrolls on the floor by the fire. They didn't bother foraging for food, but made a thin meal of the travel rations from Morlock's pack. For once, Deor did not complain.

They rose early and left the sad, hollow town behind them. They saw more during that long day as they walked. Toward evening they stopped in another, this one on a fairly wide roadway running from west to east.

"I think this is the Old Ontilian road to Sarkunden," Morlock said.

"I think it may be the big road to Sarkunden," Kelat agreed. "I don't know who made it."

"It's in very good repair."

"Well, it hasn't had much use lately, has it?" Deor snapped.

Morlock didn't answer, but started rapping on the wooden wall of what seemed to have been a sauna.

"No one's home, Morlocktheorn," Deor said.

"The wood is sound," Morlock said, "and probably sealed against water."

"What are you talking about, harven?"

"This walking is tedious and slow. Let's make a cart."

"And where are the draft animals who will pull this cart?"

Morlock grunted. "You'll figure it out," he said eventually.

Morlock started pulling the sauna apart plank by plank while Deor and Kelat ransacked the town and the nearby farmhouses for tools. The oddly shaped cart was done well before midnight; the dwarf and the master maker could work as well by coldlight as by daylight. But Morlock worked through the night at the village smithy forging chains of cunningly joined links. When Deor and Kelat awoke before dawn, Morlock was fitting the last pieces into place.

"What is this ugly thing?" Deor demanded furiously.

"Pedal-powered cart," Morlock said. "Gears and impulse-wells to magnify our efforts. Steering oar is in back, as you see."

"And I'm supposed to plant my stony ass on one of those bare boards and pedal you across the unguarded lands, is that it?"

"Refashion the seat as it suits you. We can find padding around town. Two of us will pedal while the third one steers. We'll go faster this way, if the roads don't get much worse than this one."

"And if they do?"

"We'll carry, push, or abandon it."

Deor deftly bound up their bedrolls over the wooden seats, examined the wheels, gears, and chains, muttering prayers or imprecations in Dwarvish, and finally climbed aboard. "I guess we should pedal and you steer at first? Until we all get the sense of the beast?"

Morlock nodded and they climbed aboard, piling their packs in the fourth seat. Kelat climbed aboard more hesitantly.

"Is this magic?" he asked. "I have had bad luck with magic."

"Just a new way to get work done," Deor assured him. "We'll earn every mile we make in this thing."

They put their feet to the pedals and got under way.

Their way was downhill, more often than not, but when the undulations of the land led the road upward, Morlock released some of the stored energy from the impulse wells and also changed the gear ratios. In spite of that, a couple of times they had to get out and push the contraption over the rise. Then they had the terrifying delight of the long, steep ride to the bottom of the hill, impulse collectors grinding against the wheels all the way down.

The vehicle had its advantages; even Deor was forced to admit it. The worst thing about it was the jolting. It was impossible even to get used to it, as the jolt changed depending on the road surface and the grade of incline. But they were going much faster than they had been, speeding past empty towns, gray lifeless fields, cold green woods.

Deor would have complained a thousand thousand times during the day, but he held his peace so as to not alarm Kelat. His only audible protest was when he innocently suggested that their vehicle be dubbed the Hippogriff.

They rode the grumbling Hippogriff in the day and slept hard at night, despite their thin rations. They talked as they travelled—Deor the most; Kelat very little; Morlock least of all.

They had grown so used to dead fields and empty towns that they were surprised one morning to see long tangling pillars of smoke arising from a nearby hill. The buildings there were clearly occupied, at least in the center of town. That center was surrounded by a wall, stitched together with mismatched lumber repurposed from demolished buildings, or so Deor's practiced eye told him.

"Shall we risk it?" asked Deor, who was steering.

"No," said Kelat.

"Yes," said Morlock.

Deor agreed by steering the oar toward the hill and its town.

The guards at the gate were armored with bowl-like helmets and mattress-like padding. They were weaponed with ill-made wooden pikes, and something about their slouching stance and cheery grins made Deor think these were not professional soldiers—at least, not until recently. They watched the approach of the Hippogriff with open-mouthed surprise, not even coming to guard when Deor applied the impulse collectors and braked the cart in front of them.

"Greetings, sentinels!" said Deor in what he hoped was decent enough Ontilian.

"Heartheld thingings, strangers!" one of the guards said. "Have you been come to embrickle the highhearts of High Town?"

"No, we are passing through," said Deor, his hopes of communication fading.

"Entrucklements for gift-and-get we have been bringing roadwise," Kelat remarked, surprising Deor. But of course Kelat was from here, or near here.

The guards received his remark quite cheerfully, and seemed to welcome them in about twelve times as many syllables as Deor thought was really necessary.

As the guards were laboriously opening the gate to admit the Hippogriff, Kelat said, "I told them we were just passing through, but we might have things to trade. They seem excited by the offer."

Morlock nodded and looked sour. Deor wondered why: perhaps it was just the torrent of warm stink that swept over them when the gate swung open.

There was a sort of animal pen full of odd pink and brown beasts inside the wall. Attached to it was a building that was clearly, from its stench, a slaughterhouse. There were guards armed with pikes and scythes around the slaughterhouse and the pen.

Kelat made a sound of involuntary disgust, and Morlock's bitter expression became, if possible, bitterer. Deor didn't understand why at first, and then he realized that the animals were men. Men and boys, it seemed. Although Deor was not always sure whether Other Ilk were male and female, the absence of clothing helped here.

"Let's get out of here," he said to his companions in Wardic. "These savages have nothing for us, nor we for them."

"Not yet," said Kelat reluctantly. "The Regent of the Great King will want to know about this. We . . . I should learn as much as I can."

Morlock nodded grimly. They followed their guide, pedaling the Hippogriff up the winding narrow streets of High Town.

Well over half the townsfolk seemed to be female—perhaps as much as four-fifths, by Deor's count. The women and girls were blank-faced, as if they were trying to remember something they had forgotten. None of them were armed. All the men were. None of the men seemed to be doing anything resembling physical work—fetching and carrying; cleaning; working. All the women were.

They came at last to a biggish house covered (recently) with silver paint, its front doors adorned with stained glass windows. The guard verbosely invited them to dismount and greet-and-be-greeted by the High Baron of High Town.

The High Baron of High Town was sitting on the floor of his entryway playing a game of checkers with an empty-faced young girl. He waved her away without speaking and stood to greet his visitors.

The High Baron of High Town wore splendid clothes that had clearly been made for someone else—probably several other people. His shining scarlet-and-gold tabard did not quite cover his belly; his skin showed through the lacing of his blue suede boots, and one of the seams was burst; his shining robe of office had gotten tangled with his feet, and his coronet had slipped down over his left ear. There were grease stains among the gold stitchings on his tabard.

"Bold baroner of High Town's high barony," began Kelat, "it is we who have been come to gift-and-give both things-of-word and things-of-things passing-wise from foothills coming to vale of Tilion going."

The High Baron looked upon him contemplatively for a moment or two and then said, "Perhaps one of you other gentlemen . . . ?"

"Well," said Deor with some relief, "he—" pointing at Morlock "—isn't gentle, and I'm not a man. Still, maybe we can do some talking."

"I certainly hope so. I certainly do. Some of our rustics have lost the clear path of Old Ontilian and have been become tangle-tugged in slang-sloughs lost."

"Uh. I suppose so."

"But I hope that you, gentle and man, are not considering immigrating into High Town? We have as many mouths as we can feed these days. Unless you have. . . . Perhaps somewhere safely hidden nearby . . . ? I think we understand each other."

"No," said Morlock.

"You have no females—no women or girls?"

"Not with us," Deor said.

"We will treat them well. They will live through the year and the long winter to follow, and how many people can say that in these dark cold days? The price will be as nothing, to men as devoted as yourselves."

"You waste your time," Morlock said.

"I have more time than anyone! It is a luxury I enjoy wasting. All this was my idea, so they made me High Baron, when I was only the village usurer down in Low Town a few years ago. We will accept females here in High Town, one for every two males who surrender themselves to our food pens. The women do work and have other uses; the men go to feed the community. It is the only way we survived so long as other towns faded into the dust."

"No," said Kelat.

The High Baron chuckled. "Well, I thought not. No one would carry a woman while travelling. But we will accept you as immigrants of the usual sort—straight into the slaughterhouse."

Armed men stepped out of the shadows of the hall. They wore shirts of overlapping bronze plates and carried curved swords and were not at all like the jolly cannibals at the gate.

Morlock said, in a conversational tone, "Tyrfing."

The black-and-white crystalline blade burst through the stained glass in the doors and flew to Morlock's right hand.

The High Baron goggled at the sword and the armsmen did the same. Morlock seized the High Baron by the loose skin in his fat neck and held the black-and-white blade to the Baron's throat.

"We're leaving," Deor said. "Don't try to stop us, or you'll need a new baron."

The armsmen didn't look heartbroken at this thought, but didn't try to stop them either. They backed out the door, Morlock dragging the sputtering baron along for the ride. He sheathed Tyrfing in the scabbard on his pack and sat down in the back bench, making the baron stand in front of him.

Kelat and Deor piled onto the front bench and began to pedal. Morlock steered them skillfully in a tight circle and they rattled down the same narrow street they had ridden up.

"Halt at the gate!" Kelat shouted back.

"Risky," Morlock said.

"We have to try!" Kelat insisted. He didn't say what he wanted to try; Deor thought he could guess and Morlock at least didn't ask. But he did grind the wheels to a halt just before the still open gate.

Kelat leaped out of the car. Morlock tossed him his stabbing spear and followed, carrying Tyrfing and dragging the High Baron with him. Deor grabbed his axe and stood between the gate guards and Hippogriff.

With the advantages of surprise, rage, and skill, Kelat easily slew two of the cage guards, and Morlock struck the third senseless with the flat of Tyrfing.

Kelat attacked the thin fence with the spearblade, slashing two-handed until a great hole was opened, and the naked men within peered incuriously out.

"Come with me!" shouted Kelat. "Some, at least, can escape! We will return with the Vraidish army at our backs and cleave High Town until it is neither high nor a town."

None of the men or boys within moved to escape.

"Come with me!" shouted Kelat. "What have you got to lose?"

"Everyone must die," said one. "This way, at least, my dear one is safe."

"The world is dying," said another. "Break a hole in that and I'll crawl out."

"Morlock!" shouted Deor. There were armed men coming down the hill.

"They chose this," Morlock said to Kelat. "We must go."

Weeping, Kelat turned away and threw himself into the Hippogriff, the spear clattering on the floorboards by the pedals. Deor joined him, and Morlock resumed the steering oar, dragging the Baron along as before. He released impulse energy from the wells and the Hippogriff leapt through the gate and down the hill and away into the Lacklands.

They had gone some miles and High Town had sunk beneath a ridge behind them when Morlock braked the Hippogriff to a halt.

"You're going to kill me, now," said the High Baron sulkily. "But all I did was what was best for my town. How many of them would be alive now if I hadn't led the way? In times like these, not everyone can live. Choices must be made. Don't blame me for the illness of the world."

"Get out," said Morlock, letting go of the baronial neck.

The Baron stumbled onto the grass-grown road. He turned around as if he expected to be stabbed in the back, but Morlock made no move to follow him.

"Go back to High Town, if you like," the crooked man said. "I suspect someone else is baron there now, and you will be welcomed as merely an immigrant."

He released the brake and Deor and Kelat pedaled furiously. They left the Baron standing in a cloud of dust. Deor glanced back and saw that the Baron was moving . . . but leaving the road to walk south, not returning to High Town.

Kelat laughed fiercely when he looked back and saw the same. His tears had dried, leaving filthy trails on his face. But after he laughed his look of grief and loss returned and long remained. He did not talk for the rest of that day.

"Things like that should not be," he said to Morlock that night, when they halted in the open country, many miles from High Town.

"What would you do to stop them?" Morlock asked.

Kelat did not answer.

The road was smoother now; many stretches were free entirely from grass, and they travelled swiftly. Three days after leaving High Town, they came over a rise and saw the silver thread of the Tilion in the distance. Far to the south, along the edge of the horizon, was a blue haze that might have been the sea.

"We must be careful there," Kelat said, pointing. "The bridge over the Tilion may be kept by Vraidish soldiers."

Morlock shrugged indifferently.

But the Vraids caught up with them long before they reached the Tilion. One of the towns along their way down to the river was not quite empty: there was a small squad of Vraidish horsemen there. They started shouting and pointing when they saw the Hippogriff on its wheeled flight, and Kelat wanted to pedal on as fast as they could, but Morlock (who was steering again) put the impulse collectors on full and the wheels ground to a halt.

The squad leader reined his horse in beside the Hippogriff and stared at it and all its occupants.

"Good day, sir!" said Deor in passable Vraidish. "Can we help you with anything?"

The horse soldier didn't answer him. He looked long at Kelat and then said, "Prince Uthar. You have been long missed."

"Don't call me that!" Kelat said.

"It is your right, and my duty, Prince Uthar," the soldier said.

"Is your name really Uthar?" asked Deor coolly. He didn't care for people who went by false names.

"It is!" the soldier said, slapping the shaft of his spear against his left hand, as if that made the statement truer.

"Every son of Lathmar the Old, Great King of the Vraids, is named Uthar," said the man they knew as Kelat.

"Oh," said Deor, taken aback. "That must be confusing. How many of you are there?"

"Three hundred and fifty and two."

"I mean: how many sons of Lathmar the Old?" Deor clarified, assuming that he had been misunderstood.

"Three hundred and fifty and two," Kelat repeated. "He's a hundred and thirty years old; he's had dozens of wives and a hundred concubines."

Deor almost said *Ugh*, for they ran things differently under Thrymhaiam, but then remembered that would be rude. So he said, "Um."

"The next Great King must, of course, be named Uthar," the horse soldier said. "Uthar and Lathmar have been the names of our kings since the gods fashioned the universe out of the mud of time."

Kelat muttered under his breath.

"Prince Uthar?" asked the soldier, politely but dangerously. The others in the troop had by now surrounded the Hippogriff and were looking at the occupants with cold, unfriendly eyes.

"We need use-names to be our own, since nothing else is," Kelat said, addressing Deor and Morlock rather than the soldiers. "I didn't lie to you. But there were truths I didn't tell. I'm sorry."

Morlock put his hand on Kelat's shoulder. Kelat nodded and Morlock removed his hand.

Deor was fascinated to observe that some sort of communication had occurred, and he was about to ask what they had said, but he was forestalled by the mounted captain.

"Prince Uthar, there is a reward for your recovery. I beg you will get out of that—that—"

"It's the Hippogriff," Deor said. He had his own unspoken criticisms of the wheeled beast, but he didn't like anyone else sneering at it.

"—that Hippogriff and come with us to see the Regent."

Kelat or Uthar or whoever he was said, "I have urgent business in the Lacklands and may not come."

"Prince Uthar, you understand that I ask you only for politeness' sake. The reward is food that will feed our families for a month. You will come with us."

"Where is the Regent of the Vraids?" asked Morlock.

The mounted captain said nothing until Kelat said, "Answer him."

"The Regent is overseeing the diggings north of Ontil."

"Man after my own heart," Deor said. Kelat looked at him with incomprehension, but it was not to be expected that a man would understand how much a dwarf loves the simple joy of moving soil and stone from one place to another.

"Is there a fair road to the diggings?" asked Morlock.

At first the captain didn't answer, but a glare from Kelat prompted him to reluctantly reply, "As fair as this."

"Let's go with them to your father's Regent," Morlock suggested. "It's on our way."

"But will we be allowed to continue on our way?" Kelat said.

Morlock laughed—an ugly sound to Deor's ear, and also to the Vraidish horsemen from the sour expressions on their faces.

And so from there they rode on with an escort. It perhaps lent dignity to their passage in the eyes of a watcher, if there were any. But Deor found it very disgusting. He was not terribly fond of horses in the first place, and the clouds of dust they raised on the dry road made it hard to breathe. Then there was their regrettable habit of farting, or blasting dung out their rear ends, bespattering the road and Hippogriff's wheels. At least they mostly liked to piss while at rest off the side of the road, like their riders.

But it was the riders that really disgusted Deor. They sang songs (or at least shouted lyrics); they shouted jokes to each other; they complained about their gear and the army's command; they farted nearly as often and as poisonously as their horses.

All of that could have been borne. But Deor noticed something actually intolerable: shriveled fingers of a human hand sticking out of one of their saddlebags. After he saw that, he paid close attention to their baggage, and he became sure it was all stuffed with human meat.

"Is everyone in the Lacklands a cannibal?" he asked Kelat.

The young man shook his head but did not otherwise answer. But Deor was sure that Kelat had noticed the same thing. As for Morlock, he noticed most things, except the difference between decent food and mere fuel for a bellyfire.

The long slope down to the Tilion was in their favor and they made excellent progress, often leaving their horsebound captors/guards behind to chew on the Hippogriff's dust.

At last they came to a paved roadway, and a city of tents and soldiers, not far from the river. At the horse soldiers' direction, they halted the Hippogriff at the edge of the camp and got out of it.

"Leave your things here," the captain directed.

Morlock and Deor ignored him and shouldered their packs along with their weapons.

"Your things will be safe here," the captain said.

"Will your things be safe here?" Deor demanded. "Why don't you unburden yourselves and your steeds?"

The horse soldiers eyed each other uneasily.

A tall, gray-bearded man strode up, gold sheaths on his arms and legs. "What's this noise?" he demanded. "His Majesty the Great King is taking his evening nap!"

"We discovered Prince Uthar, the one that was lost, sir," the captain said. "We claim the reward."

The older man looked with bemusement at the Hippogriff and her crew. Then he recognized Kelat. "Prince Uthar! We had given up hope for you! The Regent will have many questions."

"Ask a question of these men," Kelat said flatly. "Ask why they were roving in the Lacklands. Ask why their saddlebags are stuffed with human flesh."

"Eh?" the graybeard said. He turned to the horse soldiers. "Gentlemen, dismount."

The gentlemen did not dismount, but unsheathed their long, curved swords.

Kelat seized the stabbing spear from the floorboards of the Hippogriff. Deor shrugged off his pack, grabbed his axe, and followed Kelat into the fight. From the corner of his eye he was unsurprised to see Morlock with Tyrfing in his right hand and a cool killing look in his ice-colored eyes as he charged the horsemen.

The horse soldiers were in a bad way. They could not back their horses up, for the paling was behind them. Turning right would take them into the tangle of tents and booths; to their left was the gate and the ditch. To ride forward they would have to trample Prince Uthar/Kelat and graybeard and probably earn a few demerits or something.

In the end, that was what they chose to do, but it was already too late. Morlock dragged one man out of the saddle and threw his sword through another, who fell screaming into the mud. Kelat was facing down a cluster of soldiers to Deor's left. Ahead of him a horse reared and a horseman brandished a blade. Deor parried the blade with his axe and punched the horse in the chest with all his strength. It gave a kind of squeal and fell back onto the horse behind him.

"*Khai tyrkhodhen!*" he shouted exultantly. "*Ath Thrymhaimen! Ath! Ath!*" And he waded forward to strike again.

"*Khuf!*" shouted a voice that intended to be obeyed. "And all of you: put away your weapons."

The nascent battle died instantly. "Now you've done it!" one of the soldiers muttered to the captain. "It's the Regent!"

The Regent strode down the street of tents, her goldworked black cloak furling behind her, a gold coronet on her dark-red tangled hair, intelligence and anger mingling in her ice-colored eyes.

"My Lady Regent," Graybeard said, "these soldiers brought Prince Uthar back, but—"

Ambrosia Viviana held up a long-fingered hand and Graybeard fell silent. "No blame to you, Lord Hulmar. I think I see the seeds of this discord."

"Good evening, madam," said Deor.

"Good evening to you, Deortheorn, and to your silent friend, there. Prince Uthar—"

"*Don't call me that!*"

"Prince *Uthar*, you have long been missed. Your father was much concerned."

"He doesn't even know who I am! If he were passing by you'd have to point me out to him!"

"That's true, but he is a completist and always hates to lose any member of a set. You will account for your absence, I hope. I am not surprised to see you in trouble, seeing the bad companions you fell among—"

"Lady Regent!" called out the captain. "We found Prince Uthar, and—"

"Shut up," Ambrosia said. "Take that insignia off your shoulder. You are no longer a captain."

"But we—"

"You interrupted me *again*. Dismount from your horse; you are no longer in the cavalry."

The former captain tore the hawk insignia from his shoulder and stood silently beside his horse.

"What's the fight about, Uthar Kelat?" she asked.

"These men are graverobbers at least. They are carrying human flesh in their saddlebags."

"Salted, I think, madam," Deor pointed out.

"Does that make it worse or better?" she asked him curiously.

"Worse, in my mind. They salted down fresh kills and stored them. That indicates long-term intent. But I don't know your laws."

"My laws agree with your opinions. Gentlemen, what of it? Is Prince Uthar a liar?"

They hung their heads without answering.

"I sentence you to death," said Ambrosia conversationally. "The reward for discovering Prince Uthar will be paid to your families. Put down your weapons and go to the stockade."

The soldiers looked at each other for a moment. Without another word, they dropped their weapons.

"Hulmar, have a few of the gate guards go with them. They might need to carry a few of them. Then see about a decent burial of the bodies in their saddlebags. Incinerate them; we want no more graverobbing."

"Yes, Lady Ambrosia."

"Prince Uthar, report to Prince Uthar in Uthartown. Perhaps your friend Deor would be interested to accompany you. As for you, Vocate, perhaps you would join me for a brief conversation."

Morlock nodded and said, "Tyrfing." The sword flew to his hand, scattering blood in its wake. He wiped the sword on the flap of a nearby tent and sheathed it.

"Lady Regent," Kelat said urgently, "I have news of some import, not only for the Kingdom of the Vraids but for the fate of the wide world."

"I'll hear it in due time, Prince Uthar," Ambrosia said patiently. "Meanwhile, welcome home. Morlock, to me, please."

Deor noticed with amusement that the Vraids were more alarmed when Ambrosia said her brother's name than they had been by the flying swords or the other disasters that had befallen them.

"Well, Prince Uthar!" Deor said, as the two Ambrosii turned away for their private confab. "It's off to Uthartown for us. Will you introduce me to Prince Uthar when we see him?"

"You think it's funny," said the discontented prince, "but it's not funny."

"Oh, everything is funny, if you look at it in the wrong way. I'll prove it to you."

And they argued the point all the way to Uthartown.

CHAPTER TEN

Scenes of the Crime

Aloê and Denynê recovered seven force anchors from Earno's jaw and chest. It was messy and difficult work, but there was a grim satisfaction in it. Now they stitched the body back together like an old shirt. It was a shirt nobody was ever going to use again, but Aloê was impressed by the care Denynê took in repairing the wounds their autopsy had made. Even when healing the dead, the shriveled orange-brown woman dropped no stitches, never said and never seemed to think, "Well, that's good enough." It was only good enough when it was perfect. Whether it was from pride in her work or respect for the dead, Aloê rather liked her for that.

"So," Denynê said, holding the toothlike anchors in her bloody hand, "the murderer put a wilderment on Earno, established the stasis, cut his throat, then sealed up the wounds with the stasis field itself. When Earno woke, he knew nothing of what had happened."

"At most, he would have thought it a nightmare," Aloê said.

"How could the murderer hope to act unobserved?" asked Denynê. "Did Earno not have companions on the road?"

"At least one—perhaps two, depending on when the murder was committed," Aloê said. "Perhaps the murderer also cast a wilderment on them. Or," she added reluctantly, "perhaps they were part of a plot."

Denynê put the anchors carefully into separate jars and sealed them. "You don't like to think that," she observed eventually, when Aloê said no more.

"No," admitted Aloê. "The one companion is Deor syr Theorn, adoptive kin to my husband. The other is Noreê Darkslayer."

"Ah."

They went to wash their hands in the stream where Earno had died and sat in silence beside it for a while.

Before they had occasion to say anything else to each other, they heard a rumble of wagon wheels and hoofbeats on the Road. It was the Arbiter of the Peace, Ulvana, with a pair of her servants. Aloê had expected Oluma to be with them, but she was not.

"Fate on a dungfork," swore Aloê quietly.

Denynê looked at her, eyes wide with surprise.

"Just when we could use a gravedigger," Aloê said.

Denynê shrugged, nodded.

"Good night and greetings, Vocate," Ulvana said formally. "I understand you can use my assistance."

You unspeakable trull! Don't you see how he hates you?

"Yes, Arbiter Ulvana; many thanks. I see my other second did not choose to return with you."

Ulvana shrugged. "She said she had some other business."

"A glut of corpses in town?" Aloê said acidly. "No—forget I said that, please. I'm always speaking before I think, Arbiter."

"It's a common enough complaint," said Ulvana coolly.

"Can your servants help my other second to bring the body back into town? I'll tend to the incineration myself later on if Oluma is disinclined."

"I can do it," Denynê said, her orange-brown lips pale in the coldlights of the wagon.

"No, thank you, Binder Denynê," Aloê said. "Just tend to the body and keep it safe. At least one of his friends should be there when his body is given to the flames."

"I was his friend as well," Ulvana said slowly, "and I would like to be present."

"There you have it, Denynê. Wait for our return, please. It may be a day or two, perhaps longer."

The body, dripping cold blood, was lifted gently into the back of the cart and wrapped there with a shroud of kyllen. Denynê and the Arbiter's servants climbed aboard and drove the cart back down the Road. Aloê and Ulvana stood without speaking until they could no longer hear the cart or its horses, its lights merely a glimmer southward on the Road.

"Do we have words to say to one another?" Aloê asked at last.

Ulvana shook her head. Aloê shrugged, guessing that these words would be said in time, but not now. They mounted their horses (Ulvana taking the one that Denynê had left) and rode northward on the Road.

It wasn't long before they came to the first encampment. They dismounted and, without speaking, walked around the site. It was easy enough to find the perimeter: the Khnauronts had pissed and shitten where they lay in the night. Someone—Deor, Aloê suspected, from the neat uniformity of the digging—had buried most of the piles of dung, but there were feces smeared on the dry grass and the searing stench of urine all around the camp.

Aloê felt that such a place was a scar on the face of the Wardlands, and she was grimly aware that there were others and worse ones now. The lockhouse in Fungustown must be particularly nightmarish. The land was changing with the world, and not for the better.

But that was not her task to fix. She was here to look for blood, and there was none here. She didn't need to lift into rapture to know that this was not the murder scene.

"We may be on the Road for days," she said to Ulvana at last. "Let's turn in soon and go on in the morning."

"I have a timber lodge near here," Ulvana said diffidently.

"Excellent," said Aloê sincerely. She had a bedroll and some necessities with her, but she never enjoyed sleeping out of doors when she could avoid it.

Ulvana took her horse by the reins and led it into the woods. Aloê followed with her own. They were deep in the thin harvested woods when they came into a moonlit clearing with a bark-covered lodge in its center.

"Any of your people here?" asked Aloê.

"Should not be," Ulvana said. "We've cut as deeply as we should in these woods. In a few decades, perhaps we'll return. But I come here sometimes to—well, get away from Big Rock."

Aloê nodded. They settled their horses with some food and water in the garth and then went into the lodge. Ulvana opened the lock by sticking a long ungainly key into it and turning it with her fingers. Aloê tried not to stare; the process seemed as old-fashioned as sailing ships, but she remembered that not everyone had the master of all makers keying their houses. There didn't seem to be any protective spell on the lodge at all—not even fire-quell magic. That seemed an especially important omission when Aloê watched Ulvana kindle an open flame and use it to light a wick in a lamp filled with oil.

The lodge had a number of beds scattered around its single room, a wood stove in the center, and some shelves laden with storage jars and bottles up against one wall. There was a pump and a sink against another wall, but no obvious door leading to a privy. Aloê guessed that she would soon be reflecting nostalgically on the comforts of Big Rock Inn.

Ulvana rummaged around the shelves for food and drink and said, "I have a keg of cider and a few jars of wine. No beer, I'm afraid."

"I just drink water on a job like this," Aloê said. "I'll need to ascend into vision from time to time." Drunkenness did not necessarily prevent rapture, but it did limit one's control.

She dumped her bag by a bed and walked over to the pump. There were some mugs and drinking cans there. She would have liked to wash one before drinking from it, wash it for a year and a day in bite-foam and boiling hot water, but she didn't want to seem like a pampered princess. She blew the dust off a mug, pumped it full, drank, and then wordlessly offered what was left to Ulvana, who was watching expressionlessly from across the room. Ulvana came over and took the mug from her, drank what was left, and handed it back.

"I'll be having some wine, though," she said, as she turned back to the shelves. "Rapture doesn't suit me, I find."

That drink of water was some kind of turning point. Thereafter, Ulvana spoke to her about food, drink, sleeping arrangements, and other practicalities, as well as the task at hand. They ate fairly well: pickled cladroot and dried sleer meat, soaked in oil and fried, exchanging a word or two when needed.

After Aloê had yawned a few times and they both agreed it was time to douse the light, Ulvana said, in the quiet conversational tone they'd been using, "I hated you for years, of course."

"What I said was unforgivable," Aloê said. "I've always been ashamed of it."

"No," Ulvana said. "No. I didn't find that hard to forgive. You were right, of course, about him. He doesn't really care about any woman—except perhaps you. And that was what I hated you for. My father's family, you know, has a little money; they work in road repair and trash removal and that sort of thing. But they aren't, you know, *the thing*. But Naevros, although he has very little money and no family—he is very much the thing."

"Yes."

"I thought—if I were with him—that would sort of rub off. It seemed to for a while. Then it was gone and he was . . . well, he was rather cruel."

"I'm sorry."

"It's not your fault. That's what I realized, and that's why I stopped hating you. He probably feels like that about every woman he can have. He doesn't feel like that about you because he can't have you."

"Possibly."

"Or possibly not, of course. But that was my thinking. And then I thought: what if it had been different? What if I had fucked my way into, I don't know—being *the thing*? It still wouldn't be about me. I'd be nothing—just part of him, not anything in myself."

This struck close to Aloê's fears about herself—that she was not Aloê Oaij anymore, but only Morlock's wife. She said, "I understand."

"So I left. Came up here and worked in timber. Had my own crew after a while. I became an Arbiter a few years ago because we needed one and no one else wanted to do it."

"That's the best reason."

"So they say. It's been more good than bad. I don't call myself 'honorable' or any of that fake stuff anymore. If people think I'm honorable, I won't need it in my name. If they don't, they won't think it because I say it."

"Truth."

They were silent for a long while. Aloê repressed a yawn, understanding that Ulvana had something else to say.

In the end she said, "I was angry that they sent you at first. I thought it was a deliberate insult. Now I see. . . . I'm glad it was you. You're tired; we should sleep."

"I'm glad we're in this together," said Aloê, a little more warmly than she really felt. She felt some guilt about Ulvana, and that feeling had grown rather than diminished because of Ulvana's forgiveness.

She crawled into the bed closest to her bag, and it seemed as if Ulvana was going to say something again. But instead she just doused the light and got into another rack.

Aloê wondered if she'd happened on Ulvana's favorite bed and her hostess was going to ask her to switch. But that seemed unlikely: the bed was not terribly comfortable and not terribly clean. In fact it had an odd reek to it . . . an oily muskiness, mixed with something like sour milk.

It smelt like a man, in fact—one of these greasy young things standing outside wineshops trying to impress each other and anyone impressionable who happened by.

Ugh. Aloê almost climbed out of her own accord to try another bed. But for all she knew the next would be worse. And she was tired. She hoped her nose would go to sleep with the rest of her.

Deep in the night, she dreamed someone was deep in her. She felt his weight on her, the oily slickness of his hairless chest sliding against her as he thrust himself into her, grunting the way men sometimes do, haloed with cheap musky scent. Her dream-eyes focused on his dream-face in the dream-shadows and she realized he was Naevros syr Tol. And from the glazed expression on his sweaty face he was coming inside her.

Fuck, no! she wanted to say, and woke up as she was actually coughing out the words.

"Excuse me?" asked Ulvana. Aloê opened bleary eyes to vaguely see Ulvana standing in a doorway filled with morning light.

"Nightmare," Aloê said thickly.

"Want to talk about it?"

"Absolutely not." Aloê rolled out of bed, hawked, spat out of a convenient window, and set about her day with a deliberate fury. This was real and that was a dream—and a terrible dream, at that. Somehow the filthy scent in the bed and Ulvana's evening talk about Naevros had mingled in her mind, and the little dreammaker who lived in the basement of her brain had sent that thing up to annoy her. That was all that it was. There was nothing else about it that was real. Nothing.

They breakfasted on salted meat, pickled vegetables, and fresh mushrooms, all fried in oil. It was good, but afterward Aloê drank half her weight in water before she was free of the taste of salt in her mouth. After a minimum of ablutions, she moved with Ulvana toward the garth, where the horses were contentedly awaiting them. Ulvana had watered and fed them when she got up before dawn, and then went looking for mushrooms in the wood. A valuable companion, clearly: Aloê didn't think she could have had better luck, and she told Ulvana so. It was interesting to watch Ulvana blush at the compliment: the embarrassed girl was still alive in there, inside the lumber merchant and Arbiter.

They were travelling up the shining pale stones of the Road much faster than the captive Khnauronts had travelled down them. Before midday they came to another vile campsite. Aloê knew without sniffing around (which did not promise to be one of life's great pleasures, anyway) that this was not the murder scene. They rode on without dismounting.

In midafternoon they came to another of the old camps. Aloê felt the unpleasant sting of insight here. She dismounted and walked some distance from the campsite and the Road, ignoring Ulvana's puzzled query. She lay down on a cold patch of grass and ascended into vision.

It took a timeless time to find it, but she stayed aloft in the visionary state because she knew it was there—she could feel it. Burning with contaminated tal, some drops of blood lay on the ground, wrapped in a shadow of absence that felt like Earno.

She descended to the world that women and men think of as real and lay there on the grass reflecting. The blood was Earno's, shed in his sleep— enough to imprison the shape of his dream self there. And the taint in it. . . . It stank like the spell anchors that they had dug out of his body.

There was not enough blood present for this to be the murder scene. But they were getting closer: Earno's wound had still been fresh when he lay here.

She stood up and walked back to Ulvana. "We ride on," she said, and they did.

Before nightfall they came to the place itself. Aloê knew before dismounting. They were just beyond the woods, and the tidy heaps of earth covering the Khnauronts' dung stood out clearly against the dry green-gold grass of the plain. Sun and rain had washed away the stink of piss, thank God Avenger.

Aloê dismounted without speaking and walked away from the scene. She sat cross-legged in a field, with her head in her hands, and left her body behind.

The dry, empty field blazed with talic light in her vision: there was life everywhere: grass, bugs, worms, the long shimmering light of the living land itself, life everywhere.

Except *there*.

She drifted toward the clot of darkness in the shining web of light and life. It was another shadow of Earno, haloed here in poisoned blood.

The talic aura of the blood trapped another shadow: Earno's killer. The image was too distorted to be identifiable; it was a twisted shape overlain with many twisted shapes. The murderer had moved around Earno's body as he or she killed him.

The unheard thrum of a binding spell was still in the air. The killer must have spellbound Deor and Earno before beginning the grisly work. When they woke, perhaps they thought they'd had a nightmare.

The murderer would have established the wilderment over the two Guardians and the sentinel mannikins then cut the summoner's throat. The murderer must have quickly sealed up the wounds and established the anchor spell holding the seal. All that was clear. Then the murderer seemed to have spent some time going through Earno's clothes, or fondling his body, or something—their shadows were oddly mingled.

Repelled, Aloê's mind drifted away. She longed to ascend further, lose herself in the bright arc of the living sky. But if she did that, she might never return to her body.

She turned away from her vision, rejecting it and the world full of life's light. She opened her eyes on a coarse void of matter and energy: the real world, as some called it.

Aloê sighed and wearily rose to her feet. It was terrible to lug one's greasy flesh around after one has been floating free between heaven and earth. But that was what life was all about, apparently.

Ulvana had dismounted and was stretching her legs on the field when she caught sight of Aloê returning.

"It was here," Aloê said in reply to the unspoken but obvious question in Ulvana's eyes.

"Do you want to look around?" Ulvana asked.

Aloê almost answered, *I just did*, but then she reflected that the killer might have left something physical behind. Perhaps a signed letter expressing his intent to kill the summoner or something very helpful of that sort.

In the event, they found nothing, not even a decent set of footprints. It was after dark by the time they stopped looking.

"Let's make camp across the Road," Aloê said to Ulvana. "I don't like this place. Unless. . . ."

"As a matter of fact," Ulvana admitted, "I do have a lodge on the edge of the woods. You can see it from here."

Aloê could not see it from there, in the dim light that was leaving the world as they spoke. But she followed Ulvana's lead, both women leading their horses, and they soon came in sight of a round bark-covered lodge. There was no open garth, but there was a neat little horse barn in back.

Ulvana seemed less happy with the food in this lodge, but Aloê didn't care. The thought of squeezing more mass into her flesh was disgusting to her. She just drank some water from her bottle and staggered off to fall in the nearest bed.

And after a moment leapt out of it cursing. "Chaos bite me on both elbows!"

"What is it?" Ulvana asked, quite concerned.

The bed was polluted with the same greasy musk that had haunted her last night. Did every lumberjack in Easthold use the filthy stuff?

"Not worry," she said incoherently to Ulvana, and staggered off to another bed.

This, fortunately, only smelled like the sweat of a thousand dead pigs. She drifted off to dreams of murder—one murder after another, all of them committed by a cunning pig in quest of vengeance for the invention of bacon.

CHAPTER ELEVEN

Among the Vraids

The dark, spiralling towers of the castle glittered with the force-wefts that held their stones in place. Moving over them, pointing out various features of defense or offense, was Ambrosia's long-fingered hand. Its shadow fell on the blue brightstone trail meant to represent the River Tilion. Ambrosia leaned over the castle in her enthusiasm and invited Morlock to look at details in the courtyard.

But Morlock was stuck on a broader issue. "Is there an island in the river where you're planning to build this?"

"It's worse than that—much worse! There isn't even a river. We'll have to divert it after we dig a decent port some distance away from the Old City of Ontil."

"What will you call the new city?"

"Ontil, obviously, Morlock. Don't be so dense. We will get people to accept this new empire by pretending it is the old one returned."

"Which it will not be."

"Obviously not. Obviously not. We wouldn't want any follies like the Ontilians committed in the Fimbar Dynasty."

"Er."

"You don't know what I'm talking about, do you? Honestly, brother. You people in the Wardlands never study any history but your own, and since you don't really have any history. . . . What do you do with your time, again?"

"We enjoy dancing and other amusements."

"I'll bet you do. I'll just bet you do. Go choke on your own elbow, you supercilious son-of-a-bitch, or at least give me some advice on the supports for these walls."

"Eh." Morlock looked at the model again. "I've never constructed something on that scale. There's nothing like it in the Wardlands. I'd want Vetr's opinion: he's a good builder; it was his mastery before Oldfather Tyr died."

"It'll be something new then."

"Everything in your empire will be new. Except the name."

"And it won't be *my* empire. These fat-headed Vraids won't accept a woman ruling in her own name."

"Hm."

"Don't grunt at me. Do not do that. I'm warning you for the last time."

Morlock grunted dubiously and then went so far as to add, "But you seem to be ruling it now, while this Lathmar the Old occupies himself with breeding heirs."

"People tolerate that because it will all come to end when Uthar becomes king. Whichever Uthar it is."

"I don't understand that."

"You're not stupid enough, is the problem. If you were it would be obvious that the King of the Vraids must be named Lathmar Utharson or Uthar Lathmarson."

"It must make their history confusing."

"They don't really have history, either—just chronicles and myths."

"In the future, they will have a history."

"Yes."

"And it will be of the Second Ontilian Empire—not the Kingdom of the Vraids."

"Yes."

"Why not an Empress Ambrosia then?"

"Stop mocking me, Morlock. The fact that you're the only one who would dare do it does not mean that you get to do it all the time."

Morlock held out his hands and opened them. "I'm not mocking you. I'm saying the future is not the past. That's all."

"All right, then. Now that I've showed you my toy, tell me about this dragon business again. I don't think I like it."

Morlock told it to her again.

"Good fortune to you, Prince Uthar. I'm here with Prince Uthar to see Prince Uthar. Could you send Prince Uthar to ask Prince Uthar where Prince Uthar might be?"

"Which Prince Uthar?" asked Prince Uthar.

"Well, there you have me, I'm afraid," Deor admitted. "This lad and me are supposed to see the Prince Uthar in charge around here. The Regent requires it."

"Oh," said the Prince Uthar who was lounging behind the table. "That'll be Uthar-Null Landron." He turned to a young boy in a gold-worked tunic standing by the door of the booth. "Prince Uthar—"

Kelat drew his stabbing spear. "The next man or dwarf that says the name 'Uthar' will get this spearblade through his nose. And it you think I'm joking, remember what happened to Magister Harbim."

The atmosphere in the tent grew perceptibly chillier. The Uthar behind the table lounged more stiffly, at any rate, and glared at Kelat. The Utharling at the door suppressed a snorted laugh.

"You don't take your heritage seriously enough, young Pr—Kelat," the Uthar behind the table said sternly. "You there—Glennit. Quit your giggling and find out where Landron is. If he can't come here, come back here and lead these . . . these two back to him. Regent's orders."

"As the Regent commands!" shouted Glennit enthusiastically, and ran like a shurgit out of the booth into the dim day.

"What happened to Harbim?" Deor asked, when the silence became uncomfortable—which was right away.

"He could tell you himself," said the Uthar behind the table grimly, "if your friend there hadn't broken his jaw."

Kelat sheathed his sword and looked ashamed and angry.

"Never mind it, my friend," Deor said. "I bet it was a rotten jaw that deserved breaking."

"I don't know," Kelat said guiltily. "He was always riding me about something. Saying I wasn't good enough to be the next King of the Vraids. As if anyone ever said that was going to happen."

"How many of you are there, anyway?"

"Too many."

"Three hundred and fifty and three," said table-Uthar proudly, "as of this morning, when the King's ninth alternate wife gave birth to a son."

From the crazy look in Kelat's eyes, they were about to see the color of his spearblade again. Deor silently said a prayer to Oldfather Tyr for something to calm down the young man or at least distract him. Then he readied himself to tackle Kelat if he drew his weapon again. Prayer was all right, but Deor strongly believed that Those-Who-Watch helped those who helped themselves.

A new shape darkened the doorway of the booth: a very tall man, broad-shouldered, his back straight, and with a majestic mane of gray hair and a beard to match. Deor took beards seriously, and he felt immediately that this was a man to respect.

"My boy!" cried the old man and rushed in. "I heard you were back! We were so worried about you, your mother and I."

"You don't even remember my name. Or my mother."

"Your name's Uthar, of course. And you mother was Kyllia—is Kyllia. We had a late supper just last month. A very late supper! I think we understand each other, oh? Oh? Oh?"

"I understand you perfectly, sire."

"She's as fertile a cow as any I've put in kindle. How many of you are there? Seven?"

"Five brothers and four sisters, sire."

"Oh, the girls don't matter."

"I disagree, sire."

"Shut your mouth, you insolent little prick!" hissed table-Uthar.

The king's pale face also darkened with anger, but then he smiled. "Not at all, not at all!" Lathmar said. "The next King of the Vraids will have to think for himself."

Kelat said evenly, "I'll mention it to him when I see him, sire."

Deor felt it was time for a diplomatic stomp on Kelat's toes. He narrowly missed—the boy had superb reflexes—but his action drew the king's attention to him and away from the misbehavior of the Prince Uthar called Kelat.

Lathmar the Old looked Deor up and down and said, "Hm! You're not one of mine, are you?"

"No, sire," Deor said politely. "I'm Deor syr Theorn, Thain to the Graith of Guardians, *harven*-kin to your regent, Lady Ambrosia Viviana. I'm honored to meet you."

"Hm! From the Wardlands, eh? Wardic dwarf?"

"Yes, sire," said Deor, though he didn't really like the sound of that.

"Well, we do very well for ourselves out here, you know," the great king said. "Lady Ambrosia has hundreds of dwarves down from the mountains sometimes. They do a lot of our digging, you see."

"Yes, sire."

"I don't understand all of the digging, as a matter of fact, but the Lady Ambrosia assures me it is necessary and that it might as well be done by a pack of filthy dwarves as by honest Vraidish gentlemen."

"Majesty," whispered table-Uthar nervously.

"Oh? Oh? Oh?" the old king said in evident confusion. "Oh? Oh? Oh? Oh? Have I said something untoward? Set me straight, boys. Set me straight. Keep me honest. What was I saying?"

"You were insulting my friend, sire," said Kelat coolly.

"Uh, what? No! No! I don't think so. Was I?" The doddering old man turned to Deor with a tear in his eye.

"Don't mind it, your majesty," said Deor. "We do like to dig. And it's no fun if you stay clean while you do it; that's a fact."

"Fun, is it? Fun. Hm. I would like to have fun, I think. Perhaps I should try it. Yes, I think I will try it. You—you there. You—Prince Uthar. Get me a shovel. That's what you dig with, isn't it? I'm going to have some fun, for once."

"Alas, sire, I believe it's time for your nap," gurgled table-Uthar in a fit of desperate invention.

"Nap," said Lathmar, Great King of All the Vraids, quietly. "Nappy nap nap. Yes. I would like a nap. Where—where's my nurse? Where's Magistra Gullinga? I—I—"

The old king wandered out as abruptly as he had wandered in, and both of the Prince Uthars present drew a sigh of relief.

"They shouldn't let him wander around alone," Kelat said.

"That Gullinga frail is no better than a paper hat in the rain," said table-Uthar.

"If *she* has a son he won't be named Uthar," Kelat agreed.

"Don't be so sure. He wasn't joking about that late supper with Kyllia, although it was Kyllia from Fishtown, not your mother."

"My mother's dead."

"And resting undisturbed. I thought you'd want to know. There's not much the old fool won't stick his penis in, except—"

Table-Uthar's voice faded to a whisper, faded out entirely.

Deor turned to see his old friend Ambrosia in the doorway. He was about to speak to her when she drew the sword at her hip and struck at the gaping prince behind the table.

Kelat uttered an inarticulate cry of protest and, drawing his spear, leapt between Ambrosia and her intended victim. The blades clashed and Ambrosia stepped back, on guard, watchful.

Morlock walked into the booth and said dryly, "Kelat. Deor. Prince Uthar. Ambrosia, what are you doing?"

"What are *you* doing, Uthar Kelat?" Ambrosia said. "Unless I'm mistaken, you and Uthar Olthon detest each other. Yet here you are risking death for him. You *are* risking death—aren't you aware of it? Before your mother's grandparents were born I was learning to fence against the best swordsman in the world."

"Second-best," Deor said firmly. He admired Morlock very much, but the truth was the truth. (Morlock favored him with a rare smile, but no one else seemed to notice he had spoken at all.)

Kelat shook his head and held his ground. "I can't let that. . . . I have to do something about it."

"All right," said Ambrosia patiently. "But *why?*"

"He spoke the truth!" shouted Kelat. "Someone should make that old man keep his pants on! You can't kill someone for telling the truth!"

"A disappointing answer," Ambrosia said, sheathing her sword. "Of course I can kill someone for speaking truth. If I had killed your half-brother for doing so, he wouldn't have been the first man I killed for that very reason. A ruler of men does what she must, Kelat. You must learn that, or you will never be a ruler of men."

"So what?" muttered Kelat, and sheathed his own sword.

She shrugged her crooked shoulders and turned to open-mouthed, motionless table-Uthar. "Prince Uthar Olthon, remind me of your task here."

The hapless prince closed his mouth with a snap, opened it and closed it again without speaking, and finally managed to say, "Lady Regent, I keep track of the whereabouts and well-being of all the princes."

"And you do that from in here?"

"Lady, I recruited a cadre of the younger princes to run messages for me around the camp. They either know where everyone is or know who knows. You called it an ingenious system once."

"And so it is. From now on, though, you have a single task. You are to keep track of King Lathmar at all times and keep him out of trouble. That does not mean—" she paused to glare at Kelat "—making him keep his pants on. It does mean making sure he takes them off only in private, and does not otherwise tarnish the majestic name his grandfather wore so proudly in another age of the world."

"Yes, Lady. I will, Lady. May I use my young messengers?"

"No, your successor will need their services."

"Very well, Lady Regent."

There was a brief silence.

"Prince Uthar Olthon," Ambrosia said gently.

"Yes, Lady?"

"Where is King Lathmar?"

"I—" Olthon sighed and got to his feet. "Your pardon, gentles," he muttered, and left the booth.

"I feel like a walk, myself," Ambrosia said. "Won't you join me, my friends?"

They filed out of the booth's narrow door into Uthartown. Ambrosia strode alongside Morlock, and Deor and Kelat walked behind.

It was strange for Deor to look on the decent-sized village and know that everyone (or almost everyone) in it was named Uthar, and that each Uthar was also the son of the demented old man he had just met. There were a pair of decrepit old geezers playing drafts—sitting on the ground between a couple of booths, with a board scratched into the dirt and chunks of rock for counters.

"Haha, *Uthar*! King me, you bitch of a bitch's bastard!" crowed one of the relics.

"I'll king you with this," replied his opponent, briefly grabbing his sagging trousers at the crotch.

These princes looked far more decrepit than their father. But some of their half-brothers were playing naked in the mud nearby. Deor was no judge of human pups, but he guessed these were two or three years old at most.

"Lady Ambrosia," said Deor, "can you explain to me about all these Uthars?"

"The next king must be named Uthar, so—"

"I do understand that," Deor interrupted, earning a respectful look from Kelat. "But is it quite usual in the unguarded lands for a man to have hundreds of children?"

"Well, that's my fault, I suppose," Ambrosia admitted.

"Madam," said Deor, not knowing what else to say.

Ambrosia looked back at Deor and then quizzically at Morlock. "He fears there may be some scandal," Morlock explained.

"Oh? Well, it's not scandalous. A long time ago—well, Lathmar and I, we helped each other out of a tight place."

"Doesn't sound less scandalous," Morlock observed.

"Shut up. I assure you, Deortheorn, he was too old for me, even then. But I owed him a favor, and what he wanted in repayment was an extended lifespan. He felt he had no heir worthy of the crown, which was true enough, and he wanted to conquer an empire in the wide world beyond the Vale of Vraid. I managed to arrange it. But the effects left him—well, they left him rather single-minded. That was eighty-seven years ago, almost to the day."

"Ah."

"Things were going well enough, though. He might have seen a capable son carry his dream closer to its conclusion. Until the world began to die, and we had to turn our energies to survival."

"How are you and the Vraids doing?" Deor asked. "Our journey through the Lacklands was grim indeed."

"Morlock told me some of it. Other parts I can guess. Yes, those lands are pretty well empty. The farmers there would not change their ways. Some crops respond better to the shorter growing year—there are greenhouses and other resources. And it has been a pretty good year for mushrooms, if you can tell the good from the bad. The sea is not much harmed yet, though some waters have been over-fished."

"So your Vraids are more adaptable?"

"Not really, but they follow orders, you see, which is close enough, where I'm concerned."

Kelat grumbled, but nobody took his bait.

"Here's Prince Uthar-Null," Ambrosia remarked. "Greetings, Vice-Regent!"

Walking toward them up the unpaved street was Prince Uthar-Null, a man about a half-century old with a long, clever face and a long, thin beard and a fringe of silver hair around a shining pink scalp. Next to him walked young Uthar Glennit, whose shining eyes were fixed on Lady Ambrosia.

"Vice-Regent am I now?" asked long-suffering Uthar-Null. "Well, it sounds better than Mayor of Uthar-Town. What are my duties?"

"Every one of mine until I return. I have to go on a trip west and south, and then, it may be, to the far north. Keep a lid on things here for me, eh?"

"I'll try." Uthar-Null pointed with a disdainful thumb towards the sun. "Something about that?"

"Maybe."

"Good. Good. If anyone can do anything about it, you can."

"We'll try. This is my brother, Morlock Ambrosius, by the way: Prince Uthar-Null, Morlock."

They clasped hands.

"And me," Deor said, coming around Morlock's side. "Deor syr Theorn, at your service."

He grabbed Uthar-Null's proffered hand, although that wasn't really a dwarvish custom.

"Theorn, eh?" said Uthar-Null shrewdly. "You've come a long way from the Deep Halls under Thrymhaiam."

"Well worth it, sir. I never thought to see so many Uthars in my life."

"Nightmarish, isn't it? What the next king will do with them all is beyond my telling."

"What's traditional?"

"A quiet execution of rival heirs was apparently not unheard of. I don't think any one of us will stoop to that. But they say that kingship does strange things to the mind."

"And—pardon me for asking—why are you Null?"

"Many of us are Null," Uthar-Null said without apparent offense. "It means we are no longer in the succession. Therefore we can wield certain types of power and also marry and have children of our own, which is a great comfort I sometimes think."

"Only sometimes? Never mind: we do things differently under Thrymhaiam."

"And in the Endless Empire under the Blackthorns also, I believe," Uthar-Null said politely.

"Listen, Prince Uthar-Null," Ambrosia began.

"Madam."

"I'm going to bring an Uthar along with me. Morlock suggests young Kelat, here. I thought you might tell him your thoughts on the subject."

"Ah." Uthar-Null's clever brown eyes looked with concern at Kelat, glowering in Ambrosia's shadow. "Perhaps Prince Uthar would care to step aside."

"I would not," said Kelat. "And don't call me Prince Uthar."

"Sir," said the Vice-Regent, addressing himself to Morlock, "the Prince Uthar under discussion—"

"Arrrrrrrgh!"

"—the Prince Uthar under discussion is ill-tempered and unpredictable. He is intelligent but disobedient. He is brave but undisciplined. His every virtue has a vice. I would not trust him to carry a message to my mother, and I do not care very much about sending messages to that horrible old woman."

"He drew a blade on me just now," Ambrosia remarked.

"He did?" Uthar-Null looked sharply at his half-brother. "Why?"

"To defend Uthar Olthon."

"Olthon? But they *hate* each other!"

"Yes."

Uthar-Null threw up his hands and said to Morlock, "You see it, sir? He is not reliable, even in his hatred. Can you trust a man like that on a long road? I ask you."

Morlock shrugged his crooked shoulders, and Uthar-Null glanced aside, his features twisting with distaste.

"If it is up to me," Morlock said to Ambrosia, "I still prefer Kelat."

"It is not up to you, brother. This is my domain and my word is law, under the King's. However, in this instance, I think you're right." She turned and spoke to the prince standing behind her. "Uthar Kelat, go to your booth and pack up some things for the trip. Bring some warm clothes."

He stood there blinking at her, and she said kindly, "Hurry, now. This is your adventure. You don't want to miss part of it."

Kelat's look of adoration almost matched Glennit's. He turned quickly away and ran up the narrow dirty street, dense with Uthars.

"Uthar Glennit, my prince," said Ambrosia.

"Yes, my lady," said Glennit like it was a prayer.

"You are now the censor of Uthartown. Take up Olthon's old post, or do the job however you see fit."

"Thank you, my lady!"

"Don't do that. It's a horrible job. Soon we'll find you one more worthy of your talents. Or the world will end, and it won't matter."

Glennit went down on one knee in the filth of the street and made a fist with his right hand over his heart. Then he jumped to his feet and ran away without speaking, tears running down his face.

Ambrosia and Uthar-Null watched him go, both smiling.

"You see him as the new king, don't you?" Uthar-Null said confidentially.

"Little Glennit? Not in ten thousand years of seasoning. Oh, he will be a great man in the new empire, but not the greatest. A king needs a little orneriness in him. Morlock here might be a good one—"

Morlock grunted irritably at this blasphemy.

"—if he could bring himself to talk in words like a person. My friend, I made your half-brother Olthon the King's keeper. The old man really can't be allowed to wander around embarrassing everybody anymore."

"True, true. A good choice. Olthon is always minding someone else's business. Might as well put his one talent to good use."

"That's a good deal of the art of kingship, my friend. You'd've been a good one, if you hadn't chickened out and gone null."

"Never would have lived long enough, lady. Besides, I love my wife. Have you ever been in love?"

"Only with power, Prince Uthar-Null. Morlock, Deor, let's see what we can do to outfit you for the journey ahead. Our wealth is slender these days, but we have some dwarf-made goods from the Endless Empire that may meet your finicky standards."

"We aren't going to be riding the Hippogriff, are we?" Deor said with some concern.

"That rattletrap quadricycle beast you three rode in on? Fate and Chaos! No. Never, never."

"Horses, I suppose? Very small, very gentle horses?"

"What? No. From what Morlock tells me, I think we'll travel by galley. Have one ready for us, won't you, Vice-Regent?"

The implications of this slowly sunk into Deor's imagination.

"A galley is a boat? To go across the *water*?"

"Yes."

Deor groaned. "Maybe I should go home and see how Aloê is doing? I promise to write."

"Nonsense," said Ambrosia. "We need your sage advice and high spirits."

"I wish I was dead. Or the both of you were. I hate this trip. Each leg is worse than the last. Well, at least it can't get any worse than this."

Morlock shrugged and said nothing. But it was the way he said it.

CHAPTER TWELVE

Intruder in the Death House

T he long ride back to Big Rock gave Aloê a lot of time to think and
Ulvana a lot of time to talk.

Aloê hardly noticed the talking. She only noticed when it stopped.
Occasionally she would glance over to see Ulvana looking at her with a patient
smile.

"I'm sorry," she said the first time, but Ulvana said, "No matter. I know
there's much on your mind. If you'd like to talk it out. . . . But maybe you
don't do that."

Aloê would have loved to do that, and Ulvana seemed a sympathetic and
intelligent listener. But the matter in hand had some very dark elements she
could trust to no one. She smiled and shook her head.

They rode onward. Ulvana prattled onward. Aloê thought onward.

The crux of the matter was this: the killer was almost certainly a member
of the Graith of Guardians. She was still hoping that there was a Person
Unknown to blame—someone else besides Kelat and the Khnauronts who had
entered the Wardlands when the Wards were shattered. It was not impossible.

But! Such a person would not have been part of the dragon Rulgân's plan.
And he or she would have had to know about the plan in advance to take
advantage of it. And he or she would have had to know where Earno would
be on a given day, or within a range of days, assuming Earno was not a target
of opportunity.

She hoped he was. But she did not believe he was. And Earno's habit of
carrying a message sock gave the Graith, or at least some of its members, the
knowledge of where he was every day.

Perhaps it was someone, some rogue magic-worker with a grudge against

Earno who had gotten the information out of some innocent belonging to the Graith. She kept her mind open to this possibility, too—would welcome any sign leading in that direction.

But the most likely explanation was that Earno had been murdered by someone in the Graith. She would have trusted three people enough to talk it over with: Thea, who was dead, or Morlock and Deor, who were in the unguarded lands. So she would keep her own counsel for the present.

But her next step was clear: find out who knew that Earno would be travelling down the Road at this time. Many in the Northhold certainly. Fewer in the south. She would start there, in A Thousand Towers. Who had Earno written? Who knew of the messages? What were the messages? That would get her started.

And she would scrutinize those spell-anchors. One could not work a magic like that without leaving any traces of one's identity on the instruments of the spell. She might need help with that. She thought she would trust Noreê with that, although that bore thinking about.

And so she thought and thought.

They came at last in the evening to Big Rock, and Aloê took some comfort in the thought that she could sleep in her horrible little closet-sized room rather than in a bed soiled by the sweat of a perfumed woodcutter.

"I should go see to the incineration of Earno's corpse," she said to Ulvana.

"Surely tomorrow. . . ."

"No, his family has waited long enough. If I burn it tonight, I can send the ashes to his people tomorrow at first light."

"I'll go with you."

"Thanks. I've been a dull companion, I'm afraid."

"Silence is a skill I should learn," Ulvana said good-humoredly. "So my father always used to say, at any rate."

Aloê said something rude about Ulvana's father and the Arbiter laughed.

Big Rock was no metropolis, but it did have a death house with a furnace for cremating corpses. Ulvana led Aloê to the place, not far from the inn and the Arbiter's House.

One of the Arbiter's servants was sitting glumly on the porch of the death house. He saluted them wordlessly as they approached.

"Dull work, Gyllen?" Ulvana said briskly.

"Sad work, Arbiter. We didn't used to get so many bodies around here."

"It's truth," the Arbiter admitted, and clapped him on the shoulder as they passed.

They entered the dim atrium of the death house, lit by a single coldlight. There were two biers set up on trestles, a body covered with a shroud on each one.

"Someone must have died while we were out of town," Ulvana said, concerned. "I didn't know anyone was ailing."

Aloê was not completely indifferent to the death of strangers, but she had a great deal of work to do before she slept that night. Still, she suppressed her impatience. Big Rock was a small town, and Ulvana likely knew, possibly had loved, this dead person in life. She forced herself to be still and silent as Ulvana went to uncover the two bodies.

The first was Earno: still dead. Deader than ever, in fact: the reek in the death house was dense enough to bottle and sell as an emetic. A capable necrophor would have established a stasis spell over the body to prevent corruption, but perhaps Oluma had better ways to occupy her time.

Then Ulvana drew back the second shroud and cried out. Aloê moved forward in an instinctive impulse to comfort her, then froze when she saw the face of the second corpse.

It was Oluma.

Aloê cursed violently. She ran over to the bier and hurriedly examined the body. Dead for a day or more, she guessed from the slackness of the limbs. She had been stabbed in the back: the wound stood out like a pair of bloody lips, gaping to reveal her back ribs, shattered by the blow.

"A long knife or a sword blade," Ulvana speculated.

Aloê said nothing to that but ran to the Arbiter's servant seated gloomily on the front steps.

"Who brought the corpse of Oluma here?" she demanded from him.

He looked up at her in astonishment. He stood up to face her but did not speak.

"Answer her, Gyllen!" Ulvana commanded.

"I did, Arbiter," the servant replied, choosing to speak to Ulvana instead.

"Couldn't you see she'd been murdered, you fool!" Aloê raged at him.

"We don't get many murders up around here."

"Chaos in bright underwear! There are two murdered bodies in there right now! How many more do you want before you consider this serious?"

"I. . . ." The servant was confused. He looked at the Arbiter but evidently saw no help there. "I don't have much experience in this sort of thing. What does it matter, anyway?"

Every time Aloê thought she'd reached the pinnacle of rage, this idiot said something that pushed her higher up the slope.

"You might find it matters to you," she said grimly, "if the vengeance of the Graith falls upon your neck, Gyllen."

"But—"

"Shut up." Aloê turned to Ulvana. "May I have the services of this creature for an hour or two? I need to go out to the new murder scene. If it can be found."

"I know where it is," Gyllen said with some show of dignity.

"*Shut up.*"

"As long as you need him, Guardian," Ulvana said. "Then, Gyllen, you and I will talk."

"I'll need my other second as well—Binder Denynê. Where is she?"

"Am I allowed to speak?" asked Gyllen bitterly.

"Don't get righteous with me, you quivering pimple. If you know where my other second is, just tell me."

"She never came back to town."

"What?" Aloê cried.

"She never—"

Aloê turned away from his flat, empty mushroom of a face and ran all the way to the Big Rock House. The bald householder was enjoying the spring weather with a mug of hot cider in front of the fire in the common room.

"Goodman Parell," said Aloê, "is Binder Denynê in this house? Have you seen her recently?"

"Not for a day or two," the householder replied. "She rode out of town with you, I thought."

"If she returns, send her to find me at the Chamber of the Graith in A Thousand Towers."

"Are you leaving us, then?"

"I'm afraid so—a thousand thanks for your courtesy."

"Won't you eat something before you ride? We—"

"Can't! Thanks! Goodbye!"

She ran back to the death house, where Ulvana was having some quiet words with her servant.

". . . not if you expect to amount to anything in the Arbitrate!" she concluded forcefully as Aloê came up to them.

"Arbiter Ulvana," said Aloê, "I am sorry to leave you with my work to do, but I must move like a riptide if I am to have a chance of catching this killer."

"Say what you need, Guardian. I'm ashamed to say we haven't been much use to you up until now."

"Can you find someone to put a stasis over both these bodies, and put a guard over them until I send further word?"

"Easily. Is that really all, my friend?"

Aloê was so lonely, trapped within her thoughts and suspicions like a beast swimming in an empty sea, that the last word stabbed right through her. She seized Ulvana's hand and said, "I'm glad we're friends. It's my fault we haven't been for the last hundred years. But it won't be my fault if we're not for the next hundred."

"Good hunting, Aloê," Ulvana said, smiling. "And you, Gyllen, mind what I said."

Aloê mounted her horse and Gyllen climbed unskillfully onto the Arbiter's. At her motion, he led the way out of town, southward on the Road.

The murder scene was at the first milestone they came to. Gyllen dismounted there and pointed sullenly at a patch of grass behind the stone.

Aloê dismounted and got a coldlight from her bag. She tapped it against the milestone and it sprang into luminous life. She looked closely at the patch of ground.

Yes: someone had bled deeply here. The imprint of the body was clear in the deep, dry grass. And . . . and. . . .

She bent down and scooped up what she saw glittering there next to the bloodstain.

A spell-anchor. Like the spell-anchors she and Denynê had recovered from Earno's body—Denynê who had taken those anchors with her—Denynê who was now missing.

Was this truly one of those seven anchors? Or just one that looked like them? Had it fallen here by accident or been left here by design? More damn questions. She was sick of them.

It didn't look like the murderer had gone away through the grass on the side of the Road. Why should they? The murderer had no doubt stepped away from Oluma's corpse and walked or ridden wherever they chose along the Road.

If Aloê was right, her next stop was A Thousand Towers: to find out who had the knowledge of when Earno was passing this way. Somehow she thought the killer was down there, too. Predatory beasts hide in deep waters after a kill. Murderers would hide in a city.

"Gyllen, I am done with you," she said. "If you are lucky, we won't meet again."

"What difference does a death or two make?" Gyllen said sullenly. "The world is ending, and soon we'll all die. We should be making ships to cross the Sea of Worlds, not looking for bloody footprints."

"The next bloody footprint you see," said Aloê, "will be mine—across your face."

She mounted her palfrey and rode away southward.

The poor beast couldn't travel much farther tonight, but she didn't want to return to Big Rock. She would sleep beside the Road. She would add to her arsenal of questions. And when she got to A Thousand Towers, she would damned well find some answers.

CHAPTER THIRTEEN

The Sea Road to Grarby

"I object to water for its wetness, which is really its worst quality." Deor would have gone on, but Morlock, weary of his incessant complaints, took a handful of water from the drinking barrel on deck, formed it into a ball, and threw it at him.

While Deor sputtered and the rowers cheered and laughed, Kelat stared in open-mouthed astonishment. "How did you do that?"

Morlock silently mimed the actions of throwing something.

"No, no: I mean the water. It held together like a snowball."

"I convinced it to."

"How?"

"Water is quite gullible, in small amounts," the crooked man said.

Kelat reflected on this for a moment and said, "And in larger amounts?"

From the steering bench Lady Ambrosia said, "Moody. Dangerous. Usually beautiful, but always unpredictable. Sounds like your wife, Morlock, eh?"

Kelat was thinking that it sounded like Lady Ambrosia, but he didn't think it right to say so. Somehow Morlock had convinced her to bring him along on this journey; he didn't want to wreck anything, the way he usually managed to do.

Deor, quenched in more ways than one, came back to sit by Morlock. "*Harven*, have I been getting tiresome?" he asked quietly.

Morlock opened one hand, closed it.

Evidently Deor knew what that meant and said, "Sorry."

"Eh. Don't let it worry you."

It was the second night of their travels, and by dead reckoning they were fairly near their destination, the settlement of Gray Folk on the northeast coast of the Sea of Storms. Kelat had never been on a sea voyage that long, and he loved it. He stood by whenever Morlock and Ambrosia took the bearings of true-east and true-north with the seastone and plotted their progress on the map. He took turns at the oars. He took turns spelling the drummer who helped the rowers keep time. He stood watches as lookout. He spent time watching the different techniques of the steersman (or steerswoman, in Ambrosia's case). He wished the journey would never end.

He turned to look past the prow and sang out, "Fire on the horizon." There was a dim red spark there, where the darkness of the sky met the darkness of the sea.

"Where? What? How?" Deor demanded.

"Dead ahead," Kelat said, pointing. "Something burning. I don't know how."

"I see it," Ambrosia said grimly. "That's where Grarby ought to be. Any thoughts, Morlock?"

"Get closer," he said.

"Boat's made of wood, Morlock," Ambrosia observed. "Wood burns."

"It burns?" Morlock looked around in surprise. "Why?"

"Because. . . . Because. . . . Shut your stupid face!"

Morlock shrugged. "Closer."

"So we go closer," Ambrosia said. "But listen to me, Master Drummer and all you oarsmen! Be prepared to go to half speed."

They drove on into the dark water, and the red bud on the horizon grew into a bright, burning flower.

"Lady," said the captain, "we can beach the ship north of Grarby and march with you."

"Vornon, you're a giant," said Ambrosia easily, "but it can't be. This ship and crew must return intact to the fleet to help defend our fishing waters."

The flower grew. Its red light spread toward them, like bright petals cast on the dark water. Ambrosia ordered half speed.

She called the rowers to halt when they could actually see individual buildings on fire in Grarby.

"Haul out the skiff," she said.

The oarsman stood and moved their benches. They reached down into the innards of the hull and drew out a narrow little skiff on ropes. Morlock came over to help them lower it over the prow into the water.

"What is that?" Deor asked, in real distress.

Ambrosia stood up from the steering bench, stretched luxuriously (causing several sailors to stare wildly—including Kelat, he feared) and leaped forward to clap Deor on the shoulder. "That's the last boat to Grarby, Deortheorn! Climb aboard!"

"It'll sink."

"Then we'll swim. Get your stuff and come on!"

Deor glumly grabbed his pack and Morlock's; Kelat ran back to fetch his own and heard Ambrosia say quietly to Vornon, "You're in command now. Get this ship back and put it at the Vice-Regent's disposal. Stand by him, Vornon. It will be a long, hard year, and that brings out the traitor in weak-minded men."

"You'll be gone for a year?" Vornon said.

"I'll be back as soon as I can, but I don't know how soon that will be. Carry out my orders, soldier."

"Yes, Lady Ambrosia!"

Kelat brought Ambrosia's pack along with his and handed it to her. She grinned at him, and he felt like he'd been punched. Where was the distant, cold, often angry Lady Ambrosia he'd known all his life?

Ambrosia danced across the benches and jumped over the side, landing neatly in the skiff. "Come on!" she called.

If the skiff had been the jaws of a sea monster, Kelat would have done exactly as he did: run past the benches, leap over the side, and land right in front of her. He lost his footing and his pack almost went over the side, but she seized it and him and no disaster occurred. He hoped he wasn't gaping at her, but he couldn't stop looking at her as she turned toward the warship and called, "Come on, you two! Grarby is burning and, for all we know, the sun is not. There's no time to lose."

"That thing will sink if all four of us get into it," Deor said, not in a joking way but as if he believed it. Kelat turned to look back at him, not because he wanted to, but because he was embarrassed to keep staring at Ambrosia.

Morlock didn't reply to Deor, but he made his way somewhat unhandily down the side of the ship by way of the ropes. Once he was in the skiff he looked up to Deor and opened his hands.

Deor shrugged. "Catch!" he said, and tossed down first his pack then Morlock's. At last he followed Morlock down the ropes into the skiff.

"I think we can trust you two landsmen to row—" Ambrosia began.

"I am not a man. Madam."

"Your pardon, Deor. If you'll take one set of oars, I see Morlock is already shipping the others. Kelat, you're lookout. I'll steer."

They cast off the ropes. Ambrosia bid Vornon and his crew farewell, and they cheered the skiff on its way. Deor and Morlock got fairly soon into a rhythm with the oars and they pulled away from the warship. When the skiff was well away, they heard Vornon calling out orders, and the warship's oars began to dip and sweep. It made a long turn south, then west, back home to the cold camps of the Vraids on the northern coast of the Sea of Stones.

"This tub is going to sink," Deor muttered.

"Probably," Morlock agreed.

"*Absit omen!*" Ambrosia snapped. (Kelat didn't understand that, exactly, except it seemed to be meant to ward off bad luck.) "You should know better, Morlock."

"Every ship or boat I've ever been in has sunk, unless Aloê was in it, too," Morlock observed.

"That's not funny, brother."

"No," he agreed flatly.

"Er. Really? You mean it? Well, we all know how to swim—I hope?"

No one said her nay, and they rowed onward over the dark water toward the burning town.

The glittering red water was broken by the black-and-white furrow of a wake. "Something coming toward us in the water," Kelat called back to the others.

"A ship?" Ambrosia asked calmly.

"Something under the water."

The oars stopped rowing. Harsh ringing music: Morlock was drawing his sword. Kelat scrabbled about for his spear—where was it? Back on the warship?

The thing in the water: he could see it now. Sort of see it. It had a circular maw, ringed with knife-teeth that lifted from the water—

Morlock brushed past him and leaped off the prow of the boat, sword in hand, directly at the beast in the water.

Kelat shouted something, he never remembered what.

Morlock landed atop the scaly back of the beast. He stabbed the dark sword deep into it—there was no head—there was no neck—there was just the place behind the maw, and that's where Morlock struck. His blade went all the way into the monster until the hilts were pressed against the scaly back.

The knivish ring of teeth clenched and champed. The beast screamed and rolled in the water. Morlock disappeared.

Deor cried out and Ambrosia called out, "Steady! Ware the waves!"

It was excellent advice. The fish-beast kept on thrashing and bucking in the water. Morlock came into sight betimes, hanging desperately onto the grip of his sword, still anchored in something—the beast's spine, perhaps. Whenever he came into sight, he was already going out of sight as the fish-beast spun again and again in the water, arching its body and swinging its great finned tail.

The turmoil of the sea threatened to overturn the skiff, but it was the fish-beast's tail that destroyed it, shattering the side of the boat so that the dark sea poured in.

Kelat tottered and fell from the prow, and in the chaos of foam and bitter cold water and blood and broken wood he knew nothing for a time except the struggle to stay near the surface and breathing.

The tumult in the waters slowed, ended. The fish beast drifted in the water, as dead as their boat. Morlock was nowhere in sight.

Ambrosia snarled, "Death and Justice! If he's dead, I'll bash his damn brains in!" Her dark shape dove beneath the dead beast and returned in a moment with a choking, water-spewing Morlock.

Kelat paddled over to help but Ambrosia snarled, "Don't strain yourself. The danger's over."

"Don't *you* strain yourself, *harven*," said Deor. He thrashed his way over, their packs in tow . . . somehow all floating on the surface of the water. Their weapons were bound to the packs.

"How . . . ? How . . . ?" Kelat said, gulping as he trod water.

"Don't know! One of Morlock's little devices. Said it was best to be sure— he had bad luck on the water."

"Man thinks ahead," Ambrosia agreed, with chattering teeth. "Except when it comes time to jump on a sea-monster's neck."

Morlock had been more or less limp in her arms, but then he started and tried to get away.

"Hey, you!" she shouted in his ear. "It's over! Relax!"

"Sword," he said.

"Death and Justice! Can't you just make another?"

"Sword."

"It's—"

"*Sword!*"

"Fine! Fine! I'll get your little toy. Hang onto your pack, here. Don't let him slide off, you two."

"Lady Ambuh-buh-buh-brosia," Kelat stuttered, but she was gone under the water again.

She seemed to be angry at him, and he didn't understand it. Should he have jumped into the maw of the creature? He hadn't even had his spear. She hadn't done anything to aid or forestall Morlock either—she seemed to have stopped Deor from doing so. Why was he, Kelat, to blame?

Ambrosia reappeared with the strange crystalline sword and tossed it atop the floating packs.

"Let's follow Vornon's plan," she said, "and beach ourselves north of the t-t-t-t-town. And hope the w-w-w-w-water doesn't kill us before we get there."

It didn't, but it was a near thing. After an eternity of struggling in the cold, dark water, they finally dragged themselves onto the rocky shore. They lay there for a time, gasping. Then Morlock sat up and started fiddling with his pack.

"Morlock," croaked Ambrosia. "What doing?"

"Dry clothes."

"Stupid. Stuff's as wet as water."

Morlock looked at her with surprise. He continued opening his pack and pulled out dry clothing. With a marked absence of shame, he stripped off his wet clothes, and by that time, anyway, the others were ferociously attacking their own packs.

When they were all dressed in dry clothes and more comfortable, Ambrosia said, "So how did you do that?"

"Water's gullible. Stitch runes through the packs that convince water to stay out. Easy."

"You're easy," she jeered. "That's what the girls on the waterfront tell me, anyway."

A strange voice spoke next—inhuman, vibrant, crunching words like rocks. Kelat looked up to see a dozen mandrakes, armed with swords and spears, standing above them on the beach.

There was water in Kelat's ears and he hadn't quite caught the words. But, whatever they had said, it didn't sound friendly.

CHAPTER FOURTEEN

Empty Sock

Sunberry pie garnished with sweet cream and a cup of smoke-root tea are not, in fact, cures for grief and loneliness, and they do not answer any of life's pressing questions. But Aloê wanted them and she could get them, and they were good enough for the time being. She sat in the garden of her favorite refectory, watching the sun's pale red light disappear from the River Ruleijn below, and slowly ate her pie and drank her tea and thought many a useless thing.

She started to feel like she was being watched, though, and she looked up to see Noreê standing at the door of the refectory with one of her many thains-attendant.

She raised her cup in salute and Noreê came over. The thain stayed at the door.

"Will you have something?" Aloê said. "The owner is a friend of mine, and a wonderful baker."

"What did you want in the Arch of Tidings, Aloê?" Noreê said.

"I was trying to find out why you murdered Earno," Aloê said pleasantly. "*That* you did is pretty well established, but the Graith will want to know *why*—"

"Is that supposed to be funny?"

"Not as funny as you browbeating me, as if I were one of the thains-attendant who worship you as the incarnation of God Avenger. I am your peer and the Graith's vengeancer."

"We are not peers."

"I stretched a point. You are almost my peer."

Aloê placidly drank tea while the other woman fumed. She refilled her cup from the pot and gestured with it at Noreê, offering some. Noreê waved it impatiently away.

Eventually Noreê said, "I have a reason for asking."

Aloê said, "I have a reason for not answering. If you want to tell me your concern, I'll listen."

Noreê fumed. Aloê drank her tea. The pot was almost empty, and Aloê had just decided to get up and leave when Noreê said, "A message sock was tampered with."

"Which one? And how do you know?"

"It was the one in *stranj* with Earno's. And I know because . . . one of the thains who keeps watch on the message room is one of mine. He checks the message socks routinely, and found that Earno's had been—disrupted. Its seal was broken and the palimpsest within removed."

"And how did you know that I had been to the message room?"

"The thain on duty there tonight is another one of mine. She sent word to me of your visit."

Aloê said, "Let's go." She stood and walked away from the table, leaving Noreê to follow or not as she chose. She did eventually follow, hurrying to catch up with Aloê. By that time Aloê was at the door, exchanging pleasantries with the owner of the place. Aloê walked into the dark street with Noreê and the thain at her back. She strode ahead and let them follow her like an honor guard.

The Chamber of the Graith was nearly empty: only a few thains at the entrance, one under the dome with the broken Witness Stone, and one outside the Arch of Tidings.

"I thought Bleys might still be here, working at healing the Stone," Aloê remarked to Noreê.

"He is here most of his waking hours," Noreê conceded. "He thinks the pieces can be regrown together."

"Regrown?"

"That's what he says."

They walked on to the Arch of Tidings. There was a woman standing under the arch or entry, wearing the gray cape of a thain. Aloê didn't know her.

"This thain is one of yours?" Aloê said to Noreê.

"Yes."

"Introduce us."

"Vocate Aloê. Thain Veluê."

"It's good to meet you, Thain Veluê."

"Vocate."

"Vocate Noreê is now going to tell you to take my orders in preference to hers."

There was a brief, tense silence. Finally Noreê said, "Very well. Veluê, Vocate Aloê is tasked with avenging the death of Summoner Earno. While she is, we must all help her as we can. I must ask you to consider her orders as higher than my own, or, indeed, anyone else's."

"Except your own conscience, Veluê."

"Anyone else's at all," Noreê said urgently, as if she considered talk of conscience frivolous.

Veluê's dark eyes went from Aloê to Noreê and back again. "I will do so, Vocates."

"Thanks," Aloê said. "Show me this sock that's been tampered with."

Veluê led the way to a scrinium with several message socks in pigeon-holes. "This is the one," she said, pointing.

"Did you discover it?"

"No, to my shame. That was the day man—Curruth is his name."

"When?"

"Yesterday."

"Chaos eat his bones."

The other two Guardians looked at her in surprise.

"And mine, too. Earno's message sock was stolen, Noreê."

"Oh. Indeed."

"Indeed. And I sat in this room some days ago and sent a message to the necrophors, never thinking there might be evidence about his murder in this room."

"There still might be," Noreê said thoughtfully.

"How so?" Aloê asked. "The sigil is broken. The palimpsest within is gone."

"But message socks work because the two enclosures, and the palimpsests within them, are bound in talic *stranj*. There might be a talic impression in the message sock of the hand that removed the scrip and broke the sigil, disrupting the *stranj*."

"We couldn't run around reading the palms of everyone in the world . . . but we could start with those who likely had access."

"Yes."

"Let's do it, then."

"The impression, if there is one, will only be readable once; perceiving the talic pattern will disrupt it. Should I look for it, or should you?"

Aloê thought for a moment. "It'd be best if we look together, wouldn't you say? It doubles our chances of finding this fellow. Unless there's some reason we can't join perceptions for this purpose."

Noreê's wintry face was briefly warmed by a smile. "No, you're right. That would be best."

Noreê was the greatest seer in the world, with the possible exception of Bleys, a couple of deranged recluses in New Moorhope, Ambrosia Viviana . . . and perhaps some of the mind-sculptors in the Anhikh Kômos. Aloê never ventured on an act of the Sight in her presence without some qualms of embarrassment. But she had more important things to think about now than her ego: she braced her feet so that her body could stand in semi-consciousness and let her mind ascend the invisible steps to visionary rapture.

The eye of her mind opened and she found her talic self standing apart from the slumbrous glow of her body. Near to her in intention was Noreê, whose talic self was like a river of icy light. Aloê extended her coppery self-hood to mingle with that of the older, wiser, crueller woman. The shock of joining was deep: Aloê was used to sharing it with Thea, but Thea was gone. . . . Never mind. Never mind. They were joined.

They moved in united intention toward the violated message sock. The sigil had a spidery multibranched mark on it—the shock of spellbreak. The sock itself. . . .

She/they thought they/she saw some words! Earno's last message. They/she impressed the forms, but did not read them. Nothing is so hostile to the rapture of vision as language.

Within the sock . . . not a talic impression, but the reverse of one . . . not the image but its impress in the receptive matter of the enclosure. The sense of a specific person's absence. She/they did not recognize it. But they/she took the impress of that also.

"Return," said Noreê with her mouth, as if she were not in rapture at all. Aloê hardly heard it through her distant ears; she felt it directly in her selfhood. Which was hers alone again: Noreê had disentangled herself and descended from rapture already.

It took longer for Aloê, a timeless time. But at last or instantly the eye of her mind closed and the eyes of her body opened: she stood alongside Noreê in the hall of messages.

"It was a letter to Morlock," Aloê said thoughtfully. "Oh, Chaos on crutches. That's no good."

"Is it not?" asked Noreê thoughtfully. "I remember something about 'make you king' and 'consider Lernaion an enemy.'"

"After the Battle of Tunglskin, Lernaion said to Earno, 'They will make that crooked man king,' or something like that. Earno must have decided to warn Morlock about it. This doesn't tell us anything that I didn't already know."

"I didn't know it," Noreê said. "And it may help us more than you think. Do you bear an impress of the thief?"

"Yes." Aloê closed her eyes: the sensation was still clear in her mind. "More of an un-press—a sense of what the thief exactly is not. I'm not putting it well."

"It can't be put well."

Aloê opened her eyes to see that Noreê was smiling at her again. "Tell me something, Vocate."

"Yes?"

"You discovered this some time ago. Why did you wait to read the imprint in the message sock?"

Noreê said, "Why do you suppose?"

"I suppose that you thought I was the thief, and you wanted to test that suspicion before you revealed your knowledge."

"Your shot strikes close, but not exactly in the center ring. I feared you might be the thief, and waited until I was sure you were not. You were a good choice for vengeancer, Aloê—none better. But I didn't trust the man who proposed you. I had to be sure."

"And now you are."

"Yes. And you of me, I hope."

"Within limits. I still think you're crazy on the subject of the Ambrosii."

Noreê shrugged uneasily. "It may be so. Intuition guides me very strongly. But to surrender to intuition is also to surrender to prejudice and other impulses that arise from the dark places of the mind. Everything has its cost. But I see what I see. It should not matter for this purpose, though: I can't believe that Morlock would murder Earno and leave you to investigate the crime . . . unless you were somehow implicated. As you are not, plainly."

Aloê yawned. "Beg your pardon. A long day for me. Noreê, will you meet with me tomorrow morning and help find the thief? If he was not the murderer, he must have been acting at their behest."

"Surely." Noreê put a gentle hand on Aloê's shoulder. (The same hand had broken the neck of Osros, Third of the Dark Seven of Kaen.) "Rest, child. I'll come see you in the morning."

They walked out, exchanging a few more words as they stood in front of the Chamber. Then Noreê went her way and Aloê walked back to fetch her horse from the stable near the refectory where she had left it.

Full night had fallen, and a chilly night for spring. Horseman and Trumpeter were down and Chariot glowed somber in the eastern sky. The stars above were as sharp as silver knives; so was the wind off the river. She took part of her cloak and covered her head with it.

A single musical tone sounded, not far off in the night. She wondered for a startled moment why such a sound would make her afraid. Then the blade of a gravebolt entered her neck.

CHAPTER FIFTEEN

The God and His Enemies

"A re you enemies of the God?" the Gray Folk asked, their red eyes twitching with anger.

Deor waited for Morlock to say something, but he was sort of twitching himself. So the dwarf got up and said, "*Ruthenen!* I am Deor syr Theorn, Thain to the Graith of Guardians and cousin to the Eldest of the Seven Clans under Thrymhaiam. I greet you."

"We do not ask who you are, we ask: who are you? Are you enemies of the God, or not?"

Either the truth or a lie seemed equally likely to get them killed. Deor decided he would rather be killed for the truth. "We are not enemies of your God, but neither are we friends. He's no god of ours."

"It is enough," the leader decided. "Excantors, disarm them and keep them safe."

"Let it happen," Ambrosia suggested in Wardic, and Deor nodded. Kelat seemed inclined to follow Ambrosia's lead, no matter what the situation and Morlock—there was something wrong with him. He was in no state to be making decisions.

Some of the Gray Folk picked up their packs and weapons; the others surrounded them.

"Begin!" said the leader.

The excantors sang. It was a harsh, deep music, but not unharmonious. If there were words in it, they were in a language Deor did not know. The excantors began to march, and the four companions perforce marched with them—south and east, into the burning heart of Grarby.

They came to a jail. It was crowded with Gray Folk who jeered as the excantors chanted their way down the narrow stone hallway. There was a cell at the end; it was occupied by Gray Folk in kilts. These were hustled out of the cell and stuffed one at a time into other already-overcrowded cells.

"We must leave you here," the leader of the excantors said apologetically to Deor, "but we will return with food and other comforts. May the God not be with you."

"Uh," said Deor, driven to Morlockian levels of terseness by confusion. Were they guests or prisoners? What were the Gray Folk fighting about?

He put these questions to Kelat, but the young Vraid was as bemused as he was. "It was not like this when I was here before. The town was very quiet. I never saw a fight, much less a war."

Morlock was sitting on the floor with his arms wrapped around his knees, his luminous gray eyes fixed on something that was not present. Deor sat down beside him and said, "Morlock. . . ."

"It was so hungry," Morlock said. "So hungry. In so much pain. It could never eat enough to dull the pain. The pain frightened it. The dark frightened it. It was meant to have eyes but didn't any longer. It didn't notice the cold but it was always cold. I noticed. I noticed the cold. Then it died and it didn't want to die. But it died and died, and it keeps on dying."

"That damn sword," Ambrosia said. "He told me something about it. It's dangerous to kill with the thing."

"If—" Kelat began.

"Shut up. Deor, let him be for a while. If need be, I'll go into rapport with him and try to bring him out of it. But the fact that he's talking is actually a pretty good sign, as these things go."

There was a key rattling in the lock of the cell. Ambrosia, Kelat, and Deor turned toward the door as it opened; Morlock didn't seem to notice.

The leader of the excantors was there. He spoke to Ambrosia, "Lady, are you Ambrosia Viviana?"

"I am."

"The Olvinar would like to speak with you."

"*Hypage opisô mou*," hissed Morlock.

Deor thought he was muttering gibberish, but Ambrosia looked startled, then laughed. "I'll be careful, *ruthen*. Look after the children for me."

She left the cell with the excantor, who locked the door and silently led her away.

Halfway up the long hall, Ambrosia said, "Why aren't you chanting, if you don't mind me asking?"

The mandrake shrugged scaly shoulders as crooked as her own and said, "It agitates the godstruck. And . . . I don't think it really does any good."

"Oh. What good is it supposed to do?"

"Keep God out of your head."

"Is he often, um, in there?"

"Wouldn't be much of a god if he wasn't, would he?"

"I couldn't say. Which god is he again?"

"There's only one God!" said the excantor reflexively. "And he, uh, doesn't exist," he added lamely.

Theology was never a strong subject with Ambrosia, so she didn't inquire further along these lines. There were more immediate questions, like: "Who is this Olvinar, then? I take it he exists."

"Of course he exists. He would like to speak with you."

"Well, then."

The mandrake looked askance at her with blood-red eyes and then said grudgingly, "I must seem to you to be gibbering."

"No," said Ambrosia, lying with practiced ease. "But," she added, because the best lies serve as gilt for the truth, "I don't really understand what is happening here."

"I will tell you the tale as I understand it while we walk."

"It would be a kindness, *ruthen*."

He looked at her again, more directly this time, and said. "Then. In the old time, there was one of us, we know not his name, he defied the calling of his blood and did not become a dragon. He learned of the Little Cousins under Thrymhaiam and the Blackthorns, and he thought he would create a religion to teach the Gray Folk to fight their blood—to not surrender to the evil within them. He was our lawgiver, our temple builder. But the temple was empty, for who—what god would be the perfect being who would inspire us to be perfect?

"Then the God actually appeared?"

"He appeared, and he was evil in our eyes and stank in our snouts. Many were lost to the dragon plague then. But a new teacher arose. He taught that this was an avatar of the God, sent to show us how *not* to be, how *not* to live. His imperfection was our guide to perfection."

"Hm."

"Well, it stopped the plague. We could live, together, as ourselves, and that was something."

"And then . . . ?"

"And then came the Olvinar, the Adversary, the one called Lightbringer. He came to free us. He taught us that if we managed to kill the God, we would truly be free. It was a great word, and many received it gladly."

"But not all."

"No. Many still cling to the old foolish ways. And so we are at war with ourselves. The city burns, and we cannot cooperate to put out the fire. And the sun is dying, and some say it is because of the war against the God."

Ambrosia put her hand on the excantor's gray-plated forearm and said, "If I tried to escape, you wouldn't try very hard to stop me, would you?"

"I would not try at all," the mandrake said candidly. "I am . . . sick of it. Sick of all this." After a pause he whispered, "When the Adversary . . . when he sends us out to fight our *ruthen* kin . . . I enjoy it too much. Sometimes I . . . feel a cold thirst in my throat that I would quench with hot blood. I dream blasphemous dreams of chewing the sacred flesh of my kin . . . breaking their bones . . . licking out the burning marrow with a long forked tongue. I can't. . . . This can't go on forever. It has gone on too long. Perhaps the world really must end. Perhaps I would welcome it."

"Well, I'll go with you and talk to the Olvinar, this anti-God. Perhaps we can sort out a less permanent solution for this mess."

He nodded, clamped his long jaws hungrily a few times, and did not speak.

The Adversary lived in a house on the north side of town. It looked like a coil of great cable, wrapped around and around several storeys high, with a protrusion like a tower at the top.

There were two excantors chanting quietly at the front door. They held up their swords to salute their senior, then opened the door and stood aside.

"Go in, if you will," her companion said. "He would like to speak to you alone."

Ambrosia entered the dark doorway and heard the door closed and locked behind her. Protecting the Adversary? Imprisoning him?

The ground floor of the house was one big room interrupted by support columns. The stairway to the upper floors was exposed against the far wall.

The room was lit only in the center, where a white light-globe floated in midair. Beneath it, an old man sat at a table piled with books, light gleaming on his white hair and beard as he pored over a curious volume bound in brass.

The Adversary raised his head and looked at her with luminous blue eyes.

"Good evening, father," said Ambrosia.

"Ah! Ambrosia my dear, my very dear!" Merlin Ambrosius leapt up and ran over to greet his favorite daughter.

"Ὕπαγε ὀπίσω μου, Σατανᾶ!" she said, holding out both her hands to reject his embrace. *Get behind me, Adversary!* it meant in one of the unspoken languages from her mother's world.

"What . . . ? Ah! Ah hahahaha!" He laughed for some time rather theatrically and then said, "Very good, my dear. A most amusing reference to that somewhat obscure literary classic. That's one reason I enjoy talking to you, my dear: your suppleness of mind. Your brother would be sadly incapable of appreciating such a jest, even if he were well-read enough to make it."

Ambrosia forbore to point out that she was not joking and that Morlock had quoted that very text to her less than an hour before. She said instead, "Why are you here, father? I take it you are the great Adversary of the local god."

"Yes, yes, they flatter me with that noble title. You know the secret name of this god, perhaps?"

"Morlock says he is Rulgân Silverfoot, also called the Kinslayer."

"Yes, indeed—although what point there is in calling a dragon 'kinslayer' is beyond my telling. It's like saying, 'the one with wings—you know, the one who breathes fire.'"

"Hm."

"But, more to the point, what brings you here, my dear? I gather you didn't expect to find me here."

"Not until I saw that vile fish you made."

"Oh! Oh. You spotted that as one of mine, did you? How?"

"The thing was vicious, ugly, and a patchwork of scars. The maker makes in his own image."

"Oh, come now. I have very few scars."

"It was also in dreadful pain. So Morlock says."

"The pain of a fish. These are the trivia that your brother concerns himself with, my dear."

"He was concerned with saving me and my companions."

"Oh! Your companions, yes, I admit, I have little interest in them. But my emissary would not have killed *you*. Your blood would have poisoned him, among other things. No, I wanted you to come *here*, and here you are."

"But you can't have expected me. You came here originally for some other reason."

"And so did you, but you haven't told me either, you know. We can dance around and around the point and never come to it."

"We think Rulgân knows something about these entities that are killing the sun."

Merlin's eyebrows rose in polite surprise. "Only that? Really?"

"It seems somewhat important to us."

"I can't understand why. This world is doomed. But there are others. You were always fairly good at mathematics, and I understand even Morlock eventually learned enough to plot a course across the Sea of Worlds."

"That's your plan, then?"

"Eventually. It can't really come too soon, to my way of thinking. This world is becoming so unfriendly, what with all the cannibalism and warfare because of the crops failing year after year. And the winters lately. My dear, you have no idea how uncomfortable cold can be as one gets a little older. It's been a thousand years since I could properly enjoy a snowfall without thinking: *My joints! That old wound in my chest! My sinuses!* God Creator, my sinuses."

"Then why don't you abandon the sinking ship of this universe and swim away to sunnier climes?"

"I quite understand and resent your rodental metaphor, my dear, but the fact is that my business here is not quite finished, and I hate to leave a thing as important as this unfinished."

"If 'this,' whatever it is, doesn't impede my own plans too much, I might be inclined to help you with it. Morlock would feel the same way, I'm sure."

"Him!" Merlin shook his head. "No—the boy is soft as rancid butter.

We never should have let those dwarves near him. Besides, he knows little or nothing of lifemaking, and that is what my business entails."

"In that case, I won't be of much help, either. It's not one of my arts."

"Now that's where you're wrong, my dear; I'm sure you'll be invaluable. Won't you help me, please? And then, I give you my word, I will assist in your little quest. If you can save this world, I would be well pleased—I have nothing against it, really."

Ambrosia hesitated. Nothing was more dangerous than Merlin when he seemed plausible.

"Well," she said, reluctant to commit herself, "what is *it*, exactly?"

"It'll be easier to show you than to explain. Won't you come up to my workroom?"

They went together to the stairway. Merlin went to some effort to make himself agreeable, asking after her sister and how her experiment with the Vraids was working out, and other matters that he probably didn't care about at all.

The stairs and floorboards were made of wood, but the walls were not. It was as if the interior of the house was built to stand independently inside an already existing structure. The outer walls were like gigantic cables laid over each other. They were hard as stone, cold and somewhat oily to the touch, and their surfaces were scaled.

"First fish-beast—now snake-beast?" she speculated. But Merlin was rattling away about something and didn't seem to hear her.

The second floor was broken into a number of rooms joined by open arches. In the room where the stairway ascended, there was nothing but a three-legged table, about waist high. On it stood a fabric tent, something like a tea-cozy, but much larger.

"What's that?" asked Ambrosia.

"Ah!" said Merlin delightedly. "That is the task at hand! Let me show you." And he undid some fastenings and pulled the tent aside.

Standing on the table was a sort of egg made out of crystal. Inside the crystal were woman-shaped shadows, and a lurking flame, and a brain floating in the midst of it. Still attached to the brain by the optic nerve was a pair of eyes, bright gray like Morlock's. They searched around the room and fixed on Ambrosia in something like recognition.

"You remember your mother, my dear?" said Merlin pleasantly. "Though perhaps you haven't seen her lately."

Ambrosia would have fled back down the stairs, but they were gone. Snakelike arms unfolded from the walls and held her fast.

"She's getting very old," Merlin said apologetically. "Her people were exiled from the Wardlands so long ago, you see, and of course they interbred with the peoples they found themselves among. Well, before your mother reached sixty, less than sixty years old, mind you, she was really quite decrepit. I've tried many ways to extend her life without damaging her selfhood. My thought coming here was to implant her brain and the rest of her awareness in Rulgân's body. For various technical reasons, involving your brother and that gem he managed to implant in the beast, I have reason to believe the graft would be successful.

"But I could never get at Rulgân, you see. I bribed him with little favors— a gem that would transmit his awareness, and a spell to smash the Wards over the Gap of Lone, and a tribe of lifestealers to distract the Graith from his messenger. But Rulgân would never admit me into his presence, although he was weak enough to let me settle in this town. And he was aware of my intent at the last, and he raised up his believers against me. I've tried to fight them with a legion of unbelievers, but with a striking lack of permanent success. And it's getting late, and the world is dying, and I'm not sure I could do this type of lifemaking in another world where the laws of nature are different.

"And here you came—a gift from God Creator, if I believed in any such ridiculous myth. I think your body will sustain your mother's life for some centuries to come. Of course, that does mean we will be deprived of your charming company more or less forever. But I'm sure that's a sacrifice you'd be willing to make, if you could be brought to understand what it means to me and, of course, for your mother."

His blue eyes, colder than a winter's sky, were on her as he spoke. She had known him all her life. He had raised her and her sister until she had run away from home. She knew how he talked, and she could translate what he said into what he meant.

What he meant was, *I am going to core you like an apple and put this thing inside your corpse. And there is nothing you can do about it.*

CHAPTER SIXTEEN

Dead Ends

The healer sewing up the side of Aloê's neck was Master Snide, whose actual name turned out to be Cromber. She was surprised to find him an efficient and capable healer.

"Struck from long distance?" he asked at one point.

"Yes. I could only just hear the tone of the songbow."

"And your cloak was drawn over your head? Possibly saved your life." Cromber shook his head. "These gravebolts are well-named. They'll be giving the necrophors more work than they will us."

"I was glad to have one at Tunglskin, against the Khnauronts."

"I suppose."

"How long will you be?"

"I'm done. Stay and rest a bit, though. You lost some blood getting here. I'll make you some redleaf tea."

She had bled a good deal while searching for the would-be assassin in the shadowy street. But they had taken to their heels after their unlucky shot. No matter: she had the gravebolt. She thought she could find the songbow it matched. Raudhfax had brought her to the Well of Healing before she passed out.

Cromber brought two cups of tea: redleaf for her and blackroot for himself. They drank in amiable silence.

"How did your Wordweave game go the other night?" Aloê asked.

"Horrible," he admitted. "I'm a bad player, and a bad loser."

Aloê nodded. "This I understand. I hate to lose."

Cromber wanted her to stay in the Well overnight, but she wouldn't. It was that "hate to lose" thing. She felt she had lost a point and wanted to even the score.

She left Raudhfax at the Well and walked toward Tower Ambrose, sneaking through alleys when she could, sliding along in deep shadows when she must take a broader way.

Her thinking was this: the would-be killer would try again. The place she was most likely to go was Tower Ambrose. The assassin would wait for her somewhere near there.

Tower Ambrose was on a bluff, and it could not be approached from the south. The place she had been attacked was to the east. She stalked the person stalking her in the shadows of the River Road east of Ambrose.

The wind was high that night, and its noise covered a multitude of sounds. That was good for her, so that she could move safely in the dark. But it was bad, also: it meant that her assassin could hide from her.

She came to a halt near the place she considered optimal for her own assassination. It was near enough to Tower Ambrose that the shooter could attack someone coming from two or three different sidestreets and then escape down two or three others if need be. Yes—if they were going to try again, it would be somewhere near here. She climbed up the side of a house she knew was empty and sat on the roof in the shadow of a dormer.

She sat still for a long time. She thought of it like fishing with her hands: you had to be still, let the fish become calm and brave. Then strike when they were unaware.

The wind changed, grew quieter. The stars spun in the sky above her. Some of the lights in the city northward faded as the night got older: people were going to bed—some people.

She waited.

A man wandered by, singing a song about drunken unicorns. He got stuck on the chorus and kept repeating it. Aloê heard him saying the same line for part of an hour as he staggered slowly up the River Road.

She waited.

Dawn was not near. But the danger that she would fall asleep in her perch was near.

She thought of something she might try.

She smiled and drew the gravebolt from her cloak, one side of its gore stained black with her blood.

The gravebolt would sound as it was released from the songbow. Were they in a kind of talic *stranj*, entangled in being?

She rapped the gravebolt against the edge of the roof.

Up the street, she heard the faint chime of a songbow.

She was on her feet in an instant, running across the roof and leaping to the next house over, swinging down a drainpipe.

By then the assassin was in flight up a sidestreet. But he (she guessed it was a man) had not tethered a horse anywhere near, of course. And she was lighter on her feet than he was. He was wearing a thain's cape, she saw without real surprise.

As she got nearer to him he turned at last, deciding to make use of the weapon he carried. Had he used the thing as a club he might have had a chance, but he actually tried to fit a gravebolt to the songbow.

She threw herself at his knees and they went down together in the street.

As he was thrashing around to get free, she took the gravebolt stained with her blood and put it against his throat.

"Stop," she said, and he stopped.

"Please don't kill me," he whispered. "I was only doing as I was told."

"I—" *would very much like to kill you* "—am not going to kill you. Who gave you the orders?"

"Please. I'm afraid."

In her rage it delighted her that he was afraid, and was weak enough to admit it, too. She wanted to shake him until he broke open like a stuffed doll.

She might be able to break him. But even more than that, she wanted answers from him. She needed someone to work with her—to check her rage—to ask questions she might neglect.

Her seconds would be the people to call on here, but one was dead and the other missing. For all she knew, this quivering uncooked sausage was responsible, and that thought made her even angrier, dangerously angry.

She got to her feet and dragged him with her. "Here's an order: come with me."

Jordel's house was near at hand. She was pretty sure she could trust Jordel . . . and, if not, that was worth finding out.

Jordel was sitting sadly on his porch, a jar of wine in his hand. He took an occasional sip of wine as he moodily watched Aloê marching her prisoner up the street.

"Good evening, Aloê," he said when she was near enough for conversation. "What happened to your neck?"

"This fellow shot me."

"Oh. Should we kill him?"

"He says he had orders. I want to know who gave the orders."

"Then we can kill him?"

Aloê laughed. Her rage was receding a little.

"I think we can let him live, if he helps us."

"Oh. Do you absolutely insist?"

"That depends on him."

Jordel stood. He grabbed the would-be assassin by his left arm. "Let's talk, youngling."

They went indoors. Jordel dragged the frightened thain up the stairs to a room in the front of the house on the second storey.

"Only room with a lock," he explained to Aloê. "So we can lock him in, if need be."

"Your house doesn't have any *locks*?"

"It has *a* lock. That's more than I usually need, you know. Nothing worth stealing. Except my heart, of course. In with you," he said to the thain.

They all sat in chairs, the thain with his back to the door so that Chariot's somber light from the eastern windows would fall on his face. And they talked.

The thain's name was Dollon. He was very afraid, and he was only following orders. If they would allow him to send a message to a friend, he would be grateful his whole life long. That was what they got out of him—over and over and over.

"How long do you think your life is likely to be?" asked Jordel impatiently on the tenth repetition of the thain's request.

From below came the sounds of someone entering the house—voices they both knew, calling Jordel's name.

"Come on," Jordel said to Aloê. They left the room and Jordel locked the door ostentatiously behind him.

By then, Jordel's visitors were climbing the stairs. One was Noreê, Aloê was somewhat relieved to see, and the other was Naevros syr Tol.

Noreê had been alerted by someone at the Well that Aloê had been attacked, and she had trailed her back to Tower Ambrose. There a householder told her that Aloê had captured someone and dragged him away, and in what direction. Deduction told her the rest.

"You mean there were people watching and listening as I fought that . . . that . . . thain?"

"Many. They were discussing it in the street as I passed."

That gave Aloê an eerie feeling, thinking of all those faces in the dark, watching, doing nothing.

"As for me," Naevros said, laughing, "I was just coming by to see if Jordel had anything to drink."

"I *had* something to drink. Then I drank it. A polite guest brings something to drink, Naevros; he does not merely seek to sponge up the drippings of his host's wine cellar."

"Thanks for the lesson in etiquette, Sir Honorable Jordel of the Cowpies."

"I think it's 'Honorable Sir.' Isn't it? What's the correct usage. You're of the gentry, Aloê; you enlighten us."

"I'll enlighten you with a brick."

"You hear that, Naevros? That's the sound of true nobility—often imitated, but in the end inimitable. I remember once—"

Noreê asked impatiently, "What are we doing out here if the prisoner is in there?"

"We're giving him the chance to make a mistake," Jordel explained kindly. "So far he's made only two: failing to kill Aloê the first time, and then getting caught the second time. Now, if he gets away, we can follow him."

"That's very shrewd, Jordel!" Aloê said.

"I'm shrewder than I look. Please don't point out how easy that would be."

There was the sound of glass falling into the streets.

"Clod," Jordel said, shaking his head. "Guardians, shall we . . . ?" He sauntered down the stairway.

Before any of them reached the first storey, there was a heavy blow on the porch roof and the sound of flailing. Something fell into the street outside.

They rushed out into the street. Thain Dollon lay there without moving. His feet had gotten tangled up, and he had fallen from the porch roof to the street onto his neck. There was no question that he was dead.

"Clod!" Jordel repeated, more emphatically.

Aloê felt crushed. It had seemed, for a moment, there was a real chance of getting somewhere in this business. Now there was only one more dead body, one more dead end.

"God Sustainer, I'm tired," she whispered.

"Stay here with me," Jordel said quickly, while Naevros was only opening his mouth. "Naevros and Noreê can alert the necrophors and oversee taking the body to a suitable boneyard. Meanwhile we will eat and drink and sleep, and you will have a new idea in the morning. You always do, you know."

"Thanks, J," said Aloê gratefully. She'd been dreading the trudge back to Tower Ambrose, its dark emptiness when she arrived there.

Naevros surrendered with a good grace, shrugged, and punched Jordel on the arm. Then he turned to Aloê. With a serious look he said, "Rest. Heal. The Wardlands need your shrewdness at full strength." Then he embraced her.

"Thanks," she gasped. She waved farewell to Noreê and went in with Jordel. He fussed over her with wine and fruit and cabbage stuffed with meat and things.

Aloê didn't eat much. She was too tired, and a little nauseated. Naevros had been wearing a rather powerful scent, and it struck her as very unpleasant. It was an oily musky smell—made her think of lumberjacks, and not in a good way.

Then she remembered the scent that had stained the beds in the timber lodges not far from where Earno had died and been murdered.

And then, without really being able to prove anything, she knew or guessed something she would have preferred to never know.

CHAPTER SEVENTEEN

Miracles of St. Danadhar

"Where is Aloê?" Morlock asked in something like a conversational voice.

"She's back in the Wardlands, *harven*," Deor said gently.

"No," Morlock said thoughtfully. "No. You're back in the Wardlands. Aloê was taken by the basket-bird. I saw it fly east into the dead lands."

"That was long ago, *harven*. Don't you remember?"

"Then why am I still in prison? Did I dream all that? Am I dreaming this? Where is Danadhar?"

"You may be dreaming," Deor said. "You sound like you're dreaming. I wish you'd wake up."

"I wish it, too," said Morlock, and closed his bloodshot eyes.

"This could be worse," Deor remarked to Kelat, "I suppose. Say, if landfish were eating our eyeballs, or something like that."

"What was that name?" Kelat asked.

"Danadhar. It's someone he met the last time he was through here."

"The god-speaker."

"As I understand it, someone else was god-speaker back then. But I don't doubt that this Danadhar is god-speaker now: from Morlock's account, he was very religious. But that's right: you were around here last year, weren't you?"

"Yes, but I didn't see this."

"Understandable. In one brief stay one can never really see all the things worth seeing in a place. For instance, I spent a goodly amount of time in A Thousand Towers over the part century, but I never had occasion to see the Museum of Lithicated Teratomata or the Treasure-House of Forgotten Elbow-Guards."

"I don't mean the jail," Kelat explained patiently. "I was in a cell for a while last year—not this one—while they figured out what to do with me. I mean *this*." Kelat pointed at something on the wall.

It was some kind of memorial—an engraved plaque, riveted into the wall. Deor couldn't read all of it—the text was partly runic, partly ideogrammatic. But there was a word that might have been the name *Danadhar*, and another that was probably *Ambrosius*, and an ideogram that almost certainly represented *ruthen*.

"Hm!" Deor said eventually. "Well seen, my friend. This must be the very cell Morlock was imprisoned in all those many years ago. That means he's not as crazy as he sounds. And the event seems to be important to these Gray Folk—probably because Danadhar himself became important."

Kelat looked at him for a moment and said, "Yes, he is important. Do you mean Morlock is really more than a hundred years old?"

"Oh, yes. A hundred thirty—or twenty—a hundred and forty? Something like that. He was a horrible child, really—always blowing things up and terrifying people and saying the strangest things. Wonderful days, those were."

"Then you—"

"I'm about the same age as he—a tad older, it may be. I'd have to look at the nest records to be sure. Haven't worn as well, obviously."

"And Ambrosia?"

"She's a few years younger—she and her sister—whom I gather you haven't met."

"No. She has never been among the Vraidish tribes."

"I doubt that very much, but it doesn't surprise me you haven't seen her. She—ah—she keeps to herself."

Kelat brooded over this for a few moments, then said, "Danadhar I have met. He is very old, even as the Gray Folk count the years. And they live longer than men."

"Well—there's your father."

"Everyone knows that Ambrosia's magic is what keeps him alive. Some say it is what made him a fool."

"Um. Possibly. Longevity spells exist, you see, but they have unfortunate transformative effects; one never knows quite how one will come out, but it's very rarely for the better. That's why Those-Who-Know tend not to use them on themselves."

"How were Morlock and Ambrosia transformed? How were you? You're not crazy."

"Well, we haven't, eh, been transformed. Or maybe we have. It's part of living in the Wardlands. The land sustains you, strengthens your life. And that strength can be carried on to your offspring, which is why Ambrosia has it . . . although not in the degree Morlock has. She may age faster than he does, as the centuries pass. I know he's worried about that."

"Then she will grow old and die, just like everyone else."

"She will, but not just like everyone else. She doesn't seem to do anything like everyone else, I don't know if you've noticed."

"Yes, I had noticed that."

Deor looked sharply at the young man. He knew more about the mating practices of men and women than he did when he was a young dwarf, and he did not even need to guess that the young man was in love with Ambrosia Viviana. Fortunately, it was not his business. But he hoped that Ambrosia would deal gently with the young fool; Deor rather liked him.

There were shouts in the corridor outside—they seemed to be coming from the other cells. "Ware plague!" the prisoners were shouting, and "Call the god-speaker!" and many other things that Deor could not quite understand.

Kelat peered curiously out the narrow barred window of the cell. Deor walked over to stand next to him then grabbed a bar of the window to lift himself high enough to look out.

One of the excantors was lying supine on the corridor floor outside. He was writing sinuously, and smoke was trailing from his snout. It seemed to be lengthening a bit.

"Poor fellow," Deor remarked to Kelat. "It's the dragon sickness."

"What causes it?" asked Kelat, staring in fascination at the slowly transforming mandrake.

"Greed. Anger. Cruelty." Deor sighed. "You Other Ilk can indulge in these to your heart's content. If we do it we risk losing our hands—our kin—everything that we are."

Kelat looked at Deor's hand, gripping the bar, then at Deor's face, and nodded.

Now there was someone else in the corridor, and the prisoners began to cheer. "God-speaker! Danadhar! Save us from the plague! Save us from the Dragon!"

It was an elderly male of the Gray Folk, wearing a kilt made of weeds. He hastened to the fallen excantor and knelt down beside him.

Deor had been bitten by someone undergoing the dragon-change, once, and he called out in Wardic, "Hey, watch out there, cousin!" Then, realizing that would do no good, he said the same thing in Dwarvish: *"Vuf! Thekhma-dhi, ruthen!"*

The elderly Gray One looked up at the sound of Deor's voice. His long, terrible mouth gave a gray-toothed grin that may have been meant as friendly. Then he turned back to the suffering excantor.

The god-speaker put a long-fingered, gray-clawed hand gently on each side of the excantor's slowly lengthening face. "The choice is yours," Danadhar said, so quietly Deor could hardly hear him. "Remember that there is a choice. Will you be as you are? Will you be as you could be? Will you become what you hate?"

"I can't believe in your God!" the excantor screamed.

"What difference does that make? Belief. If I believe a stone is a mushroom, does that mean I won't break my teeth eating it? Believe or don't believe. What will you do? What will you be? What do you want?"

"There is no God. Not your God. Not any god. Not really."

"Then, for you, there is no God. So what? What will you do? What will you be? What do you want?"

"I want to kill," whispered the excantor. "I want to steal. I want to lie."

"Yes! Yes!" said the god-speaker eagerly. "So do I. But especially to kill! How I long to run down the streets of our city, my claws dripping with fiery blood, gnashing fragments of green-gray flesh in my fangs. How I would kill, in my rage and greed! What evil glory there would be in that! I saw your daughters outside."

"Be quiet!" shrieked the excantor.

"They are there, and would be easy to kill. Shall we kill them together, you and I? I will if you will."

"Be quiet," begged the excantor.

"If you go down that long, fiery path, you will have many things, but quiet will not be one of them. Nor will daughters or mates. You will be alone, in the dark, on your hoard, listening to yourself until your fire goes out."

"I can't believe in your way. I can't believe in your God."

"As if I asked you to! Belief. If the God exists, he needs your belief no more than the rain does, or the sea, or trees, or anything that is real. If he is not, he needs your belief no more than does up-downness or dark-lightness or anything that is unreal. You do the God no favors by believing in him. You do yourself no favors. Whom are you looking to please with this belief? Me? I am the one who just offered to help you kill your children."

"What am I supposed to do?" whispered the excantor.

"Choose," said Danadhar firmly. "What will you do? What will you be? What do you want?"

Now the excantor lay quiet on the stones. He wasn't breathing smoke anymore. His face seemed to be returning to its former shape. He closed his burning eyes.

There was silence in the jail.

The excantor shook off the god-speaker's hands and stood up. He turned to face Danadhar who stayed crouched there on the stones, looking patiently up at him.

"I don't need you," the excantor said.

"No," Danadhar agreed. "What will you do?"

"Leave here. I cannot fight my own *ruthen*-kin anymore. I will not."

"What will you be?"

"Not a soldier. Not a jailor." He looked at his hands. "I would like to build something. I love the smell of sawn wood even more than the smell of blood."

"What do you want?"

"To be free."

"Go and be free, my son. Leave here and build something."

The ex-excantor nodded slowly. He took off his belt of office and dropped it on the jail floor. "Thanks be to you, Saint Danadhar," he said.

"Enough of that kind of talk," said Danadhar. "Get out of here, now. Remember me to your children, eh?"

"Are they really outside?"

"They are, with their mothers and your co-mates. They're all very worried about you. Go."

The former excantor nodded and left.

"Free us, Saint Danadhar," whispered someone. Then all down the corridor the shouts broke out, "Free us! Free us, Saint Danadhar!"

"Shut up!" roared Danadhar, and silence fell.

"I find that kind of talk very disgusting," Danadhar continued, "and I will not countenance it. No! Absolutely not! Saint Danadhar will not free you. No saint will ever free you. Stop hoping for it."

He bent down and scooped up the keys from the golden belt. He walked over to the door through which Deor and Kelat were still watching him.

"Little Cousin," said Danadhar, "you tried to do me a favor just now."

Deor snorted. "Thanks for noticing, *mandrake*."

Danadhar stood back a step then smiled a long, wicked smile. "Is that offensive? I'm sorry, *ruthen*: I didn't mean it so."

"It's nothing," Deor said. "*Ruthen*, I spoke in haste: forgive me."

"I'll do a little better than that." Danadhar went through the keys and found the one for their cell. He unlocked it.

Deor released the bar and backed away from the door. The Gray One stood in the doorway.

"Here are the keys," Danadhar said, handing them to Deor. "Do with them what you will."

Deor rushed past him and unlocked the nearest cell. "Pass them on," he said, handing the keys to one of the freed prisoners, and turned back to Danadhar who was still standing at the door.

"May I know your name, *ruthen*?" Danadhar said politely.

"Deor syr Theorn, cousin to the Eldest of the Seven Clans Under Thrymhaiam. My blood is yours, *ruthen*."

"Thanks! I hope I never have a use for it. And . . . ?"

"This gentleman is Prince Uthar Kelat, son of the Vraidish King."

"Kelat. Kelat." Danadhar continued in Ontilian, "It seems to me a man of that name came to speak to the God's evil avatar some time ago. I tried to talk him out of it."

"That was me, God-speaker," Kelat said. "I wish I had listened to you."

"Oh!" Danadhar's eyes glanced aside in separate movements, which Deor recognized as a sign of embarrassment. "I'm sorry I didn't recognize you."

"It's nothing, great Danadhar. I cannot say my blood is yours; my blood belongs to my king. But my spear is yours, to strike where you say or keep it sheathed."

"Sheathed, then, new friend. There has been too much killing in the city in the past year. But we must get you your spear and whatever else you came with. And whoever else. Is there someone over there?"

"Over in the corner is my *harven*-kin, Morlock Ambrosius."

"'Was,' you mean," Danadhar corrected mildly. "That's a day I'll never forget, though it was so long ago. If—*Ruthen* Morlock! It's true!"

The god-speaker rushed past Kelat and stopped to stand uncertainly before Morlock.

Deor hoped that Morlock wouldn't spoil this odd reunion with any gibberish about the inner lives of dead fish.

The crooked man looked up and met Danadhar's blood-colored eyes. He stood and said conversationally, "*Ruthen* Danadhar. I greet you."

"*Ruthen* Morlock," the Gray One whispered. "It has been long since we last met. I have tried to keep faith with the truths you showed me on that day."

Deor glared at Morlock, but the crooked man shrugged uneasily. "I showed you no truths. I'm glad you saw some, though."

Danadhar nodded humbly and grinned his terrifying grin. "Yes. Yes. No one shows us. It is up to us to see. You are still my teacher, *ruthen*. Although— you seem no older than you did on that day."

"I am, though" Morlock said. He looked around the cell. "Where is Ambrosia?"

"The woman who was here? The Olvinar has her, I fear," Danadhar said sadly.

"The Olvinar? That is your Adversary—the anti-God?"

"Yes. He came first two years ago. He brought gifts and made friends. He called himself Lightbringer, but I perceived that was a lie. For I reasoned with myself this way, *ruthenen*: if the God chose to appear in an avatar of evil, showing us the consequences of doing what we must not do, why shouldn't the Olvinar appear in an avatar that seems good, tempting us to do what is wrong, as if we will not suffer from it? Also, his conversation seemed somewhat shifty to me. He only tells truths to mask his lies."

"Hm. I knew a man like that once. His name was not Lightbringer, though."

"He is like you in form, but taller, with white hair and a beard."

Morlock looked at Deor, a little panic showing in his colorless bright eyes.

"Morlock," Deor said. "Don't worry. If you're thinking what I'm thinking, Ambrosia is his own daughter—his favorite, from what I understand. What harm could come to her?"

"You are not thinking what I am thinking," Morlock said. "I fear it may already be too late."

In a way it was.

CHAPTER EIGHTEEN

Second Chances

I t is odd to know that one of your oldest friends is a murderer and a traitor. Aloê found it so. Everything that passed between her and Naevros now was stained with horror. And yet he was still her friend, and the rapport between them was as close as it had ever been. He had become strange to her and horrible without ceasing to be familiar.

And she found herself relying on him in ways both new and old. Noreê and Naevros both stopped by Jordel's to see her in the morning: Naevros to see how she was doing, and Noreê so that they could begin the task of finding out who had stolen Earno's last letter. Impulsively, Aloê asked Naevros to join them. Naevros was pleased, and Jordel clearly miffed. How could she tell Jordel that he was no use to her? *He* had no guilty knowledge to betray.

They rode together to Thaintower, east of the wall and north of the River Ruleijn.

"We should start with the thains who were on duty at the Arch of Tidings," Aloê said. "I suppose you have a list?"

"Yes," said Noreê. "I sent a message to Earno several days before his death. Any message he sent after that would have been written after that. And a thain on duty must have stolen the palimpsest."

"Or they may know who stole it," Naevros added.

"Or we may know, after we've talked to the thain," Aloê suggested. "'Hello, trusty thain-friend! Stand my watch for a moment while I snort down a bowl of soup.' And if the trusty friend was the thief. . . ."

"Yes," Noreê conceded temperately.

"How many of the thains in question are yours?" Aloê asked.

"All of them."

"Oh." Aloê thought of the jail in Fungustown, staffed entirely with Noreê's thains. She thought of the Hall of Tidings, staffed entirely with Noreê's thains. How much of the city did she control—or was she trying to control? The thing could become a problem. It was, perhaps, already a problem.

Aloê met Naevros' eye, and he nodded. She knew he was thinking the same thing. There was a comfort in knowing that someone else saw what she saw, was concerned by the same thing that concerned her.

Of course, Naevros was a traitor and a murderer. She did not forget that.

But how little it affected him! He sat there in the saddle, sunning himself like a cat in the thin daylight, and seemed concerned about nothing except the cut of his trousers (which kept riding up his leg as they rode). Beside him trotted perhaps the greatest seer in the world, but he was obviously not worried that some psychic effluvium would betray him as a murderer.

Of course, he was a killer. They were all three killers. The murder of Earno seemed worse to Aloê than killing in battle, but maybe Naevros justified it to himself somehow. He could truly be innocent in his own eyes. Those pretty green eyes.

She shook her head and snorted.

Naevros looked at her, glanced at her horse, and smiled to himself.

She laughed. It was funny. And he was a traitor and a murderer.

At Thaintower they dismounted and let a couple of ostler-thains tend to their horses. Then Noreê (how they knew her there! how they truckled to her!) briskly demanded to see seven particular thains in the tower atrium.

It was the third one to show himself: a fellow named Bavro. Aloê's insight whispered it to her as soon as she laid eyes on him. But, to be sure, she ascended slightly into rapture and, with great difficulty, extended her hand in greeting.

He took it. His talic self was like a glowing mist with many dark gaps—perhaps like a skeleton made of fog, but it was not a human skeleton. It was the negative of the imprint left in the message sock.

She shook loose from her vision.

"Where is the letter, Thain Bavro?" she asked.

He must have suspected why he was being summoned. But perhaps he didn't expect the question to be put so abruptly. In any case he gaped at her like a fish in a net.

"What—what—?" he said.

"The letter, Thain Bavro, the letter!" Noreê said angrily.

"The palimpsest you stole from the Arch of Tidings," Aloê explained kindly. "Earno's last letter."

"Where is it, Thain Bavro?"

"Who did you steal it for? Who are you working with?"

Bavro glanced desperately (and most revealingly, Aloê thought) at Naevros, who stood silent through all this. Whatever Bavro saw in those pretty green eyes made him quail.

"I cannot tell," he said sullenly at last. "I cannot tell."

"You will tell, Guardian!" Noreê insisted. "If not now, then later. If not to us, then to the assembled Graith on the Witness Stone."

"But the Witness Stone is broken, and—" Bavro stopped suddenly.

"Bleys tells me the Stone can be healed," Noreê said. "But we may not have to wait so long. Take off your cape of office, Bavro; you don't deserve it."

Bavro looked at each of the vocates in turn. He reached up and undid the fastenings at his shoulder, letting the gray cape fell to the floor.

"You will come with me to the lockhouse, there to await the Graith's pleasure. Guardians, will you come with us?"

"He may have hidden the palimpsest here, somewhere," Aloê said. "I'll stay and have a look around."

"I'll help," Naevros said.

Noreê nodded curtly. She took Bavro by the elbow and steered him out the door. All the thains in the atrium followed her out, the sheep following their shepherd.

"I do not like this private army she is making of the thainate," Aloê remarked.

"A thousand soldiers and one general," Naevros agreed. "Yes, something will have to be done. . . ."

After some searching and asking questions of passing thains, they finally found their way to the narrow little room that Bavro called home. They took their time searching it. It needed time: the little room was layered in dirty clothes, books, pieces of uneaten food, badly drawn pornographic art, and string, which Bavro seemed to collect obsessively.

"This place is filthier than my house," Naevros remarked at one point, "and that's saying something."

"What?" Aloê said. "Have you cast off the irreproachable Verch at last?"

Verch was Naevros' housekeeper. They had been quarrelling on a daily basis since before Aloê was born . . . usually because Verch was trying to tell Naevros how to live his life.

"He's an intolerable old queck-bug, and I should fire him, as a matter of fact. Only I've long suspected I couldn't manage without him, and now I know it. I always thought of myself as a fairly neat person; I can take care of myself handily when I'm travelling. But one little house seems to generate more filth in a day than I can clear away in three. I'm counting the hours until he returns."

"When will that be?"

"Nearly a month! He got it in his head he wanted to go south where it's warm. I could hardly say no. I hope he hates it down there."

"Couldn't you hire a housekeeper to take care of you while he's gone?"

"I—ah—I made rather a big deal about how I could take care of myself without any help. Somehow I'm going to have to figure out how to do it or I'll never hear the end of his nagging."

"If you could use help—"

"No, no. Thanks. My mess; I'll tend to it. What is *this*, do you think?" He held up a dark strip of something he had excavated from the floor. "Is it a piece of dried meat gone bad, or an article of underclothing worn far longer than it should have been, or . . . ?"

In the end they had to admit that the palimpsest was not in the filthy little room.

"Dollon was also stationed at Thaintower, I think," Aloê said. "Perhaps it's in his room. Assuming they are part of a larger conspiracy." *Headed by you*, Aloê wanted to say but did not.

"Possibly," Naevros said agreeably. "Should we search it, too?"

A cold, clear light went on in Aloê's mind.

"Or it could be in Fungustown," she said, saying something quite different from her thought. "A lot of empty buildings there."

"Er. Yes."

"Maybe I should look in one place and you look in the other?"

"Maybe you should have someone watching your back, Guardian," said Naevros drily, and pointed at the healing silk on her neck.

"Hm," Aloê pretended to consider. "Yes, that's a good point. Maybe I'll pick up Jordel on my way to Fungustown. We can cover more ground that way, too."

Naevros nodded. "You have your ducks in a row, I see. I'll carry on here. Some of the other thains may know something we want to know. And I'll plant a few seeds of doubt about Noreê's leadership, maybe."

Aloê nodded brightly and ran off. She clattered down the stairs, freed Raudhfax from the attentions of the ostlers, and galloped away toward Jordel's.

But after she had crossed a few roads and she saw that Thaintower was lost in the thicket of towers behind her, she turned sharply west and rode straight to Naevros' house, not far from the Old Center.

She believed that Verch had voluntarily left the house of Naevros for a month like she believed the sun was an orange ball of bubbling cheese—that is, not at all (although it did sort of resemble one these days). That old queck-bug loved Naevros more than his own life. So he was gone now because Naevros had wanted him out of the house. Aloê wanted to know why.

The house was locked, of course, but she had not lived with Morlock and his *harven*-kin without learning a great deal about locks—how they could be made, how they could be beaten. The locks at Naevros' house were merely mechanical—they didn't even have eyes or ears! Aloê was inside within moments of her arrival.

Inside, she found the place a bit dusty, but nothing like the sty Naevros had pretended. He'd been lying, of course. She knew it; she felt it through the bond they shared. But she might have revealed herself to him the same way: she must hurry.

First fruits of her search were scraps of a blood-stained palimpsest: Earno's letter to Morlock: the original, she thought, not the one stolen from the Arch of Tidings. The slightest ascent into the visionary realm told her that the blood was Earno's. She scanned the letter quickly then pocketed it. It was of some importance to her husband, but not for this matter.

But the full harvest of her search came in the basement. She found a bloody bagful of spell-anchors. And a body: Denynê. The body of the binder was bound: hand, feet, eyes, and mouth. And . . . it moved.

She was still alive! Aloê's eyes stung with sudden tears and she threw herself to her knees beside the bound binder.

"Denynê!" she whispered. "It's Vocate Aloê! I'm going to untie you. We must get you out of here quickly."

Denynê seemed to be sobbing through her gag. Aloê slit her bonds with the knife from her belt, cutting the gag and blindfold last.

The binder grabbed her and hugged her hysterically, babbling something into her hair.

"What?" Aloê said. "What is it?"

"I didn't believe anyone would come for me," Denynê gasped. "I thought I would die here, wherever this is, in my own filth. I thought no one cared. No one ever has. My family never . . . and then there was the Skein, and that was good. But I understand things so much better than people. They said . . . they said. . . . And now. . . . No one cared. I thought no one cared."

"I damn well do."

"You must think me disgusting. Weeping, snot-nosed coward. Out of control from fear. Not like you."

"We'll settle what you are and what I think of it when we get you the canyon out of here. Do you think you can walk?"

"Oh, yes. I did exercises as I lay here. It's very bad for the muscles to lie idle, even when you're not bound. I should be able to walk."

"You lay here and did exercises, waiting for a chance you didn't think would come, just so you'd be ready when it did. I hate to break it to you, Binder, but that's not what a coward, out of control with fear, would do. I'm going to help you up now, and we'll see what good those exercises did."

Denynê was a little unsteady on her feet, but she could move. They moved, as fast as she could, up the stairs.

Aloê was terrified that they would not get away—that Naevros would appear at the last moment and they would be foiled. She feared his prowess at the sword, his anger and shame when he understood he'd been found out. She wasn't sure she could protect Denynê or herself.

But now they were out on the street in the cool afternoon air. Aloê didn't bother relocking the door. She got Denynê up into Raudhfax's saddle and then mounted behind her.

No one shouted at them as they rode off.

Aloê was exultant. She felt like a poor man who reached into his pocket and found a fistful of coins. She felt like she had when she first dove off Cape Torn into the Bitter Bright Deep. She felt like her heart was an anvil, struck repeatedly by a golden hammer of joy.

She always remembered that feeling, in spite of what happened after.

CHAPTER NINETEEN

Enemies of the Enemy

"I'm sorry to keep you waiting, my dear," Merlin said soothingly to his favorite daughter. He was wheeling in a long table made of glass—long enough to hold a human body. Hers specifically. She could see more glassware—tubing, alembics, and such—through the open archway, where some potion seemed to be distilling itself. But her eyes kept returning to the glass egg and the long glass table next to it. That was where her father proposed to kill her.

"Don't hurry on my account," she remarked conversationally.

"Ha ha ha. Of course, you would feel that way." Now he was assembling a set of surgical tools, taking the bright pieces of metal out of an invisible box under the glass table and laying them out next to the crystal egg and the horror within it. "But," Merlin prattled on as he worked, "when I have to kill someone, I really think it unconscionable to make them wait for it. Especially when I have such warm feelings of personal regard for them, as I have for you."

"Warmly regard my vulva, you scum-bubbling bucket of rancid old pus."

"You were always a bad-tempered selfish girl. Can't you see what this will mean to your mother and me?"

"When was the last time you had a conversation with my mother, as opposed to doing things to her that you thought would be for her benefit?"

"Your mother is rather difficult to have a conversation with these days, on account of her being so very crazy. But I'm confident that when her sanity returns—"

"How could her sanity ever return when she finds you have put her into the eviscerated corpse of her daughter?"

"Now, now. Let's not get hysterical. Most of your viscera will remain intact; really that's essential for my plan."

"And you have a great deal of confidence in your plans, despite all evidence to the contrary?"

"Naturally, I adapt to changing circumstances. A plan is not a contract with the future, but an approach to a problem. As the problem changes, as circumstances change, plans must change to fit. I admit the current plan is very far from my first, best thought. I still think that the dragon's frame is most suitable for the graft, at least temporarily."

"Why not go find another one? There must be quite a few wandering around the Burning Range and its environs."

"I've tried that already, but the graft didn't take."

"I should think not. The bodies must be utterly incompatible."

"You're too material in your thinking, my dear. A shame: you were once such a promising seer. No, the barrier was immaterial. But when I tried implanting your mother into a mandrake corpse—"

"Death and Justice!"

"—I found there was a spiritual connection between the mandrake and *something else* that your mother's psyche responded to. I searched long in visionary wanderings for the answer, but eventually understood. This dragon they worship here as a god: he is connected to every mandrake in the world through some sort of device built into the temple."

"Yes, Morlock says it was a gift from the Two Powers for putting the finger on him."

"A vulgar locution. You do your teachers no credit, young lady."

"Eh."

"None of that now. At your worst you never sounded like *him*."

"Is it this mandrake device that makes Rulgân a suitable host for the *graft*?"

"At first I thought so, but now I think it's incidental. Morlock wounded him, you know, with a magical weapon, Saijok's Bane."

"I remember the story."

"It was his focus of power. It bound the two together in a way I think neither understands. Anyway, that would serve as an immaterial basis to sustain the material graft, once the dragon's brain and other traces of identity were removed. Such was my thought. But all that seems to be otiose at the moment because of this ridiculous religious war."

"Which you started."

"Now there you do me an injustice, my dear. Really, Ambrosia, you do. I came to these people, loosely speaking, who were subject to the basest superstition imaginable, and I freed mind after mind. They really looked upon me as their liberator. They call me Lightbringer, you know."

"Another alias for your collection."

"I do like it. I may start using it generally."

"Not Olvinar, or—"

"Well, that was their idea, too, but I took to it because the God was so oppressively horrible. He really is, you know. And the Enemy of their enemy . . . you know how the rest goes."

"What was the hitch, then?"

"This local god-speaker was the hitch. They hate the God, but they love this Danadhar. Hate is fairly easy to manipulate, but love is more stubborn, more selfless, more trouble all around."

"You might understand it better if you could bring yourself to feel it."

"That's good, coming from you. Bad-tempered, selfish girl." He delicately tested the sharpness of a bonesaw with his thumb and nodded, satisfied.

"So the mandrakes rallied around this Danadhar?"

"They don't like being called mandrakes, Ambrosia. They really don't."

"So?"

"I see what you mean. Well, some of the mandrakes rallied around Danadhar, and some of them rallied around their new friend, Lightbringer the Adversary. Me, in short. And this slow indecisive civil war is the result. They're so terribly reluctant to kill each other, you see. And you can't have a really successful war without a certain amount of killing."

"I know."

"Yes, I suppose you do. Meanwhile, your mother isn't getting any younger, and the sun isn't getting any healthier. I'd resolved to wait the war out— perhaps assassinate this inconvenient god-speaker—when a mantia told me that you were coming. And I think that brings us up to date."

A mantia, a spell of foretelling, was, in Ambrosia's view, a fool's game . . . but then, in so many ways, for all his cunning, her father was a fool. "So," she said, "you're ready to kill me, I take it?"

"Not at all, my dear. Also, a more charitable way to look at it is that I'm giving you the opportunity to keep your mother alive."

Ambrosia looked at the glassy egg in which shadows, flitting lights, and green-gray brain meat floated. "She won't thank you for this, Merlin. Believe me. I know her better than you do."

"You may be right, Ambrosia. I suppose you are right. But I am not doing this to be thanked. Only a fool acts with that motive, and I think you'll concede that I am not a fool."

Ambrosia never had, and never would concede this, but it hardly seemed important to say so just then. Merlin puttered around with his shining instruments of darkness for a while longer and said, "Excuse me, my dear. I have to see how that potion is getting along."

"I give you leave to go," Ambrosia said in her most regal (I-am-the-Regent-and-you're-not) tone.

Merlin snickered and ducked into the next room.

Ambrosia put her head back against the scaly wall. She did not think so much as feel. These might be the last sensations she ever had—the last things she saw, heard, smelled. . . .

A fishy, snaky sort of smell. What had he said about the fish-beast?

. . . your blood would almost certainly have poisoned it . . .

She looked down at the scaly arms imprisoning her. Did she feel a long, slow pulse within them, akin to something in the wall?

. . . your blood would almost certainly have poisoned it . . .

If the arms were alive, they could feel pain. They would react. They might react by crushing her. Yes, it would be a very dangerous risk to take, if she weren't about to die anyway.

. . . your blood . . .

Ambrosia bit her tongue—not metaphorically, but literally, hard enough to draw blood. Then again to ensure a lot of blood. Her mouth filled with it.

She spat the bright, burning blood down on the snaky arms imprisoning her.

The blood of Ambrose, the blood that betrayed their kinship with mandrakes, caused almost anything to burn. Anything but the Ambrosii themselves.

Her heart fell. The blood pooled, fuming, on hollow places in the snake-like arms, but the arms didn't react. The floor below began to burn as the blood dripped on it, but the arms holding her just went on being arms and went on holding her.

Well, it wasn't like she had another plan to fall back on. She wasn't Merlin Ambrosius, adapting to circumstances. She was Ambrosia Viviana, and she made circumstances adapt to her. She spat another mouthful of burning blood on the arms.

Then she saw their surfaces ripple like water. Perhaps the pain impulses had needed to travel all the way to the house's reptile brain, wherever that was, before there came a reaction. Perhaps the blood just needed to burn through the outer, tougher layers of skin before it could be felt. In any case, the arms were feeling it now.

She spat a third time. There were fuming craters in the snaky arms, and their reptilian muscles began to contract: she could see them move through the holes burned in the skin. For a moment she thought the arms were indeed going to crush her, but they just slid around her and contracted into the wall—trying to retreat from the fiery poison of her blood. She fell to the floor among the flames she had kindled.

But the arms carried the poison with them back into the wall. Now the wall began to ripple as the arms had rippled, expanding and contracting in pain.

Ambrosia jumped up and spat more blood directly on the walls.

Merlin came rushing in. "What have you done, you bad girl?" he screamed, just like he used to do when she was a child.

But she was a child no longer. She would have said, *Old man! You have lived long enough!* But her tongue hurt too badly to speak. But she was thinking it, and he seemed to read it in her face. In any event, he snatched up the crystal egg containing Nimue and ran away into his workshop.

Ambrosia grabbed a long serrated blade from the workbench and followed him. Behind her the walls continued to convulse and the fire continued to spread across the wooden floor.

Now she could see Merlin, through several arches, well ahead of her and running as fast as he could. But he was also having trouble hanging on to the glass egg; it almost slipped from his hands several times as she watched.

The fire was now running across the floor faster than Merlin or his daughter, and the gigantic snake or snakes forming the walls were writhing in agony. As they contracted, the inner framework of the strange house screamed: beams split and planks tore apart. A gap opened up in front of Merlin. He tried to dance away from it, but the floor was now sloping, funneling him toward the gap. He fell out of sight, still juggling the gigantic crystal egg.

He wasn't getting away that easy. Ambrosia ran down the slope and jumped into the empty darkness, brandishing her bright, serrated blade like lightning.

CHAPTER TWENTY

End of Deceit

A day and a night gone by, and Aloê at last was ready to act. She and Denynê spent the time hiding in Fungustown. She found a little house with an overrun garden and a fountain, and a little stable in back for Raudhfax. She didn't think it had been occupied long before it was abandoned—and, anyway, a nightmare or two was a small price to pay for the silence and emptiness of the streets around them.

She listened to Denynê's story, helped her heal, and wrote messages. These she brought at night to the League of Silent Women—friends of hers for long generations—and they promised to carry them for her.

They finished a lunch of spring fruits from the garden. Aloê asked Denynê, "Are you ready?"

"Let's get the bastard," said Denynê tightly. It was probably the first time she had used so crude a word. Aloê laughed and they went out to saddle up Raudhfax.

They rode straight through the city to the domed Chamber of the Graith at the ruins of the eastern wall. Aloê dismounted, helped Denynê down, entrusted Raudhfax to one of the watch-thains on the steps, and then leaped up the steps and into the shadows of the atrium.

Maijarra was there, most senior of all the thains; she stood guard alone at the entrance to the domed chamber.

"Vocate Aloê," she said, lowering her long spear and gesturing with it. "The summoners await you and your second within."

"Thanks, Maijarra," said Aloê, and strode past her. When Denynê had entered also, Maijarra shut the double doors and barred them from without.

The two summoners were standing in discussion next to the broken Witness

Stone. Denynê's orange-brown eyes were wide with interest: few outside the Graith had seen the Witness Stone, but she must have heard something of the terrible events during the last Station from her peers in the Skein of Healing. For all Aloê knew, Denynê had been among those called on to treat the spell-freed vocates. Aloê didn't remember her, but there was much from that day that she didn't remember, and some things she wished she could forget.

Bleys seemed to be desperately urging some desperate course; Lernaion's dark, somber face was etched with skepticism. Bleys broke off at Aloê's approach and turned on her in fury. "Well, here were are at your command, madam. I hope you find us prompt upon the hour and that we will not be rebuked for discussing some trivial business of our own instead of waiting in silence for your—"

"Oh, I don't mind," Aloê interrupted airily. In fact, she was as angry as Bleys was, or pretended to be. But she would not let him know that he had gotten to her. "What were you discussing?"

Bleys' mouth snapped twice like an angry dog at the end of his chain.

"Tell her," Lernaion directed.

Bleys' bald head and bat-wing ears grew red as a sunset. He pressed his lips together, as if to imprison words within. Slowly, his color cooled to something not much more ominous than his usual pale pink. Sweat glimmered on his scalp as it cooled.

"Vocate," he said quietly, "we are trying to make right what your husband made so wrong." He gestured curtly at the Stone.

Morlock's sword had shattered the Witness Stone into seven pieces. With astonishment, Aloê saw that they were now four. Somehow, three of the parts had been made to cohere—so closely that they seemed never to have been struck apart.

"Amazing!" she said in honest admiration. "Champion Bleys!"

The ancient summoner was somewhat mollified. "Thank you," he said. "But the next step is somewhat . . . well, we are at a parting of the ways. We may have to choose between preserving the wisdom already implicit in the Stone or remaking it." Then he said irritably, "Is that enough for you? Must you know still more?"

To needle him, Aloê said, "Perhaps you should wait for my husband's return. He is the master of all makers; so the dwarven masters say."

Bleys grew redder than before and seemed to swell up with angry words, but before he could say them Lernaion interposed, "The process is more like healing. When we heal a wounded mind, or a wounded brain, the process often involves forgetting. The Stone is not a brain or a mind, but it was made to work in harmony with them, and seems to function, or fail to function, in similar ways. Which would you choose, Guardian?"

"Heal the Stone," Aloê said without hesitation.

"Yes," Lernaion said. "I agree."

"The knowledge of the past that would be irretrievably lost—" Bleys began.

Lernaion raised a dark hand and silenced him. "My friend," he said gently, "perhaps you are too concerned with the past. It is for us to ensure that the Wardlands has a future."

"I'm too old for this job," Bleys said with a good humor that Aloê found surprising. "That's what you're saying."

"We are both old," Lernaion said, smiling.

"No one is as old as I am. No one in the world. So it seemed to me when I dragged myself out of bed this morning, anyway. Very well, Lernaion: I'll heal the Stone, no matter what the cost. We'll have need of it; you're right about that."

The Summoner of the City, not the oldest but the most senior of all the Guardians in the Graith, smiled with dark lips and turned unsmiling dark eyes to Aloê. "And now to your business."

"The murder of Earno," she reminded him. "Your peer."

"Yes," he conceded. "It is our business as well."

"Not everything has been explained," Aloê said, "and some may have to wait until you, Bleys, have healed the Witness Stone. But the murderer is Naevros syr Tol."

"You surprise me," Lernaion said gravely. He did not look surprised, but you couldn't go by that: his dark, narrow face kept its secrets well. Bleys said nothing at all.

Aloê described the uneven course of the investigation, including the murder of Oluma, the way she had come to suspect Naevros, the rescue of Denynê from Naevros' house, and then she displayed the original of Earno's last letter with its bloody finger marks, the stolen spell-anchors.

The summoners heard her out without asking questions. They looked at the evidence with evident interest but did not touch or handle it.

The doors of the dome chamber were unbarred and Naevros syr Tol entered. Thain Maijarra peered into the room after him, frank curiosity in her bright brown eyes, but she closed the doors and barred them anyway.

Aloê did not bother to repeat her account for Naevros. She did not meet his eye or acknowledge his presence in any way. Neither did he speak.

"Well met, Vocate Naevros," Bleys said finally. "The Graith's vengeancer here claims that you are our murderer."

Naevros still did not say anything. He seemed to be looking at Aloê but she would not meet his eye.

"Well, Vengeancer!" said Bleys. "I can lighten your mind by showing you that your suspicions are false. It's too bad that you didn't ask a few questions before you made this startling suggestion. Naevros was abroad in the Northhold before, during, and after the murder of our peer. He was seen by countless persons."

"That doesn't surprise me," Aloê said. "I saw him there myself, shortly before the slain summoner left the North. But nonetheless, I think Naevros had left the North some time before."

"You contradict yourself."

"I do not. The Naevros in the North, the Naevros you say was commonly seen, was a simulacrum. It passed by me without a glance. But you can see how the genuine article cannot refrain from gawping at me."

From the corner of her eye she saw, and with her insight she felt, Naevros recoil in pain from her words.

"A woman's argument," Bleys said dismissively.

"Yes."

"It's not proof, Vocate."

She shook her hand, still holding the letter and the bags of anchors; they rattled like dice in a gambler's cup. "This is proof. The kidnapping of Denynê is proof. The murder of Oluma is proof."

"We do not know that Naevros killed your other second—"

"I *saw* him!" Denynê shouted, her orange face tinted dark with fury. "He was standing over her body with a bloody blade in one hand and the bag of anchors in another! He chased me down and knocked me out, and when I awoke—I—I—I—"

Denynê's eyes became unfocused and Aloê guessed she was returning to those dreadful hours when she was bound, gagged, and blindfolded, waiting for death. She touched the binder's arm with her free hand, and Denynê broke off, sobbing.

"Well," Bleys said bleakly, "I don't believe it. Not yet. Why should Naevros kill Oluma but not Denynê?"

"Oluma was his accomplice. He got to her somehow, just as he got to that woman who is the Arbiter of the Peace in Big Rock. Denynê, however, was true to me. He could not be sure what she knew, and he might have seen some value in questioning her to find out what she knew."

Lernaion looked away from Aloê and glared at Naevros. His normally impassive face betrayed his anger and contempt. "Vocate Naevros, you shame us all. This was ill done."

"I will make it right," Naevros said quietly.

"Do so."

Denynê lurched against Aloê and began to cough up blood. Aloê cried out without words and grabbed the binder before she fell to the floor. Aloê looked into Denynê's tawny eyes, gaping wide with surprise and fear, and saw that it was too late. Denynê was dying . . . died . . . was dead.

Behind Denynê, Naevros stood holding a bloody sword in his left hand.

Aloê let her evidence—letter, anchors, dead witness—fall to the floor between her and the murderer.

"Won't you finish the job, Vocate?" she said, looking him in the eye for the first time that day. Her hands were empty and open, waiting. If he moved to attack her, she would close with him. No one, not even Morlock, could defeat Naevros with the sword, but she liked her chances if it came to hand-to-hand.

He did not move to attack her. He endured her gaze for a moment and looked away.

"You were foolish to entrust your evidence to us, Vocate," Lernaion said coolly. "Did you not think that Naevros might have accomplices in the Graith?"

"On the contrary!" Aloê said. "I knew that he did. For one thing, there was Dollon, the thain who tried to kill me. He broke his neck trying to escape when he heard Naevros' voice: Naevros must have had some power of fear over him. Then there was Bavro, the thain who stole the palimpsest of Earno's last letter. He obviously expected Naevros to come to his aid. Then there was all this magic." Aloê disdainfully kicked the bag of anchors where they had fallen by her right foot. "That was never among Naevros' talents. He needed help for it. I had hoped that it was only one of these *women* whom he can get to do *anything* for him." She noticed Naevros flinch when she said *women* and *anything*—exactly as she had meant him to.

"But, of course," she continued to address Lernaion, "I thought of you."

"You're boasting now, Vocate," Lernaion said shrewdly, "playing for time. We—"

"'Shut your lying mouth,'" Aloê quoted, and smiled in his face.

Lernaion froze. Then he shook his gray head sadly. "So you heard that."

"I heard it."

"It has nothing to do with this, really."

"I would need more than your word, Guardian, to accept that as true. But it doesn't matter. It got me thinking along these lines. Then there was the magic. That *is*, famously or infamously, one of Bleys' skills. And you were both here in A Thousand Towers when the palimpsest was stolen. If the thains were merely agents, as I suspected, who was their principal? A senior Guardian seemed most likely. I suspected you both, but only one was really necessary. But now I see you are both complicit."

"I didn't know about Earno's murder in advance," Lernaion said mildly.

"But you approved of it after the fact?"

"Yes."

Aloê did not expect this. She found she had nothing to say.

"We are not Arbiters of the Peace," Bleys said irritably, "nor half-witted lawmen gibbering of justice in the unguarded lands! We are Guardians. We don't judge; we defend. The Guard must be maintained."

"You have killed Guardians and the Guarded. And to justify yourself you claim you have done it to defend the Wardlands?"

The two summoners looked at each other in surprise.

"Of course," said Lernaion finally. "What did you think we did it for? Money?"

Aloê laughed harshly. "Or love? Is that what drew you to their noble cause, Vocate?" she asked Naevros. "Was that what led you to do their knife-work? Will you kill me now, too, to protect the guilty secret that you share? And to protect the realm, of course."

Naevros looked at her and took a step back. He put his right arm on the dais. He raised his sword and slashed it down, cutting off his right hand.

He held the spouting stump and the bloody sword both toward Aloê, as if they were a great gift. "Take the other hand," he said thickly, as if he were drunk. "Take everything that I am. Take everything that I could have been."

She would not pity him, not with Denynê lying murdered at her feet.

"What you are isn't much," she said coldly. "What you could have been, you cannot give me."

He fell, unconscious, across the corpse of his last victim.

She crouched down and undid her belt. It would do for a tourniquet, she hoped. As far as she was concerned, he could die. She'd prefer it that way. But he knew things the Graith would want to know, and it was clear he would talk without much prompting.

"And so, summoners?" she asked, as she twisted the belt tight around Naevros' severed wrist. "Your henchman is fallen. Your plot is exposed. But I suppose you could still try to kill me before my peers arrive."

"So you have already spread the tale?" Lernaion asked sadly.

"I told you she would," Bleys answered, sourly. "Nonetheless, madam, your peers will *not* arrive as soon as you think. We instructed Maijarra to admit no one after Naevros."

"Maijarra is a good fighter," Aloê acknowledged. "I've sparred with her myself. But my friends will be coming in force. Noreê is marshalling all her thains."

"She is not the only Guardian with a personal following," Bleys replied. "Had you not guessed?"

Aloê had not. But she should have, she realized: the actions of Dollon and Bavro should have warned her.

From outside the door, and the street beyond, there were the sounds of combat. To maintain the Guard, Guardians were fighting each other in the streets of the Wardlands' greatest city.

CHAPTER TWENTY-ONE

The Chains of the God

Danadhar and Morlock strode down the jail corridor side by side. Deor and Kelat fell in behind them. The other freed prisoners, the Gray Folk, stood by and held out their hands toward Danadhar as he passed.

"*Ar ryn jyrthin?*" Deor asked Kelat in Dwarvish: *Do you understand me?*

"Yes," Kelat admitted, in Ontilian. "The Regent wanted some of us to learn Dwarvish so that we could deal with workers from the Endless Empire. But I don't speak it very well."

"No one does—certainly not in my family. You have unsuspected depths, Prince Uthar."

"So does your mother."

Dwarvish mating practices made this insult pointless indeed, but Deor laughed politely and punched Kelat on the forearm.

They found their packs and weapons in the vestibule of the jail under a shelkhide tarp. The other prisoners waited, politely or reverently, until their saint had passed before filing out into the coldly luminous spring night.

One of them ran back inside—a youngling with a long jaw and bluish scales. "St. Danadhar!" he cried. "The Enemy! The Enemy is coming for us!"

From outside in the dark they heard the cries of terror and exultation, "Olvinar! Olvinar! The Enemy!"

"Morlock," Deor said urgently.

"Yes," said the crooked man. He drew his dark, accursed blade and ran out into the night, Deor and Kelat at his heels.

"*Ruthenen!*" Danadhar called after them, but Morlock ran on, slithering through the crowd of Gray Folk when he could, shoving them out of the way when he had to.

Soon they saw what the Gray Folk had seen and paused to take it in.

The gigantic, cable-laid house at the north end of town was moving. The tower at the top that looked like a head—that *was* a head—wove back and forth and uttered a shriek like a straight-line wind running down a mountain-side of pines.

There was red light coming from the center of the coil.

"*Rukhjyrn! Rukhjyrn!*" screamed someone in the crowd. *The dragon-sickness! The dragon-sickness!*

The gigantic snake began to move, uncoiling itself, reaching for the distant stars, shaking mundane fire from it as it moved.

"Wait!" Deor shouted, but Morlock had shouldered off his pack and was already running. There were human figures moving, dark outlines in the cascade of fire.

Morlock dashed into the burning torrent, dodging left and right to avoid planks and beams, heedless of the heat and fire.

Danadhar came to a halt beside Deor. "What happened to the Olvinar's house?" he asked, gasping.

"Ambrosia Viviana, I think," said Deor. "Look!"

One of the two human figures was trapped under something. The other was standing near, a strangely shining ovoid in one hand, a long blade in the other. And a beard—the dark outline definitely sported a beard. "The old bastard!" he muttered in Wardic.

"It is the Olvinar," Danadhar said.

"It is Merlin Ambrosius," Deor said, not disagreeing.

The trapped figure must be Ambrosia; no one else could have lived in that chaos of fire. Before Merlin could strike at her, Morlock was there. He hit the old man with the fist holding his sword. The bearded figure went flying, lost his grip on his blade, juggled the shining egg wildly, almost fell but did not quite.

Ambrosia's voice stabbed through the flames. "Kill him, Morlock! Kill him!"

Morlock raised his damned sword.

"Morlock!" shouted Deor. "No! *Xoth dhun!* The bond of blood!"

Morlock's twisted shadow paused—and sheathed the sword. He turned to where his sister lay trapped.

Danadhar ran from Deor's side into the flames. His garments were afire at the first step, but he ignored them, going to where Morlock stood.

Merlin's dark shape steadied, took hold of the shining egg with both hands. He seemed to look at his offspring for a moment, then turned away and was lost in the flames.

Together, Morlock and Danadhar hefted the burning beam off Ambrosia and she rolled to her feet. "Where is that demented old cutthroat?" Deor heard her demand.

He did not hear whatever Morlock and Danadhar said to her, if anything. The three came together through the burning wrack and out of it.

It was Danadhar, rather than Ambrosia, who collapsed when they emerged from the flames—except for those still flickering among the rags that had been his clothing.

"Haven't firewalked for an age," he said apologetically, struggling to his feet. "An intoxicating experience. Most mrmrmrblble."

Morlock took off his smoldering cloak and handed it to the Gray One.

"Yes. Yes. Thanks, *ruthen*." Danadhar took the cloak and wrapped it around his midsection as a makeshift kilt. "Wouldn't do for the Gray Folk to see their saint naked. Though they'd find a way to explain it as a miracle." He waved a clawed hand vaguely at the fire and the gigantic snake slithering off into the night. "Find a way to put this on me. 'Nother miracle o' St. Danadhar. Pardon me." He put his hands up to his snout and literally held his mouth shut for a few moments.

"I'm sorry, *ruthenen*, and new friend Kelat," he said when he released himself. "Do you not get fire-drunk?" he asked Ambrosia and Morlock.

"I feel a kind of high," Ambrosia admitted.

"Eh. I prefer a drink-drunk," Morlock said.

"We must empty a few jars sometime," Danadhar said. "*Ruthen*," he continued, speaking to Ambrosia, "I am Danadhar, god-speaker for this unhappy town. I am glad to meet you. I have heard much of your exploits among the Vraids."

Ambrosia took his proffered hand without apparent fear, which is more than Deor could have done: apparently the Gray Folk around here didn't bother trimming their nails. "I am pleased to meet you, too, God-speaker. I have heard almost nothing of you or your folk."

"That's how we prefer it, mighty Regent of the Vraids. We have few friends among the Other Ilk or the Little—the dwarves, I mean."

"You have one more as of tonight."

Danadhar spread his claws wide and placed his scaly palms on his ventral shield—evidently a gesture of respect.

"Listen, God-speaker, my brother may or may not have mentioned it, but we have good reason for trying to speak to your God. Is there any way you can get us across the battle lines? Both sides seem to respect you."

"You can speak to my God here or anywhere, Lady Ambrosia. But I take it you mean the evil avatar that lives in the temple."

"I do."

Danadhar bowed his head. "Yes," he said. "I can and I will. I must ask you not to trust him."

Kelat snorted. Danadhar turned to look at him in surprise.

"In Vraidish," Deor explained, "that means, 'I think you can count on us following your excellent advice.'"

Whether godstruck or godhater, the Gray Folk did indeed honor Danadhar. As he led the four travelers away from the fire, many of the Gray Folk who had gathered to watch went down on their knees and shouted his name. The others, godhaters perhaps, put their hands on their bellies and bowed.

One Gray stepped in front of them. He had the braided belt of an excantor, and he carried a blood-stained pike in his hand.

"Saint Danadhar," he said tentatively.

"I am Danadhar. I don't know what a saint is."

"Those Other Ilk with you—it was the Olvinar's order that they should be kept in confinement."

"The Enemy is gone. You see behind us the ruin of his house."

The excantor closed his eyes, opened them. "Then the rebellion is over."

"No," said Danadhar firmly. "If you look at that thing poisoning the temple and rebel against it, the rebellion goes on. May it never be over. Believe or disbelieve in the God, but rebel against evil when you see it—and the more powerful it is, the more you must rebel. I charge you with it, excantor."

The excantor stood straighter. "Then I must not let you pass. I must carry out the Olvinar's commands, though he is no longer here to give them."

"You must do as you think right. You may kill me, if you like, as I see you have killed others of our blood. But, unless you do, I will pass by you and bring these four to the temple."

From the way Morlock was standing, Deor knew that he was about to draw his sword. If he did, the conscientious excantor would go to seek the truth or untruth of all religions in the afterlife, of this Deor had no doubt. But would that bring the godhaters in the crowd down on them.

But the excantor lowered his pike and turned away.

Danadhar led them into the burning heart of the city where the Gray Folk fought for and against their God and each other. Each time weapons were directed at him or the four travelers, he talked calmly and rationally and urgently, and they passed on unharmed.

What he could not prevent, or did not try to prevent, was this: they were followed. The godstruck and the godhaters, silent warriors and singing excantors, every Gray One who saw them seemed to join the parade.

They came at last to the temple, stark in the moonlight.

"I will not go in with you," Danadhar said quietly. "The hate I feel for the avatar is dangerous for my soul."

Morlock grabbed him by the arm, released him. They nodded at each other. Morlock vaulted up the steps of the temple and the other three travelers followed more slowly.

"I've never met a god before," Deor whispered to Kelat. "What's it like?"

"I don't remember it very well," said the Vraid.

The interior of the temple was a study in gold and red. Gold coins and objects covered the floor of the many-pillared temple, and the whole was lit only by the fiery eyes of the dragon who lay across this immense hoard.

It was a dragon . . . and it was a device. Cables ran into the dragon's fiery eyes and into his ears. They attached him to a crystalline machine anchored to the gold-heaped floor. The machine, the dragon's eyes, and the gigantic jewel imprisoned in his metallic right foreleg, all radiated a fiery flickering light.

Angular elements moved within the crystalline device; images seemed to come and go. Deor itched to take the thing apart and see how it worked, but he put his hands under his arms and tried to quell the feeling. He avoided looking the dragon in the eye. He'd had one case of dragonspell a long time ago and hadn't enjoyed it much.

Of course, I knew you were coming, said the dragon.

Morlock grunted. "Eh. Here we are, anyway."

Then the Graith will consider my proposal?

"No."

Perhaps you yourselves will make the trade that I proposed—will guide me to a fresh world in return for what I have learned?

"No."

Will you aid me against the godhaters who would enter this temple and slay me?

"No."

Then why have you come?

"To learn what you know of the dying sun."

You ask everything; you offer nothing. We will reach no agreement on these terms, Ambrosius.

"We'll save the world, if we can. If you are in the world, that's not nothing."

If the world could have been saved, I would have saved it. I am not called the God here for no reason.

"But you are not, in fact, God," Morlock pointed out. "We may be able to do what you can't."

Doubtful.

"We destroyed the Two Powers."

They are worshipped still in Vakhnhal and through the Anhikh Kômos. Their missionaries walk west and south and north. For all I know, their apostles sail to Qajqapca.

"You see through countless eyes. Have you seen the Two Powers since they nailed you here?"

The dragon's tail moved restlessly across his hoard. *No*, he admitted at last.

"Then?"

No! Nothing for nothing! That's my law, Ambrosius.

"If the world dies, you will die and all your knowledge will be lost."

You can't save the world. Old Ambrosius could not. I cannot. No one can.

"Convince us."

Nothing for nothing.

Outside the temple, Danadhar was speaking to the crowd. They could hear no words, but they did hear the thunder of the crowd's response; it shook the pillars of the temple.

"I think your time here is done, Rulgân Silverfoot," Morlock said. "Where will you spend the last days of the dying world?"

The dragon snarled.

Morlock waited.

Deor almost spoke, but Ambrosia caught his eye and shook her head.

Nothing for nothing! the dragon said. *If I tell you what you want to know, will you help me escape from here?*

Morlock considered briefly. "Yes," he said.

The dragon submerged his snout in gold and grumbled a bit. Then he raised up his face and said, *Agreed. I will self-bind to tell you what I know. You will self-bind to assist me to escape, if there is any trouble. There is going to be trouble, from what I see out in the town square.*

"No binding magics," Morlock said. "You'll have to trust me."

The dragon glared and lashed his tail, sending gold coins skittering around the temple chamber. Morlock looked Rulgân in the eye and waited.

Agreed! the dragon rumbled at last.

"Then."

The dragon spoke.

Ambrosius, when last you saw me I was very new in my godhood. I could use the temple of the mandrakes to see through their eyes and ears, but I could not control their wills. Nor can I always do so now. I must lure a mandrake into surrendering its will to mine, a long, tedious business sometimes. The first was Skellar, who you may remember as god-speaker here on your last visit. He walked abroad, servile to my will, unable to live as a mandrake or be reborn as a dragon.

It amused me to send him to places he hated to go. For instance, he feared water, so I made him swim across the Sea of Stones. He feared the Little Cousins, so I sent him as my emissary to the Endless Empire under the Blackthorns. And he feared the cold, so I sent him north to the end of the world.

His eyes were my eyes, and his ears were my ears, but his pain was not my pain. I left him will enough to seek his own survival when threatened, but not enough to resist my commands. He spent some time in the city of werewolves, Wuruyaaria; you would

be amused to hear his adventures there, perhaps. But the geas I placed on him drove
him ever further north, through the grim, bright rind of the world where beasts become
strange, until he stood at the furthest point north where a beast with two feet may walk;
beyond was only sky, blue emptiness like Merlin's eyes.

There is a bridgehead there, where the world ends, and the bridge runs through the
sky into another world. Standing on the bridge was a thing that had neither hands nor
feet nor body nor anything that could be seen. But it was there: Skellar felt the imprint
of its angular intelligence on his own.

He stood there for a long time, void of purpose. I had told him to go north but had
not said what he should do when there.

The presence on the bridge spun a mouth made of ice in the middle air. It used the
mouth to say, "Why are you here?"

"I was sent," Skellar answered.

"Who sent you?"

"God."

"Which god?"

"The God."

"Was it one of the Two Powers?"

Skellar hesitated. "No."

"The-one-you-would-call-I," said the thing on the bridgehead, "senses an associa-
tion. Is the God who sent you the Balancer?"

Skellar thought. It was difficult for him because I had not allowed him to do much
of this since I took him over. "I don't know," he said after a time—a great deal of time,
it seemed to me, when I assimilated his memories.

"Is your God akin to the Two Powers?"

Now Skellar thought of the day when I came to his town, and the miracles the
Two Powers worked on my behalf, and how he helped them install me in the temple. So
he said, "Yes."

"You are to report to whom-you-would-call-me," the presence said.

"I don't understand," Skellar said.

The presence seized his mind, broke it open like the seal on a message, and read it.

That was when I noticed what was happening. You cannot always be looking out
of every pair of eyes available to you—not when you have as many of them as I do. But
the presence now touched the bond that pertained between me and my mandrake.

"Who are you?" the presence said to me, through Skellar.

I took the time I needed to assimilate Skellar's memories. The presence waited: they have no impatience, these things—no real sense of time.

"I am the one true God of the mandrakes," I said. "Who are you?"

"You would not understand the-one-you-call-me."

"Why not?"

"Because you would call the-one-you-would-call-me me."

"That appears to me to be nonsense, and I require the services of my mandrake."

It tried to seize control of my will through the bond, but I was ware of it and resisted. We fought much of a day and night in the arena of Skellar's mind: I watched the shadows change, grow, diminish, change.

In the end it seized Skellar's mind and dragged it from his body, over the edge of the world and across the bridge that spans the abyss.

I let the bond persist. Why not? Skellar would not be much use anymore, even if he lived, so the knowledge I gained from his suffering would be the last yield I could expect from him.

I can't tell you how much time passed, since beyond the barrier of the world I found neither sun nor moons nor stars nor anything that I could understand as marking time or change.

There are no people there. I soon understood this. Each of these presences was the same as the other—like different coins, from different places, different writing on them, but all the same, too: stack them one on another and you cannot tell one from the other.

The presence who had taken Skellar and me dragged us to a place where several other presences were. They merged or conferred or something. Now it was the same presence, but more forceful, with more knowledge. They gathered other pieces, apparently at random, and the presence grew.

They did not speak to me anymore. They made patterns of knowledge and they expected me to fit mine into theirs. Perhaps I did! Not much of what I knew would be of interest to them. But I knew that the Wastelands had been freed of the soul-killing power that dwelt there, and that the Two Powers were no longer to be found abroad in the world. Perhaps they know that now, too.

Most of what they knew, I could not understand. But I saw that they were hostile to light, and life, and they had a plot to kill the sun and pass into our world after its death.

I was losing myself in their patterns . . . becoming the kind of nothing that each of them was. I saw with my other eyes that much time had passed, and I broke the bond with Skellar. His mind may still live and suffer there, but I cannot reach it.

That was a generation of men or mandrakes ago. Now we see the sun dying, and the world with it. Is it any wonder that I seek escape?

Morlock stood listening intently, his head bowed, staring past the dragon as if he were looking all the way to the end of the world.

"Then," he said at last.

The dragon roared in fury that shook the pillars of his temple. *Will you speak in whole sentences, you vague, grunting gutworm!*

"Not about this," Morlock said. "Not to you."

The dragon grumbled into his gold and then said, *I care not. Fulfill your word or break it, Ambrosius.*

"Wait," said Kelat, causing Deor and Ambrosia to glance at him in surprise.

The dragon looked at him, a deadly amusement in his fiery eyes. *Yes, son of man?*

"You stole my mind, when I was last here. I demand . . . I demand compensation."

What I steal is mine. Your mind was mine, not yours, because I could take it. I do not buy or sell.

"Then I will kill you."

Men have killed dragons on occasion, but I have never been one of them.

"I'm with him," Deor said impulsively. "You owe the—you owe Kelat some answers. Your agreement with Morlock doesn't bind me."

The dragon looked at Morlock. Morlock said nothing. He glanced at Ambrosia. She shrugged impatiently and pointed out the door of the temple, where Danadhar's voice could be heard, a lone ship sailing against a storm of shouting.

What do you want? the dragon said reluctantly. *The gold I am leaving for my spellbound servants to bring away. Do you want some of it? Take it.*

Kelat seemed repelled. Deor could understand it. Blood has no price. . . . This grief, this shame was like that.

"Answer a question," Deor suggested.

"Yes!" said Kelat eagerly. "You put a gem in my head to control me. How? Who made it?"

Old Ambrosius, of course, the dragon said. *He, too, broke the Wards, through some knowledge of his own he would not share. I dealt with him through agents and the spellbound—never trusting him, you see. And I was right: all along he was plotting to attack me.*

"Old Ambrosius," whispered Kelat.

"Also, Merlin," Deor observed. "Also, Olvinar. And many another name."

"Lightbringer lately, I understand," Ambrosia said wryly. Morlock looked at her incredulously and she said, "Yes, I thought that would amuse you, brother."

This is very warm and cozy, the dragon remarked sourly, *and I'm sure it's very amusing. But those mandrakes outside are preparing to enter and resolve their religious disputes at my expense. They'll kill you, too, I think: the god-speaker is having trouble talking them out of it. Time to keep your word or break it, young Ambrosius.*

Morlock drew his black, shining blade and descended into the hoard. He waded through the gold until he reached the crystalline device. He paused to examine it and the shining cables passing out of it.

"This is a very intricate and beautiful device," he said.

Yes. Yes. It feels almost like a part of me. There is no chance to bring it along when I leave, I suppose?

"None. This is only the visible extrusion; it is built all through this temple."

The dragon groaned sadly.

Morlock paused again to pick up a piece of gold. "This metal seems even denser and heavier than gold," he said to the dragon.

The dragon said nothing, but opened his many-fanged mouth in a predatory smile.

"A dead dragon is heavier than lead," Morlock said. "Do you draw something from the metal that helps you fly?"

You expect an answer? the dragon said.

"You've given the answer, worm," Deor muttered under his breath. Morlock, too, seemed pleased with the dragon's ambiguous response. He nodded and flipped the coin away.

Morlock approached the dragon's face. Deor's fingers and toes curled, as if he were standing on the edge of a precipice or riding a hippogriff through the middle air. But Morlock showed no signs of fear as he came within reach of the dragon's long, wolf-like jaws. He looked closely at the cables sinking into the dragon's eyes and earholes.

"Are you ready?" he asked Rulgân, who only growled in answer.

This was enough for Morlock. Using his left hand, he gripped the cable coming out of the dragon's right eye; using his right hand, he cut through the cable with Tyrfing.

The dragon shrieked.

Morlock did the same with the other three cables, and each time the dragon shrieked fiery despair and poison smoke like mist filled the temple chamber.

The ends of the cables were still lodged in the dragon's head. Morlock gestured at one of them.

Yes, hissed the dragon.

Morlock sheathed his sword and took hold of the cable with both hands. He pulled.

The dragon roared his agony, writhing on his gold bed, pounding the pillars and the floor with his tail, sending fire and smoke throughout the temple chamber. Pillars were destroyed; sections of the roof fell in. Ambrosia, Deor, and Kelat tried to keep to the least dangerous parts of the chamber, their eyes on Morlock in case he needed assistance. He did not pause until the dragon's eyes and ear holes were free from obstructions.

The noise from within only increased the noise from without. Now Deor could hear words in the cries. "Kill the God!" "Kill the outsiders before they can kill the God!" "Vengeance and freedom!" The crowd liked that and repeated it a lot: "Vengeance and freedom!"

No sentiment could have pleased Deor's dwarvish heart more, except that he feared that he and his would be caught up in that wave of vengeance.

Rulgân rose up on his back legs, towering over Morlock. Deor rushed to stand by him, in case Rulgân attacked, and he heard Kelat and Ambrosia wading through gold in his wake.

But Rulgân didn't attack. He put his narrow, winged back against the cracked roof of the temple and pushed; the roof split apart, showering timber, stone, and mortar. The sky was open to him now: he could escape his erstwhile worshippers.

Coated with dust and grit, he was pale, like the ghost of a dragon. He looked down in fury and contempt at the four travellers at his feet.

But he roared, *If I let them kill you, who'll save the world?* He reached down and scooped them up, Ambrosia and Morlock in one clawed foot, Deor and Kelat in the other. He lifted them over his fuming head and leapt straight up into the sky.

Deor was utterly aghast. He watched with horror as the dragon's wings unfolded like sails and then beat back to drive them deeper into the sky. The fire-scarred town below spun dizzily in the dark, fell away below and behind. The stars were gone. The moons were gone. There was nothing but the stench of the dragon and Kelat's terrified face, which Deor proceeded to vomit onto. He would have been ashamed indeed, except that Kelat vomited more or less simultaneously.

"This is the worst!" Deor kept telling himself. "Nothing on this terrible journey will ever get worse than this!"

Half of the dark dragon-lit world began to grow gray. That part was the sky, Deor guessed. The still-dark part the ground. But sometimes it was above, sometimes below, as the dragon spun crazily through the air. The horizon ahead of them had rough, saw-tooth edges: mountains.

They were falling. They were falling. They were falling.

The dragon stalled in the air, just above the ground, and released them from his claws. He flew away into the still-dark east without another word.

They lay on the slope without moving for a while. Deor heard someone retching and was dimly glad that he was done with all that. Then his body was trying to vomit even though there was nothing left for his belly to give but stinking bitterness.

As they lay there, a storm walked south from the mountains. The snow-flakes began to fall thick about them as the day's light struggled to be seen in the west. They would have to move soon or freeze to death.

It was the first of Harps, the first full day of summer.

PART THREE

A Cold Summer

Some say the world will end in fire,
Some say in ice.
From what I've tasted of desire
I hold with those who favor fire.
But if it had to perish twice,
I think I know enough of hate
To say that for destruction ice
Is also great
And would suffice.

—Robert Frost, "Fire and Ice"

Endless Empire

A dwarf in a hat as bright as the sun was standing over Morlock. His red beard was braided with gold, and there was gold and silver work in all his scarlet-colored clothes. Even his boots were gilded. Of more immediate interest was the spear in his hand, its point made of mundane but effective steel.

"Shouldn't sleep here," the dwarf said in harshly accented Ontilian.

"Praise the Day, watcher," Morlock replied in Dwarvish. "I am Morlock Ambrosius, also called syr Theorn, *harven coruthen* to the Elder of the Seven Clans under Thrymhaiam." They were clearly at the foot of the Dolich Kund, "the River of Gold"—the only safe pass between the lands north and south of the Blackthorn/Whitethorn Range. It also marked the division between the Blackthorn and the Whitethorn Mountains. The dwarves of the Endless Empire, under the Blackthorn Range, never entered the Whitethorns for reasons that they did not explain. But they did recognize kinship with the dwarves under Thrymhaiam. It was not beyond belief that they could hope for help here.

"Oh," said the dwarf. He rubbed the tip of his nose with the butt of his spear, handling the heavy weapon as lightly as if it were a pen. "Still shouldn't sleep here. Other Ilk known to die in the mountains."

"Thanks," Morlock said briefly. He stood up and turned his back on the spear-carrier, partly to return discourtesy for discourtesy, but primarily to check on the well-being of his comrades.

Ambrosia was sitting up, looking on with sour amusement. She returned his nod. Deor was in a bad way, and Kelat was worse, both of them splashed with each other's vomit. It was an evil gray-green in the cold, snowy morning's light—and that was good: it must have carried a good deal of dragon venom out of their systems.

"Any maijarra leaf in your pack?" Morlock asked his sister.

"No."

"Eh."

"Can you expand on that, Morlock?"

"Tea from maijarra leaves protects against venom."

"Oh. I see what you mean. We must have inhaled a good deal of the stuff. No wonder I'm feeling woozy!"

"Yes." Morlock looked around. His pack was missing. Well, not missing exactly: he had left it on the floor in Rulgân's former temple. It was a mild nuisance, at worst, although he was sorry to lose the books he had brought with him from the Wardlands. He had also brought some maijarra leaves, knowing that they would confront Rulgân.

He eased Deor's pack off his shoulders. The eye among the fastenings recognized him and undid themselves when he spoke to them. Inside the pack was a great many things—too many, in Morlock's judgment. But there was a bundle of simples, including maijarra leaf.

"We'll need fire—somewhere out of the wind." He glanced around and pointed at a hollow free from snow.

"Right," Ambrosia agreed. "You take Deor; I'll carry Kelat."

They hustled their unconscious companions over to the hollow. Ambrosia set up an Imperfect Occlusion overhead while Morlock made a fire out of some scrub bushes. The dwarf with the sun-bright hat followed them and watched what they did carefully but didn't interfere.

Presently Morlock and Ambrosia were sipping tea from sheckware mugs. They had wrapped their unconscious comrades in their cloaks and put them near the fire so that they would not be in danger from the cold.

Morlock said nothing through all of this, and Ambrosia very little. Her red-rimmed eyes met his and she smiled furiously.

Morlock looked at the spear-carrier, who seemed to shiver within his finery, and he said, "Join us. If your watch permits."

Eagerly, the dwarf laid aside his spear and sat down at the little fire. "Thanks, bold strangers!" he said. "I thought you merely victims of dragon-spell or some other such truck, but now I see how wrong I was. What were your names again? You are called Ambrosius?"

Morlock nodded. "Among other things." He sipped his tea. The maijarra decoction was metallic and unpleasant, and in large quantities it was itself a poison. But he wasn't drinking it for pleasure. Also, it was warm.

The watch-dwarf looked at Ambrosia, who volunteered nothing and did not look at him. After a few moments he said to Morlock, "Any kinship to the Regent of the Vraids, then?"

"I am Ambrosia Viviana," said Morlock's sister in a voice colder than the white wind.

The dwarf squawked and leapt to his feet. He ran off upslope into the storm, leaving his spear behind.

"Ha," Ambrosia said, and drank her tea.

Presently the watch-dwarf returned. With him was a company of dwarves, also resplendent in scarlet and gold. In their midst was one who seemed to be half a head taller, but in fact was teetering along on boots with thick soles.

"Great Regent and true ruler of the Vraids," said the tall one, bowing as low as he dared from his perch and doffing his bright hat, "Lady Ambrosia Viviana, welcome again to the Endless Empire! Won't you come under with us and share a few words and a dish of hot mushrooms? The Lorvadh of the Year hurries hither to greet you."

"We're comfortable here," Ambrosia said, as indifferent to the dwarves' belated courtesy as to the truth. "The Lorvadh may come out here, if he chooses."

Morlock was not comfortable, and he suspected his sister was less so. But no doubt she had her reasons. He pulled some dried fish from Deor's pack and handed a piece of it to Ambrosia. She made a face, then bit a chunk off and chewed it like jerky.

The commander stuttered for a while, but as he managed to say nothing that was obviously a word, there was no occasion to answer him. He staggered off atop his stilty shoes and left his company bemused behind him. After some whispered discussion, they formed up in lines and stood with their spears upright, like an honor guard.

The dark day was approaching noon and the snow had stopped when a lone figure approached, wrapped in a cloak of blue and gold, a circlet of electrum on his head.

"Lady Ambrosia!" said the newcomer. "I ran here like a rabbit as soon as I heard you were passing though the Dolich Kund. Won't you—won't you please come under with me? I can offer you a steambath, mushrooms, beer, conversation, or simply a decent bed to rest on for a night."

"Well, I don't know," said Ambrosia. "We're rather in a hurry. What do you think, Morlock? Lorvadh Vyrn, this is my brother, Morlock Ambrosius, master of all makers and the deadliest blade in the universal world."

"Save one," Morlock pointed out.

"Honored," said the Lorvadh briefly to Morlock. "I'm sure our makers will be glad to receive you among the work levels."

Ambrosia frowned.

"Or rather—really—since you are the brother of our ally and friend the Lady Ambrosia—I cannot do enough for you, but I promise I will try. Won't you come in? I'm afraid the weather will make you unwell."

"Eh."

"My brother will be pleased to accept your invitation," Ambrosia said, rising. "And so, I suppose, must I be. Have your people bring along our baggage and our friends, won't you? Treat them kindly; the one is a king's son, the other a trusted counsellor of the Elder of Theorn Clan."

She and the Lorvadh walked off together side by side.

Morlock got to his feet. He saw the first watch-dwarf at his side, stooping to recover his spear.

"What's a Lorvadh?" Morlock asked him.

"A kind of king, I guess," the watcher said. "The Greater Fifteen elect one of their number to rule through the year."

"Hm." Morlock stooped and picked up Deor and put him over one shoulder. Then he hefted Kelat over the other. He walked off after Ambrosia with slow, short steps.

It was undignified, perhaps. But he would not leave his friends to be carried by strangers. They could bring the mere stuff: in Morlock's sense of the fitness of things, that was all right.

But he felt no kinship for them, *harven* or *ruthen*.

They stayed only a brief time in the Endless Empire under the Blackthorns. But that first day they needed baths, and food, and rest, and they got it. Ambrosia spent much of her time talking with the Lorvadh and the others of the Greater Fifteen, so the three males were often left to their own devices.

Morlock spent some time roaming the lower levels with Deor and Kelat in tow. Makers occupied a warren just above miners, and neither type of dwarf was often seen on the higher levels where the mercators and soldiers dwelled among the halls of feasting.

The makers were interested to meet Morlock, and he had some interesting conversations among them. But they had nothing to tell about the threat to the sun, or the world at large: many of them had not seen the light of the sun since they were children.

They did feel that makers should stick together, though, and they saw to it that Morlock had winter gear and supplies for the long trip north. He also made, with their help, a new stabbing spear to replace the one that Kelat had adopted. In return, he drew a few multidimensional maps for their use in creating gems, which they viewed with suspicion and interest, and they had a boisterous beery supper in which Morlock drank the masters of making and their chief apprentices under the table, even though he didn't particularly like beer.

His head was still aching the next morning when someone awakened him with a friendly pitcher of water thrown in his face.

He jumped up, snorting, and looked around to see who he should strangle. His bleary eyes focused on his sister, Ambrosia, calmly putting an empty pitcher aside on a table.

"If you're not too busy hobnobbing with the servants, brother," she said, "the Lorvadh and his councillors would like to meet you."

"Eh."

"You'll have to do better than that."

Morlock took his time: shaved, bathed, ate, and dressed himself in new clothes the "servants" had made for him. But he was still angry about the remark when Ambrosia led him up a long flight of stairs to the Council Hall under three-peaked Jyrhyrning.

There he found Kelat talking with the Lorvadh, and fourteen other dwarves dressed resplendently in a rainbow of glittering colors. There was a great table of stained pinewood with an oaken throne at one end. There were a few dwarves dressed in drab clothing sitting on stools in a shadowy end of the hall. They clutched books in their hands with arcane astronomical symbols painted on the covers. The hall was high enough in the mountain to have decent windows. These had been well made some considerable time ago, but the casings had cracked in more recent years, with the repairs done hastily and (to Morlock's practiced eye) badly. These blunders were partly hidden by velvet bunting.

He saw all this, but he did not see his friend Deor.

"Where is Deortheorn?" he asked Ambrosia.

She looked annoyed. "Deor is well. But this conversation is for the Lorvadh and his councillors to get to know you, and Kelat. There are some dwarvish astronomers, too, who have a report to give about the health of the sun."

The Lorvadh was approaching, with his hands extended in greeting. Morlock kept his eye on Ambrosia and repeated, "Where is Deor?"

"In our quarters," Ambrosia said, shrugging.

Morlock turned to the Lorvadh. "Lorvadh Vyrn: will you send messengers to bring my *harven*-kin Deor to us?"

"Er . . . I . . . I suppose it could be done," the dwarf monarch said. "Yes, of course it could be done. He could sit with the astronomers. This gathering is really for us of the *vrevnenen* to get to know each other."

"What does *vrevnenen* mean?"

"'Rulers,' Morlock," Ambrosia supplied.

"It's a word I don't know," Morlock said to the Lorvadh. "A word I do know is *harven*. It means that where Deor cannot go, I will not go."

"I'm afraid it's impossible," the Lorvadh said patiently. "I have my Master of Accountants here, my Master of Armies, my Master of Law-Speakers, My Master of Meatpackers—all the masters of the Endless Empire. Ambrosia describes your . . . your friend as a thain. I believe I know what that means. It is quite impossible for him to sit at our table."

Morlock looked at Kelat, who was just coming over, and seemed shocked at what he had heard. He looked at Ambrosia, who met his eye with knowing impatience. He deliberately looked over the head of the Lorvadh and turned away. Vyrn was saying something but he paid no heed. He left the hall and rattled down the stairs and hallways of the warrens until he came to their quarters.

Deor was there, packing their things. He looked up with a quizzical eye as Morlock entered.

"So soon?" the dwarf asked. "Ambrosia gave me to understand you might be much of the night. The Fifteen were apparently impressed by your feats at the drinking board and wanted to put you to the test."

"When you're done, we're leaving."

"I'm done. Just the two of us—er, the three of us?"

Morlock turned to see Kelat standing in the doorway. "I'm sorry," he said. "I didn't know that Deor had been excluded."

"Is that what this is about?" Deor shook his head and laughed. "Morlocktheorn, it's not as if I care. Sitting with the Fifteen Masters of the Endless Empire is not my idea of an evening's entertainment."

"Nor mine. Thanks for packing." Morlock took Tyrfing and his new stabbing spear in their scabbards and bound them to the pack Deor had made for him, then threw the pack on his shoulders. Kelat and Deor also shouldered their packs, and by that time Ambrosia was there.

"You, sir," she said to Morlock, "are the most irritating man not named 'Merlin.'"

"Eh."

"That makes it all better, of course. Well, let's get out of here before they put us to death for insulting their king." She took on her pack and they trudged to the western gate.

Waiting for them was a division of spear-dwarves clad in scarlet and gold. At their head was a dwarf wearing a silver circlet in his graying red hair and a shirt of chain mail. "Morlock Ambrosius?" he said, as the four approached.

"Yes," Morlock said flatly. If it came to a fight, he thought they could get through the gate with a little luck, and then the narrowness of the passage would be in their favor. . . .

The dwarf held out both hands, empty and palm up, a gesture of peace. "I am Fyndh, Master of Soldiers for the Endless Empire. We did not have a chance to meet in the Council of Fifteen just now."

Morlock considered for a moment, then held out his hands, empty and palm down, over Fyndh's hands without making contact.

Fyndh smiled and withdrew his hands. "Vyrn is an idiot. He inherited most of his money and made the rest by loaning it at interest. My father was a shoemaker, and I worked my way through the army from the lowest rank. We see the world differently—and I think I see it not so differently from you."

Morlock nodded, waited.

Fyndh continued, "My friends among the makers speak highly of you. I'm sorry we never got a chance to drink together. If you and your companions succeed in what you are about, you will always have friends in the Endless Empire. If not—well, we will remember you with honor until the sun goes out."

Morlock nodded and said, "Good fortune, Master Fyndh."

"To you and yours," Fyndh said. He said goodbye to each of the companions as they passed, and led his troops in a cheer as they walked out the gate and up into the pale light of the sun.

Ambrosia fell into step beside Morlock. "Fyndh will be their next Lorvadh, I think. I hope. Vyrn will never be a friend to the Vraids or the Wardlands now."

Morlock had nothing to say to that, and so said nothing. The rough, snow-stained terrain of the Dolich Kund was before them, and the sun stood dying in the sky above. It was a long, bitter road to the end of the world.

CHAPTER TWO

Fire, Gods, and a Stranger

That night they camped just past the crest of the Dolich Kund. It was a cold night: an ice-edged wind beneath searingly bright stars and Horseman, the only moon in the sky, standing somber and low in the east.

They made a fire, of course, and partial occlusions to block the wind, but Kelat was obviously down-hearted. He was possibly comparing his bed last night to the long series of cold campsites in his future.

That was bad, not just for Kelat but for all of them. Morale was important on a long journey with a small company, as the three elder companions knew well. Deor looked several times at Kelat's glum face and then finally said to Morlock, "Do the thing with the fire."

Kelat looked up, instead of down, which was a start. Morlock obligingly reached into the heart of the fire and drew forth a handful of live coals.

As Kelat watched with an open mouth, Morlock juggled the bright burning coals with his fingertips. Deor watched, too, with a knowing grin: he never got tired of this trick. Ambrosia, however, was watching Kelat's open admiration with an envious sideways glance. Eventually she reached into the fire and began juggling coals as well.

Now Kelat was looking from Ambrosius to Ambrosia with unfeigned and delighted wonder.

Ambrosia looked Morlock in the eye and lifted an inquiring eyebrow. He nodded. She tossed him a coal and he tossed one back in the air, and from then on they wove a complex tracery of red light, juggling some coals and playing catch with others, until they began to fade, and Kelat's amazement grew cooler and more familiar.

He eagerly asked how they had done it, and wondered if he could learn

257

it, too, and Ambrosia and Deor explained to him about the blood of Ambrose and their immunity from fire. In the end he was almost as downcast as he had been before, although he kept stealing glances at Ambrosia's hands.

Morlock pulled some glowgems from a pocket in his sleeve. They weren't as bright or as satisfyingly fiery as live coals, but he thought they might serve a purpose here. He tossed one to Kelat. The Vraid was startled, but caught it instinctively. Morlock showed him how to juggle it, and guided him through the steps of adding a second glowgem. He caught on quickly, not dropping them too often, and Morlock left him to practice juggling under Deor's watchful and amused eye.

Ambrosia gestured to him and they walked together into the dark beyond the range of the fire or the hearing of their two companions.

"You're corrupting my princeling," Ambrosia remarked drily.

"Oh?"

"Oh, yes. Soon he'll care about loyalty, and honesty, and wonder, and then what kind of king will he make, hey?"

Morlock grunted. "A good one?"

"Unlikely. Morality is different for kings, Morlock, than for the people they rule."

"Eh." Morlock knew little about kings, or being ruled, so he couldn't say this was untrue.

"That's easy for you to say. Too easy, as I have often told you before."

"Eh."

"Be that way, then! I suppose I have other Uthars to choose from. I could bear to fuck this one, though, and that's not nothing."

Morlock somehow disliked discussing sex with his sister, and he hadn't realized that's what they were doing. He considered long and hard and said, "Oh?"

"Yes, it's part of my deal with Lathmar the Old. I will pick the next King of the Vraids and mate with him."

"Hm."

"Yes, yes, I see what you mean, I suppose. But it's a way to wield power among the Vraids in a way that they understand."

"Is that important?"

"Not if the world ends, Morlock. If the world doesn't end, then yes, it is important. When I was a girl, growing up in that horrible little house in the woods with Merlin, I swore I'd visit every place in the world and conquer the places that seemed interesting. The Vraids will do the conquering part if I play the game right. And I usually do."

"I know."

Ambrosia laughed and put a hand on his arm. "I suppose I wouldn't find you so irritating if your opinion wasn't so important to me."

Morlock's opinion was that world conquest was a sad waste of talents as extraordinary as Ambrosia's, but he had never told her that and never would. Something about her upbringing had scarred her, shaped her, focused her on this quest for power. It wasn't for Morlock to reshape her. That wasn't his kind of making.

Before them was the dark, river-scarred, densely forested northern plain. He gestured at it and said, "What's our route north, you think?"

"We should avoid the twin cities, Aflraun and Narkunden," Ambrosia said. "I recommend a detour to the west. In time we'll come upon the Bay of Bitter Water. If it's navigable, maybe we can travel by water for a while."

Morlock grunted with a noticeable lack of enthusiasm.

"You can build a boat, I suppose? With Deor's help?"

"Yes. But I would prefer not to."

Ambrosia laughed politely at this. Then she remembered something— possibly their arrival at Grarby. "Hm," she said thoughtfully. "Hm. Well, even so, it might be safer than land. The plains near the werewolf city are dangerous indeed, and they'll be getting hungry, too."

Morlock thought about the deep, cold waves of the Bitter Water and felt a certain chill that did not come from the frosty air.

They talked for a while longer of the road ahead and then returned to the campsite to turn in.

Day followed night, and then more days and nights. They walked and walked. They gave Narkunden a wide berth, following Ambrosia's advice. The sun was a pale, white disc that a man might look at without any particular pain. The weather grew colder, a wintry sort of summer.

As they walked north, they met many animals fleeing south: white foxes and wolves, rabbits and preems, birds of every kind. And there were bears, deadly white bears mad with fear or hunger, killing recklessly among the other animals and perfectly willing to eat the four travelers.

Kelat killed one bear that charged them. They stopped to butcher it and skin it: they might need the meat or the fur on the long road ahead. Afterward they tried to fend the beasts off without killing them, but both Ambrosia and Deor had bear blood on their hands before another call passed.

Many of the days went by without incident that Morlock would afterward recall, but then came a day when they ran into creatures more dangerous than a bear.

Dawn came that day behind a dense curtain of cloud, and they kept the fire alive until the very moment they had to break camp. They walked slowly, picking a careful path across the trackless plain: the day could not have been darker without being night. The wind was bitter, but they would have to grow used to it, and worse yet.

"Is the sun dying at last?" Kelat asked.

Morlock shrugged, and no one else even did that. There was no way to answer this.

"We have been passing that tree for half an hour," Deor remarked presently.

That was different. All four travelers stopped and looked closely at the tree, black against the blue gloaming.

"I don't think it's a dryad-beast stalking us," Ambrosia observed presently.

"What's that?" Deor snapped. "And why not?"

"Dryad-beasts hide in a cocoon that looks like a tree and prey on passersby," Ambrosia said.

"Canyon keep them. Why are you sure it's not one?"

"I'm *not* sure. But my insight doesn't sense the talic imprint of an animal. It's more like. . . . What would you say, Morlock?"

"A god."

"Hell and damnation!"

"Possibly. I remember . . . I remember something like this in Kaen. It was an avatar of their god of death."

A female figure wrapped in darkness stepped out from the open air. She carried a long, bright sword in her right hand.

Morlock drew Tyrfing.

"Are you crazy?" hissed Ambrosia.

"I am Morlock Ambrosius," said the crooked man. "I will not die without a struggle, even if a god of death has come for me."

"Very noble. But we might try talking first."

"She has not come to talk."

The deathgod stepped closer. Her face was not easy to look at, but her scar-like mouth seemed to twist in a smile.

Then a new door opened in the air and another god stepped out. This figure also seemed female. Her garb was bright where Death's was dark. Her body seemed dark where Death's was pale. Her smile was equally grim, and she carried an equally bright sword in her left hand.

She held up her right hand and a mouth appeared in the dark palm.

"Stand back, sister," said the pale mouth in the dark hand. Morlock did not hear the words with his ears; they stabbed through him. He saw the others bending over in agony around him.

Death held up her pale left hand. A mouth manifested there. Its dark lips replied, "Justice, there is a time for all things to end. This is that time. It is my time."

"All times are mine," Justice replied. "Your power overmatches theirs, and this offends me."

"Justice, my beloved sister, you are among the weakest of all the Strange Gods, as I am the strongest. Do you think you can stand against me?"

"Yes."

"Then prepare yourself. But these mortals will die from witnessing our battle just as surely as they would from my blade. Look how they cower when we signify to each other!"

"I am not alone," Justice signified.

Morlock strove to stand straight when he understood Death's remark about cowering. As he did, he saw that the barren field had sprouted a shadowy crop of gods.

A door opened in the air and Morlock fell through it. He fell to ground on a narrow paved street, and Tyrfing clattered on the stones beside him.

"Are you all right?" he heard a voice saying.

Morlock looked up to see a balding, ruddy-faced stranger standing over him. Beyond him was a graystone building, rather out of place in a street full of dark wooden houses. The stranger was standing in the open door of the building, above which was a symbol of a counterweight stone on a pair of empty scales.

Morlock thought about the stranger's question and said, "Yes."

"A man of few words? All right. Here." The stranger offered him a hand to get up, but Morlock was already rising, Tyrfing in his right hand.

Morlock looked around. "Where am I?"

"Narkunden," said the stranger. "Never been here? You haven't missed much. They're talking about abandoning the town if the next winter is as bad as the last one."

Morlock grunted. "Think it will be?" he asked.

"It'll be worse. I'd bet a nickel on it, which is as much as I ever bet on anything. But they won't abandon the town."

"Why not?"

"It's not like things are better down south. If the sun is dying. . . . Some things you can't fix by running away from them."

"How do you fix them?"

"Um. Let me rephrase. Some things can't be fixed."

Morlock grunted again. "Is there a bar or a wineshop nearby? I need a drink."

"No one *needs* a drink, unless they're a drunk. Are you a drunk?"

Morlock shrugged. "If I were, would I admit it?"

"You might. Drunks come in all the types of people there are: proud, ashamed, defiant, apologetic, you name it. But I'm not inclined to help a drunk find another drink. There's some of it in my family. You understand."

"I'm not a drunk."

"Excellent. Perhaps you'll join me in a mug or two of wine? I usually partake around this hour."

The stranger stepped back through the dark doorway behind him and motioned for Morlock to follow.

The stranger didn't look dangerous. After a moment's thought, Morlock sheathed his sword and stepped through the doorway.

The interior of the stranger's house was an image of chaos: books and stones and papers and dust lying around in heaps. On one of the stone heaps was a jumble of bronze pieces that looked like parts of a skull. The room was lit, not by a lamp but by a kind of window set into the wall. But there had been no window on the wall outside, and this window showed no scene that could be local. It showed a green field in early summer or late spring; there was a large maple tree with some ropes hanging from it. Morlock would have liked to know how the window was made.

The stranger was busying himself in a cupboard and he brought back a couple of mugs filled with reddish fluid that smelled like it might be wine.

"Not very good," the stranger said ruefully. "But the best you'll find in town, I'm afraid. Any grapes they've managed to grow recently they kept for eating."

Morlock raised the mug and said, "I'm Morlock Ambrosius, by the way."

"Are you?" The stranger's vague blue eyes focused on him. "Interesting!"

"What's your name?" Morlock asked.

"Don't you know it?"

"No. Have we met?"

"I can't remember. You can't remember all the people you've met, can you? I expect someday you'll forget you've met me today."

"We have not met yet. Formally, that is."

"What? Oh, my name. I suppose you could call me Angustus. Some people do, around here."

Morlock nodded. He was used to people who travelled under pseudonyms, although he tended not to trust them. On the other hand, this fellow had more or less admitted the name was not his own. Maybe that showed he was honest after all.

"Are you a maker, Angustus?"

"No. No. No. Not really. No. I've never thought of myself that way. Although I suppose I am, sort of. But I teach at the local lyceum, at least on a temporary basis. I know a good many curious things, although it's not clear that they'll be any use when the sun goes dark. Of course. . . ."

"What will?"

"Exactly. *Nunc est bibendum!*" Angustus lifted his mug in salute to Morlock and took a drink. Morlock did the same. The wine was pretty bad, but better than nothing.

"That was Latin, wasn't it?" Morlock asked Angustus, after they had been drinking in silence for a while.

"It was indeed. *Loquerisne Latine?*"

"A little. One of my fathers made me learn it."

"Well, I commend him for it. There's not much call for it on the northern plains, I'm afraid. I teach logic, rhetoric, geometry, Old Ontilian—whatever they'll pay me for."

"There's a living in that?"

"I don't remember saying so. Now if I could teach people how to play venchball I'd have it made. The venchball trainers eat custard every night, as the saying goes. The stadia are crowded on game days, and on other days everyone seems to be talking about the next game or the last one."

"Don't know the sport. It's entertaining?"

"I'd rather be fried in oil than sit through a match. No, on game days I usually go into rich people's storehouses and steal their food."

"Eh."

"I sense your distaste, and to some extent I share it. On the other hand, a man has to live and times are hard."

"I suppose." Morlock thought of the Khnauronts' invasion of the Wardlands. He shrugged and drank again.

"How would you go north from here—if you had to go alone?" Morlock asked Angustus.

The other shook his head. "I? Would not go. Singly or in bunches. You realize that northeast of here is the dreadful city of werewolves Wuruyaaria?"

"I'm not worried by werewolves."

"If you're not worried by a city of werewolves slowly dying of starvation, I suppose there's no point in even mentioning the riptide of superpredators fleeing south in search of meat, the desperate gods afraid of losing their worshippers, the ice-monsters that rule the bitter northern edge of the world, or the Sunkillers from beyond it. So I won't."

Morlock had already met some of the gods and he took monsters on a case-by-case basis. "Who are the Sunkillers?" he asked.

Angustus pointed at the ceiling. "The guys who are doing that. Killing the sun."

"What are they like?"

"I've never met one. Not to my knowledge. A lecturer at the Lyceum has a theory that they are colonists, making the world habitable for their form of life. Another thinks it's pure malice."

"How do you know it's not a natural phenomenon?"

"Direct contact in rapture. Some of the seers didn't make it back to their bodies alive, but enough did that we know this is being *done* to us."

Morlock nodded thoughtfully and drained the last of his wine. "I know someone who says . . . it's a kind of idealism. They are opposed to biological life in principle."

"Idealism is often incompatible with life," Angustus agreed cheerily. "You may not see it that way. But as a fat, middle-aged man, I think there's a lot more to be said for kindness than correctness."

"I'm well into my second century of life, Angustus."

"Yes, the Ambrosii live long, they say. But you have the restlessness and impatience of a young man—the belief that you can change the world, or save it, at least."

Morlock shrugged. "I am not impatient."

Angustus smiled into the dregs of his wine and did not respond directly. "No, I would not walk north from here for any reason. If there were some way to fly, I might try that: I'd like to have a conversation with one of these Sunkillers. But I suppose flying is impossible. That's what they say at the Lyceum. Something about wingspans and weight ratios."

"What about dragons?"

"Dragons are mythical. Would you like some more wine?"

"No," Morlock said. He could still fell the bitter metallic burn of the stuff in the back of his throat.

"It's good to know when to stop," Angustus said agreeably, and gathered Morlock's cup from him.

The time to stop was before you began with the kind of rotgut Angustus served out. But Morlock reminded himself that the stranger had shared with him in a time of scarcity and he said, "Thanks for the drink. Maybe I'll see you around."

"Maybe. But I'm thinking of getting out of town. Things are getting weird around here."

"I thought you said that there was no point in going south?"

"There are more directions than north, south, east, and west."

Morlock nodded. "I suppose so. Good fortune to you."

"And to you."

Morlock found himself walking down a narrow street of dark wooden houses. He hardly took note of what his eyes were seeing. Something the stranger had said was taking root in his imagination. In his mind he was seeing a dry leaf dancing in the hot air above a campfire.

CHAPTER THREE

To Market, To Market

When Morlock fell into the air and vanished, Ambrosia grabbed Deor and Kelat by an elbow each. Almost as rapidly, she ascended into rapture and entangled her tal with theirs. In the next instant, the air swallowed them and spit them out on another patch of ground. But they travelled together, as they might not otherwise have done.

They hit a patch of frozen turf in the same instant, and she released her grip on the others in time to keep her own elbows from being twisted to the breaking point.

"What did you do?" Deor shouted, rolling to his feet.

"Kept us from separating," Ambrosia growled, climbing to her own feet. Kelat was already standing but she ignored the hand he was offering her. "Maybe," she admitted after a moment.

"What happened to Morlock?"

"What happened to us—only a second sooner."

They looked around. They were still somewhere on the northern plains, to all appearances. This ground was a little rougher and there was some scrub, not quite trees, toward what seemed to be the northeast. The patch was crosslit by the setting sun—along with something crouching down in it.

"God Avenger," she whispered. "Come on! Let's get out of here."

"Why?" asked Kelat reasonably.

"Werewolf over there in that dead brush."

"We can't handle a single werewolf?" the dwarf asked.

"Werewolves are like rats, Deor. Where you see one. . . ."

"I get you." The dwarf glanced around. "Some kind of city west of us."

Ambrosia would have liked to know how he did that. She saw nothing to indicate a city there. Did he hear it? Did he smell it? Was it some kind of specialized talic insight? At the moment it didn't matter, though. She said, "Then that's our next stop."

They strode westward. The wolf shape broke from cover and followed them, but they outpaced it before night fell.

Ambrosia drew to a halt and looked back uneasily.

"What's wrong?" Deor said, stopping beside her.

"Apart from *everything*? It's like this, Deor. A werewolf should have been able to keep up with us if it wanted to. Regular wolves get bored and wander off during a long chase, but werewolves are more like men."

"Stubborn, you mean."

"Yes. And there was something funny about the way the thing moved. Didn't you think so?"

Deor snorted. "I know more about things below the mountain than above it. I'm no farmer, nor *weidhkyrr*."

"A pity we don't have someone so useful with us," Ambrosia snapped back.

"It was like a child playing wolf," Kelat remarked, forestalling Deor's witty comeback.

"Eh?" She kept forgetting that he was there, and that he had things to say. "What do you mean?"

"It ran like a boy or a girl on all fours." With surprising deftness, he moved his right hand like a child galloping over the open field of his left arm.

"Yes," she agreed. "It *was* a little like that."

She decided to wait for it. The others looked at her curiously for a while then settled in to wait, too.

Presently the werewolf came over the ridge they had just passed. It wasn't surprised to see them; of course, it had scented them. It sat politely atop the ridge and waited.

"Who are you and why are you following us?" she sang in Moonspeech, the language of werewolves wearing wolf form (or "the night shape" as they call it). Deor and Kelat both jumped a bit as the howling syllables blew out of her, but they didn't run away or ask stupid questions, so that was something.

The wolf stood on all fours and sang in reply, "I am Liyurrriyu. I was sent to find you, if you are they who go to the end of the wide world."

"And if we are, and if we do, what business do you have with us, my furry friend?"

"I was sent to help you."

"Why? And by whom?"

"By the one who watches in the night and guards us against the gods. By the mighty deviser and slayer. By the one who runs with no pack and yet with all."

"What does that even mean?"

"Ulugarriu sent me—Ghosts-in-the-eyes. I am to help you, if I can."

"It's your world, too, is what this Ulugarriu is thinking." The ululation of her howl made it clear that by *your* she meant *werewolves in general.*

"Yes."

"What's in it for you?"

"Survival."

"What's in it for *you?*" Ambrosia used the short bark that designated an individual.

"May I come closer?"

"Sure."

Liyurrriyu loped downhill toward them. He (the werewolf was clearly male, and the *-u* ending to his name was masculine) sat down seven human paces away and held up his right forepaw.

But it wasn't a paw at all. It was an ape's compromise between a hand and a foot.

Ambrosia vocalized an interest in approaching nearer. Liyurrriyu tilted his head left and right in assent.

She walked over and knelt down beside him, taking his hand. It was covered in a leather glove—or maybe more like a shoe for the hand. She tugged the glove off and examined the astonishingly human hand within.

"You see how it is with me," Liyurrriyu sang in whispered vocables. "I am a nightwalker, never able to assume the day shape. But I am also a never-wolf—never able to fully free myself from the ape."

"And this Ulugarriu says he can fix you."

"*Of course* Ulugarriu can fix me. He *says* that he *will* fix me, if I do all that I can to help you kill the Sunkillers."

"Calm yourself." Ambrosia put Liyurriu's hand shoe back on his hand foot. "What do you think you can do for us?"

The werewolf growled thoughtfully. "I have lived on these plains all my life. I know many things. I can track and find. I can kill and kill and kill."

"We're all of us pretty good at killing."

"You must be better. The bitter cold in the far north is sending all beasts fleeing southward. You must swim through a wave of cruel hunters, desperate to find prey. You are prey. I am hunter."

Ambrosia had her own opinion about that, but nonetheless said, "You're hired." She rose to her feet. "Tell me about the city to our west."

"Aflraun. We're not going there, are we?"

"We are."

"Urrrr. Better that than Narkunden, I suppose. They make werewolves wear muzzles there, or swear self-binding oaths not to eat fresh meat within the city limits."

"Monstrous."

"Dried meat. Burned meat. Salted meat. They put *salt* in it, do you see? Or they stain it with smoke!"

"Each to their own."

"I suppose you've been there."

"Frequently. And I have to warn you, if you travel with me, you will see me and my companions eat those variously mistreated meats. Nerve yourself up to it."

The werewolf shuddered and sang, "I can face what I must face."

Ambrosia hoped that this was true. She had an idea to make Liyurriu acceptable to the townsfolk of Aflraun, and she suspected it would test his determination to its limits.

The next morning, before dawn, Jonon, signudh on duty for the Shortgate guards, came to a rather sleepy alert and confronted a group of travelers coming from the trackless east.

This was odd. Few lived east of Aflraun, and those that did weren't the type to travel to a city market or sample the secret joys of Whisper Street.

One was a dwarf. One was a Vraidish barbarian, from his hair and weaponry. One was a woman, crooked as an Ambrose, apparently the leader. The fourth was an odd one—as tall as the woman, but hunched over, he wore a long coat with sleeves and a wide-brimmed hat pulled down over his face. He seemed to have a pretty heavy beard.

"Greetings, travelers," Jonon said when they were in speaking range. "Do you come in peace, war, or business?"

"Peace," said the crook-shouldered woman Jonon had tagged as the leader.

"Have you got any food for trade?" Jonon asked. This was not an official question. But sometimes he made good purchases from food traders before they found out how much they could charge in the city markets.

"Food for ourselves; none to trade," the woman said, disappointing but not surprising Jonon.

"Is your companion a werewolf?" Jonon asked. This *was* an official question. Wuruyaaria had made several raids against the outskirts of Aflraun and Narkunden; more were expected. They had been instructed to watch out for spies.

"Which one?" asked the woman ingenuously.

"The one that appears to be a werewolf."

"My friend Laurentillus, here?" the woman said as if she were surprised, turning toward the shaggy one.

"If that's his name."

"Nonsense. Laurentillus, shake hands with the guardsman."

Laurentillus didn't move.

"Do the thing," the woman urged. She nudged Laurentillus in the side. "The thing."

Laurentillus started, then pulled off his right glove. He held out his right hand to Jonon. It was an undeniably human hand—calloused from much work, with an oddly hairy wrist. Jonon slapped the offered palm, causing Laurentillus to jump and withdraw suddenly.

"He doesn't seem quite human," Jonon observed.

"Doesn't he?" said the woman, deftly slipping a coin into Jonon's still-outstretched hand.

"Well, not much."

Another coin surreptitiously changed hands.

"Well, who am I to judge? Still, my men. . . ."

"How much more?" the woman asked briskly.

Jonon hated to use his position to squeeze money out of travelers, but times were hard; even meat was getting expensive. He glanced at the coins in his palm. They were foreign, of course; Vraidish by the look of them. "Two more of these," he said.

She supplied them cheerfully. He followed them through the gate, chatting of this and that. He didn't want any of his underlings to squeeze any more coins out of them.

When they were well into Aflraun, and Jonon was about to turn back, the crooked woman caught sight of something and grabbed him by the arm. "Jonon, my friend," she said, pointing at the sky over the cluttered western horizon, "what is *that*?"

He looked, but he knew what she meant even before that. "It's there sometimes, sometimes not. It keeps getting bigger. No one's sure what it is, truthfully. People say a crazy man is building something in the sky over Narkunden. Maybe it has something to do with the end of the world."

"A crazy man, you say? Tell me more."

After he parted company with Angustus, Morlock walked down to the southern edge of Narkunden and made camp in an open field. The next day he left his things under occlusion and wilderment and went into town to buy food and drawing paper. He had two or three different designs for a flying ship in his head and he wanted to sketch out some of the ideas before he chose between them.

Food was expensive, as he had feared after his conversation with Angustus. A loaf of fresh bread cost two fingers of gold. Fresh meat was cheaper, but a rather odd selection: most of it was from game animals and predators.

But it didn't matter much. Morlock was no epicure. He bought meat, bread, and mushrooms and set out to find drawing paper.

The cheapest place, so a dwarvish mushroom merchant told him, was Shardhut Scrivener's shop near the Lyceum. Paper and ink were agreeably cheap there, as he discovered, but the place was dense with dark-gowned savants from the Lyceum.

Morlock collected the supplies he needed and went to stand in line so that

Shardhut, the warty but agreeably cheerful shopkeeper, could take his money. Shardhut had three hulking assistants who didn't seem to do anything, but perhaps Shardhut didn't trust them with the cashbox. In the general confusion Morlock might easily have walked out of the shop with the goods in hand, but he had been raised by his *harven*-father with an exaggerated sense of property.

Morlock was not a talkative type, but the rest of the customers made up for that. Three of his line-mates were writing books about the end of the world, which they hoped to have completed to great acclaim before the world actually ended, and another was writing a book about how the world was not really ending, just going through a natural phase of transition, which would bring an end to all life. Another, who did not believe in the writing of books, proved through a set of syllogisms that the world's weather was no different than it had ever been, as far as anyone could tell. Another was proving through syllogisms that nothing could be proven through syllogisms.

"What's your opinion, Citizen?" asked the man behind him in line.

Morlock mulled over his options and then said, "I have heard that the Sunkillers are responsible—malefic beings from beyond the northern rim of the world."

There was general laughter at this. He was informed, on good authority, that there was no northern rim of the world and that, if there were, there could not be anything beyond it. He was asked to define his terms. He was asked for the physical evidence or at least eyewitness testimony to support his claims. Then a red-faced, red-haired academic in a scarlet gown said, "This gentleman has been talking to Iacomes."

Silence fell and every eye turned to Morlock. He said, "I did talk to a colleague of yours yesterday, but he said his name was Angustus—"

"Preposterous!" shouted the red academic. "'Angustus'! How would one even pronounce that?"

"Angustus?"

"No, it must be one of his pseudonyms. Tell me, was he a tall, dark-skinned man with dark eyes and a pleasing manner?"

"No."

"Then it must have been him! Do you know what he has been telling my students?"

Morlock didn't answer, but the red academic didn't seem to notice. "He tells my students that it's not wrong to steal if they are hungry! Can you believe it, sir?"

There was a general murmur of outrage.

"What if the students starve to death?" Morlock asked. "Whom will you citizens teach at the Lyceum?"

"It would be a great relief to have less students," remarked one of the academics. "Then I could write more books about the importance of education."

There was a general titter at this citizen's expense. "*Fewer*, Arnderus, '*fewer* students.' You can't use *less* as an adjective with a noun denoting a set of discrete objects."

"Except for numerical measurements," reminded another academic.

"Oh, yes, of course."

Arnderus turned screaming on his tormentors. He grabbed fistfuls of reed pens from a nearby stand and began stabbing at anyone within arm's reach.

"No discussions of grammar or usage, citizens!" bleated Shardhut, but it was too late; the linguistic analysis and the violence threatened to become general.

It was then that Shardhut's bulky assistants proved their worth. They waded into the fight, stripped the combatants of their goods, and tossed them into the street. In a few moments order was restored and the line to the cashbox was considerably shorter.

The conversation, when it resumed, was much more subdued, and it did not hinge on such fiercely disputed topics as the ethics of stealing or which adjective might be used with which noun. Mostly they talked about the end of the world and whether it would arrive before the next summer recess.

As Morlock was pondering the paradox of windbags who could contemplate their students starving with equanimity but were moved to blows over a point of language, he suddenly saw in his mind's eye the perfect design for his airship. He no longer needed the pens and paper. He left them on a table and walked out into the street, where the linguistic fistfight still continued. He walked past, hardly noticing, thinking of a bag of gas floating high in the air, its angry heat perpetually renewed by contact with a living mind.

❯❮

Morlock was so lost in thought that he didn't notice when his basket became lighter by a couple mushrooms. But the thief in her haste let her hand brush against Morlock's left forearm. An instant later, the thief's wrist was in the grip of Morlock's left hand. The thief gasped in pain and surprise, and the guilty mushrooms fell to the ground, where hands started to scrabble for them instantly. Morlock stomped on a few fingers, and soon he was left in peace with his thief and his mushrooms.

The thief was a young woman in an academic gown. Her face was thin and grayish, her eye-sockets shadowed with dark green, like old bruises. "I'm sorry," she muttered. "I was just so hungry. And there's a teacher at the Lyceum who says it's all right to steal if you're hungry."

"Only if you get away with it." Morlock let her go and recovered his mushrooms. When he looked up, she was still standing there, looking sadly at his basket packed with food.

Morlock was strongly opposed to theft, and he damned Angustus in his heart for setting children like this on a path they were utterly unprepared for. How many had ended up in jail or worse?

"I need the food," he said harshly. Then on impulse he took a bag of gold and tossed it to her. "This should buy you something."

She opened the bag, looked at it suspiciously. "Why are you giving me money rather than food?"

"I can't make food."

"That implies you can make gold."

"Eh." Morlock walked away.

There was a draper's shop on his way and he went in and bargained for some ulken-cloth, to be sent to his camp south of the city. It was surprisingly cheap, compared to food, but he did need a lot of it, and the deal diminished his stock of gold considerably. He went back to his camp and secured his food in the wilderment there.

He turned to face the thin-faced scholar who had followed him all the way back.

She said nothing to him, so he said nothing to her. He turned away and went down the bluff to the banks of the River Nar.

He pulled sheckware buckets from a sleeve pocket, unfolded them, and filled them with yellow mud from the river. He hauled the buckets up the bluff to his campsite.

The young scholar was sitting nearby, resting her chin on her knees.

Morlock shrugged, dispelled his occlusions and wilderments, and set about his business. He made a fire, unpacked the portable forge the dwarvish makers of the Blackthorns had given him, and while he was waiting for it to rise to a useful temperature he had a drink of that mushroomy beer that the dwarves were fond of. Morlock was not fond of it, but he did feel that any drink was better than none.

"Master," said the scholar tentatively.

"I am not your master."

"What's your name? Mine is Varyl."

"My name is my business."

"Are you about to make gold?" she asked.

"Yes."

"May I take notes?"

Morlock thought for a moment. He did some math in his head, the primitive math of economics. He almost said no to her. Then he thought of those plump, red-faced, student-hating teachers in the stationer's shop. "Eh," he said aloud.

She took this as permission and pulled a tablet and stylus from pockets in her gown.

He ended up calling her over to the forge and explaining a few things to her. Raising the mass to equal the appropriate volume of gold involved a transition through a higher space, and he was concerned that she might not be able to follow it. But it turned out that she knew a good deal of metadimensional geometry. By the time his gold was cooling next to the forge, she had pocketed her tablet and was wandering away, chewing thoughtfully at her stylus.

Morlock never saw her again. But the next day when he went down to the market to cheapen some thread, he found that the price of food had doubled overnight. Many of the buyers were hollow-cheeked young people in academic gowns who seemed to have plenty of gold.

CHAPTER FOUR

The Flight of the *Viviana*

T he round-faced man had been weeping: the marks of tears still gleamed on his cheeks, but his voice was carefully even as he said, "I'm talking about the mansion on the bluff north of town—the one with the beautiful view."

"Yes," said the hard-faced butcher, "and I'm talking about a full-grown ylka-beast on the hoof—enough to feed a family of four through a cycle of Trumpeter, if they're thrifty and are fairly fond of soup and organ meat."

"But I paid three thousand shields for this place last summer! I have a lifetime of savings in gold—"

"This is *this* summer. It's today. I wouldn't let a piece of offal out of my shop for all the gold coins in the twin cities. Straight-up trade: the beast for the property's deed. Do we have a deal, or shall I call back Master Dinby?"

"Deal," said the round-faced man glumly. "Can you have someone bring it to my house on Shull Street?"

"Delivery is extra."

The round-faced man considered this briefly, and then he leaped at the butcher, flailing with his linen-gloved hands and his silk-shod feet. The butcher, surprised, went down in front of his shop. The round-faced man was simultaneously screaming and gnawing at the butcher's wobbly neck. The resulting sound was a strangely shrill burping or farting effect. But the sight of a butcher being attacked swiftly drew other people into the fray: some defending the butcher, some more intent on getting a kick or a punch in, and still more trying to loot the butcher's stop, in spite of the armed guards within. People were rushing toward the fight with wheelbarrows of gold; they were rushing away with wheelbarrows of bloody meat; there was screaming and pleading and somewhere, unseen but heard, a chorus of women was chanting a spell meant to rekindle the dying sun.

"I was worried about trying to sneak a werewolf through town," Ambrosia remarked to Deor as they walked carefully around the fringes of the riot. "Now, not so much."

"I thought you said Narkunden was the orderly place," Deor replied.

"It *was*. You never saw so many laws and regulations. I wonder what can have happened?"

They trudged through a drift of gold-dust. Someone had been carrying it in bags that had come apart. No one passing by was even bothering to pick it up.

"Morlock may have been in town for several days," Deor observed when they were past the drift and into a quieter street.

"Yes, but he *can't* have. . . ." Ambrosia's voice trailed off.

"*Several* days," Deor reminded her.

She shook her head, not quite as if she were disagreeing.

They sneaked through the tangling streets of south Narkunden, climbing steadily higher until the buildings petered out and they passed beyond the city. There was no need for walls there, since the Narkundans feared no incursion from their trading partners to the south, the dwarves of the Endless Empire.

In the ragged field south of town was a fire; beyond it, Deor thought he could detect an occlusion well-hidden by wilderments. To the left of the fire was an odd framework, clearly a work in progress, and many bolts of ulk.

In front of the fire was Morlock, lying supine on the ground, his eyes faintly glowing in rapture. Overhead a cluster of ulken bags, strangely shapeless, floated in midair.

"Morlock," Ambrosia said drily, "if you can attend to what I say, please join us in the merely material realm. If need be, I will ascend into rapture and drag you back down."

Morlock raised one hand. The light filtering through the thin skin of his eyelids slowly faded. He sat up.

"I have approximately ten thousand questions," said Ambrosia with a dangerous tone in her voice. "If you respond to any one of them with, 'Eh,' or a grunt, or a shrug, then one of us will go down the dark canyon of death before the ailing sun sets."

"Eh," said Morlock predictably.

Ambrosia let him live, possibly because she had not actually asked him any questions yet, and in the end she got her answers.

The floating ulken bags were, not surprisingly, floating ulken bags. Morlock's cunning plan was to build a big sort of basket, fill it with the ulken bags, cover the basket with more fabric, and float all the way to the end of the world.

"What keeps those things in the air?" Ambrosia said.

"Air's hot," Morlock said.

"But it doesn't stay hot," Ambrosia said. She pointed at the babble of gasbags, even now sinking toward the ground beside the fire.

"It could," said Morlock.

"No it can't."

"How can it, Morlocktheorn?" Deor asked.

The answer was quite lengthy; the making of things was one of the few subjects that made Morlock communicative—even wordy. Deor wasn't sure he understood it. Apparently, in deep rapture, one could see the particles of air. Because they were very small, they were easier to herd about. And one could keep the warmer particles of air in one place and shove the colder particles of air away.

"How can you tell them apart?" Kelat wanted to know.

"The warmer they are, the faster they are," Morlock explained. "The trick is to see them at all, as they are merely matter. But—"

Then he and Ambrosia became embroiled in an extremely technical discussion about seeing, where phrases like "pretalic imprintable foothold" were tossed about pretty freely. Deor stopped listening, although Kelat continued to watch and listen as if it were a fencing match.

Deor walked around the camp. He found a scrap of paper on which the framework of the airship was sketched in Morlock's spare but detailed style.

He nodded with satisfaction. Deor was no seer, and was not even a master of makers. But he could follow a design that had been made by one. Morlock had collected some lumber, but there wasn't nearly enough. Then there was the question of the fabric shell for the thing. . . .

He walked up to Kelat and nudged the young man in the ribs. Kelat looked at him bemusedly.

"Can you sew?" Deor asked him.

It took a few tries before he could even get Kelat to understand what he meant, and then the Vraid was indignant. "That's women's work!"

"I'll take that as a 'no' then. Well, you're clever enough to learn. And a word to the wise: don't use the phrase 'women's work' when Ambrosia is paying attention."

"Her?" Kelat looked at the Regent, hungrily and reverently. "She's not like other women."

"She is and she isn't. Anyway, you've been warned. Come with me, unless you want to walk all the way to the end of the world."

Kelat managed to learn how to use needle and thread, despite his gonadal arrangements, and soon he and Deor were seated side by side in the field, sewing silken gasbags.

The werewolf, Laurentillus or Liyurrriyu or whatever it was, came over and was looking at their activity with interest.

Deor didn't understand a single howling syllable that the werewolf ever sang, nor was he sure the werewolf understood him, no matter what language he spoke. But Liyurrriyu was no fool and had hands. Deor taught him what he needed to know by example, and soon they were sewing companionably together.

There was no conversation, though. There could not be, between Liyurrriyu and the others, and Kelat was still intent on eavesdropping on Morlock and Ambrosia. Their argument now sounded more like a strategy session. Deor still didn't understand it, but he had a task on hand to keep him busy and that was enough for now.

They avoided town as much as possible. It had divided up into warring neighborhoods, each jealously protecting its storeholds and sources of food.

But the warehouse district in the city's center was more or less abandoned. Deor and Kelat made a journey there one day to get beeswax to help seal the gasbags. They left some gold in payment, even though they knew that gold was essentially worthless in Narkunden now. Deor didn't like the thought of stealing: the hate of it was hot in his mind.

They had little else to do, so they worked on the airship whenever they were awake. It was a weird looking beast when it was done. The gigantic frame looked like the skeleton of an open-hulled ship. It was filled with gasbags and an enclosed glass furnace to heat them. Around it all they sewed a fabric skin—tight, but not airtight, to contain the gasbags. Anchored onto the lower half of the frame was a sort of not-very-long longboat for the travelers and their gear.

"Won't we want propellers, or something?" Deor asked Ambrosia.

"What are propellers?" she replied.

He explained, sketching a little in the dirt so that the idea would come across.

"Ingenious!" Ambrosia said. "Yes, I can see how an airship might use them, but this airship won't need them. Have you looked at the clouds, Deor?"

Deor looked up curiously. The sky was half filled with clouds . . . but there was something odd about them, a twisting channel wherever the clouds crossed a line running from north to south. "The sky is cut in two," he said.

"Yes. Whatever is killing the sun is drawing air with it toward the edge of the world. If we get up that far, we can simply swim in the current."

"What about the road back?" Deor asked.

Ambrosia did not answer at first, or look directly at him. She smiled, but not at anything Deor could understand. After a while she said, "Maybe we should worry about the return journey when it's before us. One problem at a time."

Deor shook his head. He guessed that meant she thought that a return trip was unlikely—unlikely enough not to worry about.

"I think you're wrong," Deor said, after some thought. "Suppose the stream fails—at night, say? We might need to maneuver to get to it, also. We could attach the propellers to the gondola or framework—perhaps power them with pedals and impulse wells as on our lost and lamented four-wheeled Hippogriff."

"Put it to Morlock," Ambrosia said resignedly.

Morlock heard him out and agreed with a nod—didn't even say a word. It added a few days to the job, but in the end even Ambrosia agreed it was worth it.

The thing was finally done and they had loaded their gear into the gondola when Morlock said, "What should we call it?"

"It's an airship, Morlock," Ambrosia said. "That's what we'll call it."

"It's supposed to be bad luck to sail on a boat with no name," Deor pointed out. "We can use all the luck we can get."

"Any suggestions?" Ambrosia said patiently.

"*Sky-Sword of the Vraids*!" cried out Kelat. He'd obviously been holding the thought for a while.

"*Gasbag*," suggested Deor, less grandiloquently.

"*Skyglider*," proposed Morlock thoughtfully. Deor guessed he was thinking of the short-lived *Boneglider*.

"*Wuruklendono*!" suggested Liyurriu. At least, it seemed to be a suggestion.

"*Viviana*," decided Ambrosia. "Everyone agreed? Think I care? Let's get aboard and get aloft, then."

They wedged themselves into the gondola, sitting sideways, each of them at a set of pedals and manuals.

"I'll take us up," Morlock said, and closed his eyes. Presently, they saw his irises glowing through the thin skin of his eyelids.

This was the part that Deor knew but didn't fully understand. Somehow, the two Ambrosii could keep the warmer air in the gasbags and expel the cold air. Eventually, the gasbags would all be full of hot air and lift into the sky and float away, like a politician's promise.

The body of the airship began to lift from the ground.

Presently, its vast bulk was overhead and they were sitting upright. Ambrosia took her belt and lashed Morlock's left arm to the rail of the gondola. "Can't have him falling out," she observed.

Deor was not afraid of heights. He had spent much of his life in mountains, and had frequently amused himself by climbing crumbling rock faces with his bare hands and feet. He was able to look down and see clouds below him with nothing more in his mind than a mild curiosity about whether it was raining below.

What he didn't like, what he had never been able to like, what he never would like, was the knowledge that nothing was beneath him. The ground out of which he had been hatched would never betray him; he knew it too well. But he had not been hatched for the air.

Now they were getting high—several man-lengths above the ground and getting higher. Kelat was looking over the edge with considerable interest.

Ambrosia was eyeing the glass furnace overhead. Liyurriu, seated just behind him, began a subvocal murmur that carried shrill tones of panic.

Deor was afraid, too. He was afraid that the wooden frame would fall apart and that they would fall. He was afraid that the glass furnace would run out of control, the gasbags would burn, and they would fall. He was afraid that the wind would come and tip them over and they would fly out of the gondola and fall. Then the earth, whom he had betrayed by leaving, would kill him for his betrayal. He was afraid.

But he was bored by his fear. It was always the same. And would it really be so terrible to die? There were worse things, if the teachers of his youth spoke true.

He looked over the rail of the gondola.

They were now quite high and it was becoming quite cold. Kelat's teeth were chattering, and it was not because he was frightened. He looked as eager as a miner following a vein of ore. It was strangely cold. It must be—

"Ambrosia!" said Deor. "The cold air is cascading down the gasbags."

"Yes," said Ambrosia. "That—that should be fixable." She closed her eyes and ascended into vision. Deor saw blue circles through her closed eyes. But she sat upright and one of her hands rested lightly on the gondola rail; the other was on Kelat's shoulder.

She was a great seer—far greater than Morlock, who was great enough to have defeated Bleys in at least one notable test of power. Deor wondered at it, but the Sight was not one of his talents, even in the smallest degree.

The light in her eyes faded, and she opened them. The chill draft from above had ceased.

"We'll try to keep the cold air away from the gondola," she said. "It depends—"

"Madam, I don't mean to be rude, but I would hate to see you waste your time. Unless you think that Kelat can benefit by the explanation."

Ambrosia grinned. "Canyon keep you then, you stiff-necked dwarven non-seer."

"The same to you, *harven*."

They were well over the city of Narkunden now, and the face of the city bore the scars of violence. Two factions were demolishing buildings to make walls around their neighborhoods. Much of the city seemed to be empty. The docks down at the base of the bluff were burning and the bridge between Narkunden and Aflraun was broken.

"Morlock, Morlock," Ambrosia said sadly. "What were you thinking?"

Deor was stung by this. "He was thinking that many in the city were starving while others grew fat. Or so I believe, madam."

"Of course he was. But good intentions are no substitute for skill in any art, least of all the art of governance. A man named Ambrosius came to a town. His intentions were not malicious, at least not wholly so. He ignited a civil war and then went his way, and the evil he had begun continued to burn its way through the city. Am I talking about Merlin in Grarby or Morlock in Narkunden?"

"It's not the same," Deor said stoutly.

"Why not? Either Morlock knew the harm he would do by destroying the monetary system of the city, or he did not. He was either malicious or ignorant."

Deor wanted to defend his *harven*-kin. But he could not quite. Deor knew Morlock understood something of the economics of scarcity: they depended on it when they sold gems and other goods in the marketplace in A Thousand Towers. So why had he let the golden genie out of the bottle?

Deor muttered something and would have let the subject drop, but Ambrosia squeezed Kelat's shoulder and said, "What do you think, Prince Uthar?"

The Vraidish boy said slowly, "People have what they can hold. Only that."

"So? Morlock did them no harm by making their gold as worthless as paper?"

"Paper isn't worthless. It can carry a promise—a love letter—news."

"You're getting subtle, my friend. Perhaps you should go in for philosophy rather than kingship. No matter what some people have written, the two things have little to do with each other."

"I'm not interested in being king and I'm not going to be king, but you haven't seen what I mean yet."

"Maybe you haven't said it."

"People had a choice of what to do with the knowledge Morlock gave. If they used it as a weapon, it was because they were already at war. Morlock did not help that. But he did not begin it, either."

"You've given me something to think about," Ambrosia admitted, and none of them spoke for some time.

They were high enough now that the city below was getting hazy. Aflraun, across the steep river valley, was even vaguer, wrapped in its own smoke. The vistas opened up in every direction were terrifying to Deor, but he would not look away from them. He filled his eyes and his mind with cold light and empty distance. The fear didn't go away, but it began to seem a small thing— smaller, even, than he was.

They continued to rise. And they were drifting northward: Narkunden was now under their keel.

The land was a vague memory below them, and the cities on the Nar well behind them when Deor broke a long silence to say, "It is warmer."

"And we're moving faster," Ambrosia agreed. "We're entering the sunstream."

The change was gradual but unmistakable. The distant earth began to blur even more. The clouds, nearer to them now, gave their real sense of movement. The wind at their backs drove them faster, ever faster.

"This is faster than a hippogriff!" Deor called back, and Kelat laughed.

"That ridiculous cart you were riding?" Ambrosia called forward.

"No—actual hippogriff."

"What a liar you are, Deor. When did you ever ride a hippogriff?"

Deor ignored the fact that his *harven*-kin had made a remark that, under Thrymhaiam, would have entitled him to kill her with impunity. They were not under Thrymhaiam, and Ambrosia never had been. Instead, he and Kelat told her the tale, which involved telling other tales.

The wind at their backs held all through the day. They worked the pedals and manuals sometimes, to build up charges in the impulse wells and to give their arms and legs something to do: there was no room to move about the little gondola.

When the sun set, the wind faded. It did not quite disappear, and it was difficult in the dark to say how much they had slowed.

"Should we set down?" Deor called back. "Anchor and, er, stretch our legs?"

"No," Ambrosia said firmly. "It's not like we're going to crash into anything. Any progress is better than no progress; we have a long road before us."

"But . . . I mean. . . ."

"And if 'stretch your legs' is some kind of Dwarvish euphemism, then I encourage you to swing your ass over the side and let go."

"Madam."

"Deor. Should I have put it more sweetly?"

"No! I suppose you're right."

"I'll go first, if you gentlemen don't mind. I should relieve Morlock, but I have to relieve myself first."

"Only one of us is a man, madam, but I don't suppose we object."

Actually, Deor thought he could hear Kelat goggling from where he sat, two benches back, but the young fellow would have to come to terms with life's undignified details sooner or later.

"Thanks, all. You make up in gentility what you lack in humanity." She kicked off her underclothing and climbed over the side to relieve herself while Deor and Kelat looked politely away and Liyurriu watched with patient interest. When she was back aboard and dressing herself she said, "Carry on, gentles. I think we should go one at a time, lest we overbalance."

Or in balanced pairs, Deor almost suggested . . . but that might be impossible. Since his fellow males seemed disinclined to take the plunge, Deor skinned off his trousers and climbed over the edge of the gondola.

Now it was his turn to be watched with shameless and unflinching interest by the werewolf Liyurriu. It made concentrating on the task at hand almost impossible. Then Liyurriu reached forward and grabbed Deor's forearms with his apish hands. Deor was so startled he almost lost his grip—and then he realized the werewolf was doing his best to help.

Deor appreciated it. He was terrified of falling. But Trumpeter, the minor moon, was standing in the western sky right behind him, shining with bitter brightness directly into the werewolf's eyes. Deor felt he was making an unpleasant spectacle of himself. But mounting terror, in the end, came to his aid and he evacuated his bowels and bladder and climbed back aboard while his gifts were still speeding their way toward the distant earth.

"And this is the worst," he shouted back to Morlock. "The worst. Nothing on this trip will be worse than this, not if we die the second death."

Morlock, by now returned from visionary rapture, but just barely, said, "Eh." The fact that he was four benches back saved Deor from the guilt of kinslaying.

Morlock was groggily aware that Deor was angry at him, but he wasn't really sure why. He hoped it wasn't important. Perhaps Deor was simply backing into anger to avoid fear. If that were so, Morlock would fight all night with his *harven*-kin, once he shook the shadows from his head.

They drifted northward through a dark sea of air, past towering islands and continents of cloud, bright as the major moons in the west, blue and mysterious as Deor's mood in the east.

Morlock answered the call of nature with the only reply possible, and ate and drank sparingly from the stores in his pack. Kelat had cocooned himself in a sleeping cloak, and Morlock felt much inclined to follow his lead and do the same. Visionary rapture was not sleep, despite how it seemed to onlookers, and Morlock was deeply weary.

But there was something he must attend to first.

He climbed onto his bench and stepped across to Kelat's. The Vraid started and pulled back the hood of his sleeping cloak to peer curiously at Morlock.

"You," Morlock said to the werewolf on the next bench. "What are you, really?"

The wolvish face looked on him, its reflective eyes as bright as little moons. After a moment, it opened its jaws and said carefully, "Liyurriu."

"I didn't ask your name," Morlock said. "Though I don't doubt you are lying to me about that. I asked *what* you are."

The wolvish eyes looked at him. The wolvish mouth did not answer him.

"You may not speak this language," Morlock said. (He was speaking the vulgar Ontilian they used in Narkunden and Aflraun.) "But I think you understand it. You showed me you did when you told me your name just now. Do you understand me?"

Liyurriu did not say anything, but after a moment he nodded curtly.

"Will you tell me *what* you are?" Morlock asked.

Hesitantly, the wolvish head shook: no.

"Will you tell me why you are here?"

Liyurriu shook his head again—reluctantly, it seemed to Morlock, but definitely.

"Is it because you cannot? I can see that you might be able to understand a language but not speak it. We can bring Ambrosia out of her vision so that she can translate. Or you can tell her rather than me. Will you?"

A long pause. Liyurriu closed his moonbright eyes, opened them. A slow shake of the head.

"Then." Morlock reached down and grabbed the werewolf by the scruff of his hairy neck.

"Morlock, no!" Deor screamed.

When Liyurriu realized what Morlock was about, he slashed with his claws and snapped with his jaws, but Morlock easily avoided these dangers and tossed Liyurriu off the airship. The werewolf body fell, writhing like a snake but silent as a stone, into a bank of cloud and out of sight.

Deor roared and grabbed for Morlock, as if he would send him by the same path. Morlock stepped back to his own bench and sat down.

"Are you completely crazy?" shouted Deor, and Kelat, too, was looking at him as if he were a dangerous lunatic.

"Kelat," he said. "*Harven* Deor."

"Am I *harven* to a murderer?" Deor continued, hardly less loud than before. "What in the Canyon do you think you are doing? Which one of us will you throw out next?"

"None of you," Morlock said. "As for Liyurriu, he is not what he seems. He should never have been with us."

Deor glared at him for a while, saying nothing. Morlock met his gaze and said nothing more.

Kelat finally broke the silence, saying, "What do you mean? Liyurriu was not a werewolf?"

"Eh."

Deor unleashed a thunderblast of semicoherent Dwarvish profanity.

Morlock ignored him and addressed himself to Kelat. "Your question does not have a yes or no answer. Liyurriu, as you may think of him, did not exist."

Kelat sat back and pondered this.

"Do you mean he was a mere illusion?" Deor said in a more nearly reasonable voice. "Impossible, Morlock. He did work on this airship. He—" Deor's voice choked off and he turned away.

"His physical presence was real," Morlock said, "but it was not inhabited by a mind. Not as your bodies are—as mine is."

"What do you mean?" Deor demanded. "What *can* that mean?"

"His body was simply a sort of puppet, controlled by another mind far distant from here. A seer of great power."

"Who? Why?" Deor demanded.

"That was what I wanted to know," Morlock reminded him. "It is what Liyurriu would not say."

Kelat asked, "Did you see it in your vision? Is that how you know?"

"Yes." In his mind he could still see the tethers of talic force glimmering through the world, east and south. That was where the puppeteer of Liyurriu-puppet was.

"Why didn't Lady Ambrosia know it?"

"She has long known it, I think."

"Then she must have had some purpose in concealing it. Shouldn't you have . . . er . . . consulted with her?"

Morlock reflected briefly and said, "No."

Kelat reflected briefly and then climbed into the now empty bench behind Deor.

Morlock shrugged. It was no skin off his walrus. If it helped the boy sleep better, then it was all to the good. He wrapped himself in a cloak and courted sleep. It came quickly, and he was wrapped in a darkly golden dream where he lay beside his darkly golden wife, when his sleep was shattered by Deor's voice.

"Whazzit?" he said, or words to that effect.

Deor was sitting in the bench Kelat had vacated, leaning over so that his head was near to Morlock's.

"Morlocktheorn," Deor said.

"Deortheorn," Morlock replied.

"Why did you give the knowledge of goldmaking to the Narkundans?"

"Ah." It was an unexpected question, but his *harven*-kin deserved a fair answer. He thought it over for a while and said, "I was angry at those smug pink parasites."

"Excuse me?"

"Those teachers who hated teaching, swarming around the stationer's shop, talking about money as if it were virtue, arguing fine points of grammar while others were starving."

"Oh. Oh. I shall have to apologize to Ambrosia, I think."

"About what?"

"We had an argument about something, and I'm beginning to see her point a little."

"She usually has one," Morlock said.

"Yes. Do you think Liyurriu is dead?"

"The entity who was using Liyurriu is not dead. The body may or may not survive the fall."

"We're miles in the air, Morlock."

"Werewolves drink strength and health from moonlight, it's said, and Trumpeter is bright tonight. But there is no Liyurriu, Deor. That person does not exist."

"Eh," said Deor pointedly, and climbed past the snoring Kelat to his own bench.

Morlock shrugged, descended again into the depths of his cloak and sleep. His dreams this time were dark and cold, and Aloê showed herself in none of them.

CHAPTER FIVE

The Wreck of the *Viviana*

They flew the blood-warm wind from the dying sun northward, day after day. At night they drifted. Sometimes they drove the propellers with the pedals and manuals to have something to do and to keep warm. Sometimes they talked, although infrequently. They watched the distant land and the bright ring of the horizon and they waited for the end—of their journey, of the world.

They saw below them a great tidal wave of beasts fleeing from the bitter blue death that roamed the north. From their airship miles above they could see it, black, brown, and red against the pitiless white and silver of snow and ice.

North of the great migration, there were still shapes moving in the wild, wind-carved wastes of snow, but they could not quite see them or understand what they saw.

And there was a long, straight line running ahead of them, all the way to the northern horizon. When they talked, they talked a little about that.

"You know what it is," Ambrosia said eventually. (Morlock was in trance, keeping the *Viviana* aloft.)

"I do not know what it is," Deor replied emphatically.

"It's the weight of the sun's death. It's the footprint in the snow of the warm air we're riding north."

"Ah," said Deor and Kelat in chorus and with equal satisfaction.

The Ambrosii grew hollow-eyed. It was hard to spend much of a day in visionary rapture, day after day. It made the soul's relationship to the body more tenuous. If the bond finally broke, that was death. They were not about to die. But they were not well either.

One day, around noon, Deor said, "We're lower than we were. Are the gasbags getting cold?"

Morlock looked up into the body of the airship. The glass furnace was still burning its fuel. He looked back at Ambrosia. Though deep in vision, she looked at him with eyes closed, the dim glow of her irises visible through the lids. She shook her head. And the ship still seemed to be buoyant.

"Unlikely," Morlock said. He glanced all the way around the horizon and added, "Look north."

"The sky seems . . . bigger there," Deor called back. "Or the land higher."

"The sunstream is dropping down—carrying us closer to the Soul Bridge?" Kelat asked.

"Likely," Morlock said.

He wondered if the very sky curved down at the edge of the world, closing in the world's air like a glass bowl enclosing water. The idea gave him a breathless, locked-in feeling that he disliked strongly. He said nothing of this, however.

As *Viviana* flew lower, they could see the wild beasts of the snow fields better. But it was hard to understand what they saw. Many shapes were white-on-white, their borders hard to distinguish. Others glittered like glass in the bitter, pale sun.

"Are those *plants?*" wondered Kelat, as they flew past a dense, tangled chaos of bitterly bright ice things.

"Of course!" Deor said. And Morlock agreed: it was very like a forest seen from above, except that it was a forest after an ice storm, with no green or brown to be seen. There were skeletal shapes of black, though—very like thin tree trunks and bare, wintry branches.

"What kind of creatures would feed on such plants?" Kelat wondered.

"Ice-bunnies?" speculated Deor. "Frost-deer?"

"And who feeds on the ice-bunnies?"

"Us, maybe. A nice frost-bunny stew sounds good right about now, doesn't it?"

"Not really, no."

Morlock noticed that the glittering plants did not grow near the narrow road leading into the deep north. Nor did the hulking white shapes tend to travel there.

"What's that?" Deor called back, pointing to the east. "Quake sign?"

Morlock looked at a long, serpentine break in the snow crust. "Hope so," he called back. But he didn't think so. Fault lines from an earthquake would have been more angular.

Later, when Morlock was in trance, keeping the *Viviana* aloft, Deor made some reference to "throwing more of us off the airship."

Ambrosia, who had stepped past Morlock to talk to the other males, said, "You're still angry with Morlock about Liyurriu?"

Deor was taken aback. After a moment he answered, "Yes."

"You realize there is no Liyurriu? He was simply a fraud, sent to beguile us?"

Deor said slowly, "If you say so."

"I do say so. It stood out like Chariot in a cloudless winter sky when you looked at him in the talic realm."

Deor lowered his head. He was remembering the werewolf sewing beside him—holding his arms when he was hanging outside the gondola. It had *felt* as if there was someone behind those moonlit eyes. "Why didn't you notice it, then?" Deor asked. He could hear the anger in his own voice, but he couldn't keep it out.

"Of course I noticed it. I suspected it when we met, and confirmed it that first night, when I stood watch while you were all sleeping."

"Why didn't you say anything?"

"I thought Liyurriu might be useful. Even an enemy can be useful, if you know him for what he is. And it was not clear that Liyurriu (or his puppeteer, rather) was an enemy."

"Then Morlock was wrong."

"I didn't say so. He doesn't trust people who lie to him; it's a fool who does. Liyurriu could have been sent by someone who wants the world to end, to wait until we were vulnerable, then turn on us and kill us."

"Who would want that?"

"The people Morlock calls the Sunkillers."

"Surely there are none in our world? That's why we are going to find theirs."

"It's not sure at all, Deortheorn, if I may call you so."

"*Harven.*"

"There *was* one in the world, our world. I'm pretty sure there was. The Balancer, the unbeing that lived in the Waste Lands. Did Aloê ever tell you about it?"

"I heard something about it," Deor admitted.

"It had a relationship with the Two Powers. It was to keep them working, engaged in the destruction of the world. It was some plot of the Sunkillers, who lived in our world before the sun was born, and ached to return. That plot failed; this is another attempt, it would seem."

Deor thought long about this. "So you think Liyurriu was sent by them, or one of them—by the Sunkillers?"

"No, I don't. I doubt one of them would trouble to learn the night speech of werewolves, for instance. But what if I were wrong? I was willing to take the risk; Morlock wasn't. A difference of opinion."

"And of method."

"Because he acted arrogantly and alone, without saying a word to anyone? So did I, you know. And he gave Liyurriu, or whoever was pulling Liyurriu's strings, a chance to speak up. Whoever they are, they should not have tried to bandy words with Morlock Ambrosius."

There was an implied rebuke there, Deor decided. If the stranger behind the Liyurriu-mask should have not bandied words with Morlock, still less should his *harven*-kin, perhaps. And, if he was going to do it, he might as well do it to his kinsman's face.

He turned away from Ambrosia and his own thoughts and looked off *Viviana*'s left bow . . . "port" they'd say on a sea ship, although he never understood why.

There was a glittering ice-forest there, running west as far as Deor could see. They were flying low enough now that he could see things moving among the crystalline leaves. Icy birds? Perhaps. He couldn't quite catch their shapes.

Ambrosia and Kelat continued to talk in low tones behind him. They were not saying much, but the way they were saying it made him wonder if they would be mating soon. He hoped they wouldn't do it in the *Viviana*. He never enjoyed witnessing the mating of the Other Ilk—it was so violent, so hard to distinguish from an act of hate.

In the event, he found that he need not have worried. The *Viviana* had not long to live.

The first sign came that night.

Morlock was awake; Ambrosia was in trance. Deor had thought and thought and thought about what she had said to him earlier. So he nerved himself to stand up on his bench.

The moonslit snows below were bright as a skull's teeth, ready to devour him if he fell.

He sneered at them and gently stepped onto the bench where Kelat was snoring. The boy didn't waken.

Ambrosia was still sitting on the bench behind Kelat. Her closed eyes glowed eerily in trance. Even more eerily: she raised her right hand in greeting as he passed. Morlock couldn't do that in rapture. If Noreê or Illion or any of the great seers of the Wardlands could do it, Deor had never seen it. But it was effortless for Ambrosia. He raised his own in reply.

"Excuse me," he said gruffly, as he stepped past Morlock's bench, and then he seated himself on the vacant bench behind Morlock.

Morlock was enjoying some dry bread, salted meat, and a mold-speckled slab of pale, crumbly cheese. He held his hands out to Deor, silently offering to share.

Deor took a piece off the moldy end of the cheese. They sat there, chewing and not talking. Deor enjoyed a good talk, but he had grown up among seven clans of dwarves whose notions of conversation more nearly approximated Morlock's. And it was easeful to sit there, not saying anything because nothing needed to be said.

Then: something needed to be said.

Chariot shone brightly over the western horizon, and Horseman stood high overhead, eclipsed by *Viviana*'s bulk but adding its light to the world. Except for color, it was nearly as bright as day . . . and in this northern icescape there was little color to be seen.

So Deor saw quite clearly when a cloud of the fluttering things left the ice-forests below and arrowed toward low-flying *Viviana*.

"Morlock!" Deor shouted, and pointed.

Morlock looked, saw, stood. "Rouse Kelat and my sister, if you can." He ran forward recklessly, drawing his sword as he went. He stood on the prow of the gondola, his sword, bright with reflected moonlight, in his right hand; his left hand grasped the rigging.

Deor followed with more cautious speed. His shout woke the already twitching Kelat. Deor turned to look at Ambrosia, wondering what to do. He feared to touch her, lest he be drawn into her vision. Also, he had to admit to himself, he simply feared to touch her.

She raised both her hands now. He took that to mean, *Stop. I know what I'm doing.* He didn't doubt it. The Ambrosii always knew what they were doing. But they didn't seem to ever know what the other was doing.

Deor turned to look outboard of *Viviana*'s gondola.

The flying things were nearer now, the nearest ones enough to see. They weren't like birds—more like insects. They had great membranous wings that flapped so swiftly that they seemed to glow in the moonlight. Heads with many eyes, glittering like polished diamonds, turned on their narrow necks jerkily, as if moved by ill-made gears. Their long, curving bodies were filled with some dark sloshing fluid, clearly visible through the transparent chitinous plates they had for skin. They kept their long, spiny legs folded up over their great bellies, like self-satisfied club men after a good dinner. At the end of each broad tail was a long, glittering sting.

The foremost was heading straight for Morlock. Of course it was.

Deor watched, motionless, as the crystal beast arrowed in, swinging the fat weight of its body to direct the sting at Morlock. Then the dark fluid in its center seemed to boil, and a jet of it came out of the sting as it drove it to strike.

Morlock dodged the sting and its venom, if that's what it was.

The dark fluid fell among the ropes. The ropes stiffened and shattered like glass.

Morlock slashed with Tyrfing and shattered the icy wing of the beast.

It tumbled away in the night, silent, strangely like Liyurriu, striking a few of its fellows and taking them with it as it went, but there were more, so many more.

Then all of Deor's ancestors roared in his ears. He was a Theorn of Theorn clan, and his *harven*-kin was fighting for his life—for all their lives. So what if it was futile? So what if they all died? No dwarf lives forever.

He seized his axe and flourished it. "*Ath, rokhlan!*"

"*Ath! Ath!*" Morlock replied. He waved his sword at the moon in the west. "*Khai, gradara!*"

Deor leaped forward to stand beside Morlock on the prow, now swinging a little because of the shattered ropes.

Ambrosia spoke. "Ware impulse!" her toneless, entranced voice said.

Morlock and Deor had time to look at each other when the airship lurched forward.

They tumbled together back onto the empty bench at the front of the gondola.

There was a humming in the night: the *Viviana*'s propellers were spinning. Ambrosia was releasing the pent up energy of the impulse wells.

The cloud of icy insects was left behind, glittering in *Viviana*'s airy wake.

Deor, looking back, shook his free hand at them and shouted derisively.

Morlock tapped his shoulder and pointed ahead.

Another cloud of icy insects was rising to approach their prow.

"Gleh," said Deor.

"Yes," said Morlock. He jumped up on the bench and swarmed up a surviving rope using his feet and his left hand. As Deor watched, open-mouthed and uncomprehending, he swung Tyrfing with deadly force, shattering the keel of the airship and severing its fabric envelope. He climbed up onto the broken keel and slashed again and again. He shattered the glass furnace, scattering its long-burning maijarra coals among the ulken-cloth gasbags and the gondola. Gasbags were drifting away in the dark air.

"Deor! Kelat!" he called down. "Come on!"

Someone using Deor's voice said, in a remarkably cool tone, "Come on and do what exactly, *harven?*"

"Grab a gasbag and ride it down to the ground."

Of course. Of course. Deor looked about him sourly. Ambrosia was already swarming up the ropes. Kelat saw this and immediately followed suit.

The gondola was burning. The gasbags in the *Viviana*'s heart were afire. Ice-spewing crystal insects the color of moonslight were closing in on them from all sides. This was not the time to calmly discuss alternatives. If they had been just a little lower, Deor would have jumped, and to Canyon with the gasbags and Morlock's kindly meant suggestion. But they were still high enough to kill a falling dwarf. Deor thrust the axe handle into his belt and climbed up the ropes. He grabbed the first gasbag he came across. (Was it a good one? How could he tell?) He kicked off from the *Viviana* and drifted away into the moonslit void.

He was the first away. Morlock was still busy hacking away at the airship's shell. Ambrosia and Kelat were quarrelling about something. Irritably, Ambrosia seized a gasbag and drifted away from the dying airship. Kelat followed, gripping the seam of a gasbag with one hand, his sword with the other. Morlock at last grabbed a gasbag and kicked off.

The *Viviana* was now heeling badly, lit with internal fire in the bitter, night-blue air. Burning balloons were leaking from her wounded belly. The clouds of ice insects met her in midair and attacked.

Then, and only then, did Deor understand what Morlock had done. Abandoning the airship and scattering burning globes through the night air gave some cover for their escape.

Away from the glass furnace and the kindly tending of the seers, the bitter night air cooled Deor's gasbag quickly. His descent became something more like a fall. Soon he let go of the balloon and tossed his axe well away from him so that he would not disembowel himself on impact. The bone-white ground leapt up at him, and he committed himself to the care of his ancestors.

The surface was so soft that he didn't even feel his boots strike it. He passed from a world of moonlight to a world of darkness in an instant. He ground to a halt, not because his boots had struck earth at last; his fall simply seemed to have compacted a little island in the snow.

Deor took a cautious breath. There was little air to breathe: the snow had collapsed around him and he was quite thoroughly buried, perhaps to a depth that was twice his height, perhaps more—certainly not less.

But now he knew what he was doing. He started making a way for himself with his hands and feet, compressing snow, making a kind of slope to crawl out of the hole. It took time, but he wasn't worried. It was no worse than travelling over the glaciers of Mundjokull, though perhaps a little colder. A lot colder. No matter: he knew what to do and he did it. On the way up he came across his axe. It made him heavier, but he was glad to see it.

He broke back to the surface at last, after many a recollapse of the snow around him. The wind-carved crust of snow was very tenuous, but it could hold him if he stretched out his weight carefully.

He saw three other snowholes with floundering figures in them: his comrades.

Beyond them all, encircled by glittering clouds of ice-bugs, the *Viviana* fell from the night-blue sky. Horseman, rising in the west, lit her with fierce light; beyond her in the eastern sky, Trumpeter seemed to watch somberly. Her front section completely empty of balloons, the rear section in flames, she dropped prow first toward the snowy fields and crashed, the remains of her wooden framework and gondola screaming on impact before silence fell, even the fires silent, quenched by the bitter, moonblue snow.

Deor watched it all through a haze of tears. He had hated the journey on the *Viviana* more than any other he had ever taken. But she was the work of their hands and minds, fearfully and cunningly made with great labor, and she had died protecting them. He wiped the tears away and snarled at himself for a fool. But he did not look away until the fires were gone and the ice insects had flown off again.

Deor crawled across the surface crust to where Morlock and Ambrosia were arising from their own impact craters, crooked shadows in the moonlit snow.

"What now, Ambrosii?" he called.

"The wreck of the *Viviana*," said the shadow with Morlock's voice.

Of course. Their packs, if they could recover them.

"And maybe we can salvage some of her for snowshoes," he said, thinking aloud.

"A good thought," Morlock said.

Deor looked at the ruins of the *Viviana*, half sunk in snowdrifts.

"She was a brave ship," he said, and—Canyon keep it!—his voice broke in mid-sentence.

The shadow that was Ambrosia turned to look at him. "Yes," she said. "I should have known better than to name her after a woman so mortal and so crazy. But maybe that's why she was so brave."

"Could be," said Deor with Morlockian gruffness, and crawled off to help Kelat out of his snow pit.

CHAPTER SIX

The Narrow Road
to the Deep North

Their packs survived more or less intact. Morlock and Ambrosia had placed fire-quell magic on them, as they did out of habit with most things they wore, and the only losses were from the crash. In Morlock's, for instance, the impact had shattered a jar of some horrible mushroom liquor he had received as a gift from the Blackthorn masters of making.

"Eh," said Morlock. "I could have used a drink."

"You drink too much, *harven*," Deor said.

Morlock shrugged and turned away to harvest fabric and wood for snowshoes.

They each made their own snowshoes, even Kelat, who proved to be quite good at it.

"If you couldn't make snowshoes and walk away," he explained to Deor, "you were trapped all winter long with the other Uthars."

"But it can't snow so very much on the north shore of the Sea of Stones, where Uthartown is," Deor objected.

"Uthartown is wherever the Uthars are. It must have had fifteen different locations that I can remember."

"Sixteen since you were born," Ambrosia interjected.

Deor's eyes crossed at this and Morlock smiled to himself. Deor understood travel, and tolerated it fairly well, but the idea of a home that was *not always in the same place*: that was unthinkable to many a dwarf.

Morlock cut cloth from the shell of the *Viviana* and made it into face masks for each of them.

Ambrosia and Deor took theirs without comment, but Kelat objected. "I don't like things on my face—I don't care how cold it gets."

299

"Your face cares," Morlock retorted. "We are nearing the edge of the world, where men may not dwell."

"Even Deor and I don't like it much," Ambrosia said. Kelat laughed, and did not put on his mask. The others did, though.

The track of the sunstream was easy to read on the moonslit face of the snowy plain, and they shuffled across the empty white fields to reach it.

The snow crust there was deeper and more stable. They pitched camp for the night.

"We should have brought firewood from the *Viviana*," Kelat said.

"No fires on this trip," Morlock said.

"What keeps us from freezing at night?"

"You will, Prince Uthar," Ambrosia said. "You're a furnace, burning fuel night and day. Did you know it? All we need do is contain the heat that you, and I, and the others here generate as a matter of course. Morlock or I can shepherd that heat, keeping it within a shelter, as we kept it in the balloons of the *Viviana*."

Kelat looked relieved at this, but Deor gave a sidelong glance and said, "I don't like it, *harven*. Long watches in the visionary realm are a burden you have already born to your harm. Kelat and I will go fetch some firewood."

Ambrosia said flatly, "No. We can't carry firewood enough to last us to the edge of the world, and we're unlikely to find any on the road, unless you think you can make a bonfire out of ice-trees. This is the only way, Deortheorn," she added in a gentler tone.

"There's another way," Deor said stubbornly. "Share your burden. Teach us how to do it."

Morlock met Ambrosia's eye. She nodded briskly. "The Sight is a treacherous gift for a ruler," she said. "But *harven* Deor has a point."

"I always have a point," Deor admitted, "though I usually manage to stab myself with it."

They set up their occlusion and ran a census on their food. It wasn't much to reach the end of the world with, much less to walk all the way back.

Deor said to Kelat, whose face fell approximately one face-length when he saw how small the rations would be, "Well, look on the bright side. We may not have to walk back."

"Because we'll be dead, you mean?" Kelat said calmly. "That might be just as well. Starvation's an ugly death."

Morlock was impressed with the youth's steadiness. He did childish things, like refuse to wear a face mask in the coldest air in the world. But he was not a child.

"If it comes to that," Morlock said, "there are ways to survive without food."

Deor stared at him. "Oh?"

"Yes. We might absorb the tal of the local beasts and plants directly. It would keep life in our bodies, anyway."

"What's the downside? I can tell by your face there's a downside."

"It may change our bodies."

"Ach. Well, troubles never come singly."

"And a stitch in time saves nine."

"A stitch or nine is exactly what you'll need when I'm done with you, *harven*," Deor said mildly.

They each ate something and then Ambrosia and Kelat wrapped themselves in their sleeping cloaks and lay back to back. Deor stayed awake for a while and Morlock took him through the first lessons of the Sight. It did not go as badly as it might have, and Morlock was strangely moved to think that his *harven*-kin and oldest friend might become a dwarvish seer—a rare thing in the world, if not absolutely unheard of.

Morlock watched intermittently all through the night. The occlusion, in fact, trapped most of their heat, but he set a sentinel mannikin to wake him every few hours to make sure the shelter had not grown too cold.

When day came they struck camp without eating and began the long walk northward on the narrow road paved with ice and the sun's death. The cleft of the road was always before them; their path ran a little below the level of the snow fields, and there was often drifting snow to contend with. The day was but little warmer than the night; the heat drawn away from the sun seemed mostly to stay aloft. Kelat rarely wore his face mask but Morlock didn't warn him again; he was not the boy's mother.

They walked, with a few breaks, until sunset. Then they made camp, ate a little, and Kelat and Ambrosia stayed up while Morlock and Deor turned in.

And that was how it went: day after day in the endless plain of snow and ice. The biggest difference most days was in who would hold the watch at night.

They talked some as they walked. But, in truth, a time came when they had said most of what they had to say to each other, and each walked with his or her own thoughts.

Morlock's daydreams largely focused on Aloê. Rarely in their marriage had they been apart so long or so far. His longing for her was by now the principal concern of his waking life. It dwarfed hunger, thirst, cold, and fear. The hope of her, the golden warmth of the thought of her, kept him moving. The only way back to her was ahead. His long, regular strides were like the beat of a song, a song that had one word: *Aloê . . . Aloê . . . Aloê. . . .*

It was not all monotony, though. Occasionally, there were monsters.

One day they found they had passed from the flat, snowy plains to a bumpier region of snow-covered hills. The hills bristled with black-hearted ice trees. The bloodless sun above lit the hills with searing brightness. Morlock drew his mask over his eyes and stared down at the ground. So he wasn't the first to see it.

"Morlocktheorn," Deor said at his elbow. "One of those hills is moving."

Morlock looked up and saw: a hill that stood just to the left of their path lurched up from the ground. They could see sky beneath it through three stumpy legs or roots that still touched the ground.

"Is it a plant?" wondered Deor. "Or . . . ?"

It pulled one of its legs loose from the ground. The leg looked oddly like one of the trees on the beast's back: crystalline and spiky, veined with darkness.

A second leg came loose, and then the third.

Morlock remembered shapes he had not understood when seen from the air: vast hill-sized shapes moving through the snow. This. These, rather: they should assume that all the hills were the three-legged hulking beasts.

It took a step, and the ground shook. The step was toward them.

"Move," said Ambrosia, but they were all moving already.

Now more hills were shaking, streams of snow flying off them in the wind like strands of white hair.

"Think they eat things like us?" Deor speculated.

"Does it matter, if they kill us first?" Kelat replied.

"It may to them. Think how disappointed they'll be! 'Oh, no! Dwarf-meat again!'"

"That what your mother used to say, you think?"

Deor glanced at Morlock, rolled his eyes, and laughed with (it seemed to Morlock) ostentatious politeness. Morlock decided he should tell Kelat about dwarvish family life so that he could make his banter more on point.

The hillbeast who had first awakened was moving faster now—as fast as they were, shuffling along on their snowshoes. It seemed to be picking up speed as it went, and now there were others bumbling along behind it. The hillbeasts on the eastern side of the road were trundling into motion also.

"Should we kick these shoes off?" Ambrosia, who was in the lead, called back.

Morlock had been thinking the same thing, but on impulse he shouted back, "No!" He waited a moment for his half-formed idea to emerge fully into being and then continued, "Slow start; slow stop."

"Right!" Ambrosia called back after another moment. She leaped off the narrow road to the north and ran westward through the field of shuddering beasts.

"Deor! With her! Kelat, with me!" Morlock shouted. He leaped off the road, running eastward.

The cold—cruel enough on the snowy road carved by the sun's death—bit deeper than ever in the snowy fields. Morlock was glad of his mask—wished for something better. He wondered if impulse wells could be adapted to turn impulses into heat. Hm. . . . If you put impulse collectors in the shoes. . . .

A hillbeast roared behind him. Once, in a very different land than this, Morlock had heard an elephant scream when it stepped on a poisoned stake. If a thousand elephants made of glass had stepped on four thousand poisoned stakes, it might have sounded something like the hillbeast's rage.

"What are we doing?" Kelat wondered aloud, shuffling along beside him.

Morlock looked at Kelat, noticed something about his face, decided it wasn't the time to mention it. "We're sowing confusion," he said, and jabbed a thumb over his lower shoulder.

Kelat spun about and gasped. He grabbed Morlock's arm and Morlock halted, looking over his shoulder.

One of the hillbeasts pursuing them had blundered against a hillbeast that was just beginning to rouse itself. The hillbeast in motion staggered back and raised the long lip of its gigantic body, exposing the vast mouth between its spiny root-like legs. The mouth had no teeth, but it did display a long, snakelike, thorny tongue. It screamed its thousand-glass-elephants-in-agony scream and stabbed the offending hillbeast through its side with the long, indefinitely extensible tongue. Black matter spurted out of the wound, and the attacker rolled its tongue in and out of the wound, slurping up the clumpy black fluid, whatever it was. Now the offending hillbeast, offended, struggled to its rooty feet and stabbed its attacker with its own tongue.

The beasts about them were rising up also.

"Come," said Morlock. "We'll run until we have pursuers and double back—"

"I see!" shouted Kelat, evidently delighted, although his face didn't change expression much.

They ran back and forth for much of the day, sowing chaos among the hillbeasts. Sometimes they caught sight of Ambrosia and Deor doing the same. But as the sun began eastering, Morlock led Kelat away northward through the fields, successfully avoiding the attention of the hillbeasts, who were mostly busy feeding on each other.

They saw Deor and Ambrosia running parallel to them on the far side of the road. As dusk rose, blue from the earth, into the sky, they met on the road and set up occlusions for shelter.

The others wanted to talk about the adventures of the day, but Morlock overrode them all, saying to Kelat, "Let's have a look at your face."

Startled, Kelat raised a gloved hand to his face. "What's wrong with it? It doesn't hurt."

"Feel anything?" Morlock asked.

"Uh. . . . No."

"It's frostbite," Ambrosia confirmed, looking at the hard, white skin that showed wherever his golden beard didn't. "Oh, Uthar."

"Sit down," Morlock directed. "Take your gloves off and hold your hands over your face."

Ambrosia sat next to him and closed her eyes. In moments she was in visionary rapture.

"It's starting to feel better," Kelat said.

Morlock didn't doubt it. Ambrosia could herd the warmth from Kelat's hands and his core to thaw his frozen flesh. But if the tissue was dead . . . dead was dead.

Morlock sat, shucked his pack, unpacked his food, ate his cursory meal in three bites, and then filled his belly with water, wishing it were wine.

"I'm going to be all right," Kelat said tentatively. If it was a question, Morlock didn't answer it. He put his food and waterbottle away and unfolded his sleeping cloak.

Ambrosia descended from vision. She opened her eyes, looked at Morlock, and shrugged.

Morlock tapped his nose, meaning, *What about his nose?*

Ambrosia shook her head. It was dead (or so Morlock guessed).

"We should take care of it now," Morlock observed.

"*You* are sure of that," she said.

He thought this remark over. Morlock was sure, and Ambrosia was likely sure as well. But Kelat would not be.

"What do you mean?" the young Vraid said. He was still obediently holding his hands over his face. If he had as obediently worn his face mask, he would not be facing mutilation now. On the other hand, if he were merely obedient, he wouldn't be much use on a quest like this.

"Your face will be well enough, though it will have some bruising for a while," Ambrosia said. "Your nose is in a more serious condition."

"What's wrong with it?"

"We'll know in a couple of days. You can lower your hands now."

They talked even less than usual that night.

The next day, Kelat wore his face mask. Morlock and Deor talked over the idea of using impulse wells to heat clothing in winter. It was purely theoretical, since they had no impulse wells or the means to make them at hand, but it was a way to combat the perpetual gnawing chill, if only in imagination. It seemed to raise everyone's spirits.

At the end of the next day they inspected Kelat's face again. The bruising was horrific: blackish purple smeared across his face, darkest on the nose. The very end of his nose was a greenish gray: gangrene was beginning.

They showed it to him in a mirror and explained what it meant.

"Cut my nose off?" he said, obviously surprised at the thought of it. "Can't you heal it? Surely you can heal it! I've seen the wonders you can do when you try."

"The flesh is dead," Ambrosia said with unwonted gentleness. "I'm sorry, Kelat. But dead is dead. It will have to come off."

Kelat looked at each of them, as if he expected someone to disagree. He shouted, "No! No! I'd rather die."

"No, you wouldn't," Ambrosia said impatiently.

"You don't know—"

"It's you who don't know, sir. That's why you are in this uncomfortable position. But that's all that it is—not a matter of life and death."

"It is to me!"

"Kelat, my friend," Morlock said. "There are things worth dying for. We all believe that, or we wouldn't be here. But vanity isn't one of them."

"This isn't vanity."

"It is."

Silence.

"Let me go away," the young man said quietly. "Let me go away and die in the wilderness. You can keep my rations and have . . . have that much good from this mess."

Ambrosia's eyes filled with tears and she looked at Morlock.

"No," he said pitilessly. "You have not yet been of much use on this quest, young Prince Uthar, but what use you could be you still can be. We didn't bring you along to judge perfumes or the bouquets of fine vintages, you know."

Kelat glared at him with hatred.

"But if you insist on leaving when the journey is at its most dangerous," Morlock continued, "you must, of course, take your rations. If you find the courage to live, out among the snows, you'll need them."

"Shut up! *Shut up!*"

Silence again.

"I'll kill you someday," Kelat remarked in a conversational tone.

Morlock shrugged his crooked shoulders, and there was no more talk of Kelat wandering off in the night to die.

They lay Kelat on his back. Ambrosia fed him a painkilling drug she had in her pack, and they arranged shears, bandages, snow, and herbs near at hand.

But when she lifted up the shears, her eyes grew wet again and she whispered, "Oh, Morlock. Oh, his beautiful face."

Morlock was not attached to the young man's beautiful face and he didn't like the way his sister's hands were trembling. He took the shears from her. He put his left hand over Kelat's eyes, to restrain him physically and to keep him from flinching, and swiftly snipped off the gangrenous nose. Deor deftly caught it, and Ambrosia and Morlock busied themselves with sewing up the edges of the wound and bandaging it before Kelat lost too much blood.

"You've redleaf?" he asked her at one point.

"Yes. We'll have to give it to him to chew; we can't make tea."

Then they were done. Kelat would have gotten up groggily, but they made him lie down again. "Rest!" said Ambrosia. "It's all any of us can do tonight."

Kelat lay back down and saw Deor awkwardly holding the severed nose.

"Might need it," Kelat said thickly, as if he had the worst cold in history. "Make soup out of it."

Deor reflected briefly and then said deliberately, "Snot soup? I remember—"

Kelat gasped, then laughed, spraying blood out of his mouth and nose hole. "Sorry!" he said as the others cleaned him up. "Sorry!"

"My fault," said Deor, not very sincerely to Morlock's eye.

"Snot soup," Kelat whispered, and chuckled. He said no other word until morning.

The drug that Ambrosia had given him made Kelat sleep, but his sleep was restless and he kept waking and dozing all through the night. At no waking moment did he get the cruel relief of forgetfulness, the delusion that it had all been some terrible dream: it was always the pain in his face that woke him.

The next day he rinsed his mouth with melted snow, forced himself to eat a few bites of food, and then bound on his snowshoes and shuffled with the others along the narrow road northward. He wore his mask, of course. In fact, he had decided he would wear it, or something like it, for the rest of his life.

The pain was pain. He didn't relish it, but he could bear it. The shame of his stupidity—that would be with him for the rest of his life: every time he looked at a mirror; every time he chose not to look; every time someone looked at his face; every time they chose not to look.

The day was cold and searingly bright. He was so sick of the endless cold, the endless snow and ice. And now the shame, like vomit, filling his gorge. Maybe death was better than this.

But he would not be weaker than the others. Not again. Whatever burdens they bore, he would bear them, too. He would show them, and himself, that he could.

He found himself walking next to Morlock, with the others some distance ahead.

"I'll never forget what you said to me," Kelat remarked quietly.

Morlock looked at him with those gray eyes, bright and cold as the horizon, and waited. There was a calm in him that nothing could touch. Kelat envied it and hated it.

"I'll always remember," Kelat continued, "that you gave me something to live for, even if it was only hate."

Morlock relaxed indefinably. "Well. I have natural gifts in that direction. So Ambrosia is always telling me."

"And you're not worried about me acting on the hate?"

Morlock shrugged his crooked shoulders. Kelat waited, but he didn't say anything more. They walked together in silence for a long while.

That afternoon, as the sun was eastering, Kelat was walking alone while Morlock and Ambrosia conversed in low voices ahead of him. He couldn't catch everything they were saying, but finally he heard Morlock say, in an annoyed tone, "People are born every day with faces worse than he has now."

Ambrosia replied heatedly, "Those people are not the King of All the Vraids."

"Is Kelat likely to be?" Morlock sounded surprised.

"Someone has to be. You can say it doesn't matter, that a civilized people wouldn't care what its leaders looked like. But the Vraids are, at best, semicivilized."

"A civilized people doesn't have leaders," Morlock replied.

Ambrosia laughed, taking it as a joke. Morlock did not laugh, and Kelat wondered why. She glanced back toward him and he didn't meet her eye, or give any sign he had heard them. He didn't want to betray any sign of weakness. He was painfully aware that this was itself a sign of weakness, but he couldn't help that. It was his only way forward, his only plan of action.

At dark they pitched camp, ate a few bites from their dwindling stocks of food. Then Morlock and Deor turned in while Ambrosia stayed up to keep watch in visionary rapture.

"You should sleep, too," Ambrosia said to Kelat, who had made no move toward his sleeping cloak.

"You were going to teach me about the Sight," he reminded her.

She almost spoke, stopped herself, looked at him (he was glaring though his mask), and nodded.

For some reason, he found it easier to focus on the spiritual exercises than before. And once he felt himself floating above his body: not cold, not in pain, not ashamed. He turned toward Ambrosia and saw her talic presence, like bright, fiery flowers. Behind her lay a shadow, still as death.

Then it was gone, and he was in his body again.

"That was extraordinary," Ambrosia said, and seemed to mean it. "Rest now. Meditate on what you've learned, and even more what you've unlearned."

He nodded and turned to wrap himself in his sleeping cloak.

Thus ended his first day as a noseless freak.

The end of the world seemed a world away. Morlock remembered seeing it from the gondola of the *Viviana*, but he didn't truly believe in it any more. It was just necessary to keep on walking and walking until they froze or starved or were killed by monsters. He remembered the reason why they were there. He remembered it the way he remembered being warm, or drunk, or the afterglow of sex. These were historical facts. But they had no relevance to his life now.

Loneliness was as much a part of this journey as the deadly cold and the hunger. Paradoxically, there was also a lack of solitude. They were always in each other's company, and they grew weary of each other's faces and voices. By mutual consent they started spending more time alone—leaving many paces between each other, the little company strung out on the long, narrow road.

Morlock's antidote through this time had been thoughts of Aloê Oaij. But by now all those thoughts were a little threadbare, and they did not keep the chill of loneliness out anymore. He felt as if she were talking to him constantly, but he couldn't understand what she was saying. That meant thoughts of her were laced with frustration as well as comfort. Then one morning he woke up and the words were gone. Her voice was gone. He could not remember exactly what her voice sounded like. That was a bad morning.

When they took breaks from walking, one or more of them would leave the road. Originally these were opportunities to relieve themselves—at least in Morlock's case. But eventually he started to leave the road just to be away from the others, to be free from the boredom that was as mindless and intense as rage.

There was little variety in the harsh, white landscape—even the hills were often shadowless, if the day was cloudy. But it was something slightly different. On the long, tedious trek north, even little reliefs were welcome—necessary.

One day, as Morlock walked around a small hill on the east side of the road, he was surprised by the sight and sound of something new. It was a kind of flower grown from ice. It was a little like a woodland tulip: seven petals surrounding an open face. It was about as high as his knee, and it was emitting a low, silvery tone, like a wind-chime in the chill, persistent breeze.

As he took a step closer, the tone changed, became deeper somehow.

That was interesting, and it had been so long since something interested him that he stepped still closer. Then the tone changed again. It was fascinating, and the sound was reminding him of something; he wasn't sure just what. He stepped closer and saw that a second glass flower was rising up from the snow to join the first. The tone it emitted was like and unlike the first. Together, they made a sound that was very pleasing, and increasingly familiar to him.

He took a step closer, and a third glassy flower rose from the ground to stand with the others.

The music was warmer now, as warm as a human breath in the icy air.

He stepped forward.

Now there was a crown of woodland tulips the color of glass, their faces toward him, singing a wordless song in a voice that he knew.

It was Aloê's voice; he recognized it now.

He recognized something else. The tulips lying on the ground had been concealing something: a sac of darkish fluid set into the snow. In the sack were floating half-melted (or half-digested) ice insects.

They had been drawn by the music, as he had been drawn. They had gotten too close, as he was getting too close. And they had been swallowed by something, some mouth beneath the snow crust. He thought he could feel the surface shifting slightly underneath his snowshoes as he stood there amazed.

He thought of stepping backwards instead of forwards. He thought about it for a long time. But he didn't do anything about it. The thought of step-ping backward and losing the sound of Aloê's voice was inexpressibly painful to him. But that was only part of it. His legs were not under his control. They were numb, almost, but not with cold. What if the sound was vibrating the strings of his nerves and overmastering his ability to move? Had he been stung by something, and was he feeling the effects of the venom? Was this binding magic of a kind his talismans did not protect him from?

He managed to not go forward. But the truth was, he could not go back.

He thought of drawing his stabbing spear. But as soon as the thought entered his mind, there grew up an impassable gulf between intention and execution. Nor could he speak, to call Tyrfing to his hand.

So he stood there, bathed in the voice of his beloved wife, expecting death.

A howl broke the spell—a long, ululating, meaty howl from a wolvish throat. The ice flowers rippled like water. Some turned away in the direction of the howl; others stayed, gazing at Morlock. But the music, and the magic, was broken.

"Tyrfing!" shouted Morlock.

The deadly crystalline blade flew around the hill to his outstretched hand. He stepped forward and swung the blade like a scythe, mowing down the ice flowers. They shattered like glass and their voices fell silent. The howling, too, had ceased.

Morlock felt something moving under the snow and waited for the flower beast's mouth to appear. He was disappointed when it didn't. He stepped forward and slashed through the stomach sac, letting its dark fluids and half-dissolved contents flow into the surrounding snow. The movement under the snow stopped.

Morlock took three long steps back and turned to face the howler.

It was Liyurriu. The left side of his face was smashed flat, like a clay figure that someone had dropped on the floor while it was still wet and then stepped on. There was a definite list to his four-legged stance. But Morlock knew those ape hands and feet.

"Stay where you are," he said to the werewolf. "The weapon in my hand can sever your life from your body, however they are bound together."

The werewolf promptly sat and proceeded to gnaw a tangle from its curling, hair-like fur.

The beloved voice of his sister fell unpleasantly on Morlock's ear. "What in Chaos are you doing here, Morlock?" Nonetheless, he was glad she was here to act as interpreter. Deor and Kelat were at her side.

"Almost getting killed," he said. "Watch out for singing flowers."

"And why are you menacing the entity who, apparently, saved you with another kind of singing?"

"You know why."

"What's to be done, then?"

"I want Liyurriu here to tell us what he is and who sent him."

"And if his answers don't suit you . . . ?" began Ambrosia, with a dangerous tone in her voice.

But the werewolf was already ululating a long and, to Morlock's untrained ear, rather repetitive reply. Ambrosia heard him through, sang a few howls herself, each one of which got a copious response from Liyurriu.

"First," Ambrosia said at last in Wardic, "he says that he is sorry he didn't trust you with the truth back in the airship."

Morlock grunted. "I'm not interested in apologies."

"*He* is. I'm giving you the barest summary."

"Thanks."

Ambrosia continued, "He is sent here, he says, by a lifemaker in the werewolf city. The maker—"

"What's his name?"

Ambrosia uttered a kind of howl.

"That sounds just like his name," Morlock said.

"No, no—they're really quite different. Listen, I'll sing it again more slowly—"

Morlock held up his free hand. "Never mind. We can go on thinking of him as Lurriulu—"

"Liyurriu."

"—yes. I doubt that I'll ever have the need to speak Werewolvish."

"You never know, Morlock. Anyway, what would your Oldfather Tyr say to hear you dispraising the study of languages."

"As a matter of fact," Deor observed, "he was not fond of wolves."

"So be it! Liyurriu was sent by this lifemaker to aid us. He's worried about the end of the world, you see, as well he might be."

"Eh. Wouldn't a werewolf like it if the sun never rose?"

"I asked about that. Werewolves get cold, too, it seems. Also, no sunlight would be bad for the prey, he said.

"Us, in fact."

"Yes. He admitted that, too, by the way. He's being very candid, Morlock."

"Understood."

"He'll help us if he can. If we tell him to go away, he'll go away. If you wish to dismember him, feel free to do so; the body is only an avatar."

"Eh. He may have a dozen more."

"He said he has more, yes."

"What do you think?"

"I think he could have let you die just now, and then come after us one by one on the road. I thought you were high-handed before, but your suspicions were reasonable, given what we knew then. Now we know more."

"Another mouth to feed," Kelat pointed out.

"Uh—Prince Uthar makes a good point—"

The werewolf sang.

"'This avatar does not need food,'" Ambrosia translated. "Any other objections?"

Deor shook his head slowly. Morlock said, "No." Kelat said nothing.

"Now we are five," Ambrosia said happily. "It'll be nice to have someone else to talk with. Let's get going!"

Ambrosia came up with a novel method of varying the monotony of their companionship. There was no reason why they couldn't establish two shelters every night rather than one, and they could vary the numbers in each shelter: two in one, three in the other, one in one, four in the other. They could roll dice or draw lots to decide how many shelters and who slept in each one. Conceivably they could even have five different shelters, although that might be putting undue stress on the seers who kept them alive each night.

It was amazing what only a night or two of these arbitrary separations did for their companionship. They talked more during the day. They resented each other less at night. Kelat already believed that Ambrosia was wiser than everyone else, but she was always outdoing herself in his estimation. He did not say anything about this, however, and his expression could not have betrayed him, as he wore his mask all the time now.

Until the third night of shelter switching, when the gods of chance or fate assigned Ambrosia and Kelat to the same two-person shelter. Morlock, in the other shelter, was seer for the night.

"Come, Prince Uthar," she said briskly once they had eaten their meager meal. "Off with the mask and I'll check your wound."

"I've been taking care of it," Kelat said sullenly.

"I'm not much of a healer, but I'm better than you are. You'll concede that, I hope."

"Yes."

"Then: off with it."

Kelat took his mask off, feeling more naked than if he'd taken off his breeches. She swiftly unbandaged his face and looked at his wound. "Good," she said. "You *have* been taking care of it."

"I don't want to be—" He snapped his mouth shut.

"—any more of a nuisance that you've already been?" she guessed.

"Something like that."

"On a long enough trip, everyone takes their turn at being a pain in the ass. Don't let it worry you. Morlock was sort of an idiot about that glass flower, but you don't see it bothering him."

"I don't see anything bothering him."

"And you'd like to be like that? I suppose I understand. When I was young and foolish, I felt the same way. But in the intervening years, I discovered two things. One is that things bother Morlock more than he lets on. He just doesn't show it the way we do because he wasn't raised by men and women. The other thing was: I'd rather be *me* than anyone else in all the worlds."

"Of course," he breathed. It was a confession of his adoration. He knew it, only after he had spoken, and she knew it, too, he thought. Her radiant gray eyes fixed on his and she smiled. He reached reflexively for his mask, but she reached it first with her long, clever fingers and tossed it across the shelter.

"If you touch that thing again tonight," she said, smiling angrily, "I'll strip your clothes off and toss your bare ass out into the snow."

"I don't want you to have to look at the hole in my face," he said, turning away from her. "My beautiful face," he added bitterly.

She took him by the chin and turned that face toward her again. "I'm older than you are," she said, "and I know that something can be broken and still be beautiful."

"Like me."

"Like your face. *You* are not broken. I've seen you struggling with this, becoming a man under the weight of it and . . . and other things. But yes. I still find your face beautiful."

She kissed the wound where his nose had been. He felt with horror her soft, firm lips on the ragged, seeping edges of his wound. He was shocked to the core, and without thinking he pushed her violently away. She landed on her elbows next to his discarded mask, her eyes wider and more luminous than ever and a crazy, terrifying grin on her face.

"That's the way you want to play it, eh?" she said.

She launched herself with her elbows and landed on top of him. He tried to hold her away from him, but she was so strong. . . . Plus, she cheated by tickling him where his leg met his hip, which never failed to make him convulse (although he had no idea how she knew that). She rewarded herself with a long, wet kiss (on his mouth this time, thank the Strange Gods), and he could not even try to hold her away any longer.

"I'm not worthy of you," he whispered in her ear.

She laughed wickedly and the sound stabbed him with pleasure. "That's not your problem, Uthar. The only thing you have to decide is whether you want to fuck me."

"Always have," he whispered.

"Then get your damn clothes off. No, never mind!" Her left hand danced across the fastenings for his clothing while her right hand did the same for hers. In seconds they were rolling around unclothed on the floor of the shelter and he was exulting in the sacred, unspeakable beauty of her nakedness: rosy ivory skin shading to golden brown on her arms and face, iron muscles moving under her sheath of female softness, mouth wet on his, tongue searching desperately for his, then he was on her, ungracefully, eagerly, and she guided him with her clever hands, and her pubic hair scratched along the shaft of his penis as he sank into her, and she was hot and wet, hotter than the dying sun, wetter than the sea.

The world was silent. There was no sound anywhere.

Uthar moved his hips as far back as he dared; he felt he would die if his penis didn't stay inside her vulva. Then he rode that silken slide of ecstasy down to its end again, and one more time, and then his body was shaken by a storm of orgasm. It was pleasure enough to unhinge the mind, yes, and it was a relief, yes, and it *hurt*. It hurt the way it hurts when you've been carrying something for too long, so long you've almost forgotten what it was like before you were carrying it, and then you set it down, and it's wonderful to be free of it, and only then are your muscles free to feel pain.

He lay atop her, gasping out words of love and worship, and the world wasn't silent anymore.

He heard his beloved's voice as if from far away, through the golden fog of carnal ecstasy: "Well. That wasn't so bad. How soon can you go again?"

It was a long night, and yet too short.

In morning's blank, ugly light her beauty was still sacred, transcendent, superbly practical. She set about the tasks of the morning as if they had sex every night.

As the others were still disestablishing the occlusion over their shelter, and somewhat out of earshot, he said to her, "If—"

She said, "I'll tell you when I'm done with you."

And that was what he had to hold onto that day. She was not done with him. She had never, in the course of the entire night, said that she loved him. And of course, love had little to do with her choice of a life-mate. And would a demimortal like her condescend to be the life-mate of a wholly mortal man whose life was so much shorter than hers?

The worst possible way to look at it was this: she was mating with him because, nosed or noseless, he was the only eligible man for thousands of miles. This was all the more possible, since he'd heard her remark to Morlock something about "my brother, a dwarf, and a meat-puppet that looks like a werewolf." Kelat wasn't any of these things; hence, last night—and tonight, possibly, and perhaps an indefinite number of nights. Then nothing, when she had a longer list to choose from.

It was worth it, he decided. He'd have given up a thousand noses to have what he had with her now, however long it lasted.

The random assignments of shelter mates continued. When Kelat and Ambrosia had a shelter to themselves, they coupled like murkles in heat. Otherwise, they were companions on the road, no different than the others. Kelat assumed that the others knew, but nevertheless no one ever referred to it, giving the affair a pleasing quality of sneakiness and privacy.

One day, Kelat was concerning himself with numbers (the bites of food left in his disturbingly light pack; the odds that he and Ambrosia would pair off tonight), when he saw a piece of ice falling from the sky.

The weather had been as monotonous as the road north: clear and cold. He wondered if this was the first blast of an ice storm . . . but the sky was cloudless; the silver sun glittered on the ice, almost an arch, or a. . . . There were scales or something on the arch. . . .

Liyurriu snarled and ran forward, but it was too late: the gigantic ice-dragon's tail slammed down and trapped the Ambrosii and Deor beneath it.

The werewolf ran on. Kelat threw off his pack and ran after him, drawing his spear as he went.

The ice dragon's gigantic wolflike head slithered into view. It was almost impossible to see its glassy outlines against the white snow. But Kelat could see hollow fangs that dripped with something like venom. . . .

Liyurriu had closed with the dragon's head and seemed to fly up into the air. Then Kelat realized the werewolf was climbing something—some feathering, or icy plates on the side of the serpentine head.

He kicked off his snowshoes and leaped for the same—hoping it was there rather than actually seeing it. He landed a foot or two off the ground, sliding across a piece of nearly invisible ice, leaving scars from his cleated boots. He jumped at the next feather, and the next, until he was beside Liyurriu in the back of the thing's gleaming, surprisingly narrow neck.

It was ware of them, and the head began to twist around. That was good because it was turning away from their companions, still trapped under the tail. It was also bad because they nearly fell off. Liyurriu and Kelat both grabbed for the nearest dorsal plate and managed to hang on.

The werewolf put his misshapen jaws to the back of the glassy neck and gnawed at it.

Kelat saw his purpose. Break through the scaly skin—sever the spine. If it was like dragons of a more familiar kind, that might kill it.

A jet of translucent shining ichor sprayed out of the dragon. Liyurriu tried to dodge aside but could not. The jet fell across his foreleg and it shattered like glass. Liyurriu fell silently away, and the task was left to Kelat.

He could see no other method than Liyurriu's, nor did he expect any different fate than Liyurriu's. That didn't bother him. It was wonderful, after a lifetime of being a spare part that no one would ever want, to know his purpose in life: he was born to love Ambrosia, and to die defending her.

What did worry him was the thought that he might fail. He must not fail.

He stabbed with his spear deep into the ice-dragon's neck, dancing away from the jet of freezing ichor and steam that sprayed out. Then he did it again and again. The jets were smaller, easier to avoid, flowing through the several holes he had made. He cut a channel between them, and the deadly muck flowed away thickly down the side of the beast.

There was a strange weightless sensation, as if he were flying. Then he saw that he was: the dragon's head was in midair. The beast was lifting itself up, perhaps to crash its head down and shake him loose. If so, he had moments, perhaps only a moment.

He stabbed into the glassy trench he had made, as near the center of the neck as he could tell, as deep as he could drive the spear's blade. And he struck! He struck something.

His hands, drenched in ichor, were numb and void of feeling. But they still gripped the shaft of his spear. He drew it out and stabbed again and again and again. The dragon's head struck the snowy ground and the shock threw him off it.

He tried to get to his feet, but his body would not respond. He saw that the spear-shaft in his hand was broken a handsbreadth below where his hands still gripped it.

He craned his neck to look at the ice-dragon. It was lying near at hand in a steaming pool of its own glassy ichor. Its eyes were open, filled with rainbows in the sun's pale light. But it wasn't moving. He guessed it was dead.

Ambrosia came running up to him.

"You stupid son-of-a-whore!" she screamed. "I'll kill your stupid, nose-less face!"

That was when he knew that she loved him. It was terrible to lose her, and the world that was suddenly his, in that moment. But the knowledge was something he could carry with him into the darkness, and he hugged it close to him as his awareness ebbed away.

When Morlock dragged himself out from beneath the dead ice-dragon, he heard Ambrosia screaming and got up to run toward her. But he was stopped by the sight of Liyurriu's body, shattered like a clay figurine, past all repairing.

Its eyes were open, though, and they were on Morlock.

"Shall I sever your life?" he asked, drawing his deadly dark sword.

"You forget," said a voice, speaking flawless Wardic through Liyurriu's unmoving jaws, "that this body is not truly alive. It will be no more use to you and yours, Ambrosius, and I plan to abandon it."

"Then."

"Good luck at the end of the world, Ambrosius. I will know you if we meet again. But you won't know me." The voice laughed a little through the werewolf's deformed, unmoving jaws. Then the wolvish eyes closed and Liyurriu was silent forever.

Morlock looked about and saw that Deor was already with Ambrosia by Kelat's fallen body. He strode over and said, "Dead?"

"No," Ambrosia said tonelessly. The focus-jewel hanging from her neck was glowing, as were her closed eyes. "Help me."

Kelat's hands and forearms were bone-white with frost, as was his left leg. There was no doubt what help Ambrosia wanted: she must be concentrating the heat in his body on those frozen areas, thawing them out before they died.

He lay down in the snow and summoned deep vision as fast as he was able. If Kelat could be saved, time was their enemy.

Kelat awoke to the cheery light of a fire flickering on the shelter walls.

That was odd. But it was pleasing. He thought he would never see fire again. He thought he would never see anything again.

He tested his hands. They ached unbearably, but he could move them. His leg, too.

"Oh, you'll live to fight another dragon someday, if that's what you're worrying about, Prince Uthar," he heard Deor remark.

Kelat lifted his head. "Name's Kelat."

"Yes, but Ambrosia suggested we start calling you Uthar instead. It's all those other Uthars who'll have to change their names, from the sound of things."

Kelat considered this in silence. It seemed rather momentous, but in a distant way. Being alive—and not seeing his arms and leg go the way of his nose—all that seemed more important, was certainly more immediate.

Morlock and Ambrosia were lying still on opposite sides of the fire. Their eyes were not lit up with vision. They were just sleeping.

Kelat gestured at the fire. "What . . . ? What . . . ?"

"My pack," Deor said. "It was almost empty anyway, so I'll distribute what's left among the other three. The seers are out, as you see, and we have to get through the night somehow. I had some fun designing the occlusion so that the smoke departs but most of the heat remains—but I suppose you don't care about that."

"Keeps me alive. I care."

"Some food will help, too. I was all for making werewolf sausages out of that dead meat-puppet, but Morlock seemed to think the meat might not be healthy."

"Ugh."

"Well, that *was* what he actually said. I take it you agree. You want a mouthful of flatbread and dried meat? It's what we've got, so that's kind of a rhetorical question."

"Water more."

Deor unfolded a flatware bowl and got him some melted snow.

"We're going to make it, I think," Deor said to him while he drank. "I didn't think so before."

"Make it a while longer," said Kelat. He tried to think of himself as Uthar. He was still thinking about it when he fell asleep.

They did make it.

One pale, unremarkable morning they ate the last crumbs of their food and struck their shelters. They trudged up a steep ridge and, at the top, looked all the way down to forever: the wintry sky of that harsh summer faded to a misty blue like evening below. The land ran raggedly up to the edge of the sky and stopped. At the very end of the world, the winds from beyond the edge had scoured the stone free of snow.

But they no longer needed the track of the sun's death in the snow to lead them. There, on the blue-black stone at the ragged edge of the world was a bridgehead. Beyond it a bridge extended in a long, curving arch beyond the eye's ability to follow: paving stones black and white gave way at some indefinable point to patches of light and darkness.

"The Soul Bridge," Ambrosia remarked.

Morlock nodded. There was nothing else it could be: the bridge the Sunkillers had made to invade the world, the way Skellar had been sent beyond the sky by Rulgân.

They saw no one there at or near the bridge, but their enemies were not material entities. Morlock kicked off his much-repaired snowshoes and drew Tyrfing, which was also not a material entity (or at least not merely material). He strode down the far side of the ridge and walked up to the bridgehead, Ambrosia at his side, the others close behind.

As he got closer, he did see someone or something: a vaguely manlike body, half-buried in snow, sprawled next to the bridgehead.

"Skellar," he called over his shoulder.

Ambrosia grabbed Morlock by the elbow. He turned to look at her. She was in rapture, eyes closed and faintly glowing, the focus-amulet at her throat throbbing with pulses of light.

The light faded. She opened her eyes.

"Then?" he said.

"The body is not dead, but neither is it the residence of a soul any longer. There is nothing else alive between here and the edge of the sky except us—and except that." She pointed at the Soul Bridge.

He grunted. "Alive?"

"It is tal interwoven with matter, like your blade Tyrfing there. Or, for that matter, like you."

"Odd, but not unexpected. What's troubling you?"

"That." She pointed at something on the first step of the bridgehead: sheets of crystal, pinned with something like ice to the stone. There was dark writing on the crystal in a language that he knew, by a hand that he recognized.

It was a letter. And it was addressed to him.

CHAPTER SEVEN

The Graith Divided

The battle outside the Dome of the Graith grew louder, but it was hard to tell who was winning. Apart from cries of pain, no one spoke: there were no pleas for mercy, no offers of quarter, no boasts or war cries.

"Aloê," Lernaion began.

"Shut up, and I mean both of you. Any talking you do you can do to the Graith at Station. It sounds like it won't be long now."

"You're very confident your allies will win."

"Fairly confident. You'd better hope I'm right. If that door opens and your servant Maijarra lets in your band of thugs, then I'll kill you both and have done."

Lernaion allowed himself a cold smile. "Very confident. But how will you justify yourself to your peers in the Graith."

"I have the Graith's mandate, you old fool! I am the Graith's vengeancer, and you three are the murderers of a summoner. Your lives are mine whenever I choose to take them."

Bleys was looking toward the double doors. The sound of the battle was fading, gone. Booted feet came striding up the hallway.

The doors were unbarred from the outside and Maijarra swung them open. Her silver spear was deeply stained with blood.

Aloê tensed and Bleys laughed aloud.

Through the open doors strode Noreê, Jordel, Illion, Styrth Anvri, Sundra, Callion, Keluaê Hendaij—bloody weapons in their hands, grim looks on their faces. The Awkward Bastards were victorious, but not triumphant. Aloê knew how they felt.

"Vocate Maijarra!" cried Bleys. "How could you betray us?"

Maijarra's milk-pale face was motionless, unmoved. "I am thain to the Graith of Guardians," she said, "not to you."

And, at Aloê's command, she put the summoners in chains and led them away to the lockhouse.

The trial of the summoners had to wait for the healing of the Witness Stone. (Illion and Noreê were taking up that task.) But other strings in the conspiratorial web snapped more easily.

Aloê got a writ of authority from the High Arbitrate and rode on Raudhfax up to Big Rock to apprehend Ulvana. She anticipated some difficulty finding Ulvana: the woman must have heard of Naevros' exposure, and she had many places to hide in.

But when Aloê arrived at Big Rock House, the householder told her that Ulvana was being held prisoner at the Arbiter's House . . . by Noreê, who had appeared with a company of thains the night before.

"Thanks, Goodman Parell," Aloê said.

"Will you be staying with us long, I hope?"

"Only overnight, I think."

"Are you going to the Arbiter's House instanter?"

"Yes, goodman, if that means what I think it means."

Parell hesitated a moment and said, "Will you please tell Vocate Noreê to have her things removed from here? It's just that—well, if she wants an explanation, I will make one to her."

"I'll tell her, Parell."

"Thanks to you for that. Vocate, I don't know if I'm too old-fashioned or not old-fashioned enough. . . ." His voice trailed off.

"Which would you rather be, goodman?"

"What? What? Oh, too old-fashioned, I suppose. I'm too decrepit to be taking on modish airs—wearing purple shoes and talking about the latest ballads as if I could tell one note from another anymore. But I tell you, Guardian, in the old days it was not done. Your Graith didn't ride into a town like they were a conquering army and we were peasants who had to . . . well, do something peasanty. But I suppose I'm talking too much."

"Not too much for me. Say it loud and say it often, goodman."

"Have been. Good day to you, Vocate."

"Good day, Parell."

Aloê left the inn and walked across the way to the Arbiter's House. There was a cloud of thains surrounding it, leaning on their spears. There were no townfolk in the street.

A thain held out his spear to prevent Aloê from entering the Arbiter's House. "You'll have to wait here, Vocate. And leave your weapon. Vocate Noreê's orders."

Aloê always carried her songbow of the runic rose these days, slung over her shoulder. She took it in her hands and struck the thain blocking her to the ground. The others started forward but she ignored them, bending over to rip the gray cape from the fastenings at the fallen man's shoulders.

"I expel you from the Graith," she said to him, as he stared vacantly up at her. "Hinder me again, and I'll expel you from the Wardlands. Resist me, and I'll banish you from the land of the living. Now get out of my way. Get out of my way, all of you."

They hesitated.

She grabbed the spear from the ex-thain and said, "By God Avenger, from this moment forward you will give way before a red cloak if it's only hanging on a clothesline. Clear off!"

The fallen man scrambled to one side and the rest stood back, their eyes resentful. She felt they were yielding to her personally, not to the principle. And that wasn't enough. But it was a problem for another day. She cast the spear into the dust of the street and walked past them into the Arbiter's House.

Noreê was walking toward the door, and her pale eyes crossed gazes with Aloê's in an almost audible clash. "You had some trouble getting in?" asked Noreê.

"Yes. Your private army is a problem, Noreê. For the Guarded—the Guardians—the Guard itself."

Noreê waved a scarred, ice-pale hand. "A temporary measure. I've no longing for kingship, I assure you."

"What if others long to make you king?" Aloê replied.

"Nonsense. I'm no Ambrose. You came to talk to Ulvana, I guess?"

"I don't speak nonsense, Noreê. I'm telling you something you need to hear. And, yes, I came to speak to Ulvana. If it suits you to permit it, of course."

"You have the wrong idea about me, Aloê. I was maintaining the Guard before you were born."

"As Merlin was before you were born. It is *you* who has the wrong idea about *you*, Guardian. Look to it."

Noreê's pale eyes looked on her patiently and her pale lips actually smiled. She had heard what Aloê had said; she did not regard it in the least.

"This emergency will be over soon," she said, patting Aloê on the arm. "Let's not quarrel about it."

It was maddening to Aloê that Noreê didn't take the issue seriously—as if it were a matter of taste, like a disagreement about after-dinner cheeses. If she would not listen to Aloê now, there would come a time soon when she must be made to listen.

They went together, but not in the same mind, to the Arbiter's Hall of Audience.

Ulvana was sitting in the Arbiter's chair. There was no one in the room with her; she was not reading or writing or doing anything—just sitting there with a vacant look on her face.

"Ulvana," said Aloê, "the Graith of Guardians has a claim of vengeance against you. I have a writ from the Arbitrate deposing you from your rank as Arbiter and waiving vengeance on your behalf. Do you have anyone else who would choose to act for you?"

"No," said Ulvana in a monotone. "My family has washed their hands of me. My life is yours."

"The Graith will give you death or exile, on my recommendation. Will you answer my questions?"

"I don't care. Yes. Ask them."

"Did you participate in the murders of Summoner Earno and of Necrophor Oluma Cyning?"

"No! Not exactly."

"Did you participate in *any* way in those murders? Did you know about them in advance? Did you assist the murderer afterwards?"

Ulvana looked down for a moment, saying nothing. Then she raised her head again and gave each of the Guardians a defiant look. "The murderer. The murderer. Can't you say his name? Is he nothing more to you than that?"

"Tell me his name. Tell me what you know about this business, and I will exercise the Graith's mercy. If not, I will execute the Graith's vengeance."

"Mercy!" said Ulvana, and laughed sobbingly. "Mercy! What can you do to me that's worse than what you've already done?"

"Why, I don't know," said Aloê courteously. "I would ask Earno and Oluma what they think, only they're dead, you see."

"It had to be you," Ulvana moaned. "The both of you. The unattainable ice princesses, white and black. The ones he never felt worthy of, so that he had to grovel in the muck. Muck like me. Like me."

"Listen, Ulvana, I'm no princess. I work for a living. And I'm not unattainable; just married."

"To that thing. That Morlock. He's probably had you both."

Grim, white-haired Noreê, one of the great seers of the world and one of the three Victors of Kaen, snorted with surprised laughter. She turned away to regain her composure.

"Here's where it stands with me, Ulvana," Aloê said. "I am the Graith's vengeancer. I could kill you now, if I chose, with only the Graith to answer to."

"Go ahead. I want you to. I'm sick of everything."

"I could, and I may do the same thing to Naevros syr Tol."

Ulvana grew very still.

"Or," Aloê added, "I could exile you both. Strictly speaking, that prerogative rests with the Summoner of the City, but he is in disgrace at the moment and the Graith has delegated his power in this matter to me. I can kill you, and I assure you it will be an easy death. But I would prefer to send you into exile. With Naevros, if possible. But I need a reason to do so, a reason for the Graith to forego vengeance. Tell me what happened. Make me understand."

"He'd hate me," Ulvana said, looking at something far beyond the walls of this room. "He'd hate me for the rest of his life."

Taking a risk, Aloê said, "He hates you now. If he loved you, he would not have put you in this hole. The question is not what he wants for you. The question is what you want for him—and what you still may get from him. If he dies, all hope dies with him. If he lives, someday he may turn to you. Who else would he have?"

Ulvana completely broke down, weeping into her hands for what seemed an endless time. At last, she told Aloê everything she knew.

Naevros had come back into her life a year ago, riding up to Big Rock from A Thousand Towers on some sort of business. He said he had come to respect her for making her own way in the world—that he was sorry for the way he had treated her—that he hoped it could be different now. He deployed as many lies as he needed to seduce her again, and Aloê got them all from Ulvana.

It was about five months ago that he revealed he had an ulterior purpose in resuming the affair. That was when she knew everything he'd said was a lie. And he knew that she knew—smiled to himself as he watched her realize it. But she had already yielded her pride to him, and found that she couldn't reclaim it—didn't want it.

Ulvana said, "I could feel again—really feel—surrender myself to it—not have to, to watch myself and correct myself, but be what I was meant to be! I don't suppose either of you can understand that."

Aloê wasn't interested enough in the subject to express a thought on it. What she wanted to know was what Naevros had said and done before the murder. She said placatingly to Ulvana, "We want to understand your experience so that the Graith can judge you fairly. What did Naevros say to you about the plot? What did he want done?"

Ulvana sighed. "He said he and his allies had a plan to save the Wardlands, but that it was risky, and not all of the Graith would be willing to take the risk. He said that he was to eliminate the Summoner Earno, and perhaps others if it came to it. He said—he said—I was the only person he could trust!"

"I'm sure he did."

"Are you? Are you? I wish I could be. I had timber lodges near the Road, and he knew it. I knew the lands all around here, and he knew it. I was Arbiter of the Peace, charged with investigating murders hereabouts, and he knew it. But I think he trusted me, too. Don't you think so?"

"He must have, to let you so deeply into his counsels."

"Yes. Yes, exactly!" Ulvana's reply was frantic—so frantic that Aloê wondered if she was also worried about the alternative: that Naevros told her so much because he planned to stop her mouth with death when he was done with her.

"What did he tell you about Oluma Cyning?"

"Nothing, except that he had corrupted a necrophor and that she would assist in the investigation of Earno's murder. Or do you mean afterward? When he. . . . When he. . . ."

"Tell me about all of it."

"Well—he told me what I told you. When the necrophor—"

"Oluma?"

"Yes, her. When she came to town she told me what she knew about the plot, and warned me not to trust the healer—"

"Denynê."

"Yes, her. The necrophor warned me not to trust the healer, as Naevros had been unable to get at her."

"Seduce her, you mean?"

"I suppose. I suppose that was what she meant. She laughed when she said it."

"Oluma herself succeeded at that, didn't she?"

"Yes." Ulvana wrinkled her nose in matronly disapproval. "She bragged about it to me—thought it was funny. That's what the whole business was for her; a grim sort of, of lark."

"But Oluma didn't manage to drag Denynê into the conspiracy?"

"As far as I know, she didn't try. She wasn't that interested; it was just one more game in all the games she was constantly playing. I shouldn't have been surprised that Naevros had to kill her."

"But you were surprised?"

"Yes, it. . . . I was surprised, yes." And frightened, too, Aloê thought, looking at Ulvana's face now and remembering it then, when they had found Oluma in the corpse-house. Frightened that Naevros was getting rid of his fellow conspirators: that was Aloê's guess. Ulvana lived simultaneously with two different versions of Naevros: the hero of her love-romance, and the cold-hearted seducer and murderer.

"What was your role in all this?" Aloê asked. "What did he want you to do?"

"I showed him the . . . the lay of the land, I suppose. He spent some time at my old lumber camps. He wanted me to report to him how the investigation went. And, of course, he stayed with me after it, after the thing."

"After he had murdered Earno."

"Yes, that. He could not afford to be seen—there was a simulacrum of himself he had left in the North to give himself an alibi. So he was with me for a number of days. That was. . . . That was a good time."

Because she'd had her beloved all to herself, Aloê thought. And, of course, he would have been at his most charming; his plan depended on keeping Ulvana happy.

"Did you attempt to mislead me at any time?" Aloê asked.

"Only by omission. Naevros warned me about that in a letter, as soon as he found out that you would be the Graith's vengeancer. He said I should act as I would if . . . if I were not involved. He said you would know if I did not. He rates your cleverness very highly. More highly than he does mine. And he's quite right, of course. I still don't understand what you discovered in our journey together. Was it something you saw in your vision? He said he had a way of concealing his talic imprint from a seer. Did it fail him?"

"No. Tell me, Ulvana, why did Naevros create such an elaborate murder plan? Why not arrange something less spectacular, something that might have passed as an accident?"

"Oh, that wasn't his idea. His partners—his seniors, he called them—they insisted on it. They said they needed to be sure they put Earno out of the way; he was blocking some important task they had in hand. And if an attempt was made and failed, it might draw suspicion."

"If you strike at the king, you must kill him," Noreê said, somewhat blasphemously. Ulvana started a little in her chair: she had forgotten the older vocate was there.

Aloê met Noreê's cool gaze and they both nodded: they were done here.

"Ulvana," said Aloê, "I'll consider your case and consult my peers in the Graith. In the meantime, you must be under guard. The thains here, or some others, will take you to the High Arbitrate in A Thousand Towers."

"I don't wish to go there. I don't want to see those people."

"You must go somewhere, and you can't stay here."

"Yes. I see that. I don't want to stay here, either. Aloê, I've answered your questions; won't you answer mine? What did you discover that led you to Naevros?"

Aloê hesitated before answering. But there was no obvious reason not to tell her.

"It didn't mean anything to me at the time," she admitted. "But there was a scent in one of the beds I slept in at your logging shelters—a sort of sweet musk."

"Oh," Ulvana said quietly. Then, "I gave him that scent. It was a present."

"I noticed it on him later when I met him in the city. That was what helped me guess. The proof came later." Aloê thought of Denynê and frowned at a painful memory.

"He said he would wear it in the city," Ulvana said. "But I wasn't sure. . . . I wasn't sure whether that was only one of his lies." She looked sharply at Aloê and seemed to be about to speak. Aloê looked straight into her eyes and she flinched.

"Did you always despise me?" she asked plaintively, as Aloê turned to go.

Aloê considered the question fairly. "No," she said. "No, when I met you again in Big Rock, I sort of liked you. But that wasn't really you, was it?"

"It used to be," Ulvana said sadly. "Until a year or so ago."

Aloê shook her head and strode away through the door. Noreê followed her out, and the thain outside folded the door shut, closing Ulvana in alone.

"I'll have some of my thains escort her down, if you like," Noreê said.

"They're not *your* thains, Vocate," Aloê said.

Noreê smiled and nodded: a mere detail to her. "Ommil," she said to the thain on guard, "take a couple of the others and escort Ulvana down to the High Arbitrate in the city tomorrow morning."

"Yes, Vocate," said the thain.

"What did you think of Ulvana?" Noreê asked as they turned away and walked into the street.

"Pitiable. But I didn't pity her."

"Yes. My long-dead father would have called her a real woman."

"Oh? Why?"

Noreê shrugged, a gesture that reminded Aloê oddly of Morlock. "That is easier to know than to explain. She lives through her man; that is part of it. He is everything, and she is content to be nothing, if he only notices her. She is completely selfless."

"I'd say she's completely selfish."

Noreê laughed. "You are contrary today, Vocate. How can she be selfish? She gave up everything for that man."

"For a price. As long as she got what she wanted, nothing else mattered: Earno's life; Oluma's life; Denynê's life—anyone else's; her principles as a member of the Arbitrate; the safety of those who trusted in her; her independence and fortune, so proudly won over a century of work. She threw all that away to satisfy an urge."

"You speak unkindly of love," Noreê said, not as if she disapproved.

"I'm not talking about love at all. Naevros purchased her with a fantasy, the way he might have purchased a meat pie with money. He offered her the pretense of love, which was enough for her. For that she sacrificed everything, not for him."

"Are you going to talk to him now?"

Aloê nodded.

"Perhaps I should ride with you," Noreê suggested. "The presence of his two unattainable princesses might unnerve him."

"What is a princess anyway?"

"A sort of female kinglet, I think. They have them in the unguarded lands. They are much sought after as mates, apparently, and people kill dragons and things to woo them."

Aloê, who'd had occasion to kill a dragon herself, revolved this notion in her mind. "Odd," she said. "Yes: let's try to shake him up."

They rode down to the city the next morning and arrived at Naevros' house in the afternoon.

There was a cloud of watch-thains on the street outside Naevros' little house. Aloê was surprised to see them there. Naevros had been released from the Well of Healing after swearing a self-binding oath to appear before the Graith when summoned. No guards were needed, but here they were.

Plus, they wore different badges, as if they belonged to different graiths. One group had green armbands; another sported red caps; a third wore purple leggings.

She rode Raudhfax through the milling crowd as if they weren't there, causing a number to jump out of the way. She dismounted and strode toward the front door, ready to throttle anyone who hindered her.

She heard a timid voice say, "Your pardon, Vocate, but you are not allowed to enter." She turned and prepared to leap at the speaker like a lioness taking down a deer . . . but he wasn't speaking to her. A herd—no, three distinct herds of thain—were surrounding Noreê, who looked at them curiously with her dark blue eyes.

"Here, you," Aloê said to them as a body, "get away from her."

"I'm sorry, Vocate," said a freckly fellow in purple leggings, "but our orders are that no one shall enter this domicile saving yourself."

"Ours, too," supplied a pimply youth with a green armband. "And ours!" chimed in a girl in a red cap, and in general all the cattle mooed the same song.

"Whoever may have given you those orders, and those badges of rank to go with them," Aloê said, "you can't suppose that their instructions are binding on us. Stand out of her way."

"Sorry, Vocate. Orders."

The herds lowed in unison: orders, orders, orders.

Aloê was about to lay a few of them on the ground using her songbow as a club when another voice spoke, breaking the spell: "Don't trouble yourselves, vocates. I'll come down to you." It was Naevros, standing at the window above his front door.

Neither Aloê nor Noreê responded, but Naevros disappeared, and in a moment the door opened and Naevros stepped out of it.

The thains stood out of his way as if he were carrying a bowlful of plague-infested pus. He was not. He carried nothing: not a sword at his hip, not a cloak on his shoulders against the chill of the summer day. His clothes looked old and ill-matched; there were buttons missing from the shirt and threadbare patches on the trousers. His reattached left hand hung from the end of his arm, barely moving. It had a slightly bluish look to it. He did not offer it, or the other hand, to Aloê or Naevros, but he did acknowledge their presence with a nod and a glance of his green eyes, which is more than he did for the thains.

"Let's go down to the Benches and have a bite to eat," he suggested. "I don't suppose I'll have many more chances to eat there, one way or the other."

They agreed and they all walked together down the street to Naevros' favorite cookshop.

"How's Verch?" asked Aloê.

"Gone. Forever, this time," Naevros said. "I fired him. I'd sell the house if I could find a buyer. I'll need all the money I can get in the unguarded lands. Unless you plan to kill me."

"You'll have the option of exile, of course," Aloê said.

"I'll take it. Or did you imagine me drowning my sorrows in a pool of my own blood?"

Aloê noted the bitter bantering tone in his voice and chose to ignore it. "No," she said frankly.

He winced and sighed. "Well, I suppose it's too late to pretend now that I'm something other than I am."

They sat in the garden, empty of other patrons as the blue chill of evening approached. Without looking at the server, a young woman with streaked hair who looked at him with sad, sympathetic eyes, Naevros ordered pork seared with cherries and thrummin on the side. Noreê had a plate of jeckfruit and grondil. Aloê ordered chicken and mushrooms, and they shared a carafe of the house wine.

"I suppose you've come to break down my resistance," Naevros said, when they all had a glass. "You want to ask me questions, expecting no answers, just hoping to plant doubts that will soften the real examination on the Witness Stone. Is that it?"

"What if it is?" Aloê replied.

"If it is, to hell with it. Ask me your questions. I'll answer. I'm not going to put on a defense. I did what I did, and I'll pay for it without whining."

Perhaps only a little whining, Aloê thought to herself. Naevros favored her with a green glance, and she wondered if he had understood her unspoken response. It repelled her, but their rapport was as strong as ever. Aloud she said, "I know what you did, and most if not all of your fellow conspirators. What I don't understand is why you did it."

"Don't you?"

"No."

"A simple reason, for a Guardian. I did it to maintain the Guard."

She looked at him without speaking.

"No, really!" he insisted.

"You'll have to put some more lines in the drawing, Naevros. I don't see what you're getting at. How did murdering Earno help maintain the Guard?"

"I don't know all the details. But Lernaion and Bleys had a plan to save the Wardlands from the effects of the dying sun. Earno was planning to interfere with it, or they thought he was. So he had to be killed."

"Why would you believe them?" Aloê asked.

Naevros seemed genuinely surprised. "Wouldn't you?"

Aloê looked away instead of answering. She wondered if he had always been this stupid and she hadn't noticed it, or whether something had happened to him. She marveled that she had ever felt torn between this clever, shallow, pretty man and ugly, powerful, crafty Morlock Ambrosius. She missed him very much at that moment, and there was a shrill, fearful quality to the feeling. She was worried that the loss was permanent, that he would never return from the journey he'd begun.

She pushed the feeling away. The food came then, and she managed to ask Naevros a few more questions through the meal, but she didn't learn much, and she was increasingly convinced that she never would learn more from Naevros.

After the meal the two vocates parted company with Naevros and rode westward to the lockhouse in Fungustown.

"Would your father say Naevros was a real man?" Aloê said, breaking a long silence.

"Unquestionably. Why?"

"He seems the mirror image of Ulvana. He killed and lied and betrayed every trust so that he could have what he wanted."

"A hero's mantle, you mean? Yes, I agree with you there."

"And what good would it have been to him if he had it?" Aloê asked. She felt the cool pressure of Noreê's regard and turned toward the older woman. "Do you mean this was really about me? He was trying to impress me?"

Noreê laughed in surprise. "Your insight is sharp, Vocate. That is what I almost said. But I didn't say it because, on second thought, it seems to me too superficial. Naevros always seems to have a woman against whom he measures himself and whom he tries to impress. If it weren't you, it would be someone else. If you had ever yielded to his charms he would have despised you the way he does every woman he has seduced, and he would have found some other bitch-goddess to pray to."

"I don't like that term applied to me," Aloê said quietly.

"I don't, Vocate. I apply it to his idea of you."

Aloê thought she was right and yet not all right. Still, it was a trivial matter to waste the dying sun's light on.

They arrived at the lockhouse to see Bleys. He was the last Guardian in the lockup; Lernaion, Naevros, and the thains had all sworn self-binding oaths to appear at Station; only Bleys had refused.

The thains at the lockhouse door were divided among the purple-legging crowd, the red-cap crowd, the green-armband crowd, and some thains who had not yet been branded by their masters.

"Guardians," said Aloê, "do not hinder me or Noreê or any vocate going about her self-set tasks, and you may remain. If you challenge me, you will curse the day you chose to pledge yourself to the Graith."

"That is agreeable with our orders, Vocate Aloê," said one of the green armbanders, and the rest of the gray-caped chickens took up the chorus: orders-squawk-orders-squawk.

Aloê dismounted in their midst, waded through them, leading Raudhfax by the reins, and finally tied up her palfrey outside the lockhouse.

Noreê left her horse in custody of one of the unmarked thains—one of her own, no doubt—and strode through the crowd to follow Aloê inside.

"Some of the other vocates disliked the thought that I had sole mastery of the prisoners," she explained, "so they recruited their own thains and sent them to assist."

"You see what you've started. Will every vocate now have a personal army of thains to do her bidding?"

"Perhaps they should," Noreê said good-humoredly. "This is only for the emergency, Aloê."

"After this one there will be another."

"Perhaps." Noreê seemed determined not to fight with her, so Aloê gave up—for the moment.

The entrance to the basement was guarded by thains with an ill-assorted rainbow of badges. Aloê brushed them aside and descended, taking a cold-light from a pocket of her cloak as she descended the crumbling stairs to the basement.

A dizzying wave of stink swept over her. The sting of urine was in her eyes and nose, and it wasn't the most alarming thread in the reek. . . .

She took the songbow from her shoulder and gripped it in her hand like a club. The hot smell of fresh blood rode the foul air.

The chaos of the basement made no sense to her eye at first. She had stumbled over a bundle of something at her feet before she realized it was a bundle of limbs—a Khnauront, lying on its side, its throat cut from ear to ear.

"Call your thains," Aloê said over her shoulder.

"Oh, there's no need for that, Vocate," said Bleys' warm voice from across the dim basement.

Aloê lifted the coldlight high to see better and caught sight of the summoner across the floor of the basement, strewn with dead Khnauronts. He was holding a bright piece of metal in one hand and with the other was pulling at the nose of a Khnauront to expose his bare neck. Two quick slashes and the Khnauront was spraying blood, dark in the bluish light. Bleys released him and he fell on his side.

The summoner stepped over to where the last Khnauront was sitting upright, his back against the far wall. He looked at Bleys and his bloody little piece of metal incuriously.

"Don't!" shouted Aloê.

"With you in a moment, my dears," called Bleys cheerily. He slashed the throat of the last Khnauront and let him fall. He dropped the piece of metal beside the dying body and then picked his way carefully across the carnage toward the thunderstruck vocates.

"You don't need to thank me," Bleys said, as he got nearer. "Although I don't think it would be a good idea to take my hands." He held them up: they gleamed with blood. "After a few days of probing their minds, I determined that these objects could be no use to themselves or anyone else, and decided to get rid of them . . . since the Graith, in its usual way, could not decide what to do with them."

Aloê exhaled, then, more reluctantly, inhaled.

"I assure you, these things were not human—merely machines for turning food into shit, as the saying goes. What can I do for you, my dears?"

Aloê said, "I wanted to urge you to swear a self-binding oath so that you could be released from this hellhole."

"I'm afraid I can't, my dear," said the smiling, blood-stained old man. "Before either of you were born, I had a counterspell against binding spells engraved on my collarbone. That prevents me from swearing a self-binding oath; you can ask Lernaion about it, if you like."

"Ur. Well, maybe we can find more acceptable quarters for you."

"These quarters are perfectly acceptable to me. I'm not particular about things. Perhaps you're thinking about the nightmares from the decaying fungus, but really I don't mind them. If you ever get to be my age, which I do not wholeheartedly recommend, you'll understand how pleasant it is to have a vivid dream, even a nightmare, awake or asleep."

"If some of the upper floors are intact, I'm sure you can have your nightmares and cleaner air to go with them. We must have you alive to testify, Bleys."

"I'll drink to that, as your husband might say, my dear. Yes, I can't wait to testify. The sooner young Illion is done with healing the Witness Stone, the better I'll like it. Shouldn't you be helping him, Noreê, instead of playing chief jailor to an old man?"

"I intend to," Noreê said quietly.

"Wonderful."

"You could tell us something of what you have to say now," Aloê observed.

"But would you believe it? Should you believe it? I would not recommend it, if I were some third person with your best interests at heart (as I am not, of course). No, you will have to wait. Because it's very important that you believe what I have to say." Bleys absentmindedly wiped his hands on his white mantle of office. "I wonder what's for supper?" he said wistfully. "Could one of you ask about it for me on your way out?"

Bleys got his wish a pair of months later. They were very long months from Aloê's point of view. Most of the vocates started recruiting personal forces of thains, and many had companies of them marching through the streets.

Aloê and Jordel watched them pass by one day from the second floor of his house.

"I suppose they all have to swing their feet at the same time," Jordel said, "if they're going to walk so close with everybody's elbow up everybody else's ass. But I tell you, Aloê. . . ."

"Tell me, J."

"I think that they're doing it to threaten people."

"I think they're doing it because they're afraid."

"I think that we're saying the same thing."

Fear was in the eyes of the thains marching, and fear was in the eyes of the Guarded, watching from the windows in their houses and towers, and fear was in the eyes of the vocates marching at the head of their companies on the long-awaited day of Station.

Since Lernaion, the Summoner of the City, had been charged with Impairment of the Guard, it fell to the vocates to summon themselves to Station. But when Illion gave word that the Witness Stone was healed, Noreê sent her thains as messengers to summon the members of the Graith. Whether they loved Noreê or hated her, the vocates obeyed. Many whispered to each other that she would be chosen as the new summoner, to fill the place left vacant by Earno's murder.

On the chilly summer day of the Station, Aloê rose before dawn. She was staying with Jordel again because the empty ancientness of Tower Ambrose distressed her. They walked together, without a single thain-attendant, to the Chamber of the Graith. They met Illion, also walking without a thain, and Styrth Anvri, Sundra, Callion, and Keluaê Hendaij, who contented themselves with a single thain-attendant each.

But the streets adjoining the Dome were a solid mass of gray capes and clashing badges. Aloê was idly considering the possibility of making her way through the crowd on stilts when Jordel began to shout, in a shocking stentorian roar, "Make way for the Graith's vengeancer! Make way!"

The thains-come-lately looked over their shoulders aghast and pressed back against those nearest them. Cracks opened up in the wall of gray capes, and the vocates plunged into them. Jordel continued his shouting, and soon they could hear his brother Baran doing the same in another part of the crowd, and Illion began shouting it, too, and no one in recorded history had ever heard Illion shout anything, and eventually they were on the other side of the crowd, climbing the stairs into the Chamber.

A few vocates were standing before the open double doors to the Chamber proper: Rild of Eastwall, resplendent in purple leggings; Gnython the Rememberer, wearing a green armband on both arms; Kothala of Sandport, sporting a red cap, and a few others.

"Fine ladies and gentlemen," Jordel rasped (his voice still ragged from shouting), "perhaps you could tell your underlings not to block the streets. There's more than one way to impair the Guard," he added.

That spurred them to action; it takes fear to motivate the frightened, Aloê thought. They rushed away to give orders to their disorderly followers.

The pale sun had climbed more than half way up the cool blue sky before the vocates were assembled at Station, and the Guardians accused of Impairing the Guard stood, with folded hands, awaiting the Graith's judgment. Aloê was obscurely pleased that Naevros had rallied for the occasion. If his clothes were not new, they looked it. His wounded hand looked almost healthy, except for the angry red line where it had been reattached to his arm. He held himself like a person who mattered. But he did not wear the red cloak of his office, and neither did Bavro wear his gray cape.

Lernaion did wear his white mantle of office, however, and Bleys presumably did, too, but it was hard to tell whether the oldest Guardian's cloak was actually white. His clothes were filthy; his person was filthy; Aloê could smell him from where she stood at the Long Table, halfway across the great Chamber of the Graith. If he was at all embarrassed by his condition, he didn't show it.

Since the Summoner of the City was among the accused, Noreê stood forward to convene the Station. No one objected to this—at least not out loud. But Aloê could not have been the only vocate who thought their peer was taking too much on herself.

"Vocates," she said, actually rapping the Long Table with the silver staff of exile, "stand to order! We are come here to settle the fates of our members, accused of Impairment of the Guard and murder of the Guarded. I called you here because the Summoner of the City is among the accused and may not speak here, except in his own defense. If you prefer that someone else preside here, I will stand back."

Silence.

"Go ahead, Noreê," suggested Gyrla.

"Thank you, Guardians," Noreê said. "I call on our vengeancer, Aloê Oaij."

All faces in the room turned to Aloê. She'd thought much about this moment. It was a chance to wax rhetorical, to magnify herself in the minds of those who are impressed by torrents of well-chosen words. The last trial for

Impairment had happened around the time she was being born, but she had read about that case and many others.

In the end, she eschewed any attempt to soothe or startle her listeners with rhetoric. She stated plainly what the conspirators had done and how she had discovered it. She concluded by saying, "The only witness I see who is not present is Ulvana, late of the Order of Arbiters. She was under guard at the High Arbitrate; perhaps she could be sent for."

"That won't be possible, I'm afraid," Noreê said. "I received word from the High Arbitrate last night that Ulvana had committed suicide."

Aloê felt a sudden stab of grief and pain at this. She was also angry: that the message had come to Noreê and not her; that Noreê had not bothered to tell her until now. The pale cold Guardian loomed over them all these days, sole ruler of the Wardlands. It would have to be stopped somehow.

"Did she jump or was she pushed?" Aloê snapped back.

"If I understand you, Vocate Aloê, you are suggesting that the High Arbitrate may have killed Ulvana in secret to prevent her testimony today."

"It seems possible, at least."

"It seems irrelevant, at best. Unless her testimony is key to your case."

"No. I have stated my case. It is time for the witnesses to ascend to the Witness Stone."

"May I speak?" Naevros called up from the floor.

"You may speak in your defense after you testify on the Stone," Noreê said.

"That's just it. I don't intend to present a defense. Neither does my junior colleague. We will accept death or exile at the Graith's choosing, or your vengeancer's alone."

"Hm." Noreê allowed herself a cold smile and turned to Aloê. "What do you say, Vengeancer?"

"I'll abide by the Graith's decision, or exercise the prerogative if we can't come to an agreement. But I think the accused should stand together in punishment; they are all equally guilty."

"We can save part of a day if the summoners also waive their defense," Noreê said, without much sign of hope. "Lernaion, what say you? Do you admit your guilt?"

"I defer to the judgement of my elder peer," said Lernaion.

"Bleys: will you admit your guilt?"

This was the moment that horrible old man had waited for. He did not speak at first, but pretended to consider. Then he lifted his head high and cried out, "Waive my defense? I might do so for the good the Graith and the Guard, to which I have devoted the entirety of my very long life. But I will not waive, for the convenience of you, my fellow Guardians, or for the well-being of anyone in the world, my defense of the Wardlands. Everything, everything that the dedicated young vengeancer has told you is true. And it is not all. I have many secret deeds of blood and fear to my credit. I have killed—extorted—threatened—seduced—corrupted—stolen. These are crimes, if you please, if we stood in one of the courts of the unguarded lands. But we do not. All that I have done, all that I have ever done, was done to maintain the Guard."

"Summoner Earno," said Noreê coldly, "you may speak in your defense after you testify on the Stone—"

"Is that a threat?" shouted the red-faced old summoner. "I tell you, young Noreê, that I have come here expressly to testify on the Stone! I will speak, not in my defense, but in the defense of the Wardlands and in defense of my colleagues too shamed and bemused to speak for themselves. I have suffered; I have been beaten; I have endured night and day the torments of nightmares in that hellhole you consigned me to; I have kept the thin, fragile thread of life unbroken in my ancient body for this, and this alone: to speak and be heard where I could not be silenced! Lead me to your Witness Stone and let the Graith read the truths written in my heart!"

His voice broke on the last word. Aloê, glancing around the Long Table, saw that many of her peers were visibly moved at Bleys' performance. That was the first time she suspected that the murderers of Earno would escape exile.

"The Stone is in its usual place," Illion pointed out mildly. There were a few laughs at this, but most of the vocates still seemed taken with Bleys' dramatic performance. He strode over to the dais of the Witness Stone and laboriously climbed the steps to reach it.

"You will wait for us to establish rapport with the Stone first, Summoner Bleys," Noreê called down the Long Table.

"Take your time," replied the great seer calmly.

Illion was standing next to the Stone: he placed a hand on it, and his eyes began to glow with rapture. He held out his other hand to Baran, who stood by him. Baran took the hand and closed his eyes. In time, he too showed the signs of visionary ascent.

It did take time, but one by one the vocates, of varying levels of skill, joined the rapport with the Stone. The only exception was Gyrla, who jumped down contemptuously without saying a word.

They were one, in the end, though all were different, and Noreê spoke in them and through them, saying, "Put your hands on the Stone, Bleys, and accept rapport."

Bleys smiled—they felt rather than saw it—and placed one finger on the stone. Rapport was instantaneous; he was already in the visionary state.

Bleys said with his mouth, "I am innocent of Impairing the Guard. All I have done, all I have enlisted others to do, I have done to defend the Wardlands."

They heard the words only vaguely with their ears. They knew them for truth in their hearts.

All stood separate in their shared mind for meditation then. Aloê had time to think: *What he believes is true is different from what we may know to be true. He may have Impaired the Guard without intent.* But she also knew that most of her case against him was already undone, irrelevant in the face of his shocking admission.

"Why did you murder Summoner Earno?" she finally found the strength to ask.

The great seer turned his attention toward her, and it seemed that she was alone with him.

"I have been waiting for someone to ask me that, my dear. Thank you. Once when I was walking the long roads in the empty lands east of the Sea of Stones, I met an odd entity, a sort of unbeing. . . ."

Aloê later learned that others had asked the same question, or a similar one, and that all the vocates had been drawn into Bleys' meditation as if each alone was in rapport with him.

It seemed to her that she could see with his eyes, that she ached with his feet, grew short of breath and chill as shadows rose from the dusty earth of the empty lands. She knew somehow that it had been many years ago—shortly after the death of the Two Powers in Tychar.

The unbeing came upon Bleys as he was making a fire to warm himself. He sensed it with his insight. It tried to kill him with a weapon that had no name—but she recognized it. It was a kind of mist that came from nowhere and everywhere. It began to break down Bleys into his component selves, as acid breaks down a piece of meat.

But Bleys was not a piece of meat. He stepped outside of his body into vision and let his body dissolve and reform itself in the presence of the deadly fog, unconcerned with its fleshly agony.

In vision, Bleys saw-without-seeing the unbeing who attacked him.

He wove a path of vision around it in fifteen dimensions so that the unbeing was bewildered and could not dispel his mind as it was trying to dispel his body.

For a timeless time he meditated on the unbeing and its nature. Then he struck back, causing a little fog to condense in the locus where the unbeing presented itself.

The presence of physical matter distressed and excited the unbeing very much.

Bleys realized that the unbeing was the same type of entity that Aloê and Ambrosia had encountered in those same lands. (There was a side corridor of memory in Bleys' meditation where Aloê saw herself as he saw her, and the cool, ironic lechery of his regard made her feel greasy.)

They duelled that way for a long time with weapons of being and unbeing, of making and unmaking. But eventually their duel became a kind of conversation, where actions bore symbolic meaning.

Bleys learned that the unbeing was only one element in a class of unbeings beyond the northern edge of the world. They had once been in it, but the advent of sun and of material life had driven them out in repugnance and hatred for the new-made world. The Two Powers had been fashioned as an experiment in destroying material life, but had failed because the unbeing sent to keep them in balance had succumbed to materiality.

Bleys revealed that he was a member of a class of beings, some of which had defeated the Two Powers.

The unbeing reiterated its urgent need, shared by all of its cohort, to wipe the slate of the world clean of physical life. Because it had no thought that information should be withheld, it shared various scenarios of world-cleansing.

Bleys was curious about the domain of the unbeings in the far north. Apparently it was a fragment of this world that they had managed to sever free, redrawing the borders of the sky so that it would not be tainted with light and life. So it persisted, a fragment of a world drifting alongside its former home in the Sea of Worlds.

A thought came to Bleys that shocked even him. But he tested it over and over, and there was no flaw that he could see.

He asked the unbeing if it could teach him the skills to redraw the border of the sky and separate a part of the world into its own world.

The unbeing knew part of that knowledge and shared that with him, but the knowledge was too great for any single element of the unbeings to contain its entirety.

Bleys told the unbeing that if he and his fellow beings could know those skills, they would no longer resist, would even assist the project of the unbeings.

That was when the great collaboration began. Bleys and the unbeing fashioned an un-object of many dimensions. With it, he could communicate with the unbeing wherever he was, wherever it was.

Aloê never found the words to explain the un-object to anyone else, but she didn't need it explained to her: it hung in lightless luminescence at the center of her own mind.

With shock, Aloê realized that Bleys had incorporated the un-object into the Witness Stone itself. Even now, even now. . . .

As she let her awareness expand she became aware of many listeners, the class of unbeings in the far north beyond the wide world's end, the Sunkillers.

And over the years Bleys, with increasing single-mindedness, pursued his collaboration with the unbeings. His plan was simple: the ultimate protection for the Wardlands was to remove the adjoining lands from existence entirely. Then the Wardlands could persist as an island in the Sea of Worlds, perhaps with an artificial sun and other conveniences, and the Sunkillers could have the rest of their world to themselves.

Of course that meant that everyone and everything in the world that lived and felt and was a being would die. That was what had shocked Bleys about his own plan . . . at first.

But only at first. He was not a purveyor of justice or an avatar of mercy.

He did not judge; he defended, and this was the ultimate defense, a final solution to the problem of the unguarded lands.

He enlisted others in his project: Lernaion, who took a long time to convince. Lernaion took upon himself the task of enlisting Earno, but he had bungled it somehow. Aloê sensed Bleys' rage more clearly than the details of the failure. But probably Earno was hopeless anyway. He had travelled too much in the world to sacrifice it willingly. He seemed to think he had some obligation to it, or to the people in it, that rivalled his obligation to the Guarded.

Lernaion and Bleys enlisted Naevros to do their knifework. Bleys had long ago noted Naevros' susceptibility, and the whirlwind of thoughts surrounding the vocate's seduction were tinged with cold pleasure in Bleys' mind.

Now the unbeings, the Sunkillers, were concerned. They knew from their allies in the Wardlands that beings had been sent to investigate the sun's death and that some of them were those who had destroyed the Two Powers. The unbeings did not understand and would not understand independent agency and free will. They looked on the actions of the beings approaching them as a betrayal by their allies. The unbeings would be angry, extremely resentful, if those others were not stopped somehow.

To save the Wardlands they must recall their colleagues from the edge of the world and make plans for life after the death of the sun.

Aloê felt the insidious, inevitable pull of the logic. It vibrated in her mind—in the pattern of the un-object that was party to and basis of their rapport. Aloê resisted it, rejected it. Suddenly she became aware of others doing the same. She fought harder, fought free, was alone in her own mind at last, not subject to rapport.

She descended from the visionary state.

As soon as she had pulled the world of matter and energy around her like a blanket, she shouted at Bleys: "Bleys! Break the rapport and let the vocates go or I'll smash your Stone for you again!"

"If you like, my dear," said Bleys warmly, and the light in his eyes died. His smile, however, lived on. The vocates, as they returned to full awareness, began to shout and question and argue, and that went on for hours. But Bleys had already won: he knew it, and Aloê did, too. The vocates were frightened, and the way to drive frightened people was with more fear.

CHAPTER EIGHT

News from Home

The four companions stood at the edge of the world and looked down at the letter.

"A trap, you think?" Morlock asked.

"Certainly," whispered Deor in mock terror. "If you pick that up, a thousand Sunkillers will rush out from underneath it and begin biting us on the toes!"

"I suppose our friend and *harven*-kin here," Ambrosia said, "is not aware that many magical traps are set with a kind of bait, and that picking up or accepting the bait activates the trap."

"Not his kind of magic," Morlock agreed.

"Oh," Deor said, chastened. "Sorry, Ambrosii. How can we tell?"

The Ambrosii looked at the glimmering page, the dark writing on it.

"You're sure that it's Aloê's hand?" Ambrosia said.

"Yes. Aren't you?"

"I wouldn't know, brother. She's never written me a mash note."

Morlock shouldered off his pack and went through it, pulling out a tablet and stylus. "Show me what you see," he said.

On the malleable surface, Ambrosia deftly sketched an image of the letter, including the script on its first page.

"That's what I see," Morlock said. "It is not an illusion. I see no sign of a physical trigger. Is there a talic presence?"

"The whole bridge is a talic presence, brother."

"Eh. I'm going to open it."

"Go ahead. I'll remember you as you were."

Morlock crouched down. Pulling his knife from its sheath on his belt, he used its blade to flip over the first crystalline sheet.

Beloved, the letter began, *good morning, or whatever time it is when you read this. I have had a bad dream. Unfortunately, it's not the kind I get to wake up from.*

"Aloê wrote this," Morlock said.

"Good," Ambrosia said.

"Not really," Morlock said, and continued reading.

I write you through the agency of the unbeings beyond the northern edge of the world, and at the request of the Graith of Guardians. They ask you to return without attempting the passage of the Soul Bridge or the rescue of the sun.

I'm going to paint you the whole picture. This is going to take a while.

It did. Aloê told him about the conspiracy to murder Earno, and how she had uncovered it, and about Bleys' defense of himself and his colleagues before the Graith.

The Graith acquitted him, I am ashamed to say, Aloê wrote. *At least it was not unanimous: Jordel spoke at length, which is perfectly usual, and quite seriously, which is perfectly unusual and was doubly impressive because of that. Illion pointed out that the Graith has the obligation to defend and avenge its members, and that it is a tactical as well as moral mistake to allow our murders to go unpunished. Gyrla made a powerful case against trusting Bleys under any circumstances whatever. But, in the end, the Guardians were relieved that something was being done, that something could be done, to protect the Wardlands from the impending death of the world, even if it made them complicit in that death. Bleys and Lernaion are summoners again; Naevros and Bavro have sworn off the Graith. The alliance with the unbeings beyond the world has been affirmed, and Noreê and others from New Moorhope are already working on the magics needed to redraw the border of the sky and separate the Wardlands from the dying world.*

The Graith's message to you is this: on pain of exile, you must return and refrain from harming our new allies or interfering with their plot to kill the sun.

My message to you is a little different. Come home now. The greatest danger to the Wardlands is not the dying sun, or the unbeings who would kill it and us, but the Graith itself. There is a cancer in the order, and the great task before us is to cut it out—to break the Graith, if need be, before the freedom of the Wardlands is sacrificed to mere safety. We few who see this need you beside us in that struggle.

Come back to me. I say it like some stupid fisherman's stupid wife. Come back to me.

With love and urgency, I remain

Aloê Oaij, Vocate to the Graith of Guardians

"I have to think about this," said Morlock.

"Of course," said Ambrosia. She opened her mouth to speak, but closed it without saying anything.

Morlock turned away from the others and walked along the ragged edge of the world. The wind from the gulf to the north was cold, but no colder than his thoughts.

He had defied the Graith before and returned to honor in its ranks. The Graith was not an army, with military discipline; it was the duty, as well as privilege, for the vocates called to Station to think for themselves, to act in accordance with those thoughts.

But the Graith was changing. He had noticed it himself, and those changes seemed to have gathered momentum in his absence. Aloê thought there was a real risk that he'd be exiled. He had to trust her judgment. If he tried and failed, his life in the Wardlands would be over. What did that leave? Life in the dying world, or escape across the Sea of Worlds to some place he had never known.

And he would be alone. That was clear to Morlock. She said she wrote as a lovesick fisherman's wife, but she didn't, really. She was a Guardian before she was a wife. Her loyalty was to the Wardlands before him.

On the one side, there was a life with Aloê. On the other side was the death of the world.

He thought about the Lacklands and their sparse cannibal denizens, the Vraids on the shores of the Sea of Stones, Danadhar and his Gray Folk in burning Grarby, the master makers under the Blackthorn Range, the frightened, shattered city of Narkunden, all the lands he had seen in Laent, and all the lands he had never seen in and beyond it: all those people, dead in a darkness that would never end.

They would all die someday, it was true, no matter what he did. It was possible that what he was doing was futile anyway. Would he throw away life with Aloê for nothing?

He wondered what he should do. He wondered what he would do.

He looked back at Ambrosia, standing with her head held high on the bridgehead of the Bridge of Souls. It occurred to him that she was afraid; she never bothered to look fearless otherwise.

He walked back to the others. Through the mask, Uthar was staring at him. Deor looked at him and looked away.

"Morlock," said Ambrosia briskly, "we've talked it over while you were off pondering. Of course, I must go across the Soul Bridge instead of you. Except for the fact that your talic self can bear Tyrfing, that was always the better plan, and I see now it was inevitable. I ask only that you wait here and help the others retrieve my spirit if things get rough on the other side. Your Graith can hardly object to that. Is that acceptable to you?"

"No."

Half a world away, the Graith stood at Station in their domed chamber. Bleys stood at the Witness Stone, bound and interwoven with the un-object of the Sunkillers. His open eyes were glowing in visionary rapture.

"Ambrosius is walking beyond the world on the Soul Bridge," he said. "Summon our champion. We must aid our allies."

CHAPTER NINE

Ghosts and Shadows

"The bridge," Ambrosia said, "is a means for drawing tal out of the world—perhaps from the sun itself. That was why Skellar found it possible to go out but apparently did not make it back once Rulgân abandoned him."

Morlock grunted. "I'll say my goodbyes now, then."

"Shut your stupid face. When you go into vision, wait for me. I'll establish a rapport with you, and we may be able to sustain contact while you pass beyond the world. If we do, I can draw you back."

"Then."

Morlock took Tyrfing in his hand and lay down in the snow. He looked at Skellar's eyes, still glowing red beneath the lids, and closed his own. He summoned the rapture of vision.

Slowly, he felt himself rise from his body, his talic self a torrent of black and white flames. Tyrfing rose with him.

A non-word impinged on his awareness: he was aware of Ambrosia's talic presence, a whirlwind of green and gold.

He ascended the Soul Bridge and followed it northward, into and beyond the sky.

Time was hard to gauge, so he didn't. But the bridge grew more solid under his burning feet with each stride he took. That meant there was less matter, more tal. He saw designs in the stones, too—blocks of tal, they must have been, with a smear of matter.

The edge of the sky was like a curtain of darkness. The bridge went on and Morlock with it.

The tal drawn from the sun, from the sky, was all around him. He felt renewed, euphoric, as if he would live forever. He tried to fight the feeling, but it was stronger than he was. He drifted in it, a fire within the fire.

Then the river of tal was gone. All light was gone. He was beyond the world.

With his inner eye he saw everything but understood nothing. He was like a baby just entering the world. Forms had no meaning.

Then something stabbed him. That had a meaning.

He swung toward the threat and brought Tyrfing to guard. He tried to understand what he was feeling. It wasn't pain: his body was on the other side of the sky. But it was a kind of suffering, and a kind he had felt before.

Before him he seemed to see a warrior made of light, armed with a sword made of mist. Then he remembered. He remembered the prison without walls in Tychar, the island surrounded by a lake of mist. When he walked into the mist it rendered him down, somehow . . . broke him up into the components of himself until there was no self anymore. It had been agony. He could not feel pain in his vision, but the distress of unbeing was equally bad.

He remembered the anger and shame he had felt as they had dragged him back to the island, to the prison, to himself.

He dropped the point of his sword and stabbed wildly at the shining warrior.

The warrior's parry was late—perhaps he was surprised. Tyrfing's point didn't strike home, but its harsh blazing edge struck the warrior's bright shoulder and rasped along it.

In his inner ear, Morlock heard a Guardian screaming.

Morlock withdrew to guard and thought.

What was this warrior? Who was this warrior?

He thought he knew. He remembered what Aloê had written in her letter—not to mention the letter itself. The Graith had used their link with the Sunkillers to send her letter to the end of the world, and they must have sent more militant aid by the same route. And who would they send?

It was Naevros—his talic self, anyway—that Morlock was facing.

Morlock held his sword athwart his talic self, then raised it high, then dropped it to guard—a kind of salute.

A fragment of time, and the warrior opposite did the same. He was Naevros. He must be.

And yet. . . . And yet. . . . The shining surface of the warrior, like plate mail forged from glowing glass, was unlike any talic avatar Morlock had ever encountered in vision. And the voice he had heard in his inner ear was not Naevros'. If he had to put a name to it, it would have been Rild of Eastwall.

Were the other Guardians there, in rapport with Naevros, protecting him somehow?

Was Aloê there?

He hoped not, but his choice was made. He dropped his sword to attack; the other parried and riposted with the blade of mist; Morlock circled away from the stroke and stabbed the shining warrior in the side.

A new cry of pain: Vocate Vineion, howling like one of his own dogs. Morlock thought he saw him briefly, peering in pain through the crack on the glowing glass plate.

Naevros spun, struck Tyrfing aside, and lunged. The blade passed through Morlock's talic self again: he saw the black and white flames of his talic being fade into gray lines where the sword of mist had passed.

Morlock moved back and brought up Tyrfing to guard. Naevros pressed his attack and Morlock contented himself with defense for a while.

They had done the best they could bringing Naevros here. He was the greatest swordsman alive.

And yet. . . . He also thought they had made a mistake. A timeless time ago, when he left the world and came to this place that was and was not a world, he had been utterly bemused.

But a fencing match, a fencing match with Naevros in particular, that was something he understood: a long, coiling argument that ran back and forth with flashing swathes of rhetoric and sharp, pointed periods. He had done this. He could do this. He understood this. And it gave him time to ponder the un-world of these unbeings.

Why hadn't they attacked him with weapons of their own when he came through the gateway in the sky? He saw them all around him, lattices of tal framing emptiness, moving about the coarse, invisible landscape, staying still, appearing and disappearing in irregular rhythms. He felt their malice and their hate; he heard many more of their thoughts than he understood, but he knew this fight between Guardians was important to them. But they made no move of intention against him, or to help Naevros.

Perhaps they could not. Perhaps the brawling, stabbing, clawing of material survival was so alien to them that they could not participate in it.

They needed Naevros to do their knifework, as Bleys and Lernaion had. Morlock wished he could speak to the man that had been his friend and his enemy, his mentor and his rival. He would have chosen to fight alongside Naevros rather than against him.

Then he remembered that Naevros had killed Earno. Blood for blood, life for life: that was law in the Deep Halls of Thrymhaiam, where he had grown, like a mushroom, in the dark. Naevros had placed his bet; he would have to stand the hazard of the cast.

For a timeless moment, peering past the shining warrior, his enemy, he saw the Sunkillers, appearing and disappearing in the dark lands beyond, and he understood something. They were enacting the passage of a higher dimensional object through a two-dimensional plane. In his mind, the various shapes of the object took solid form. Transfixed by fascination, he was nearly destroyed.

The sword of mist passed under Tyrfing and through the centrality of his self.

Death was near. He knew it, and his enemy knew it. He struck back with all the force his fading will could command, and several of the glass plates shattered in screams of pain. Past them he could see Naevros' unprotected talic self: a coil of shining, steely lines. Morlock brought back Tyrfing as Naevros twisted the misty blade in his selfhood; he struck through the shattered plates, stabbing at Naevros.

Now it was Naevros' pain he heard echoing in his mind's ear. The misty blade withdrew: Naevros backed away.

Morlock watched wearily as the shining plates protecting Naevros began to reform. More Guardians were being drawn into rapport to protect Naevros. How many could they draw on? How many were party to the vile alliance with the Sunkillers? Most of the vocates, by Aloê's account. He hoped she was not one of them.

He became aware of another being. Not the angular lattices of tal that composed the Sunkillers, and not the shining warrior of the Graith, no part of his own black-and-white talic emanations. This being was more like a rusty, dark stipple on the surface of the darkness, oozing like a serpent among the lifeless stones, nearly as lifeless as the stones themselves . . . but not quite. There was a smear of bloody light there, the merest trace of life.

Native to this place? Impossible. An infection from the world, travelling with the sun's life along the Soul Bridge? Perhaps. Skellar had done it. . . .

And, of course, this was Skellar! Or what was left of him, not fully alive or dead, body and soul almost untethered, but keeping each other from dying. The way Skellar oozed among the rocks reminded Morlock sharply of how he had groveled in his bed of gold all those years ago, when he had been god-speaker in the town of mandrakes.

Skellar felt his regard, and fled. Or . . . led? The snakelike talic avatar paused at one moment, is if to allow him to pursue it.

Morlock did follow. A thought was in his mind. What was renewing Skellar's tal? Feeble as it was, it had not been snuffed out, and his body was not sustaining it. He must have a source of tal. Perhaps he was preying on the Sunkillers. Or perhaps he had found the outlet for the river of life, the tal stolen from the sun.

Naevros followed also, striding across the dead, dark world in his suit of light. He was slow at first, surprisingly slow.

Skellar disappeared over a ridge of dead stone. Morlock ascended above it and saw a valley of stars below.

Morlock descended after Skellar, whose rusty tal stood out like a shadow in that life-filled place.

The stars were bulbs of sunlife—smaller in diameter than Tyrfing was long. They seemed to grow from a tangle of thorny tal lattices, hedges of cold unlife caging hot sunlife.

This was what they did with the river of tal that they were stealing from the sun. These things were like jars, or something, restraining the dangerous tal of the sun and keeping in from infecting the un-world with material life.

Morlock wasn't sure it was working. As he stood there, he saw a new bulb slowly start to take new form among the thorny lattices. Other thorns turned toward it, like flowers turning their faces to the sun. They might not be alive . . . but they looked like they were.

Skellar's rusty avatar coiled about a low-hanging globe and grew a little brighter. That was how he had stayed alive. His body wasn't feeding his talic avatar; his talic avatar was sustaining his body with tal bled from the sunglobes.

Morlock became aware of Naevros' approach and turned Tyrfing toward him. The shining warrior came straight at Morlock—lunged—recovered—parried Morlock's attack—riposted.

Slow, slow—indefinably slow. How close was the rapport between Naevros and the other Guardians? Was there resistance to his will—misunderstanding of a swordsman's moves?

Morlock circled around the shining warrior, stabbing and slashing. The warrior, who was Naevros, but only in part, swung about to meet his attacks but could not disguise his lumbering, his failure to attain Naevros' deadly catlike swiftness.

This was not like every other time Morlock had fought Naevros, half in jest and half in earnest. This was all in earnest, and Naevros' magic armor was like weights on his hands and feet.

Then, and only then, did Morlock fully realize that he *had* no hands and feet—not in this fight. His body was on the other side of the sky, at the end of the world. He held Tyrfing by his bond with it and with his will.

Morlock rose from the ground and struck downward. The shining warrior raised his misty sword too slowly and Tyrfing only glanced off it to land squarely on the glassy crown of the warrior's faceless head. The glass shattered; Tyrfing penetrated deep within it, and Morlock had the satisfaction of hearing both Bleys and Naevros cry out in a harmony of pain.

One for Earno! He would have shouted it if he could. *Blood for blood and life for life.*

He spun about the shining warrior in midair, stabbing and slashing, shattering plate after plate of the warrior's armor.

Finally Naevros was moved to take a risky step. He turned the misty blade on his own armor, prying it apart as if he were opening a shellfish. The Guardians sang out, a choir of agony, but then Naevros' avatar stepped forth, a wiry skeleton of steel, unprotected from Morlock's sword but unencumbered now.

Naevros flew through the dark air and met Morlock in the empty sky. They circled around each other, striking when they could.

Morlock discovered something: now the advantage of speed belonged to Naevros. Tyrfing was made of matter, at least in part; it took an effort of his mind, and expense of his tal, to move it. Whatever Naevros' sword was, it was something else: weightless, freighted with death. Naevros could move it as quick as his thoughts. The advantage was slight: just enough to kill Morlock.

Morlock took refuge in the thorny lattices holding the bulbs of sunlife. Naevros' speed would matter less there, he hoped. Also, Morlock could bask and heal in the tal leaking from the sunbulbs. But so could Naevros, of course. . . .

Naevros' wiry, shining avatar landed among the thorns and stabbed through them at Morlock.

Morlock vaulted over the thorns and tried to catch Naevros while he was entangled in them.

Naevros slashed with his misty sword and slid through the gap he had made in the wall of thorns.

He swung his sword as Morlock landed, sweeping it through the thorny lattices as if they were dry grass.

Morlock dodged the blow and struggled to bring up Tyrfing in time to parry.

Now a sunglobe was between the two swords, the disruptive blade of mist and glittering unbreakable Tyrfing.

It shattered between them and its light and life and tal were released in a single instant.

The thorny lattices were on fire—actual red fire, as ordinary as bread and water. Another sunglobe burst, and another. Morlock was dazed, exalted, dazzled.

Trapped in the burning lattices, surrounded by exploding sunglobes, Naevros writhed in agony.

The whole valley was exploding. Light was leaping into the lightless sky. The unworld was distorting under it, and Morlock knew he had to flee or die. He left Naevros dying there and arced through the empty sky toward where he thought the gateway to his world might be.

Except the dark sky was no longer empty.

A bright, white eye opened in the dark world. The Sunkillers scattered across the dark plain fell away before its glance, stretching like shadows at sunrise, and Morlock felt the shape of the dark world change around him. Naevros was gone. Skellar's bitter, rusty ghost was gone. The Soul Bridge was going; he felt/heard it fragmenting behind him in the tide of sudden light.

The eye looked at Morlock, and the monochrome flame of his talic self flared back, back toward the gulf between the worlds.

He raised Tyrfing in defiance and salute. *Khai, ynthara!* he said or thought. *Praise to you, Day.* He fell back into a nothingness he feared and hoped was death.

A world away, Naevros syr Tol stood on the Witness Stone and screamed. His eyes filled for a moment with sunlight, and the Guardians looked away, unable to bear the light. His voice trailed off. His hands dropped. His eyes faded. He fell to the floor. By the time they reached him, he was dead, or at least no longer alive.

PART FOUR

Fall

We're getting a bit short on heroes lately.
—Ian Anderson, "A Cold Wind to Valhalla"

CHAPTER ONE

The Way Back

The blue, empty sky at the end of the world blinked and was suddenly gold. Deor felt the heat of a thousand summers on his face, a bright light that baked him to his chilled, gray bones. He wondered if he would die of it. He did not think that he cared. It was wonderful to be alive, even for a moment, after so much death. It was something to be warm after so much bitter cold. It was something to know that Morlock had defeated the Sunkillers, even if he never talked to his *harven*-kin again.

Then the moment passed and the bolt of light from beyond the end of the world spread out into the sky above, and Deor heard his voice laughing. It was a kind of light, pleasant cold, like on Cymbalsday morning. That was a traditional day for snowball fights, so he made a snowball and hit Kelat in the face with it.

The Vraidish prince shook the snow off his mask and laughed. He grabbed some snow and replied in kind. His aim would have been perfect if Deor had been even five feet tall, so the dwarf took the precaution of ducking behind a snowy hill before the Vraid struck again.

Deor looked around, hoping to enlist Ambrosia and Morlock in the ongoing snowfight.

Morlock's body still lay beside Skellar's on the bridgehead at the end of the world. The bridge beyond was gone, shattered by the freed sunlight.

Deor dropped the snowball he was making and ran over to where Ambrosia was kneeling beside her brother.

She turned her face toward Deor. Her eyes were closed and he could see her blue irises shining through the thin skin of the eyelids. She was still aloft in rapture. She spoke, in the toneless voice of the enraptured, "He is falling through the void. There is no here, there is no there. Falling. Many are lost, but he is not lost yet. I am losing him. I am losing him. Help me. Deor. Uthar. Help. . . ."

"Kelat!" shouted Deor, and the Vraid was there, his brown eyes wide with concern.

"I don't know what to do," Deor said to Ambrosia.

She lifted her hands blindly, trapped in her vision. "Your strength to mine. We may hold him. We may draw him back."

"Or?"

"Or we may fall with him into emptiness."

Fall with him into emptiness! Would the gateway in the west open for a soul lost, falling endlessly, at the northern edge of the world? Deor doubted it. It would be the second death for him, damnation, trapped in the earth where Those-Who-Watch could not see him or bless him.

But it was Morlock. It was Morlock. Better to be damned than to go back without him, to explain to Aloê, to Vetrtheorn, to everyone, *Yes, he is gone. Perhaps I could have saved him but I was afraid. . . .* That would be damnation.

He grasped one of Ambrosia's outstretched hands, and Kelat took the other. The males kneeled beside the woman in the melting snow.

Then the prison of Deor's skull broke open and his soul was drifting free in the endless air over the edge of the world. He didn't like it. His body was gone and he seemed to himself a shell of silver scales with nothing inside. He didn't like that either.

He wasn't alone, though. He saw a green-and-gold whirlwind that he knew immediately was Ambrosia. Beyond her was a kind of coppery lightning bolt that he recognized as Kelat.

They moved together through the abyss, guided by Ambrosia's will. The dome of the sky was close enough that Deor could see/feel its curve.

Ambrosia focused on an entity adrift in the gulf between the end of the world and the end of the sky: a flickering of black-and-white mingled with white-and-black. Morlock.

Deor stood in the air where he was, at Ambrosia's unspoken command. Kelat passed onward with her, until he, too, was told to stop. Then Ambrosia went on alone into the gulf until she was almost as distant as Morlock, and the bond with her grew as tenuous as an old man's memory.

From far away, Deor heard Ambrosia speaking without words to Morlock. He tried to add his unvoice to hers, was unsure if it had any effect.

There was a time, and then another time, and Deor blinked and found he was awake.

He sat up gasping. The bond was broken. Had they failed?

The first thing he noticed was that he was lying in the snow alone. He looked about and saw that Ambrosia and Kelat were setting up an occlusion and talking in that intimate way they had when they thought that nobody could hear them. Deor's hearing was quite acute; his intolerance for the mating habits of the Other Ilk was equally sharp. Fortunately he had great skills at not noticing what he didn't want to notice.

Morlock was on his feet, dragging Skellar's body up on to the bridgehead of the broken Bridge of Souls.

"Here, you!" he called, leaping to his feet. "Wait for me!"

Morlock waited, and Deor, as he caught up with him, gathered up Skellar's dangling feet. "What are we doing?" he asked.

"Skellar is dead at last," Morlock said. "I thought I would toss it over the edge of the world."

"Better than burying it in snow for ice-dragons to gnaw on," Deor agreed.

They carried the dead mandrake to the edge of the broken bridge and tossed it off. They watched in silence until the body was lost in the misty blue gulf below.

"So," Deor said. "You made it back, *harven*."

"Yes."

"Did it work?"

"Eh."

"Not good enough, *harven*. Try again."

"The Soul Bridge is broken. The wound in the sky seems to have closed. But we don't know if the sun has been permanently harmed, or if the Sunkillers will try again."

"If you had to guess?"

Morlock shrugged. "They may have other problems for a while."

"Then we go home."

Morlock looked a while longer into the misty gulf. Then he turned his back and walked away from the end of the world: homeward, as Deor supposed.

A year and fifteen days later, on the tenth day of Harvesting, the fourth day of fall, four ragged travelers walked up the long slope into the northern edge of the Dolich Kund.

The watch-dwarves on duty were playing dice on a flat stone in front of Northgate. One raised his eyes to look at the travelers with friendly curiosity as they approached and then said in Ontilian, "Hey! I know you!"

The woman in the group said, "I know you, too, watcher, though I'm afraid I don't remember your name."

"Kudh Spearholder, Lady Ambrosia," said the watch-dwarf with the sun-bright hat, doffing said hat and bowing low. He snapped a few crunchy Dwarvish syllables at his fellow watchers and they leapt to their feet.

"Lady Ambrosia. Sir Ambrosius."

"Don't call me that."

"Lord Ambrosius."

"Morlock."

"A beautiful name. A golden name."

"Eh."

"Noble travelers, the weather is warmer than it was when I shared your fire a summer or two ago, when it seemed the world was dying. But won't you come in and accept the best of what we have to offer? The Lorvadh has standing orders that any of you, any one of you, who cares to pass through our territory be treated with the highest honor. He would himself be honored to see you again."

"We're not sure we'd be honored to meet him," Ambrosia said. "Sorry if that wounds you, Kudh Spearholder."

"Oh, you're thinking of old Vyrn, last year's Lorvadh? He's no longer a master. He found it cut into his moneymaking. Spends his hours wallowing naked in gold coins, I've heard. No, Fyndh is the new Lorvadh, and there's some talk of keeping him in the job next year, too."

"I'd be glad to meet with Fyndh again," said Ambrosia. "And Morlock has some business to discuss with the master makers under the Blackthorns."

"Then we part company here, my friends," said Deor. He had promised himself he would never set foot in the deep halls of the Endless Empire again.

"No, don't get weepy on me. Kelat and Ambrosia, I'll see you soon, I hope. Morlock, I'll meet you back in Tower Ambrose. I mean to stop by Thrymhaiam on the way and give them the news there, so you may reach the city first."

Morlock grabbed his forearm, saying nothing of course. Kelat stuttered out something behind his mask. Ambrosia nodded warmly and said, "Travel safe, Deortheorn. We'll expect you at the wedding."

"That will depend," Deor said and turned away to march up the slope. His enthusiasm for the mating rituals of the Other Ilk was limited.

He turned back to have a final glimpse of them, but they had gone inside the deep halls by then, and the watch-dwarves had gone back to playing dice. He did get a little weepy then, although he didn't know why. Only later did he understand. Perhaps he had felt the future without understanding it. He never saw any of them again.

Morlock stayed on, enjoying the hospitality of the Endless Empire only long enough to make a new nose for Uthar Kelat.

The young prince was resistant to the idea at first, but Ambrosia insisted. "My friend," she said, "if you had lost your nose bravely in battle, it would be one thing. But your kinsmen will be cunning enough to sniff out a nose lost to frostbite—a fool's injury, or so those who have never seen the deep north might think it. No, you'll wear your nice nose and like it, my friend, or we will never be married."

Kelat's noseless face was torn with mixed emotions. "If I marry you, do I have to be the next King of the Vraids?"

"Not exactly. You get to be, which is somewhat different."

Uthar Kelat was unconvinced, but he consented to wear a nose.

Morlock had made a wooden leg or two in his time, but replacing a facial feature required developing new skills. He got quite good at creating life-like noses out of wax, but the problem was that none of them looked really convincing against the mobility of Kelat's face. But the master makers of the deep halls under the Blackthorns put their heads together with Morlock, and together they developed a nose of wax and fungus, with pseudo-muscles woven of spider silk. Morlock sealed the pseudo-muscles to the real muscles of Kelat's face, and wove the scarred edge of Kelat's skin together with the false nose. The result was a masterpiece of making, its greatness revealed by the fact that no one would ever be able to tell it was made at all, unless they already knew.

"That's your wedding gift," Ambrosia said when they parted company. "Don't bring anything else."

"Bring it where?" asked Morlock, confused.

"To the wedding, brother. I didn't get to go to yours, but you will be at mine. Give me about a year to set it up—that should be enough time."

Morlock's wedding had been a dinner at which he and Aloê had told their friends they were married, but he knew they did things differently in the unguarded lands, especially royal families. He nodded, hugged his sister, and turned away.

Kelat was waiting to shake his arm in the Vraidish fashion. "Thanks," Kelat said.

"Watch out on hot days," Morlock said. "I don't think the wax will melt, but. . . ."

"Oh," Kelat raised his hand to his face. "I'd forgotten about that. Thanks for that, too, then."

"What else?"

Kelat threw up his hands in exasperation. "You figure it out! When you do, remember I said it. Good fortune, Morlock."

"And to you and yours," said the crooked man, and turned away toward the crooked, high horizon.

He crossed the Dolich Kund and then struck westward through the foothills of the Whitethorns. It was a meandering path, but it suited him. There was fruit and game, and the early autumn weather was warm and golden. He even came upon a hill town that had people dwelling there, although he made a long detour around it.

He came to the Gap of Lone from its northern edge, and one afternoon, as he was about to turn from the rough hills into the flat plain of the Maze, his eye caught a searing glint of something polished or crystalline atop a nearby hill.

It was odd. No one dwelt here. No one built here. But the thing that he saw didn't look natural. He was tempted to go look more closely at it. The longing to go home tugged him in the other direction. But home had waited a long time already, and he was still a vocate to the Graith of Guardians: they would want to know if someone was settling in these slopes, so near to the Wardlands.

He climbed the hill.

The thing at the top was an oblong box made of crystalline stones. Inside the box was a body. He recognized it long before he reached the top of the hill. It was, or had been, Naevros syr Tol.

Naevros lay, as if sleeping, encased in the stone. The sunlight made the crystal glow, reminding Morlock of the armor his avatar had worn when they fought beyond the wide world's end. The body was dressed with Naevros' customary elegance, but his cloak was not the red cloak of a vocate. It was the black cloak of an exile, separated from the Wardlands by the First Decree.

Morlock stood there for a long time, gazing on his friend and enemy. He had no words to say, no prayers for the dead. He remembered the murder of Earno and his hands clenched. Then he remembered long hours of talking, laughing, drinking, fencing. He would say no curses either. Naevros was dead and, it seemed, exiled; the thing was done.

He turned to go.

Noreê stood below him on the slope. There was a black cloak in her hands, a red cloak on her shoulders. She looked at him without anger, almost with pity. "He meant something to you—didn't he?" she asked wistfully.

"Yes."

"And to me. He isn't dead, you know. But his spirit is gone."

Morlock thought back to the burning valley beyond the edge of the world. "He's dead."

Noreê looked away. "They put him out here," she said, "because the body still breathes, once a day or so. They put a black cloak on him because they said. . . . Well, he earned it."

"And worse."

"But Bleys is still summoner, and Lernaion. There is no justice, only defense."

Morlock waited.

"I cast a mantia that told me you might come this way," Noreê said. "I . . . I used a path-magic to draw you here, too. I wanted to be the one to tell you, and I wanted to tell you here. Now . . . it's not as I imagined it. But never mind."

She turned to face Morlock and held out the black cloak toward him. "The Graith sends you this."

He took it by reflex, looked at it uncomprehendingly. It was cut just like a vocate's cloak, but it was black, not red. It was the cloak of exile.

He raised his eyes and looked into hers. "They can't," he said.

"They did."

"I have a right to defend myself."

"You have no rights in the Wardlands. You are an exile. Three vocates died during your duel with Naevros, did you know that? Many were hurt. All were frightened, and frightened people are easy to lead. . . ."

He ran past her down the slope.

"Don't go back!" she called after him. "I don't say it as. . . . Don't go back! Don't try to go back!"

He ignored her. He ran with long, even strides down the slope until he reached the plain of the Maze. He felt the talic resistance before him, felt with his insight the shifting path that would lead him, by slow gradual steps, toward the other side.

He ignored it and walked straight against the talic wall of the Maze. It was difficult, but there was a fierce satisfaction in taking each step. He was in a mood to fight something; the Maze would do. When he reached the other side they could kill him or treat with him. But he was determined to lay his defense before the Graith. Someone, someone would listen to him.

Alarm bells were ringing in the Gray Tower over the Gap of Lone; he could hear them from afar. He saw Guardians in three colors of cloak standing at the tower's base. In his fierce battle with the power of the Maze, he didn't bother to identify any of them. He would see them face-to-face soon enough. He held the black cloak aloft in a gesture of defiance for them all to see.

He was about a thousand paces from the end of the Maze when his left leg suddenly went out from under him. He fell into the dark, golden grass of the plain and didn't understand what had happened until flame began to smolder around him. Then he realized: someone had shot him.

It must be a gravebolt, to strike from such a distance. It had passed through his left thigh; the wound was deep, but it had not severed the great artery of the leg.

His Ambrosial blood was spreading fire in the dry grass of the plain. The gravebolt, too, was burning. But before it was consumed, he saw the runic rose carved on the shaft.

On a warm autumnal day, Jordel stopped by Aloê's new house to have breakfast and say, "You don't have to do this."

The one irritated her as much as the other, but it was the last day she would endure either one for a while: she was already packed for her journey north. Her ostler had already saddled Raudhfax, in fact.

"That's a complicated teleological question," she said.

"I didn't ask a question."

"You implied one. Can a mantia be broken?"

"I always try to avoid mantias, myself. Hate causal loops."

"I'll remember that."

Jordel finished the rolls and tea that Aloê had made for her breakfast and said, "There! Ready to start?"

"I suppose so. Are you coming along?"

"Of course! Unless you'd rather I didn't. Baran's coming, too, although he discreetly waited outside."

"Why didn't you?"

"I was hungry."

Aloê looked at her friend narrowly. "I thought you wouldn't want to be seen with me, J?"

He made a disgusted face. "That kind of stupid, sloppy thinking is precisely why I came! You are my friend. You are my peer in the Graith of Guardians. You stood by me in some rough times. I stand by you."

"Even though you disagree with me?"

"I don't know that I do disagree with you. I simply say *you* need not do this."

"Ever had a horse that was dying, J?"

"Yes. And, if you want to know, I always pay a professional horse-knacker to put them out of their misery for me. It's a trivial comfort, but it helps me sleep better."

"This'll help me sleep better."

"I'm not arguing with you, am I?"

"You are, in fact, arguing with me."

"Well. You started it!"

She kissed his forehead, in preference to kicking him, and walked ahead of him out the door, where Raudhfax was awaiting her, along with Baran and the brothers' two horses. Jordel's was an ungainly, sway-backed, yellow nag that began to dance with joy as soon as he saw Jordel approaching; Baran's was a stalwart brown stallion with an ill-tempered eye, a bit like Baran himself.

"Thanks!" she said to her ostler. "Take care of the house for me, won't you? I won't be more than a halfmonth or so."

"Take your time," said the ostler, and turned away as they rode off.

They did not, in fact, waste much time on their trip north. It wasn't a pleasure excursion.

They found Bleys already in residence at the Gray Tower. He greeted them in the atrium with an unpleasantly warm smile.

"I wondered if you would really go through with it, my dear," he said.

"Call me that again and I'll cut your throat. I'll do it personally, too—not through an assassin."

His smile disappeared, reappeared. He turned away.

"Does everyone in the Graith know about that damned mantia?" she muttered to Jordel and Baran.

Jordel hah-hummed for a bit, and Baran finally said, "Yes. You should not have consulted Noreê. It's the type of story that would amuse her."

Noreê was also the greatest seer Aloê knew, apart from the unspeakable Bleys. Perhaps she should have consulted Illion, but he was undergoing the rigors of ascent to the rank of summoner—the one good thing to come out of the Graith recently, she thought.

On the afternoon of the day the mantia had foretold, she stood at the base of the Gray Tower, along with Jordel, Baran, Bleys, and a handful of thains.

Then she could almost smell the lyrea leaves she had burned to summon the mantia; she could feel herself floating free from her body, in time, not space. She could see herself doing what she was about to do.

"There he is," said Jordel quietly.

Too far away to tell who it was, she nonetheless knew who it was. On his shoulders was a weather-worn cloak of red; in one hand, a black cloak of exile.

She took up her songbow. She spun a gravebolt in her right hand until its impulse well was full. She fitted it to the bow and waited.

Morlock wasn't following the shifting paths of the Maze. He was breaking across them. She guessed he must be furious, afraid.

He held the black cloak aloft and she knew he was furious, defiant. He had a right to be furious. He and his companions had saved the world that she and the Graith would have let die. He didn't deserve this. But the Graith had decreed it: he was an exile, too dangerous to be allowed back into the Wardlands. Some feared that he was ambitious to be king. For some, it was bad enough that he could make the attempt. Some hated him, like Bleys, for their own reasons. Some feared him, especially after the battle with Naevros, when some of them had died, dropped dead from the dais under the Dome of the Graith.

Some of those things might change in time. But an exile who returned to the land was killed. That was the First Decree. He could not be allowed to return.

She took aim with the gravebolt.

In her vision of the future, she had seen herself doing these things and she had wondered why—*why* would she do this, *how* could she bring herself to do this? But the more she thought about it, the more reasons she thought of.

Not hate or fear. She had been afraid that terrible day of the battle beyond the edge of the world; she had felt pain, as Morlock's damned sword shattered the soul armor they had made to protect Naevros. But she'd been glad the Graith and the Sunkillers were defeated, glad that the world would go on living.

But if he came back now, he would be killed. There was one way that she knew to keep him from coming back. She knew it would work because she had seen it in the future. Causal loop: knowledge of the future creates the future. . . .

She took aim with the songbow. She could see him quite clearly now. She remembered what they had meant to each other, even though she couldn't quite summon those feelings now. She didn't feel anything, really. She wasn't telling herself this was for his benefit. But if he came back, and they killed him, and she could have prevented it, how could she live with herself? She was doing this for herself. There was work to do in the Graith, in the Wardlands, and it needed her. She had to be alive and reasonably sane to do it.

He was not very near now—still a thousand paces from the base of the Tower at least. But close enough. She was confident her bolt would fly true. She had already seen it all. She let the bolt fly; the bow sang gently in her hand.

"A hit," Jordel said calmly, as if he were the judge of an archery contest.

Yes: a hit. Morlock had fallen over. She had been wounded herself; she knew what his mind was doing now. He would look to see what had hurt him. He would look at the gravebolt that had passed through him—*through his leg*, she thought. He would see the runic rose on the bolt and recognize it.

He was motionless for a long time, so long she feared he was dead. (And how would she live with *that*?)

Then he rose to his feet. He was too far away for her to see his face, but he was looking toward them here, that was obvious.

If she knew him from a mile away, then he ought to know her. She stood away from the group so that he could see her better.

He stood still for a long time as the fire from his Ambrosial blood spread through the plain around him.

At last he moved. He took the red cloak from his shoulders and tossed it away into the burning grass. He took the black cloak in both hands and bound it across his shoulders. He turned and limped away into the west, trailing blood and fire behind him as he went. She stayed watching until he was out of sight. She stayed there, not watching, until the sun set in the east and the bloodfires lit the blue autumnal land below like bonfires.

Jordel touched her shoulder. She turned toward him.

"You did the right thing," he said. "Come. Let's go eat."

"That's not what you said before."

"I always say that."

"I mean . . . about it being the right thing."

"I didn't say it was wrong. I said *you* didn't need to do it. Now that you've done it, you don't need to feel bad about it. You probably saved his life."

"I don't feel bad about it. I don't feel anything."

"You will. Come on. It's cold out here."

It was cold. Inside the tower there would be—a fire.

"Let's stay out for a while longer," she said. She was starting to feel something, and she didn't like it.

The thains and the summoner had all gone in. Jordel and Baran stayed out with her, although she didn't ask them to. She was always grateful to them for that.

But when she had mastered her feelings, she went in and got something to eat. You have to eat.

Morlock Ambrosius, wearing the black cloak of exile from the Wardlands, limped into the night. Eventually, he took a strip from his shirt and bound up his leg to slow the bleeding, but he didn't bother to do anything else to it. It would heal or not heal. He was indifferent to it. Eventually the bleeding stopped, but the pain went on for a long time. He was aware of it without the slightest desire to do anything about it.

Another day of aimless walking and he found himself at night in a town on the coast of the Narrow Sea. Some of the buildings were lit up, so not everyone here was dead. One of the buildings had an open door, so he walked into it.

There were empty benches and tables. He sat down on a bench.

A man came up to him and said, "What can I do for you?"

That struck Morlock as funny, and he laughed.

"Maybe you've had too much to drink already," said the man.

Morlock looked at him. He looked around. The place was an inn or something.

Now there was someone else there. There were two men, one bald, one black-haired, both with red-brown faces and black eyes. "He's been in a fight," the bald man was saying. "Look at that bandage on his leg! Listen, we can't have him dying here."

"He's not dying. He's just hungry and thirsty. Right, friend? You want something? You've got money to pay for it, something to trade?"

"Money," Morlock repeated idly. He should have some fingers of gold from the Endless Empire. He took a couple from a pocket and looked at them with vague interest.

"See there!" said the man with black hair. "I bet you won that fight you were in, friend. What'll you have? Food? Drink? Both?"

He was hungry. And you have to eat.

"Drink," said Morlock Ambrosius.

Sigil

I, Deor syr Theorn, told this tale at your request, the true tale of our *harven-kin's* exile from the Wardlands. It is a mostly true tale, I think: I talked to many people, even some I hated, to learn the things I put in it. Other things I had to guess at. That's true in any history, and don't trust the historian who says differently. I began the tale long ago but finished it only tonight. You may no longer remember that you asked for it. But I think it's a tale that you need to hear.

Wyrththeorn, you are the youngest of my many sons, and you have caused me more worry than the others put together. From the time that you were hatched, I constantly found you causing some kind of mischief with your clever fingers, your crafty mind, your crooked, insistent urge to know and do.

I have here beside me a letter from Rystyrn, your most recent master in the arts of making. He says that he will not have you in his shop. You are disruptive; you are defiant; you cause dangerous fires with your experiments in making; you disturb the other apprentices with your odd remarks about geometry and ethics. He says you cannot be taught, and it is almost true: you cannot be taught *by him*. And he is the last master of making under Thrymhaiam who would consent to take you as an apprentice, and then only because your *ruthen*-kin, the Eldest of Theorn Clan, begged him to. Your shadow walks before you, my son, and it is very dark.

There is only one other person in my life who has caused me so much wonder, amazement, and grief.

And so, Wyrth, if you have read this far, I give you a choice. In the morning, go to Master Rystyrn and make your humblest apologies. Be a good student to him, and he will be a good master to you, and someday you will have a place of honor under these mountains.

Or leave these mountains. Leave the Wardlands. Find our *harven*-kin Morlock in the unguarded lands, as I long ago tried to do and failed. We hear many tales of him these days, and few of them good. But all agree that he is a wonderworker beyond compare, even beyond what he was in his youth, when the greatest makers of Thrymhaiam already acclaimed him as their master.

Stay or go. I know you will be a trouble to me wherever you are. It's that way with everyone I love.

Appendices

The Lands of Laent during the Ontilian Interregnum

Laent is a flat or shield-shaped land mass bordered by ocean to the west and south and empty space to the east; north of Laent is a region of uninhabitable cold; south of Laent is a large and largely unexplored continent, Qajqapca. Beyond that is believed to be an impassable zone of fire.

Along the western edge of Laent lies the Wardlands, a highly developed but secretive culture. It has no government, as such, but its borders are protected by a small band of seers and warriors called the Graith of Guardians.

Dividing Laent into two unequal halves, north and south, are a pair of mountain ranges: the Whitethorn Range (running from the Western Ocean eastward) and the Blackthorn Range (running from the Eastern Edge westward). There is a pass between the two mountain ranges, the Dolich Kund (later the Kirach Kund). North of the Dolich Kund there are only two human cities of any note, Narkunden and Aflraun. The rest of the North is a heavily wooded and mountainous region inhabited by humans and others of a more or less fabulous nature (e.g., the werewolf city of Wuruyaaria).

The Whitethorn Range, by custom, forms the northern border of the Wardlands. The Blackthorn Range is divided between the untamed dragons and the Heidhhaiar (the Endless Empire) of the dwarves.

Immediately south of the Whitethorn Range was the wreckage of the old Empire of Ontil, ruined by its rulers' ambitions, ineptitude, and misused powers. A period of general chaos and more or less continuous warfare obtained in these lands until the advent of the Vraidish tribes and the rise of the Second Empire of Ontil (ongoing in the present story).

South of the former Empire of Ontil lay the so-called Kingdom of Kaen. The ancient cities of the Kaeniar considered themselves at perpetual war with the Wardlands, which lay just across the Narrow Sea. The Wardlands, however, took little notice of the Kaeniar or any other domain of the unguarded lands.

The region between the Grartan Mountains and the Whitethorns was called the Gap of Lone by inhabitants of the unguarded lands. Inhabitants of (and exiles from) the Wardlands called it "the Maze" because of the magical protections placed on it.

Immediately south of the Blackthorns was a wooded region of extremely poor repute, Tychar. Farther south was the Anhikh Kômos of Cities, Ontil's great rival who unaccountably failed to take advantage of Ontil's fall to extend its domains. The largest Anhikh city, where the Kômarkh lives, is Vakhnhal, along the southern coast of Laent. Anhi may or may not extend its domain to the Eastern Edge of the world—accounts differ.

APPENDIX B

The Gods of Laent

There is no universally accepted religious belief, except in Anhi, where the government enforces the worship of Torlan and Zahkaar (Fate and Chaos).

In Ontil an eclectic set of gods are worshipped or not worshipped, especially (under the influence of Coranian exiles from the Wardlands) the Strange Gods, including Death, Justice, Peace, Misery, Love, and Memory.

In Kaen, each city and many places in the country have at least one local god, whose priesthood serves as one of the two branches of government (the other being the military and civil power of the tirgans). There is, at least in theory, a higher rank of national gods, and an upper echelon of universal gods, although their actual existence has been disputed by a significant minority of Kaenish heresiarchs.

In the Wardlands at least three gods, or three aspects of one god, are worshipped: the Creator, the Sustainer, and the Avenger ("Creator, Keeper, and King").

The dwarves of the Wardlands evidently assent to these beliefs. (At any rate, they have been known to swear by these deities.) But they have another, perhaps older, belief in immortal ancestor spirits who watch the world and judge it from beyond the western edge of the world. The spirits of the virtuous dead collect in the west through the day and night and pass through at the moment of dawn, when the sun enters the world and the gate in the west is opened. Spirits of the evil dead, or spirits that have been bound in some way, may not pass through the gate in the west. Hence, dwarves each day (at sunrise, or when they awake) praise the rising of the sun and the passage of the good ghosts to Those-Who-Watch in the west.

APPENDIX C

Calendar and Astronomy

1. *Astronomical Remarks*

The sky of Laent has three moons: Chariot, Horseman, and Trumpeter (in descending order of size).

The year has 375 days. The months are marked by the rising or setting of the second moon, Horseman. So that (in the year *The Wide World's End* begins) Horseman rises on the first day of Bayring, the penultimate month. It sets on the first of Borderer, the last month. It rises very early in the morning on the first day of Cymbals, the first month of the new year. The other two moons set simultaneously on this occasion. (The number of months are uneven—fifteen—so that Horseman rises or sets on the first morning of the year in alternating years.)

The period of Chariot (the largest moon, whose rising and setting marks the seasons) is 187.5 days. (So a season is 93.75 days.)

The period of Horseman is fifty days.

The period of Trumpeter is fifteen days. A half-cycle of Trumpeter is a "call." Calls are either "bright" or "dark" depending on whether Trumpeter is aloft or not. (Usage: "He doesn't expect to be back until next bright call.")

The seasons are not irregular, as on Earth. But the moons' motion is not uniform through the sky: motion is faster near the horizons, slowest at zenith. Astronomical objects are brighter in the west, dimmer in the east.

The three moons and the sun rise in the west and set in the east. The stars have a different motion entirely, rotating NWSE around a celestial pole. The pole points at a different constellation among a group of seven (the polar constellations) each year. (Hence, a different group of nonpolar constellations is visible near the horizons each year.) This seven-year cycle (the Ring) is the basis for dating, with individual years within it named for their particular polar constellations.

The polar constellations are the Reaper, the Ship, the Hunter, the Door, the Kneeling Man, the River, and the Wolf.

There is an intrapolar constellation, the Hands, within the space inscribed by the motion of the pole.

This calendar was first developed in the Wardlands, and then it spread to the unguarded lands by exiles. In the Wardlands, years are dated from the founding of New Moorhope, the center of learning. The action of *The Wide World's End* begins in the 407th Ring, Moorhope year 3242, the Year of the Hunter.

2. *The Years of* The Wide World's End

407th Ring, 2843 N.M.: Year of the Door

   1. *Cymbals.*

New Year. Winter begins.
1st: Chariot & Trumpeter set. Horseman rises.
8th & 23rd: Trumpeter rises.

   2. *Jaric.*

1st: Horseman sets. 13th: Trumpeter rises.

   3. *Brenting.*

1st: Horseman rises. 3rd & 18th: Trumpeter rises.

4. *Drums.*

1st: Horseman sets. 8th & 23rd: Trumpeter rises.
Midnight of 94th day of the year (19 Drums):
Chariot rises. Spring begins.

5. *Rain.*

1st: Horseman rises. 13th: Trumpeter rises.

6. *Marrying.*

1st: Horseman sets. 3rd & 18th: Trumpeter rises.

7. *Ambrose.*

1st: Horseman rises. 8th and 23rd: Trumpeter rises.

8. *Harps.*

1st: Horseman sets.13th: Trumpeter rises.
Evening of the 188th day of year (19 Harps):
Chariot sets; Midyear—Summer begins.

9. *Tohrt.*

1st: Horseman rises. 3rd & 18th: Trumpeter rises.

10. *Remembering.*

1st: Horseman sets. 8th & 23rd: Trumpeter rises.

11. *Victory.*

1st: Horseman rises.13th: Trumpeter rises.

12. *Harvesting.*

1st: Horseman sets. 3rd & 18th: Trumpeter rises.
6th: Chariot rises, noon of 281st day of year. Fall begins.

13. *Mother and Maiden.*

1st: Horseman rises. 8th & 23rd: Trumpeter rises.

14. *Bayring.*

1st: Horseman sets. 13th: Trumpeter rises.

15. *Borderer.*

1st: Horseman rises. 3rd & 18th: Trumpeter rises.

407th Ring, 2848 N.M.: Year of the Kneeling Man

1. *Cymbals.*

New Year. Winter begins.
1st: Chariot, Horseman & Trumpeter all set.
8th & 23rd: Trumpeter rises.

2. *Jaric.*

1st: Horseman rises. 13th: Trumpeter rises.

3. *Brenting.*

1st: Horseman sets. 3rd & 18th: Trumpeter rises.

4. *Drums.*

1st: Horseman rises. 8th & 23rd: Trumpeter rises.
Midnight of 94th day of the year (19 Drums):
Chariot rises. Spring begins.

5. *Rain.*

1st: Horseman sets. 13th: Trumpeter rises.

6. *Marrying.*

1st: Horseman rises. 3rd & 18th: Trumpeter rises.

7. *Ambrose.*

1st: Horseman sets. 8th and 23rd: Trumpeter rises.

8. *Harps.*

1st: Horseman rises.13th: Trumpeter rises.
Evening of the 188th day of year (19 Harps):
Chariot sets; Midyear—Summer begins.

9. *Tohrt.*

1st: Horseman sets. 3rd & 18th: Trumpeter rises.

10. *Remembering.*

1st: Horseman rises. 8th & 23rd: Trumpeter rises.

11. *Victory.*

1st: Horseman sets.13th: Trumpeter rises.

12. *Harvesting*.

1st: Horseman rises. 3rd & 18th: Trumpeter rises.
6th: Chariot rises, noon of 281st day of year. Fall begins.

13. *Mother and Maiden*.

1st: Horseman sets. 8th & 23rd: Trumpeter rises.

14. *Bayring*.

1st: Horseman rises. 13th: Trumpeter rises.

15. *Borderer*.

1st: Horseman sets. 3rd & 18th: Trumpeter rises.

The Wardlands and the Graith of Guardians

Accrding to Gabriel McNally's reconstruction (generally accepted by scholars of Ambrosian legend, always excepting Julian Emrys), the Wardlands were an anarchy with no formal government at all. According to legend, the Wardlands had not been a kingdom since the golden age at the beginning of time, when the King (usually identified with the divine aspect known as God Avenger) ruled in person in Laent and elsewhere. Since then it has been considered blasphemous, or at least irrationally presumptuous, for any person to assert a claim to rule the Wardlands. Those who try to do so are exiled or (in extreme cases) killed.

What in other cultures would have been state functions (national defense, dispute resolution, even road building and repair, etc.) were carried on by voluntary cooperatives: the Arbiters of the Peace, the Guild of Silent Men, the League of Rhetors, etc. Most famous in the unguarded lands was the Graith of Guardians, sworn to maintain the guard.

The Graith had three ranks of Guardian: the lowest and most numerous were the thains, wearing a gray cape of office. They were hardly more than candidates to the Graith proper, and they undertook to obey their seniors in the Graith, even more senior thains.

Vocates, in contrast, were full members of the Graith, privileged to stand and speak at the Graith's councils (known as Stations). Their only obligation was to defend the Guard, and the Guarded, as they saw fit. Their cloak of office was blood red.

Most senior in the Graith were the Three Summoners. They had no power to command but were generally conceded the authority to lead the vocates of the Graith proper. The Summoner of the City convened and presided over Stations of the Graith. The Summoner of the Outer Lands was charged with watching for threats to the Guard from the unguarded lands. The Summoner of the Inner Lands was charged with watching for internal threats: those who would try to disrupt the fertile anarchy of the Wardlands and establish the sterility of political order.

The greatest danger to the anarchy of the Wardlands was obviously the Graith itself. Members of the Graith were pledged to abide by the First Decree, which forbade any acquisition of power or authority over those under the Guard. Nevertheless, Guardians were exiled more often than the Guarded for political aspirations to government (euphemistically referred to as "Impairment of the Guard"). Power corrupts, and the Guardians wielded power more often than their peers among the Guarded.

Note on Ambrosian Legend and Its Sources, Lost and Found

Readers of these collections of Ambrosian myth and legend are already aware that Morlock's exploits beyond the northern edge of the world were not the end of his career as a hero. It took centuries for that to be evident to his contemporaries, however—or even to Morlock himself, and in that time his path took a number of severe turns, some sinister, some comic, many disgraceful.

The dwarves of Thrymhaiam cultivated his legend (as they are wont to do for their kin, whether *harven* or *ruthen*), but as far as they were concerned this was its final episode, and the various verse retellings of his deeds in the struggle against the Sunkillers apparently took the tone of an obituary, with one famous exception. We know that Defender Dervanion wrote up an account for the Graith of Guardians, although we don't know if it went into general circulation, and the anonymous Seventh Scribe of New Moorhope wrote an alliterative epic of the entire matter, including the *Balancer of the Two Powers*.

All of these sources have been lost. What we have is a series of verse plays in Late Ontilian, which may have been based on one of the talkier Dwarvish song cycles, and an epic, if that's not too strong a word, in rhyming verse by the pseudonymous Ninth Scribe of New Moorhope, and the Khroic *ekshalva* about Morlock, which purport to be based on direct visionary contact with the events they narrate.

I am not going to discuss the issue of whether the Ontilian plays are based on Dwarvish sources or whether they derive from a lost Mandragoric account of Morlock's life. First, because Dr. Gabriel McNally and Reverend L. G. Handschuh have debated the matter at length in the columns of the *Journal of Exoplenic Folklore*, and their total inability to reach any kind of agreement indicates the matter is undecidable at our current state of knowledge. Second, because I don't care.

I don't care about the overly solemn lost Dwarvish song cycles, and I don't care if there were any Mandragoric analogues or parallels, and I don't care about the lost epic of the Seventh Scribe, and I really have no interest in daydreaming about the papers that may or may not be filed in the distant and inaccessible archives of the Graith of Guardians.

The only one of these lost sources that I regret is a version that is supposed to have been made in old age by Deortheorn for the benefit of his last son, Wyrththeorn. It would be good to have because Deor was a witness of and participant in many of these events, and someone who knew Morlock well enough not to idealize him. And it must have been Wyrth's first real introduction to the career of his *harven*-kinsman Morlock. It must have had a great influence, and the time would come when Wyrth had a great influence over Morlock, both drunk and sober.

Some have questioned my attempt to re-create Deor's lost account using the Khroic *ekshalva* as sources. Dr. McNally, indeed, has warned me that he will count me with the dead if I continue: he'll never speak to me, write to me, or mention my name again on Facebook. That's too much to hope for, but it would be reason enough to forge ahead on a task which has sometimes proved difficult.

Other reasons include the fact that I have a contract and have already banked the advance. But, though satisfyingly cynical, that doesn't really account for my intermittent but persistent thirty-year quest to tell this particular story.

I think one reason I kept at it was an attempt to understand *why*: why the young hero Morlock syr Theorn became the old, embittered wonderworker and part-time monster Morlock Ambrosius. Maybe this is misguided: myth is multiform, and there's no reason that characters have to be consistent between different versions. But if there was a Morlock, he took some particular path from his alpha to his omega, and this is my attempt to trace that path.

This reminds me of something Reverend Handschuh says about the Ambrosian cycle. He's one of its most severe critics and considers it mere romance, not true epic. Like his hero W. P. Ker, and like many another gentle well-read scholar, he prefers the harsh, unforgiving world of classical or Germanic epic. In that tragic vision of life, heroes face their fate without hope of redemption or escape, and Reverend Handschuh rather scorns Ambrosian legend for its lack of tragic doom. "There is always hope," he writes. "There is always hope."

He means it as a criticism, but I don't think it is a criticism.

About the Author

© *J. M. Pfundstein*

James Enge lives with his wife in northwest Ohio, where he teaches classical languages and literature at a medium-sized public university. His first novel for Pyr, *Blood of Ambrose*, was nominated for the World Fantasy Award in 2010. He is also the author of *This Crooked Way* and *The Wolf Age*, not to mention the Tournament of Shadows trilogy (consisting of *A Guile of Dragons*, *Wrath-Bearing Tree*, and the thing you're reading here). His shorter fiction has appeared in the magazine *Black Gate*, in *Swords and Dark Magic* (Harper Voyager, 2010), in *Blackguards* (Ragnarok Publications, 2015), and elsewhere.